PENGUIN BOOKS

MARIE BLYTHE

Howard Frank Mosher is a 1981 recipient of the Literature Award bestowed by the American Academy and Institute of Arts and Letters. A Guggenheim fellow, Mosher is the author of five critically acclaimed works of fiction, including *Where the Rivers Flow North*, which was made into a movie, *Disappearances*, *Northern Borders*, and *A Stranger in the Kingdom*, for which he won the New England Book Award for fiction in 1991 and which has just been filmed. His most recent book is *North Country: A Personal Journey Through the Borderland*. Mosher lives with his wife and the two children in Vermont, near the Canadian border.

MARIE BLYTHE

A Novel by
Howard Frank Mosher

PENGUIN BOOKS

PENGUIN BOOKS
Published by the Penguin Group
Penguin Books USA Inc., 375 Hudson Street,
New York, New York 10014, U.S.A.
Penguin Books Ltd, 27 Wrights Lane,
London W8 5TZ, England
Penguin Books Australia Ltd, Ringwood,
Victoria, Australia
Penguin Books Canada Ltd, 10 Alcorn Avenue,
Toronto, Ontario, Canada M4V 3B2
Penguin Books (N.Z.) Ltd, 182–190 Wairau Road,
Auckland 10, New Zealand

Penguin Books Ltd, Registered Offices:
Harmondsworth, Middlesex, England

First published in the United States of America by Viking Penguin Inc. 1983
Published in Penguin Books 1985

10 9 8 7 6 5

LIBRARY OF CONGRESS CATALOGING IN PUBLICATION DATA
Mosher, Howard Frank.
  Marie Blythe: a novel.
  I. Title.
PS3563.O8844M3   1985   813'.54   84-26461
ISBN 0 14 00.7659 X

A portion of Chapter One appeared originally in *Country Journal*.

I would like to acknowledge the generous help given to me during the writing
of this book by the John Simon Guggenheim Memorial Foundation.
                                                                    —H. F. M.

Printed in the United States of America
Set in Video Compano

For Phillis

MARIE
BLYTHE

Chapter One

In the spring of 1899 six families set out on foot through lower French Canada. They left at dawn in a hard rain, walking south beside their oxen along the St. Francis River, and as they departed they sang a song their ancestors had sung more than a century ago on their way to Canada from France, a rondel in two parts with the men singing the verses and the women joining in with the refrain.

Despite the rain it was a morning of high promise. The air was fresh with the scents of thawing mud and running water. The mist over the river was full of the harsh, eager calls of wild ducks and geese which by nightfall would be halfway to Hudson's Bay. Heading south through the rain, the singing people were full of hope.

They traveled by easy stages, pausing often to rest, since the track they followed was too muddy for carts and everyone had to carry as much as possible. The men carried lumbering tools, the women carried household utensils and extra clothing tied up in quilts, and the dozen or so children who had survived the smallpox epidemic that had ravaged the settlements along the St. Francis the previous winter carried sacks of bread to eat on the way.

The rain drove harder, saturating the dark woolen coats of

the travelers. Under her dark shawl, Marie's hair was matted like the coat of a black water dog. Before she had walked a mile her wooden shoes and high woolen stockings were plastered with mud. Her waterlogged jacket was as ponderous as an ox yoke, but the rain was not cold and she trudged along contentedly, glad to be out and moving after the long Canadian winter and interested in all the spring sights along the river.

At the foot of a stretch of broken water, men in skiffs were removing salmon from gill nets strung across spruce poles jammed into the river bottom. Other men were out in the fields plowing with oxen. Near the far end of a field across the river Marie saw a man plowing with a team of horses, which were still so unusual along the upper reaches of the St. Francis that she mistook them for cow moose broken to plow. She spotted a blue heron standing on one leg in a reedy inlet, a pair of kingfishers chattering low over a cove, and a great fish hawk with a white head rising from a backwater with a large fish twisting in its claws.

Everywhere there were signs of spring. And everywhere, nailed to trees and stumps and fence posts and the weathered sides of barns and even houses, there were handbills advertising jobs in the States. Even before the epidemic, times had been hard for lumberers and subsistence farmers along the St. Francis, and by noon, when the people stopped by the river to eat, another twenty families had joined their procession.

It was still pouring. The rain was coming so hard by now that no one bothered to make tea, although Marie's father managed to kindle a small warming fire in the hollow trunk of a dead paper birch tree. Marie stood close beside him, holding a soggy piece of bread and staring at a yellow handbill nailed to the birch trunk. It was tattered and faded, but above the faint printing was a lithographed drawing still discernible as a village with a double row of houses and a long building of two stories with many windows. Two mountains rose above the town, one at each end, and stretching away from it was what appeared to be a lake or a broad river.

Claude Blair grinned as he fed the fire bits of damp bark. "The States are full of opportunities, eh, Marie?"

Marie was not sure what an opportunity was—she thought it might be something good to eat, like the maple sugar candies in the shape of leaves her father brought her from the Hudson's Bay store in St. Francis—but she nodded and grinned at Claude, who lighted his pipe and began smoking it upside down in the rain.

"Eat your bread, Marie," he said. "It's dripping on the ground."

Without taking her eyes off her father, she ate her sopping bread. When Claude rubbed his hands near the fire, she rubbed her hands. Then she began to smoke an imaginary pipe upside down in the rain until he noticed what she was doing and laughed.

When they started out again a short time later, the entire inside of the birch tree was on fire. Orange and blue flames lapped over the shattered top of the trunk fifteen feet above the ground. Marie looked back over her shoulder at the tree, burning brightly in the rain like a gigantic candle beside the river.

The handbill curled at the bottom and was consumed.

Early in the afternoon they turned away from the river onto a logging trace leading up a steep wooded ridge. In places, slippery ledge rock shelved down across the trail, and Marie had to cling to the slick, ropy tails of her father's oxen. Claude Blair walked beside the rear ox, a big, oxlike man himself with dark curly hair and mild blue eyes that missed nothing in the woods. Tiny and dark and as silent in the woods as her St. Francis Indian ancestors, Marie's mother brought up the rear. She carried a cedar board about four feet long by a foot and a half wide tied to the bundle on her back. From time to time she coughed softly in the rain, which turned to huge wet flakes of snow as the families approached the height of land above the river.

The snow collected on the stiff branches of stunted spruce

trees rooted tight to the granite spine of the ridge. It built up in small wet piles on the curved ends of Marie's shoes. It clung to her cheeks and eyebrows and lashes, and then abruptly it changed back into rain again, and the rain seemed even colder than the snow. All afternoon the people walked through the woods in the rain.

At dusk they came out of the trees into a cut about as wide as the river by Marie's old home. Two glistening rails extended as far as they could see in both directions. The rain had tapered off and the sky was a clear evening green, but most of the families sagged down with their loads in the wet brush on the edge of the woods, too weary to move a few steps farther into the clearing. Except for the water dripping off the trees it was quiet. There was not much conversation, and there had been no singing since early morning.

"Look, Marie," Claude said. "The stars are coming out. See the old man's violin?"

Marie looked up where her father was pointing and found the outline of the violin. Nearby she found the old woman's loom and not far from the loom the ferocious *loup-garou* Hector Napoleon, part wolf and part man, pursuing the lost Indian boy across the sky.

"There's Hector," she said sleepily. "There's that boy."

"There's the boy's father getting ready to shoot his bow and arrow at Hector," Claude said.

Marie had no trouble locating the father, but she wasn't certain about the bow and arrow. She'd recognized the bow and arrow beyond doubt only once, when Claude had pointed them out to her on a silver and blue Stars of the Heavens quilt for sale at the Hudson's Bay store. She wondered whether she would be able to see them from the States. Then she wondered whether she would be able to see any of the stars there.

She was just going to ask her father about the stars when she heard a low noise like spring ice starting to shift on the St. Francis. Far down the cut to the west a light appeared. The rumble gathered into a steady roar like all the ice on the river letting go at once. The light grew brighter.

"Here comes the train, Marie," Claude said excitedly. "Here comes the train for the States."

They rode in three locked cattle cars, concealed in great piles of straw and surrounded by bellowing oxen tied to the slatted sides. The cars smelled of damp straw and manure. They smelled strongly of steaming wool and of too many people packed too close together. The oxen bellowed and roared. Marie's heart beat fast as the train swayed and rattled south through the night toward the States.

"Go to sleep, Marie," Claude said. "You're all right. By morning we'll be over the line."

She reached out and groped for her father's hand but instead her fingers came to rest on something smooth and hard; it was the cedar board her mother had carried to the train. She ran her fingers gently over the surface. "You're all right," she said. "We'll be over the line by morning."

She fell asleep to the swaying of the car and dreamed that again she was waking from a raging fever in the dead of night, in the dead of the previous winter, to see her father digging by lantern light under the floor of their cabin. When he finished he went to the door and looked out into the darkness. It was perfectly still. The ground was frozen eight feet deep. The river was locked in tight from bank to bank. Even the rapids in the bend below the cabin were frozen silent. "It's starting to snow," he said out the door to no one.

By morning the storm was a blizzard, and it continued to snow hard all day and into the next night, as Claude dug twice more in the floor of the cabin. It snowed throughout the following day and night. It was still snowing lightly at dawn of the third day while Claude dug for the fourth and last time. He finished just as the traveling mercy sister arrived from St. Francis, having waited out the blizzard wrapped up in her blue coat in a blowdown like a spruce grouse.

In the middle of the morning he strapped on his snowshoes and took his bucksaw and felling ax to the woods. An hour later he returned with a flat slab of white cedar. He had chosen cedar, he explained, because it flourishes in wet places and endures all sorts of weather and does not rot quickly in the ground. With the painstaking concentration of a person who cannot read or write well, he inscribed four rows of letters on the face of the slab with his carving knife. In part to avoid tempting fate, in part to have one intact record of the entire family, he added Marie's name, his own, and Jeannine's at the bottom. He rounded off the top of the marker with his draw-knife so it would shed rain and snow. And when he finished he announced that in the spring they would go to the States.

"We'll take this with us," he said, staring at the names of his children on the marker: *Ti* Claude, Gaston, Gabrielle, Baby Ste. Simone.

Claude and Jeannine had both contracted smallpox in their childhood and were now immune, and with Sister Thérèse's help Marie sustained the disease with only a small scar below her left ear. Yet just as the epidemic marked a critical point in Claude's life, causing him to decide to leave Canada forever, so it left Marie with an ambition of her own: to become a beautiful white mercy sister, like Sister Thérèse, and travel from place to place nursing sick children and sleeping in the snow like a grouse. At the time, though, she said nothing about her plan to either of her parents, but confided it in secret to the marker.

Later Marie dreamed that she was walking in the rain with her parents. In this dream they were heading across flat, open terrain toward a line on the horizon. The line shimmered darkly like a heat mirage on the St. Francis in raspberry time, and like a mirage on the river it receded before them as they walked toward it. Marie knew that the States lay just across the line but it continued to recede with the horizon, and although they seemed to walk forever they never drew any closer to it. . . .

"This is it," her father's voice said in the dark. "This is the line, Marie. Be very still."

Voices approached from outside the car. A chain rattled and bars of lantern light fell through the slats and slid over the ceiling above Marie's head. The horns of the cattle shone in the lantern light. Marie's heart beat fast as she burrowed into the straw. She felt an almost overpowering impulse to get out of the car, and her breath came short and hard but she managed not to move or cry out.

"Canadian cattle," a voice said.

"How many?" a second voice asked.

"Twenty in each car. Three cars."

"Is the hay for them to eat on the way?"

"Yes."

"Very good. Then you won't be charged duty on it. Only on the cattle themselves. Twenty cattle in this car?"

"Twenty."

"Very good."

The chain rattled, and it was all Marie could do not to burst out of the straw and rush for the door. Bars of light glided over the ceiling. The voices passed on to the next car.

"Did you hear what they called this filthy straw?" someone nearby said in a low voice. "They called it hay."

"They called the oxen cattle," someone else whispered.

"Maybe they weren't referring to the oxen," the first voice replied.

"Aren't they supposed to weigh animals and give them ear tags?"

"Of course. They've been bribed. Do you think they'd let us in otherwise?"

"Maybe they'll weigh us and give us ear tags."

"Shut up. They'll hear us."

"What difference does it make? They've been bought off."

Gradually Marie's heart slowed down and she became aware of a throbbing ache in both her feet. During the night they had swollen up from walking all day in the rain, so she reached down and pulled off her heavy wooden shoes. She took off her damp stockings and wedged them into the toes of the shoes.

Then she waited, breathing lightly and quickly, hoping that no one would put a tag in her ear, until at last the train gave a lurch and was under way again.

"This is it," Marie said to the cedar marker. "Get ready for some opportunities."

At dawn the train stopped high on a mountainside to take on water from a wooden tank whose top was out of sight in the mist. A man unchained the doors of the cattle cars, and the people got out to stretch their legs. Claude took Marie through the thick mist to drink from a fast, icy brook. "We're up in a cloud," he told her, but she thought he was teasing.

While the men carried water to the oxen, the women walked up the brook into a thick stand of firs and spruces, where they washed beside a deep green pool fringed with snow and changed into their best clothes. Shivering in the cold, Marie put on her red and blue holiday dress, still wet from the rain the day before. Her feet had swollen too much to fit back into her shoes, which she held one in each hand. Jeannine, who was still coughing at intervals, wore her green holiday dress with white piping at the sleeves and neck and hem. All the other women who had brought holiday dresses put them on. In the meantime, the men had washed in the brook below the tracks and changed into sober dark suits and white shirts with ruffles.

As the train headed down the mountain, Claude picked up his daughter and pushed between the oxen to the side of the car so she could see what the States looked like. The mist began to tatter apart, revealing a beautiful country of wooded hills with pastures and meadows just starting to turn green running high up the hillsides between the woods. And the trees were not just softwood trees, like the unrelieved fir and spruce and cedar woods on the St. Francis, but hardwoods and softwoods mixed in together, and the hardwoods were a lovely light gold with tiny new leaves just coming out of the bud. Yet there was still spring snow along the north sides of the hedgerows and stone walls, and the mountains that closed in the country to itself on all sides were still white with spring snow partway down their sides. Then the sun rose, and for a few moments the snowy mountains turned a deep fiery pink.

"Look, they're burning!" Marie said, and Claude laughed and told her that the fire was only the sunrise reflected on the snow.

An hour later the train stopped briefly on the edge of a village of white houses and large brick buildings arranged around a long rectangular green lined with elm trees just leafing out. On the green under the elms Marie saw a soldier dressed in gray and holding a long knife. He stood motionless, looking into the distance. "That's a statue, Marie," Claude said. "He can't hurt you. He's made out of stone. I believe it's President Washington."

Marie looked skeptically at the statue. She had great faith in her father, yet she could hardly believe that the man with the knife was made of stone; and a few moments later she was more alarmed still because it seemed as though the whole village was sliding out from under her. She grabbed her father tightly and shut her eyes, and when she opened them the village was moving fast away from her.

"It's all right, Marie," Claude said. "We're just backing up."

The train backed north out of the village and through a cedar swamp, on a spur track beside a slow dark river. It was a big swamp, much bigger than the cedar swamp where Claude had cut the marker. Marie was disappointed because she had hoped they would stop in the beautiful farming country or the village.

The train backed slowly along the river. In places the steep blue clay banks were covered with moose tracks, and Marie looked hopefully into the woods for a glimpse of a moose. Watching the cedars and tamaracks from the backing train gave her the sensation that the trees were moving and she was standing still; but before long the trees began to give way to low alders and red osiers, and except for a few scattered islands of tamaracks nothing reached higher than ten or twelve feet. The sun went under a cloud, the surface of the river turned a flat toneless gray, and for the first time since leaving the cabin on the St. Francis, Jeannine Blair spoke.

"Look, daughter," she said in a harsh whisper. "This is the place I told you about, where the *loup-garou* sleeps by day. Perhaps we'll catch a glimpse of him."

Instantly Marie shut her eyes. Many times her mother had frightened her and her brothers and sisters with tales of the vast bog somewhere to the south of their home where the *loup-garou* slept under the dark water, emerging at night to roam the sky for disobedient children who had wandered away from their homes into the woods. In the deep secret heart of this morass, Jeannine claimed, nothing at all grew, neither hardwood nor softwood trees, bushes nor berries. "No, not so much as a single partridgeberry," she said grimly, staring at her terrified children with eyes as bottomless as a dark night in deep woods.

"Except for the werewolf himself," she intoned, "the heart of the bog supports no life. No birds, no fish, no turtles, even, which can live almost anywhere there's water. The rivers flowing into this place lose themselves hopelessly a dozen times and never rise with a freshet or fall with a drought. The water is more poisonous than seawater."

At this point in the story Claude would usually wink at the children to let them know that they should take it with a grain of salt; but it was well known to everyone on the upper St. Francis that Jeannine's mother had been a witch and that Jeannine herself could keep the stub of a candle burning all night by merely staring at it, or make a pot of beans walk right off the edge of a shelf.

"Of those persons so foolhardy as to venture near the home of the *loup-garou*," she would continue, "few emerge, and those who do have no memory of their past lives. In the center of the swamp there is no night or day. Only the absence of all light, sound, life, direction, and time."

But when Marie finally dared to open her eyes again the train was out of the swamp and moving along a narrow blue bay between two soaring mountains still capped with snow; and just ahead, where her father was pointing, wedged onto a tongue of land separating the bay from a great lake running between other mountains as far to the north as she could see, was the village from the yellow handbill on the birch trunk, sparkling in the morning sunshine.

She stood with her parents and the other people on the platform of the railroad station, with a wooden shoe in each hand, looking down at her bare feet. They were as wrinkled and white as tripe, and she wanted to keep them out of sight under her dress but it wasn't long enough to conceal them.

Up and down the street the houses gleamed in the sunshine. They were the light golden color of the new spring leaves, and although they were all patterned in the same style, with two stories and steep slate roofs to shed the snow, there were many small, pleasing variations in the carved scrollwork running along their eaves and doors and windows. Neat yellow picket fences separated the front yards from the street, which was paved with a greenish crushed stone that set off the pastel yellow houses to their best advantage. Marie looked at the houses with great interest. Except for St. Francis, which was just a dozen log houses along the river by the Hudson's Bay store, and the place with the long green the train had passed through, she had never seen a village before; now it appeared that she was going to be living in one.

On a knoll at the foot of the western mountain sat a much larger house of three stories. It too was painted pale yellow, and it was flanked by spacious lawns with many tall sugar maples just leafing out. On the hillside between the west end of the street and the drive curving up to the big house was a building with four tall windows full of small panes.

At the opposite end of the street, the long two-story building from the handbill stretched far back between the north row of houses and the gigantic lake. The long building was yellow and so was the covered bridge leading to the lumberyard and sawmill across the bay at the foot of the eastern mountain. The sawmill and the open-sided pavilions above the lumber were yellow. The ventilators on the long building, the soaring brick chimney behind it, the railroad station, and the platform the people stood on were all painted yellow. With the exception of a cluster of small houses with battened vertical siding just above the sawmill, everything in the village that paint would stick to was the same shade of pale yellow; the small houses were painted no color at all but were as new and raw-looking as the boards in the lumberyard.

Marie looked from her wrinkled feet to the yellow village, then back at her feet, then again at the village. That is when she first saw the blurred faces behind the dusty windows of the big two-story building across the street. There were dozens of them, staring out at the people crowded onto the platform in their best clothes, many of whom, like Marie, were holding their shoes in their hands because their feet had swollen. For perhaps a full minute the blurred faces looked at the Canadians and the Canadians looked back at the faces. Except for a low steady humming from the long building and the occasional lowing of the oxen in the cattle cars, the village was as quiet as the mountains above it.

Then the faces faded away.

"Look, Marie," Claude whispered.

Coming across the street toward the platform, walking purposefully without hurrying, looking carefully at the newcomers without appearing to stare, was a man in a blue coat. Like Marie's father, he had dark hair and blue eyes, and he was about Claude's age, forty or so. Although he was not as big a man as Claude, who stood two or three inches over six feet and weighed well over two hundred pounds, he was well set up and moved with decisive energy so that the green gravel in the street crunched briskly under his shining black boots as he approached.

"Good morning," he said in good French in a voice that

inspired confidence. "My name is Captain Abraham Benedict. I'd like to welcome you to Hell's Gate."

Claude and some of the other men lifted their hands to their hats and said good morning. Some of the women curtsied and wished the Captain good morning, though Marie noticed that her mother did neither. Captain Benedict bowed gravely, and immediately Marie gravely bowed back, imitating his bow exactly. Claude was embarrassed, but Captain Benedict laughed and winked at her. Then he politely invited the Canadians to go into the railroad station, where breakfast was waiting for them.

They sat at long trestle tables laden with more food than Marie had ever before seen in one place at the same time. There were huge platters of roast beef and ham and chicken. There were deep dishes of baked beans. Other dishes contained hot vegetables. Rolls warm to the touch were heaped in wicker baskets lined with white linen napkins. Great yellow blocks of butter sat on slivered ice in shallow trays, and women in long white aprons brought steaming pitchers of tea and coffee. One of the women smiled and spoke to Marie, who looked blankly at her.

"She's speaking English," Claude whispered. "I think she's asking if you want more tea."

Marie nodded, looking at the aproned woman with considerable curiosity. Until that moment she had supposed that all people everywhere spoke French.

As they ate, Captain Benedict moved from table to table, greeting each family individually. With him was a very lovely woman in a white dress, with light golden hair piled high on her head. Tagging along behind came a yellow-haired boy, looking as though he would rather be someplace else.

"This is my wife, Rachel, and our son," Captain Benedict told the Blair family.

Claude had taken off his cap before sitting down to eat, but as he answered the Captain's questions about Canada and the trip down, he respectfully touched his fingers to his forehead several times.

Suddenly Marie noticed that the boy was mimicking her father's gesture, not in the spontaneous way she had imitated the Captain's bow, but mockingly, with exaggerated obsequiousness. She was so astonished by his rudeness that she choked on her tea and began to cough uncontrollably.

Claude patted her back and her mother stared hard at her, but Marie continued to cough until Rachel Benedict knelt beside her. "What's your name, dear?" she asked when Marie finally caught her breath.

Staring into her empty tea mug, Marie said her name.

"You're very pretty, Marie. You have beautiful blue eyes. Can you look at me with them?"

"Yes, madame," Marie said.

But she could not bring herself to look at Rachel Benedict, who was by far the most beautiful woman she had ever seen, with golden hair and large brown eyes with golden glints in them; and she continued to stare into her tea mug as though reading a fortune.

Rachel smiled. "How old are you, Marie?"

"Eight years, madame."

Rachel put her arm around her son and drew him toward her. "This is Abie, Marie. He's ten. I think you and he will be great friends."

Marie, who wanted nothing so much as to drown Abie Benedict like a cat at her first opportunity, did not think so; but suddenly he did something that confused her greatly. Reaching out quickly, he touched her dark, curly hair, the way a child might touch a strange doll on a store shelf. And in her surprise and confusion, she began to cough again.

"I know just what will soothe that cough," Rachel said. She rose, picked up a small pitcher on the table, and poured some milk into Marie's tea mug. "Go ahead," she said kindly. "Drink it."

Marie looked at her father, but Claude was busy talking with Captain Benedict. She looked at her mother, who stared back at her without expression. On the upper St. Francis, cow's milk was thought to be hard for children to digest, and although Marie knew what milk was, she had never tasted it.

Marie took a sip; it tasted warm and chalky. Rachel nodded encouragingly. Against her better judgment Marie raised the mug fast, before she could change her mind, and drank the milk in three gulps.

Instantly she realized that she had made a bad mistake. Snatching up her shoes, she jumped to her feet and started toward the door, but before she reached it she was sick down the front of her holiday dress. She was sick again on the platform and again in the gravel street. She was sick behind the long two-story building, retching on her hands and knees like a poisoned dog until there was nothing left in her stomach to be sick on; and then without knowing how she had gotten there she was running inside the covered bridge, still holding her shoes.

When she was sure that she was out of sight from the street, she paused to catch her breath. Inside the bridge it was quiet and dim and a cool breeze blew in on her heated face through a narrow window that ran the entire length of the north wall. Inhaling deeply, she looked north up the long lake between the mountains and wished she and her father and mother had never left Canada.

Walking slowly, stopping frequently to inhale the breeze off the lake, she moved deeper into the dusky bridge. A brown and white pigeon fluttered from its perch in the webbing of the rafters over her head, startling her momentarily. Looking up at the crisscrossed timbers, she had an idea.

Near the far entrance of the bridge she found a slanting beam running up the inside wall. Pushing her shoes ahead of herself, she scrambled up it to a wide timber forming a long shelf above the window. Here, high in the bridge, she stretched out with her back against the wall and shut her eyes. She could hear people calling her name but she did not reply; she was too sick and dizzy, too humiliated, too confused by all the events of the past twenty-four hours. She could still feel the swaying of the cattle car beneath her, and she fell asleep to the swaying of the car in the maze of rafters.

Once she heard a wagon rumble by below but she did not come fully awake. Later the metal roof of the bridge began to snap in the heat and she dreamed that the *loup-garou* was walking back and forth just above her head, looking for a way to get in at her. She lashed out with her arm, knocking one of her shoes off the ledge onto the walkway below, but still she slept on. . . .

"Marie. Come down, Marie."

Inside the bridge it was nearly dark. Claude Blair was standing below in the dusk, calling to her, and now Marie wanted only to crawl down into his arms and be held. "I thought you'd drowned, Marie," he said over and over, hugging her and scolding her at the same time. "I found the shoe and thought you'd drowned."

"I wasn't drowned," she said sleepily as he carried her out of the bridge and started up the hill past the sawmill. "I was just sleeping."

She could smell the dark, warm scent of his pipe tobacco as she snuggled against his jacket, and she was very happy to be held and carried and scolded; and then she was even happier. "Look!" she said, pointing over his shoulder. "They do have them here after all."

Claude stopped and turned around. "Have what, Marie?"

"The stars! See the old man's violin over the mountain?"

Claude looked up at the emerging stars and began to laugh. "Of course they have the stars," he said, hugging his daughter. "Why, Marie, the States have as many stars as opportunities. More of both than we could ever count."

Chapter Two

"Roots go to water," Jeannine Blair announced the next morning.

Taking Marie firmly by the hand, she led her from the base of a tall black spruce tree behind the house up the slope toward the spring that supplied their water. Midway between the tree and the spring she knelt and dug down a few inches into the brown needles with her kitchen knife until she came to a slender root, which she severed with a hollow-sounding snap. Walking backward toward the spring, she pulled up about twelve feet of the root. Then she cut it again and looped it over her arm like a lariat while Marie watched with great fascination.

For the rest of the day Jeannine soaked the spruce root in a bucket of water. Not once did she speak or let Marie out of her sight, and although Marie was immensely curious about the root, she knew better than to ask about it but quietly helped her mother put their new home in living order. It was a well-built, tight house of four rooms with a lean-to for wood attached to the back, nothing like the elegant yellow houses across the bridge but a great improvement over their log home on the St. Francis, and she was very proud to be living in a real house and eager to help scrub the plank floors with a sandstone brick and wash the windows and sweep the dooryard around the stoop. Yet she could not stop wondering what Jeannine intended to do with the root, coiled up like a sleeping snake in the water bucket.

That evening, after Claude had returned from his first day of work in the woods and they had eaten supper, Jeannine sewed a strip of flour sacking six inches wide around Marie's right ankle. Without explanation or comment she wound the smaller end of the saturated spruce root five times around the padding, sewing each loop carefully to the loop below with heavy black thread. The larger end she tied to her own left wrist. Marie looked inquiringly at her father, but Claude only grinned and shrugged, and soon afterward they all went to bed in the room next to the kitchen, Jeannine and Claude in the high double bed by the door, Marie in the small low bed by the window. Outside, the breeze off the lake blew through the branches of the spruce tree and Marie fell asleep quickly and dreamed that she was back in Canada and the *loup-garou* was dragging her off into the woods by her ankle. When she woke at dawn the loops had shrunk tight to the burlap padding, which they gripped like five strong fingers. And then Marie understood the purpose of the spruce root. It was to prevent her from running away.

Later that day Marie pleaded with her mother to free her, promising to stay near the house. But nothing she said made any impression on Jeannine, who, having lost four children in Canada, did not intend to risk losing her last child in the States. From that day on Marie had to go everywhere her mother went, tethered by the ankle like a young ox.

Sometimes at night after her parents were asleep she tore at the sewed loops until her nails broke, or tried to bite the root in two. But it was no use; the fibers were as tough and sinewy as rawhide. And although Claude sympathized with his daughter, he did not intercede on her behalf since he believed that it was not his place to interfere with the way his wife brought up their family, however large or small.

To Marie, the worst part of her restriction was the mortification she had to endure. Each morning after Claude left for work with the other men, she and Jeannine went down the path from the house to the sawmill, where they stacked a homemade hand sledge on flat runners with discarded slabs of wood from the previous day's sawing. Marie dreaded these wood-gathering expeditions because both the sawmill crew and the other Canadian women stared at her and her mother; years later she thought that much of the great pride that was both a strength and a weakness to her throughout her life stemmed from those terrible early-morning excursions on the spruce root to the mill.

Soon after their arrival Claude spent a Sunday building an outdoor clay baking oven shaped like a beehive. Every day from then on, after the kitchen floor had been scrubbed, Jeannine made a fire of black alder sticks inside the new oven. When the sides were heated all the way through she raked out the ashes and put in two long loaves of bread. In Canada, Marie had loved to help her mother bake bread; now it was one more chore she dreaded because of her humiliation over the root.

Worst of all were the family's weekly shopping trips to the village. Each Saturday after work the Canadians received their wages in pale yellow squares of Benedict Company scrip redeemable for goods at the company store. Then they would put on their best clothes and walk down across the bridge with their families and make their purchases for the coming week. The store was an exciting place, even larger than the Hudson's Bay store in St. Francis, but Marie's great fear was that she would be seen there by one of the Benedicts, particularly the rude boy with yellow hair.

Still, Marie's new life in the States was not all grim. Sometimes on rainy days Jeannine took her up the brook behind the house to catch a mess of trout for supper. Later in the summer they picked red raspberries high on the mountainside where the men had been logging. Often in the evening Jeannine and Marie caned chair seats for the factory, and then when he wasn't too tired Claude would tell stories about Aunt Odette's talking cat and Jean Labadie's imaginary black dog, which Marie later repeated word for word to the cedar marker inscribed with the names of her brothers and sisters.

Claude had set the marker in the sandy ground on the slope behind the house, and Marie frequently had a chance to visit it while her mother worked in the garden. Besides the old Canadian fairy tales, she told it about the yellow village and the twin mountains and the lake. But as the weeks passed and she became immersed in her daily routine, she forgot exactly what her individual brothers and sisters had looked like, and connected them more with the shapes of the letters in their names.

Fall arrived. Marie helped her mother harvest the garden. They moved the seasoned wood into the shed and went up the mountain with the sledge for balsam boughs, which they interlaced all the way up the sides of their house to the windowsills against the impending cold weather.

When the fall foliage was at its peak and the mountainsides over the lake were solid walls of red and yellow, a family of gypsies visited Hell's Gate. The first indication of their presence was the clamor of spoons being beaten on tin pans in quickening measure as they swirled down the long single street between the yellow houses, vivid as colored leaves blown off the mountains by the wind. Marie was delighted when they continued past the factory, crossed the bridge, and set up their tattered tents below her family's doorstep on the edge of the lumberyard.

With them the gypsies had brought a performing bear, which climbed up a pole with faded red and green stripes. It was a mangy, flea-ridden bear with decaying teeth from eating too many sweets, and it did not go up the pole with much conviction, but besides its climbing routine it could sit up on its thin haunches and beg and shamble along on its hind legs while a gypsy boy held the chain fastened to its collar and a young man played a guitar. Soon a large crowd had gathered from the village. Marie and her mother watched from the edge of the dooryard.

Under the direction of a loud, burly, vigorous woman of about fifty, with several gold teeth and hair the color of polished copper, two dark, slender young women opened canvas knapsacks crammed full of cheap hand mirrors, colored glass jewelry, mouth organs, magnifying eyeglasses, and many other tawdry and marvelous items that seemed far too numerous to have fit inside the knapsacks, which were still bulging. The young man who had played the guitar built a fire and began brazing tinware brought by the villagers. The loud woman set up a makeshift easel and painted portraits for fifty cents apiece. While she worked, she told fortunes in English or French to anyone who asked to have his fortune told and some who didn't. At dusk the boy who tended the bear set off pink and yellow skyrockets over the bay until Captain Benedict rode across the bridge on his Morgan mare and told him to stop before he set the village on fire.

Early the next morning Marie stood just outside the door of her house, watching the gypsies break camp in the mist before sunrise. The big woman with copper hair came up the path and helped herself to a pailful of water from the spring behind the house. On her way back she paused on the edge of the Blairs' dooryard and scratched one large bare foot with the toes of the other. "Well," she said in French, "what is it you want to know?"

"How much longer will I have to go on this cord?" Marie asked immediately.

The gypsy woman looked at her steadily, her eyes as gray and still as woodsmoke on a cold windless morning. Now she was scratching the other foot.

"What cord?" she said, her gold teeth flashing dull in the gray light.

Marie looked down at her ankle. The burlap padding was

still there, but only a short hank of the spruce root was trailing away from it. It had frayed in two of its own accord, though she had no idea when, since as soon as she took a tentative step she could still feel the drag, like a tooth that continues to ache long after it has been pulled. She started to say something, but the woman was already on her way down the path, and ten minutes later the gypsies had all vanished in the mist.

For days afterward Marie wished she were a gypsy, stood on one foot like the big woman, and pretended to lead a bear by a chain and to shoot off showers of colorful skyrockets. One morning she woke up to discover that the top of the mountain across the bay was covered with snow. The bay froze a week later, and Jeannine took her to jig through the ice for perch, as they had done in a cove near their home on the St. Francis.

The day before Christmas it snowed hard. By twilight, when the Canadians began to gather in their holiday clothes in Armand St. Onge's dooryard, a foot of new snow had fallen. The hanging meadows high on Kingdom Mountain faded from lavender to violet to purple as the people headed down the path past the sawmill and across the bridge and along the snowy street toward Captain Benedict's house, where they had been invited to spend Christmas Eve. Lighted lanterns covered with red and green paper hung from the stone pillars at the foot of the drive curving up to the house, which in Hell's Gate was known as the Big House, and the tall windows on each side of the door glowed through the falling snow. Marie's heart beat fast as they walked past the lanterns under the jaw of a whale inverted above the pillars, which she half believed was not a whale jaw at all but the legs of a *loup-garou* that Captain Benedict had killed when Hell's Gate was still a wilderness. She remembered how she had been sick the day she first came to the village, and hoped the Benedict boy would not stare at her. Yet at the same time she was eager for him to see her in her new holiday clothes and immensely curious about the inside of the Big House.

Rachel Benedict greeted them at the door. She wore a

white dress again, and her golden hair shone beautifully, but Marie was even more impressed by the high winding staircase behind her, with its polished banister festooned with fir boughs. White birch logs were blazing in a fireplace at the foot of the stairs and another great fire had been kindled in the parlor, where the Benedicts received their guests under a fir tree ten feet high decorated with dozens of tall white candles that gave off a spicy scent as they burned. Marie had never seen a tree inside a house before and supposed that it had grown there.

Captain Benedict gave each family a sealed yellow envelope containing a Christmas bonus of scrip. In return the Canadians presented him with hooked rugs, quilts, and maple sugar molds carved into the shapes of beavers, bears, and moose. After the exchange of gifts, Abie Benedict came into the room, dressed like his father in a blue coat and dark tie, and passed around cut-glass goblets of punch and Christmas cookies sprinkled with red and green sugar crystals. He grinned at Marie, who looked away and refused to take a cookie. But while she pretended to be intently studying a long spear on iron hooks over the mantel, which her father told her was a harpoon for killing whales, she watched Abie out of the corner of her eye.

When everyone had taken something to eat and drink, Armand St. Onge opened a black case resembling a hatbox and took out his concertina. Pamphille Bonaventure had brought his violin, and while he and Armand played a fast reel, Claude and some of the other men joined hands and danced a stepdance with grave expressions on their faces. Then the men and women lined up in two rows opposite each other and danced together, and finally Marie did a jig alone, in her new blue and yellow dress and white stockings and red dancing clogs with large copper pennies nailed to their soles for taps, which Claude had made as a surprise for her in the evenings after she had gone to bed.

"Your daughter's going to be one of the great ones," Armand

said to Claude afterward. "If she lives, that is," he added super-
stitiously in a lower voice.

"She'll live, all right," Claude said. "She lived through the
smallpox, didn't she?"

Armand, who had lost nine children in the epidemic, smiled
sadly. "I hope so, Claude," he said.

Meanwhile, Rachel Benedict took Marie by the hand and led
her through the dining room and hall and up the twisting
staircase past the fragrant boughs to a broad landing at the top
of the stairs. While Marie sat on a love seat with a high, carved
back, Rachel lifted the lid of a leather-covered chest and began
to show her the most marvelous things she had ever seen.
There was a glass jar filled with small shells of all colors; a huge
tooth bigger than the palm of her hand with a picture of a ship
carved on one side and a great fish on the other; a bottle with
a real ship inside, tiny but perfect in all details; and, best of all,
a shell as large as Marie's head, with fluted chambers tinted
rose and orange, like the colors of a brook trout in spawning
time; when Rachel held it against her ear, Marie heard from
deep inside it the sound of the wind blowing through the
woods.

"Marie, how would you like to come here and live with me
sometime?" Rachel said.

Until now, it had never occurred to Marie that she might live
anyplace but home. She found the idea both frightening and
exciting and was unsure what to say, but just then her father
called her, so she stood up and started back down the stairs.
Claude was waiting with her coat and boots in the hall by the
fireplace. She did not see Rachel again in the bustle of getting
dressed, but as she walked back down the drive she could not
stop thinking about her invitation to live at the Big House and
the wonderful shell with the wind imprisoned inside it.

At the foot of the hill someone began to sing "Bring a
Torch." Someone else joined in; then everyone was singing. It
had stopped snowing, and the night was so cold the breath of
the caroling people hung on the air like smoke as they walked
down the street. In some of the houses curtains were drawn

back and villagers looked out, as they had looked at the Canadians the morning they got off the train and stood on the platform uncertainly in their best clothes and bare feet. To Marie, that seemed like a long time ago.

It was house-painting time in Hell's Gate. Every year during late July, each building in the village received a coat of the specially mixed yellow paint Captain Benedict ordered from a wholesaler in Burlington; then for two weeks the resinous, promising scent of fresh paint hung over the peninsula like an invisible mist.

Out in the garden, where she was supposed to be picking potato bugs and crushing them under her bare feet, Marie inhaled the heady odor of paint from across the bridge and wished that she could help paint the houses or go to the woods to help her father. She was growing tall, like Claude, and like him she had a tendency to daydream about the future. Father Boisvert, the traveling priest who visited the Canadians once a month, said that she had learned her catechism faster than any child he could remember, and it had already been established that when she turned twelve she would go to the convent in Montreal to prepare for the sisterhood. She knew she would miss her parents, but as the time for her to leave drew closer, her desire to see some of the rest of the world increased. The priest had told her about the great organ at the Cathedral of Mary, Queen of the World, which he described as a vast chest of shining pipes that sounded like a thousand violins playing together. She often imagined herself singing and dancing to this remarkable instrument in her white sister's habit and red dancing clogs. And this, the pipe organ, is what she was daydreaming about in the summer of 1900 when she heard Armand St. Onge shouting her father's name on the path behind the house.

"It's Claude," he shouted as he ran into the garden. "It's Claude Blair!"

Jeannine came to the back door, her hands stained bright red

from the raspberries she was preserving. "What about him?"
she said sharply. "What about Claude?"

Panting for breath, Armand stared wildly at Jeannine. He
stared at Marie, standing in the potato plants. He looked back
at Jeannine. "His hitch came loose on the mountain, Jeannine,"
he blurted, and then he began to weep.

Like most accidents in the woods, Claude's had occurred so
suddenly that no one was ever exactly sure how it had happened. About halfway to the top of the mountain, a granite
boulder as large as the Blairs' house overlooked the trail. On
its top grew a beech tree, whose dark exposed roots extended
down over the sides of the huge rock, clasping it in a rigid
embrace. A small spring flowed out of the ground at the base
of the boulder between two of these great knobby roots, and
here Claude had often stopped on his way up and down the
mountain. He would sprawl on the ground and drink from the
tiny pool between the tree roots, looking down into the clear
water at the coppery beech leaves strewn over the bottom like
arrowheads; or, if he was in a hurry, he would bend over and
scoop out a few quick swallows with his cupped hands. From
this spot the town was visible, and sometimes in the morning
the yellow train would be coming up the bay, small as a toy
train; Claude liked to look down at the train after he drank.

Here, too, in the late afternoon when her chores for the day
were finished, Marie often waited for her father to return from
the woods. As he came down the trace with his oxen she would
run to him and ask what he had brought her, and he would
shake his head and slap his thigh as though disgusted with
himself for forgetting again. She would continue to look at him
solemnly until he roared with laughter, and then from his
jacket pocket he would extract the smooth bracket fungus or
squadron of British soldier lichens or fragment of rose quartz,
or the blue jay or partridge feather he had picked up in the
woods, and she would take it and examine it gravely and thank

him while he shook his head with delight and roared. Then he would hand her his goad, and while she stood by the yoke of oxen he would sprawl out on the ground and drink like one of his own animals from the tiny pool between the tree roots.

The pool between the roots was no larger than Claude's red handkerchief but it was always full, even after several men had drunk from it. Its runoff trickled down the trail for a hundred feet or so, making a dark spot in the summer and freezing in the wintertime to a light blue-green glaze, which the drovers negotiated by fastening grip chains around the logs in order to prevent them from sliding forward and crushing the legs of the oxen.

It was here, on the trail below the spring, that Claude's accident had taken place. Somehow the braking chain had not held, and the butt maple log he was bringing off the mountain had slithered sidewise, fast as a striking snake, throwing him into the boulder and killing him instantly.

Marie did not cry much after the funeral was over. She had been taught from an early age not to. But as the days passed she sank deeper and deeper into a remote solitude in which she neither laughed nor smiled nor spoke except when absolutely necessary, even to the marker.

Father Boisvert was alarmed by the great change in the girl and did everything he could think of to console her and help Jeannine. Although he was seventy years old, he did not look much more than fifty, and he came to Hell's Gate each Saturday to help the Blairs in whatever ways he could, chopping wood, working in the garden, talking with Marie, taking her fishing.

All his life Peter Boisvert had loved to fish, and like his biblical namesake he was an accomplished fisherman. On long clear afternoons out on the bay in a small boat, or high on the mountain brook, he taught Marie to think like a fish—"Where would you lie if you were a trout, Marie?"—and at the same time talked to her about God and His infinite wisdom, telling her that God had loved her father so much He had called him to heaven early. He told her marvelous stories about the saints, particularly St. Joseph, the patron of all animals, who had once rescued Ethan Allen's daughter Fanny from a monster that had risen out of Lake Champlain to devour her, after which she converted to Catholicism and went to Montreal to become a nun. But Marie no longer had any interest in joining the sisterhood, and, although she did not say so, she blamed God bitterly for taking her father away from her. Finally it occurred to the priest that he might reach her by telling her his own story.

Peter Boisvert had been born in the year 1830 in a farming community southeast of Montreal, in the broad valley of the St. Lawrence River, the son of a flax farmer and the youngest of four children, all boys. His mother had died when he was an infant. In 1837 his father and many of his neighbors joined the Papineau Uprising, in which thousands of French Canadians armed themselves and rebelled against British rule, an insurrection that was enthusiastic but short-lived. One morning in the summer of that year, soldiers in red coats swept through the flat countryside around his home, setting fire to field after field of flax and hay and hemp and tobacco. "Go south, to the States," Peter's father said to him. "Tell no one anything."

A few minutes later Monsieur Boisvert was shot defending his dooryard. His three older sons were captured, shut up in their father's smokehouse, and asphyxiated as an example to the rest of the villagers of the fate of all rebels who objected to the protection of the Queen, though Peter did not learn this until years later.

Unable to tell one direction from another in the thick black smoke, the boy walked east, then north, instead of south. When the sun finally reappeared, just before setting, it was as small and red as a copper penny on a hot stove lid. That night he slept in some cattails beside a drainage ditch. The next day he wandered into a vast marsh, from which he emerged famished and half blinded by mosquitoes on the third morning.

He found a lane, followed it through an orchard and a hay-field to the rear of a long brick building, went to a small wooden door, and knocked. After some minutes a monk about fifty years old appeared and asked him his name. His face caked with ash dust and swamp mud, Peter stood silently and shook his head.

"Where do you come from?" the monk asked kindly, suspecting the answer all too well.

Remembering the last words of his father, Peter again shook his head.

"Who are your people?"

Nothing.

The monk thought for a moment. Then he said, "Are you hungry?"

Peter nodded.

He never forgot his first meal with the monks, he told Marie. It was Canadian pea soup, as thick as rich stew. When he finished eating, he brought in kindling for the refectory wood-box.

"Where are you going from here?" the friendly monk asked him. Then, immediately, because he did not expect a reply: "Would you like to stay with us for a while?"

Thinking of pea soup with dark chunks of ham immersed in it, Peter nodded again.

He stayed with the monks for the next five years, cutting wood, helping in the dairy and the garden, working in the fields and orchard. They liked him for his intelligence and energy and for his naturally serene temperament but considered him too active for the contemplative life of the monastery, and when he was twelve they sent him to Sherbrooke to be trained for the priesthood. Some years later he was ordained and assigned to a parish not far from his original home, a robust young man full of vigor and dedication, with the great faith and commitment to life of many persons who have lived through genuine horrors.

One afternoon in the summer of 1862 a Yankee came galloping into Father Boisvert's Canadian parish on a fine black horse. It was haying time, and he stopped at every farm to talk with the men in the fields. He was recruiting hired help to work in the States, he explained, and to any able-bodied man between twenty and forty who would sign up to go, he promised a draft of fifty dollars on the Bank of Lower Canada. Times had improved for the Quebec French since the Papineau rebellion. Hippolyte Lafontaine had risen in Parliament to deliver his brilliant speech in French in defiance of the law forbidding that language; but the old seigniories south of the St. Lawrence had been divided and subdivided and subdivided yet again between sons and grandsons and great-grandsons, and at farm after farm the man on the black horse was successful in his recruitment.

Father Boisvert was alarmed by the imminent emptying of his parish. He couldn't blame the men for wanting to go, though, and it occurred to him that wherever they were headed, their spiritual needs in that place should be regularly attended to. His superiors in Montreal agreed. "Make sure you bring them all back after the harvest," the Monsignor told him. And early in July, when the hay was in the barns, he departed with two hundred and seventy men from his parish and several adjoining it.

They left early in the morning, walking through yellowing fields of stubble in a light mist. That night they slept in a beech woods near the border, which they crossed the following morning, twenty-five years after Peter had started out for the States through the smoke of his father's fields as a boy of seven. They walked through Highgate and Swanton and St. Albans. They walked through Milton and Winooski, stopping on the way to cut hay for farmers whose help had left to fight in the Civil War. Continuing down the Champlain Valley, they picked apples near Shelburne and dug potatoes at Shoreham. In late September they reached Rutland, where they were quartered for a few days in a mammoth brick building near a railroad.

One evening the man on the black horse appeared again and informed the Canadians that more jobs were available for those who wanted them. He did not explain what they would be doing, except to say that it was outdoor work farther south and that they would be furnished with proper clothes and boots. Anyone who signed up to go would receive an additional bonus of fifty dollars. More than two hundred men agreed to stay on. They boarded a train that night, and the following week they were a thousand miles away, wearing new blue jackets and firing muskets across a field at a yelling swarm of men dressed in gray and firing back at them.

Without knowing it, the Canadians had enlisted in the Grand Army of the Republic, and though he had signed nothing, and carried no musket, Peter Boisvert was with them.

He was in the South for the next two and a half years, serving as chaplain and field nurse to his company, which consisted entirely of French-Canadian enlisted men and American officers. The men had little real notion of why they were there but fought courageously and sent most of their pay, when they received any, back home to Canada. Father Boisvert was wounded at Chancellorsville, captured at Vicksburg, and later escaped back over the lines near Atlanta, though not before serving as nurse and spiritual guide to a battalion of French-speaking Confederate troops from Louisiana, with whom he retreated south before Sherman, walking in the smoke of burning fields again, after a quarter of a century, although this time it was cane and cotton being destroyed and the devastated area was three hundred miles long and sixty miles wide.

After the war, the priest had stopped briefly at a Burlington hospital to visit wounded soldiers. There he had met Monsignor DeGoesbriand, who persuaded him to continue his ministry in the States by traveling to out-of-the-way places that had no church, which he had been doing ever since.

"So you see, my young daughter," he concluded as Marie looked at him with a mixture of wonder and puzzlement, "how important it is, no matter how sad or discouraged we may be, to maintain a little faith in something at all times—even if it's only in the importance of going fishing. Shall we go fishing now?"

She nodded solemnly, still thinking about his story, which, though it had little effect on her at the time except to distract her momentarily from her grief, was to become one of the main influences of her life.

To bring in enough money to live on, Jeannine went to work doing housecleaning for village women. Leaving home early in the morning with Marie beside her, she swept her way out of the door and across the yard. She continued to flick her broom at a pebble here, a leaf there, as they went down the path past the sawmill and lumberyard and across the bridge to clean the homes of women whose language they could not understand. Unlike some of her Canadian neighbors, Jeannine had not tempted fate by saying she would never work out in the village; yet she hated having to do someone else's housework, particularly in the homes of the German cabinetmakers, whose kitchens were redolent with unfamiliar, strong odors of cabbage and liverwurst and vinegar and whose heavy dark horsehair furniture covered with stark white lace antimacassars and lamps and curtains fringed with dark amber beads oppressed one's spirits like a funeral procession.

The jobs Jeannine and Marie were able to get were invariably the hardest and dirtiest. They hoed out henhouses and scraped stovepipes. They broadcast ashes on gardens and draped rugs over clotheslines and flailed them with brooms. Aggravated by the ashes and soot and dust, Jeannine's chronic cough grew rapidly worse; by the winter solstice, she was leaving a trail of bright red splotches in the frozen snow from her house to the village, like a wounded deer.

At Christmas, Rachel Benedict sent each Canadian family a box of oranges wrapped individually in thin sheets of red and green paper. Marie sold their box door to door in the village for scrip to buy flour and pork.

After the first of the year Jeannine did not work at all, and they lived mainly on yellow perch and smelt, which Marie caught through the ice on the bay. Sometimes as she stood with her wooden jigging stick in her hand, holding the fish eyes she used for bait under her tongue to keep them from freezing, children from the village skated nearby. Once Abie came with them, and when he saw Marie popping fish eyes into her mouth he jeered at her until Ned Baxter's son, who at twelve was already as tall as most men, made him stop. But when he offered to let Marie try his skates, she turned her head away silently, since she knew that her mother would disapprove of her playing with the village children.

Even to her husband, Jeannine Blair had always been inscrutable. She had never talked much, and since the epidemic she had spoken hardly at all. Her own mother, who had died of smallpox while still a young woman, had been a full St. Francis Indian, and Jeannine had been raised by a dour, stern grandmother to whom cleanliness was not next to godliness but inherent in it, a stay against the Canadian wilderness, and whose own grandmother had been a Daughter of the King, one of the thousands of orphaned teenage girls shipped to Canada from France in the seventeenth century as wives for the early settlers.

Except to frighten her children, Jeannine hardly ever told stories, but back in Canada she had told Marie and her brothers and sisters a remarkable one about this great-great-great-grandmother. She had been married the day she stepped off the ship in Quebec City, which happened to be two days before her fourteenth birthday. The following winter, when she was fifteen years old and already carrying her second child, her husband had cut himself badly with his ax, almost severing his foot at the ankle. It was a hard winter in a country of hard winters, the vast north shore of the St. Lawrence two hundred miles above Quebec, almost in Labrador; and with the father unable to hunt, the family was in danger of starving.

The girl-grandmother, who had been raised in an orphanage in Paris and until eighteen months ago had never seen a spruce tree, or a trout, or even a river, baked several loaves of bread, which she left with her injured husband and infant. Then she left the house on snowshoes with her husband's musket and skinning knife. Three days later she returned with the frozen hind quarter of a calf moose she had walked down like an Indian by tracking it through heavy snow and sleeping in windfalls by the trail at night. On the third day, moving in short circles and lying down frequently, the exhausted moose had begun to founder in the snow. Exhausted herself, Marie's pregnant great-great-great-grandmother had shot it at point-blank range, gutted it, and eaten part of its heart for strength before cutting it up. She had secured as much of the additional meat as possible high in a spruce tree and then dragged the hind quarter home.

Marie had often asked to hear this story repeated but her mother had told it no more than two or three times, and never since coming to the States. Yet Jeannine taught her to fish, and to trap muskrats and minks along the brook, and where the best berries grew, and one evening the previous spring she had taken her down to the bay to see a great flock of snow geese coming in for the night, which was the most exciting experience of Marie's young life.

Although it had been a warm evening, the mountaintops were still covered with snow and the ice had been out of the bay less than a week. As the white geese came soaring down out of the warm blue dusk with their black legs stretched comically out in front, Jeannine had told her to put her hands behind her. Then, side by side, with their hands and arms behind their backs so as not to alarm the geese, they had walked slowly into the water. The hard yellow sand beneath their feet sloped very gradually, and they walked far out among the cruising, swanlike birds, which tilted their large heads sideways to observe them and honked companionably to each other, like Armand St. Onge's tame gray dooryard geese. For minute after minute, while their legs turned numb in the icy water, Marie had stood with her mother in the midst of the geese, until the bay was white for hundreds of feet around them. Only when it was too dark to see the birds had they walked back to the shore and gone home. But Jeannine had never told Marie why she took her to see the snow geese, or alluded to them once afterward.

Since their arrival in Hell's Gate, Marie's mother had not bothered to learn more than a dozen words of English. She had never permitted Marie to associate with the village children, and because of the epidemic, there were no Canadian children within two or three years of her age. After Claude died she refused all help from everyone in both the village and the Canadian settlement, returning all gifts of hot dishes and bread and desserts left on her doorstep to the doorsteps of their donors. When Rachel Benedict visited after the funeral, Jeannine did not invite her into the house; and as the embarrassed wife of the factory owner began to reiterate her proposal to take Marie into the Big House, Marie's mother shut the door in her face.

Jeannine had never shared any of her husband's natural faith in opportunities of any kind, though she did not seem to be pessimistic by nature either. In fact, it was impossible to tell most of the time what Jeannine was thinking, except that her face had the slightly abstracted, intense expression of someone who habitually thought a good deal; and as spring approached and the ice began to turn dark before breaking up, she reluctantly told Father Boisvert to go ahead and make immediate arrangements for Marie to attend the convent in Montreal, since she had no doubt that she would die from her consumption before the first leaves were on the trees.

Also, she was concerned that they were running out of food.

One day there was nothing left in the house to eat but a few sprouted potatoes. Jeannine had been unable to get out of bed for a week, and Marie had stayed close by, keeping the stoves stoked, cleaning the already immaculate kitchen, sweeping the snow off the doorstep. Early that morning, however, she made up her mind to spend the entire day ice fishing. Twice the previous winter she and her mother had walked the five miles to the mouth of the Lower Kingdom River and fished through the ice off the railroad causeway. Both times they had caught one hundred or so yellow perch weighing from a quarter of a pound to half a pound apiece. If she had good luck today and caught just half that many, she could sell them from house to house or at the store in the village for enough scrip to buy some flour and maybe a little beef to make her mother a broth. She hated to leave Jeannine alone, but the ice might go out any day, so if she went at all, it would have to be now.

She boiled two potatoes for her lunch and two for Jeannine's. She brought in several armloads of firewood, gathered together the ax, a knife, a dozen tip-ups, and a pannikin to keep her fishing holes clear of ice and to boil tea in at lunchtime, got her snowshoes, and, telling her mother not to worry about her, headed down toward the bay, pulling her gear behind her on the hand sledge.

It was quite warm and snowing lightly, big flakes of spring snow like the snow that had fallen on the ridge she had crossed two years ago with her parents and the other Canadian families on the way to the States. An inch of wet snow had accumulated on the ice, and a set of deer tracks, still sharp, ran south down the bay in the direction she was heading. There were not many deer in Vermont around the turn of the century. Marie had seen only three in her life, and at first, as she trudged south in the animal's tracks, hauling the sledge over the wet snow behind her, she thought little about them. Compared with the tracks of a moose they were small, almost tiny.

She had already reached the mouth of the river, cut twelve holes in the ice with the ax, and caught several fish before it occurred to her that the tracks must be very fresh to show up at all in the sugar snow. Next she thought about meat, which she had not eaten for months. A deer wouldn't go nearly as far as a moose, but two people could live on it for a long time, and she could make a broth for her mother from the meat. She wished she had a gun. Then she thought about her great-great-great-grandmother walking down a moose, and remembering that story gave her an idea.

There was no time to deliberate. If she waited any longer, the tracks would fill up with snow. She collected the tip-ups she had just set out and put them back on the sledge. She checked to make sure she had put the matches and tea in her jacket pocket before leaving home. With the ax over one shoulder and the rope from the sledge over the other, she set out again on her snowshoes, following the tracks south along the frozen river. She had no idea whether she could overtake the animal, or kill it if she did. She didn't know if she could drag it home on the sledge if she managed somehow to kill it. She knew only that she was hungry for meat and her mother was very ill and one deer would do far more for them than a hundred fish.

A mile upriver, the tracks veered to the right, angled up the railway embankment, and disappeared into the vast cedar bog where Jeannine had said the *loup-garou* lived. That was the end of that, Marie thought, shuddering. As soon as darkness came, Hector Napoleon would run it down and devour it on the spot. Badly disappointed, she started back along the river until she came to the causeway. There, to her great surprise, she picked up the tracks again. For some reason the deer had not gone far into the swamp but had come back up to the mouth of the river and then headed off almost due west along the south base of Kingdom Mountain. After a moment Marie turned west, crossed the causeway, and followed it.

The deer kept close to the foot of the mountain, trending west by northwest, as though it sensed the danger of the bog. Even if the *loup-garou* did not exist, as Marie's father had privately assured her it didn't, the bog was a bad place for a deer or a person to go, especially in winter, since around the edge it was full of deadfalls buried just under the snow, and farther in there were few stands of softwood trees for shelter in case of a blizzard, and in spots throughout its entire expanse springs ran just under the ice and you could break through into deep water or a quicksand-like muck and drown in two minutes.

It occurred to Marie that the sooner the deer knew she was following it, the quicker it would tire itself. She began to walk faster. A mile west of the causeway, the tracks turned to the south and entered a dark green island of cedar trees just inside the bog. If it had bedded down in the cedar brake, she might be able to creep up on it. Yet she did not want to drive the deer deeper into the swamp, where she dared not go after it, so instead of following the tracks directly toward the cedars she cut out around them and approached the island of trees from the south, hoping to push the deer back toward the mountain.

The back of her neck tingled and she could feel her heart beat quicker as she started into the snowy swamp, but she doubted that the *loup-garou* would bother her in the daylight, and by now the falling snow had let up enough for her to see the south shoulder of Kingdom Mountain, which would serve as a landmark to guide her back to safety.

The deer crashed out of the trees while she was still two hundred yards away. To her relief, the tracks headed northwest again, skirting the foot of the mountain. They were farther apart now, and she knew that it was running.

Late in the morning, five miles from the causeway and ten miles from the village, Marie rested for the first time. She still had not seen the deer, but she had heard it again twice and thought it was growing tired. It had probably already come a long way over the ice when she first picked up its trail, because the third time she jumped it, she found where the deer had been lying down.

The sun had come out and was melting the new snow, which in turn had begun to melt the top layer of the old snow underneath. Just ahead, the deer had entered a dense stand of skunk spruces and started up the back side of the mountain in a northerly direction. The wet snow glittered on the limbs of the spruce trees. High above, the hoarfrost on top of the mountain sparkled in the sun. Marie started up into the woods after the deer.

Under the dense branches of the softwoods the snow on the ground had not melted at all. It was good walking for both the animal and the girl, but the trees were so thickset that their spiky dead lower branches caught on her jacket and leggings and snagged the rope fastened to the sledge and the sledge itself. After five minutes of this she realized that she had to make another decision: she would have to abandon the sledge or stop tracking the deer and retrace her path to the causeway. If she left the sledge in the woods, she doubted that she could find it again. But she had come too far and the deer meant too much to her and her mother to give up the hunt now. She tipped the sledge up against a large spruce, untied the rope and coiled it over her shoulder, picked up the ax, and moved on up the mountain.

The tracks were closer together now, so apparently the animal was walking again and not greatly alarmed. Soon after she had discarded the sledge she came to a spot where the deer had stopped and pawed through the snow to uncover some reindeer moss, though whether it had eaten any was hard to tell. It occurred to her that it must be very hungry, perhaps even starving—why else would it have come down over the ice past the village in the first place?

Thinking of the deer eating reminded her of the boiled potatoes in her pocket. She did not feel hungry but knew she should eat something. She reached into her coat, took out one of the potatoes, and ate it like an apple as she followed the trail.

She continued through the woods, heading due north now. In the hot sunshine, the snow had started to melt even under the softwoods, and although her snowshoes still supported her easily on the softening drifts, the deer was beginning to sink through in clearings where the sun penetrated at full strength. Realizing that the break in the weather was to her advantage, Marie walked faster, deliberately snapping dead twigs in order to frighten the deer into running. She knew that in order to wear out the deer, she would have to keep moving herself, and although she was very hot and thirsty, she continued to walk fast, reaching down now and then and scooping up a mittenful of snow to keep her mouth from drying out. Inside her woolen blanket coat, she was sweating.

Toward the middle of the afternoon she found a shallow depression in the snow where the deer had lain down again. Half an hour later she came to another dishlike indentation. Despite the heat and her thirst and a growing lightheadedness from exercising hard after weeks of eating nothing but potatoes and fish, she began to trot.

By now the softwoods were dripping steadily; every time she brushed against a tree, wet snow cascaded off the branches onto the ground. The packy snow caught in the meshes of her snowshoes and weighed them down. Every twenty feet or so she had to stop to clear off the accumulation, using one snowshoe to scrape the other. Running and stopping, running and stopping, she was not aware that she had reached the top of the north shoulder of the mountain until suddenly below her she saw the lake. It was late afternoon, and three or four miles to the south, the yellow village shone in the last low rays of the sun. Marie had tracked the deer in a complete semicircle.

The tracks angled down through the woods toward the lake. As she started after them, Marie came across a fresh yellow stain in the snow where the animal had nervously stopped to pee. Halfway to the bottom of the ridge she jumped it yet again.

It was twilight when she reached the frozen lake. She had already made up her mind that if the deer swung north, toward Canada, she would have to give up the chase and return to Hell's Gate, since even if she followed it north and killed it, she could not possibly hope to drag it more than a few miles without the sledge. If the deer turned south toward the village, she was determined to stay on its trail.

It had not occurred to her that the deer might head directly across the lake, and when she saw the tracks running due east toward the foot of Canada Mountain, looming purple and shadowy a mile away over the ice, she did not know what to do. Then, thinking of her great-great-great-grandmother tracking the moose as a young girl, she started to trot again, moving east over the ice, on the trail of the deer. From time to time she had to go out around dark pools of standing water where the snow had melted on top of the ice. The spring thaw was here at last.

By the time she reached the opposite shore it was nearly full dark, and although some of the stars were out, she was able to follow the tracks only as far as the first stand of softwoods, thirty feet above the lake. There in the darkness of the trees she lost them.

Now that she had made up her mind to remain on the trail she did not hesitate at all. In the last dusky light she cut a heap of dead lower branches, which she transferred to a sheltered spot near a brush pile forty or fifty feet inside the woods. The ground was not level there, but the mountainside was so steep that she doubted she could find any level place. Using one of her snowshoes as a scoop, she scraped as much snow as possible away from a hemlock stump on the opposite side from the lake. With strips of yellow birch bark for kindling, she built a small fire, not for warmth, since it was well above freezing, but to boil tea. Then she removed her snowshoes.

With the tea, which she drank very hot, she ate the second potato. Once she looked up through the branches of the trees, thought she glimpsed Hector Napoleon, and looked away fast; but when she worked up courage to look again, she saw that it was only the Eskimo fisherman, and she remembered that Hector did not appear in the winter.

Comforted by the fire and the hot tea, she was suddenly sleepier than she could ever remember being. Intending to sleep for an hour or so and then refuel the fire, she curled up in her blanket coat in the brush pile and did not wake up until dawn.

During the night the temperature had remained above freezing, and the first sound she was aware of was the steady drip of thawing snow. For a moment she actually thought she was back in Canada, waiting for the train with her parents and the other people and listening to the rain running off the trees. Then she remembered the deer and feared that its tracks would be gone, melted away with the thaw. She jumped up and waded through soggy snow up to her knees to the edge of the woods. To her enormous relief she found the trail immediately, each deep indentation where the deer had put its hoofs shadowed blue in the early light. She returned to the brush pile, strapped on her snowshoes, and started up the mountainside through the thick woods with the rope and the ax.

Five minutes later she found where the deer had bedded down for the night, in a copse of fir trees. Although she could not tell for certain, the trail leading out of the firs seemed very fresh. Now the deer was sinking into the snow almost up to its belly at every step.

Halfway up the mountain, the snow was harder. It was colder here, and it grew colder still as she climbed higher. The branches of the small spruce and fir trees were covered with thick white rime. Marie's breath condensed and froze on the inside of her coat hood. The air seemed to be full of invisible icy particles. Above her she saw nothing but swirling clouds and steep rock walls, glazed green and blue with frozen springs. The wind gusted hard, pushing her in against the mountainside.

The deer had been balked by the cliffs and had turned along their base, paralleling the lake far below. It was foundering badly now, although the snow was no longer wet but packed hard from the high winds.

Sometimes the clouds dipped down and enveloped Marie, and she had to wait for them to blow by. Ice collected on her eyebrows and lashes and seemed to line the inside of her nose and throat and lungs. Still, she seemed to be climbing, though she could not really tell. Her cheeks stung fiercely until she remembered to rub snow on them. Several times she thought she could hear the deer plunging through the snow ahead of her, just out of sight in the clouds, but in the wind she could not be sure what she was hearing. She knew that deep, dangerous fissures cut into the rocky upper slopes of Canada Mountain. In the wintertime these chasms were often concealed by treacherous snow bridges. She made up her mind to take ten steps, ten times; if she did not see the deer by then, she would start back down the mountain.

Before she had gone fifty paces, she realized that she was already descending. Her snowshoes slipped on the slick surface of the snow, and she had to take them off and dig footholds with the heels of her boots to follow the deer's slanting descent across the steep slope. Sometime later she dropped back below the treeline. A rift opened in the clouds; far below her, she caught a brief glimpse of the town and realized that she had somehow followed the deer directly over the top of the mountain.

She descended out of the clouds into a thick forest of mixed hardwood and softwood, where her father had once come to cut logs. Today, though, the woods were quiet. Under the trees the packed snow was littered with bits of bark and twigs and evergreen needles, and although Marie had not yet seen the deer, she found imprint after imprint where it had fallen and skidded on the littered snow. Half an hour later, when she approached the gigantic boulder where her father had been killed, the animal was falling every hundred yards or so.

As Marie came around the corner of the boulder, the deer was kneeling on its front legs, drinking from the spring. It drank in long deep gulps, the way her father had after working all afternoon in the woods. She believed that she could probably kill it with the ax now; the animal apparently no longer had strength enough to stand, much less run away. But she could not bring herself to strike it while it was drinking since she believed that it had made the terrific climb up and over the mountain to have this drink, knowing that whatever was following it would not give up and would eventually overtake and kill it.

The deer raised its head. It did not seem surprised to see her, and although it made a weak attempt to stand as she started toward it, it only foundered deeper into the drift at the base of the rock. With the ax gripped firmly in her hands and her hands behind her, the way her mother had taught her to approach anything wild, Marie took one step at a time until she was less than two paces away.

As she had thought, the deer was very small compared with a moose. It did not even seem to be as large as the other deer she had seen from a distance. It reminded her of a large, panting dog.

"Stand up," she said. "I'm not going to hit you lying there like that. Stand up."

But the deer would not stand, and now it was no longer looking at her but off at the far mountains across the lake. Marie did not believe she could kill it while it lay in the snow, refusing to look at her, until she thought of her great-great-great-grandmother, who perhaps had not wanted to kill the young moose either but had no choice. For a moment then it seemed to her that she actually was the girl-grandmother. She raised the ax and brought the blade down sharply with almost but not quite all her strength, as her mother had taught her to strike a chunk of firewood, cleaving the animal's skull to the jaw and killing it instantly.

She had helped her mother dress several moose, so she knew how to gut out the deer. She threw the innards and its sex organs (it was a male) in a steaming pile on the snow, and although she could not bring herself to eat the heart as the grandmother had done, she put it and the liver in the tea pannikin to take to her mother. She tied the rope to the deer's neck, and before heading down the mountain she lay down near where the deer had lain and drank from the spring, looking at last fall's coppery beech leaves strewn over the bottom and drinking deeply of the beech-flavored water.

It seemed much colder. A hard crust had formed on the snow, and as Marie pulled the deer's carcass along behind her it kept sliding into the backs of her legs and tripping her. Twice she fell, the second time cutting her cheek on the icy crust. After that she tried to let the deer down the slope in front of her, keeping just enough pressure on the rope to prevent herself from going too fast; but although it did not weigh much more than eighty pounds now that it was dressed, it was still too heavy for her to manage this way for long. In exasperation she gave it a terrific shove down the trail. It gained speed rapidly and at the first bend skidded off into a ravine and lodged in a deep drift. She was twenty minutes getting it back up onto the trail, where, panting and lightheaded, she braced it against the uphill side of a big maple tree. Then she sat down in the snow and began to cry.

But soon she got up and, thinking again of the girl-grandmother, took a small bite of the deer heart. It was terrible, like eating something's living flesh, and she threw it into the woods. She tried to think of what the grandmother would have done in her place and couldn't imagine.

Without knowing she was going to speak, she said aloud, "You aren't that grandmother. You're Marie."

This was a peculiarly comforting thought, just as earlier that morning when she killed the deer it had been comforting and useful to think that she was like the grandmother. Thinking of herself as herself, yet also as a person somewhat separate from herself, she concentrated on what she, ten-year-old Marie Blair, could do to get the deer down the mountain, and had an idea that would have seemed ridiculously farfetched to most adults but made perfect sense to her.

She dragged the animal back onto the trail and folded its stiffening legs under it. She removed her snowshoes and slung them over her shoulder by their straps. Then she straddled the carcass and rode it down the trail. It was an exhilarating descent, and it did not seem strange in the least to her to ride into the cluster of battened houses and up to her dooryard, where she dismounted and dragged the deer the rest of the way to the lean-to.

She was very excited and proud as she burst through the kitchen door, already calling to Jeannine about her good luck. And since the room was still quite warm and her mother was sitting up in bed looking into the kitchen from the adjacent chamber, Marie continued for some time to try to tell her about everything all at once: how she had picked up the tracks on the bay, followed the deer along the edge of the bog and behind Kingdom Mountain, slept out overnight in a brush pile, and then tracked it over the top of Canada Mountain that morning.

Dark-faced and diminutive, propped up on pillows and staring into the kitchen, Jeannine appeared to be listening impassively. Her black eyes were wide open, and she looked no different than ever until, pausing for breath, Marie noticed the thread of dried blood emerging from her mouth and running down over her chin and neck and over the edge of the bedcovers into a coagulated pool on the floor. Then she realized that the deer would do her mother no good at all, and all that she had accomplished in the past twenty-four hours had come to exactly nothing.

Marie knew what she must do. With her father's claw hammer she pried up several boards in the kitchen floor, as she had seen Claude do during the epidemic back on the St. Francis. She got the garden spade from the lean-to off the back of the house; then, since the ground outside was still frozen, she began digging her mother's grave under the kitchen floor. Like all the soil near the lake, the earth under the house was loose and sandy, and the digging went quickly. Once when she paused for a drink she glanced in at her mother, propped up on the bed like a stuffed figure. Her jaw had started to sag slightly, so that she appeared to be grinning. After that, Marie dug quicker, and by midday the grave was ready. Wasted by many months of consumption, Jeannine weighed only about sixty pounds, and compared with getting the deer carcass off the mountain, it was a simple matter to pull her body across the floor and ease it into the opening. Then she laid a quilt over her mother, shoveled the earth back in, dumped what was left over in the garden plot, and replaced the floorboards.

She spent most of the afternoon cleaning, sweeping the kitchen floor, scrubbing it with soap and water and one of the red sandstone bricks, scrubbing the bloodstain on the floor of the bedchamber. When the house was in order she washed herself thoroughly. She put on her holiday dress and her boots and coat and went up to the cedar marker above the garden. In the woods beyond the marker, it was already growing dusky.

Kneeling and brushing away the snow that had drifted partway up the board, then tracing the carved indentations lightly with her fingertips, Marie solemnly told her brothers and sisters and father that Jeannine was dead. She explained that she had been obliged to bury her beneath the kitchen floor because the ground outside was still frozen, and since she thought they would be interested, she told them how she had walked down the deer. "It isn't nearly as big as a moose, though," she added, so that they would not suppose she was boasting or be envious of her accomplishment. "I'm going to give it to the St. Onges."

She paused to consider how to phrase what she had to say next, as her fingers continued to move gently over the names. "I have to go away," she said finally. "Not to the convent with Father Boisvert. I'm not sure where, or how long I'll be gone. But someday when I'm too big to be off anyplace, I'll come back and tell you about my travels. I promise."

She stood up, feeling the warm south wind on her face. By dawn, she thought, the ice would be out of the bay. Thinking of Father Boisvert had reminded her that it was important to maintain faith in something, however small. "Well," she said to the marker as cheerfully as possible, "spring's coming."

She walked down to the lean-to and dragged the deer next door to the St. Onge place, leaving it at the stoop where they would be certain to find it. Then she walked quickly down the path toward the covered bridge. The long street was deserted. It was suppertime in the village.

At the far end of the two rows of houses she turned south along the railroad tracks. It was quite warm, and she could smell rain in the strong wind coming up from the south, and although she felt very sad, she was also excited, since she thought that many new opportunities might be in store for her, if she could only maintain a little faith.

As it grew darker, and she could no longer see where she was walking, she found the ties with her feet. She walked on into the night for what seemed to her a long time. Then she saw a light.

It was a campfire on a knoll near the causeway, and she approached cautiously for fear it might be a tramp's fire until she heard the guitar music. In the flickering light she made out a bulky figure facing her across the fire. It was a woman, and she was stirring something in a pot. When she lifted her head, she looked straight into the darkness toward Marie.

"Why are you spying on us?" she said harshly, her gold teeth flashing in the firelight. "Haven't you had your supper?"

Chapter Three

"Well, parrot. Are you happy to be coming home again?"

"Certainly not, Pia," Marie said in English. "My home is with you and the others, where we stop at night."

"How foolish!" Pia said in her harsh, good-natured voice. "Your home is here, in this outlandish yellow town. You're no more a real gypsy than you are a real boy."

"I'm a gypsy and my home is with you."

Pia stooped. With a grunt she lifted a half-grown snapping turtle off the spur track by its tail. "What do you know about being a gypsy?" she said.

"How to dance with the bear to the guitar," Marie said promptly. "How to throw handsprings and leap high like a trout and turn over in the air and land on my feet. How to venture into strange villages to sweep out chimneys and hide articles for you to find by divination and report back conversations to assist with your fortune-telling. All those things, and more besides."

"Not a one of which is worth knowing," Pia said. "Enough of this nonsense! You must be part gypsy after all to run on so. Be still now. I want to admire this outpost again. In all my travels I've never seen anything remotely like it."

It was springtime once more, and Marie and the gypsies were

standing on the causeway at the mouth of the Kingdom River where Marie had found them two years ago. As she gazed up the bay at Hell's Gate, the village looked exactly as it had looked on the day she buried her mother. She, on the other hand, had undergone a remarkable alteration. Instead of a dress, she now wore a scarlet pair of boy's belled trousers and a boy's shirt dyed turquoise. Her hair was cut short, and although there were still patches of snow here and there on the mountains, she was already barefooted. In her left ear she wore a small gold ring.

Looking at the tiny community between the twin mountains, Marie thought back over her travels with Pia and her family. The past two years had been hard ones in many ways, moving from one new town to another in all kinds of weather, knowing nobody and regarded suspiciously by nearly everyone; yet they had been good years too. She liked masquerading as the gypsy boy Mario. She liked caring for the bear. Best of all she liked the gypsies themselves, who were not really gypsies at all but itinerant Italian stonecutters who had picked up tinsmithing and peddling as sidelines during their travels. There were Pia's two older sons, Robert and Ernest, who were master craftsmen, and their wives and children; a younger son of about twenty, named Ethan Allen; and Pia herself, the big smoky-eyed woman who had asked Marie if she was hungry the day she ran away from Hell's Gate.

"This Captain you've told me so much about," Pia said as she stared at the village. "He owes you something, parrot. Just what, I'm not yet certain, but he most surely owes you a debt for bringing you and your family here and not taking better care of you. Now, go with Ethan to the village and do as he tells you there. But first listen carefully. . . ."

It was late morning by the time Marie and Ethan Allen started down the track toward the village. Turtles as big around as molasses kegs appeared and disappeared in the bay. Blue dragonflies with iridescent wings hovered above the reeds. Dawdling along in their ragged, dark cloth jackets, stopping to look at everything, Ethan and Marie now resembled railroad tramps more than gypsies.

An exuberant young man who had little interest in cutting stones, Ethan read all the time, the stranger the book the better. Before he had turned fifteen he was a clever illusionist and could manipulate a deck of cards or a cloak or a rope as though these things were alive, and he could fix any clock ever made, but he never stuck with anything for very long and his family worried about him constantly. He was fond of saying that people liked to be cheated, to which his mother would reply, "They don't, but you like to cheat them." In all ways, he was more a mountebank than any of the rest. He was very good-looking and had a girl friend in every village on their circuit.

As they walked along beside the ties, Ethan sang and whistled and laughed. Over his shoulder he carried a thick coil of strong rope and a burlap sack. Marie carried a wooden brush with stiff wire bristles. Ahead the village shone pale yellow in the sunshine.

Against his mother's express instructions, Ethan stopped to dig turtle eggs in the sand beside the tracks. When Marie objected, he said disrespectfully, "How will the old woman know what we do if we don't tell her? She's a vexatious, prying old woman, begrudging us a few eggs that don't even belong to her. Besides, if we don't take them, the skunks will just come at night and dig them up for themselves."

It was nearly noon when they arrived at the village and walked up the knoll under the double row of horse chestnut trees the gypsies had brought to Hell's Gate several years ago and sold to the Captain as American chestnuts. They sat in the shade of one of the two big entrance pillars to the carriage drive, and Ethan reached into the sack and got out a stone jug, from which they drank a refreshing beverage of cold water slaked with molasses and a touch of vinegar. Ethan pointed up at the whale's jaw towering above the pillars. "Look at that obscene monstrosity," he said. "What sort of man would put such a grotesquerie over his gateway, making guests feel as unwanted as outcast Jonah? Surely this Benedict is crazy; I've always thought so. Isn't he crazy, Marie?"

"No," Marie said. "He isn't crazy at all. He's a very good man."

"He's crazy," Ethan said lazily, as though the point wasn't worth debating.

Marie looked at the jawbone. In the glaring noon sun, with yellow roses climbing partway up both sides, it did not seem intimidating. She looked beyond to the roofs of the Big House. From the foot of the drive they appeared very high and steep. Under the beating sun the gray slates glistened like ice.

The factory whistle blew for noon.

"Imagine coming and going like a train to an impertinent whistle," Ethan said. "I could never do that. What if a man wanted to dig turtle eggs?" Then he said, "Look down the hill. Here comes that crazy swaggering Benedict."

Abraham Benedict was not swaggering. He had never swaggered in his life. He walked purposefully, without hurrying, and looked exactly as he had looked the first day Marie saw him. He did not seem especially surprised to see two strangers sitting at the entrance of his drive.

"Good morning, governor," Ethan said, without getting up. "Chimneys need a whisking out?"

The Captain stopped beneath the jawbone. "It's five past twelve," he said, without consulting his watch.

Ethan shrugged. "That's all right. We work right through noon, not by the hour. Two bits a flue."

"You said good morning," the Captain said. "It's five past noon now. It's afternoon." He did not speak rudely. The correct time was a fact, important to him if not to the gypsy.

Ethan grinned. "Yes, governor," he said indulgently. "About those chimneys now."

The Captain looked at the seven large brick chimneys above the Big House. He seemed preoccupied and did not answer immediately.

"Nothing like a good hot chimney fire to clean out a dirty

flue," Ethan said. He stood up and put the jug in the sack and slung the sack over his shoulder. "Come along, boy."

"We aren't going to have any chimney fires," the Captain said emphatically. "They were all cleaned last fall. But if you want to brush out the winter's buildup, that's fine. I'd appreciate it."

He started toward the house, then turned and smiled at Marie, reminding her of how he had smiled and winked at her the morning she got off the train in Hell's Gate with her parents. "What's your name, son?" he said kindly.

"Mario," Ethan replied quickly. "His name is Mario, he's very shy. He doesn't talk at all. His mother was startled by a serpent thirty feet . . ."

But Abraham Benedict shook his head, told Marie to be careful on the steep roofs, and started up the drive to the house.

Ethan and Marie followed him to the portico in front of the large front door, then went around past the conservatory to the kitchen. Ethan reached in the sack and, with a flourish, took out a chunk of spruce pitch, which he rubbed on the bottom of his bare feet and on Marie's, lifting each foot up in turn and holding it across his knee while he smeared on the pitch, like a man shoeing a colt.

"Are you afraid to go on high, as mad Ahab implied?" he asked, looking up at the towering roofs.

"No, Ethan. Of course not."

"Good."

He fastened a short stick shaped like a bobbin to one end of the rope, tossed it over the low kitchen room, went around to the other side, and held the rope tight while Marie climbed up hand over hand.

She scrambled up the hot slates to the ridge and fastened her end of the rope to the kitchen chimney so Ethan could climb up to join her. From there they scaled a gutter pipe to the roof of a second-story porch. Another pipe led to the high upper roof of the house.

As Ethan tied the rope under her arms, she could smell the hot pitch melting on the bottoms of their feet. He boosted her up to the great central chimney, where she balanced for a moment, out of sheer delight in the view and the day and herself, before starting her long dark descent.

The inside of the chimney was nearly as spacious as a well. Except for the layer of soot that had accumulated over the winter, the walls were remarkably smooth. Bracing herself with her feet and shoulders, she brushed her way quickly down into the darkness while Ethan paid out rope.

She continued sweeping until she reached a side flue, through which she crawled into a fireplace in a large room paneled with bird's-eye maple veneer. From the toilet articles on a vanity made of the same kind of wood, she deduced that she was in Rachel Benedict's bedroom. She brushed off the bottoms of her feet, walked on her toes to the door, and looked out into a long hallway. No one was in sight.

She returned to the hearth and tugged on the rope. It whipped out of sight like the tail of a snake. A minute later she retrieved it from the main flue, with the sack attached. She untied the burlap bag, empty now, and carried it down the hall, walking very quietly. On the landing at the head of the great spiral staircase, in front of the window giving onto the secluded sleeping porch and overlooking the town below, sat the dark trunk. Very slowly, Marie lifted the lid, removed the beautiful pink shell, and slipped it into the sack. She closed the trunk lid gently and was about to return to the bedroom when she heard voices from downstairs, in the direction of the dining room.

"Rachel," the Captain's voice said, "this is the second time in as many terms, and that's twice too often. I'm going to put him to work on the rough-mill floor under Ned Baxter the first thing Monday morning. Maybe if he learns what it is to work, he'll be grateful to go back to school in the fall."

"He's a bright boy, Abraham. I don't know what the trouble is."

"I don't dispute that he's bright. He's your son, isn't he? Of course he's bright. And maybe his intelligence will turn into wisdom someday and maybe his heedlessness will turn into courage. But not if he doesn't learn to stick with things and see them through. Because he's also a very indolent boy and in some ways a weak-willed boy. It's as simple as this—if we let him shirk now he'll shirk later."

"I can't condone sending him to the factory. There must have been fifty accidents there over the years."

"Yes, and that's fifty fewer than at any other woodworking factory that employs as many men as I do and has been in business half as long. Ned will put him to work tailing the cut-off saw or doing some other safe job. He won't be in any danger, I assure you."

"Isn't there an office job he can do?"

"No!"

The Captain's reply was not loud, but it was very sharp and quick.

"There isn't," he continued. "I won't have the men say I gave my son a sinecure as a reward for being expelled from school."

For a time it was quiet. Marie began to think that the conversation was over or that they had gone somewhere else to continue it. Just as she was getting ready to return to Rachel's room, the Captain spoke once more.

"Maybe you're right, though, about not sending him to the factory. Maybe he'd only find some way to fail there too. But I'll promise this much, Rachel. When he starts school again in the fall—supposing we can find a school that will take him— he's going to stay there at least a full year."

"I'm sure he will, Abraham," Rachel said in a soothing voice. "I'm sure this time he will. I'll talk to him about it very seriously. And thank you for understanding him."

"Oh, I don't claim to understand him. Only you seem to be able to do that. But I suppose I should be grateful that one of us does. For the time being, at least, that will have to be enough."

A door closed, and there was no further conversation from below, so Marie went back to the bedroom, fastened the sack containing the shell to the rope dangling in the fireplace, and tugged for Ethan to pull it up.

Two minutes later she was sweeping again, and by the middle of the afternoon, when she finished the last chimney, she needed no disguise. She was black from head to foot, and her nose and throat were clogged with soot. She hadn't overheard any further conversations, but she was sure that Pia would find what she had to report useful.

Abie Benedict was bouncing a hard rubber ball off the back wall of the kitchen. He had grown much taller in the past two years, and she doubted if she would have recognized him except for his yellow hair. "Hello, sweeps," he said without interrupting his game. "Tell me my fortune."

Ethan looked at him appraisingly. "Do you really want me to?"

"Why not?" Then Abie turned to Marie. "I can lick you, sweep's boy."

He made this declaration cheerfully enough and then returned to his game, but she gave him a long hard look and continued to stare at him while Ethan went to the back door for his payment.

"Now, then," Ethan said as they headed back down the tracks toward the camp, "relate all that you heard in your odyssey through the flues of the great yellow house."

She repeated the argument between the Captain and his wife, and when they arrived at the mouth of the river Pia made her tell again what she had heard and done. After Marie finished, Pia looked at Ethan, who nodded. "That's what she told me," he said. "No significant differences."

"I'll determine what's significant and what isn't," Pia snapped. "What are these so-called insignificant differences?"

"None," Ethan muttered.

"Ah!" Pia said. "You did well, parrot, despite that one's jealousy. Now go wash yourself. This evening we'll all go into town together."

"But what are we going to do with the shell, Pia?" Marie asked.

"Put it back where it belongs, of course," Pia said harshly. "Go wash."

Just at sunset the gypsies burst onto the long drowsy street of the village, appearing with an enormous tumult of drums and clattering pans and spoons beating together, as though they had suddenly fallen out of the sky, yet with the slightly bored air of being on their way to somewhere infinitely more important. While the men built a fire in the middle of the street in front of the factory and the women unpacked their knapsacks, Marie coaxed the bear to climb up its striped pole. It was a very old bear, and after hauling itself up partway, it clung there by the nubs of its claws and looked around as though perplexed not to have found a bees' nest, until Marie tugged on the chain to remind it to come back down. Nor was it any longer able to dance unassisted to Ethan's guitar, but had to shamble through a ponderous waltz with its huge cracked pads resting on her shoulders. Most of the bear's teeth had rotted out from the steady diet of gumdrops, licorice whips, and peppermint sticks fed to it by curious children, and its breath reeked like an unlimed privy. As they lumbered through the dance, Marie had to keep her head turned away, giving the animal, which was cranky from old age and boredom and the hardships of constant travel, frequent opportunities to snap at her ears.

Yet although it was growing senile, the bear never failed to attract a good crowd, and once they had gathered, Ethan drew a large circle in the sand of the factory yard and Marie did handstands on his hands extended high over his head and double somersaults off his shoulders. In a loud harsh voice like his mother's, he announced, "See Mario, the wrestling gypsy boy, contend in the ring. Pit your biggest boys against him for a wager."

A group of boys stood nearby, watching her acrobatics. "Step up, Ned," Abie Benedict said to a well-built boy about his age. "You can toss that spindling gypsy out of the ring. If you won't, I will."

The rugged-looking boy grinned and stepped into the ring. Marie recognized him as the son of the mill floor foreman, Ned Baxter.

"No punching, no kicking, no biting," Ethan intoned. "The first one with two feet out of the ring loses."

While Ethan made his wagers, Marie looked at young Ned Baxter carefully. She was certain that she could beat him without any difficulty, as she had beaten dozens of other country boys who had come into the ring against her since her wrestling lessons with Ethan had first begun.

"Go!" Ethan said, and after a startled pause, Ned ran at her with his head down.

She waited until the last possible moment, then dropped flat on her back, lifted her feet, caught the charging boy cleanly on the breastbone, and used his momentum to flip him over her out of the ring.

Quickly Ethan stepped up to protect her from possible retaliation, but when Ned recovered his breath he laughed goodnaturedly and said she'd beaten him fairly and that he'd give a dollar to learn that trick.

He turned to Abie. "All right, Ab," he said. "See what you can do."

Again Ethan took wagers, though not so many as before. "No punching, no kicking, no biting," he repeated.

"One minute, please. I'd like to place a wager."

Through the ring of people stepped a man in a blue coat. He spoke quietly, in a confident tone, and although it was getting dusky Marie saw immediately that it was the Captain.

"How much do you want to bet?" Ethan said.

"One hundred dollars," the Captain said without hesitation.

A murmur went up from the crowd. Ethan shrugged and smiled. "I don't have one hundred dollars," he said. "I don't have half that much."

"How much do you have?"

"Thirty dollars. Maybe thirty-five."

"Fine. I'll wager my hundred against your thirty."

Ethan glanced again at Abie, who was standing just inside the ring and grinning at Marie insolently.

"Go!" Ethan said suddenly, and this time Marie didn't wait; she was on Abie like a cat, and they were rolling in the ring.

Abie was considerably bigger than she was, but that wasn't unusual. Nearly all the boys she wrestled with outweighed her, and many were stronger. What surprised her was how quickly he moved, not giving her the slightest chance to get him in one of the disabling holds Ethan had taught her. She had expected him to be slow and soft from the soft life he led, but he was the quickest boy she had ever fought. All he lacked was experience. It was his inexperience, his uncontrolled desire to win at any cost, that caused him to wind his arm around her neck and start to choke her; and then before Ethan could pull him off, her own instincts took over and she drove her knee hard between his legs. He let go instantly and gave a yelp. Leaping to her feet, she grabbed a handful of his thick yellow hair, dragged him to the edge of the ring, and pitched him out almost at the feet of his father—who without a word counted one hundred dollars in yellow scrip into Ethan's hand and walked up the street toward the Big House.

She looked at Abie, writhing on the ground and moaning, and felt no pity for him. It had taken her four years, but at last she had gotten even with him.

The next afternoon, while the two older gypsy men went to speak with the Captain, who had asked to see them in his office, Pia paid a social visit to Rachel Benedict. With her she brought Ethan Allen and Marie, dressed as a gypsy boy, and while Ethan regulated the Captain's twenty-four clocks, the two women sat on the horsehair love seat on the landing at the head of the long curving staircase and drank tea. Marie perched on the old trunk by the window.

"You must be very lonesome here," Pia said after a while with a bluntness too natural to offend most people, much less a woman as gracious as Rachel.

Rachel smiled. "Sometimes."

"That's to be expected. Who can be friends with the big boss's wife? It's like being friends with a gypsy. Impossible! But tell me about those Canadians across the roofed bridge. Do they ever come calling on you?"

"Only on Christmas. The rest of the time they keep mainly to themselves. My husband encourages them to maintain their customs."

"Nonsense," Pia said, getting out a tablet and a soft pencil and beginning to sketch Rachel's portrait. "He wants to keep them under his thumb, and that's the best way. I know all about it. As long as they go around gabbling in French like a flock of foolish geese and make a cake that looks like a log every Christmas, your husband knows they won't give him any trouble."

"Why, I don't think that's it at all," Rachel said. "What trouble would they want to give him?"

"Look over there where they live, Mrs. Benedict. They haven't even asked to have their houses painted like the rest of the village."

As Pia talked, her pencil moved so fast Marie could hardly follow it. "It isn't very surprising about your husband, though. Mine was the same way, except in his case it was women he wanted to keep down. Especially me. That's why he let me prattle with fortune-telling. He thought that if I was busy pretending to look into the future and find things that had never been lost, I'd stay in my place and let him kill himself in the stone sheds. My father brought our family here when I was a small child, and he did the same. He died before he was my age. Two of my brothers died too. My sons would have followed if I hadn't exerted myself and pulled them out of there as soon as their father died."

Rachel nodded sympathetically. For a while it was quiet; then she said, "Recently I lost something."

"Of course you did," Pia said, her pencil flying. "People are always losing things. What was it?"

"A seashell."

"Look for it where you lost it."

"Where I lost it?"

"Certainly. Whenever you lose something, go back and look for it where you saw it last. Do it now."

"It was in that chest."

"Get up, boy," Pia told Marie.

Marie stood up and Rachel opened the lid of the trunk. Inside, resting on a folded white linen tablecloth, was the missing conch shell, its whorled chambers glowing orange and pink, like a January sunset over the south shoulder of Kingdom Mountain.

Rachel smiled. "Thank you," she said.

"Don't thank me," Pia said, handing her the finished portrait. "You're the one who found it."

Rachel sat back down on the love seat and admired the portrait. "I'm flattered," she said. "This looks like me at seventeen."

Pia frowned and finished her tea. "It's what you look like to me this afternoon," she said irritably. "Now don't talk any more about my work. I can't stand to discuss it. Tell me why that shell means so much to you."

Rachel, who liked Pia very much, smiled and used a gypsy trick herself by answering one question with another. "What do you see in your teacup?" she said.

"Wet leaves. That's all I ever see. You can't predict the future by looking into a cup of tea, Mrs. Benedict; and while we're on the subject, I'll tell you that we don't burn the clothes of our dead or hold our own courts or steal children, and I went through the eleventh grade at Barre Academy and would have graduated, probably at the head of my class, except that's the year my father died and my mother and I both had to go to work in a bakery."

Pia paused.

"But what is it you want that you don't have?"

Rachel smiled at her.

"Another child?"

She nodded.

"Yours hasn't turned out exactly the way you expected, has he? Oh, don't take offense. None of mine did, either, and I kept trying and hoping for a girl, thinking at least then I'd have someone to talk to someday; when this one came and I saw what was between his legs I could gladly have drowned him." Without pausing more than a second or two, Pia said, "Does your husband want another child too?"

Rachel hesitated, then nodded.

"He hasn't stopped sleeping with you in despair, has he?"

"No."

"Thank heavens!" Pia said with relief. "That's usually the end of everything good in a marriage when that happens." She sighed. "Well, you know what they say about marriage, Mrs. Benedict."

"No, what do they say?"

"You don't know that old rhyme? It goes like this:

"Ice cream is a very strange thing,
And so are codfish balls.
But the people that people marry
Are the strangest thing of all."

Rachel laughed, and then for a minute the two women sat silently. Marie looked from one to another, wondering who would speak next. She was enormously interested in their conversation, and had memorized every word to repeat to herself later. She hoped they would visit all afternoon, but already Pia was scratching one foot with the other.

"Well," Pia said finally, "you'll probably get what you want, Mrs. Benedict. Most people do, if they'd only have the sense to recognize it, much less appreciate it, when it comes.

"Now then. Do you know what your husband wants with my sons? They've been tied up with him half the afternoon."

Rachel shook her head. "No, he hasn't told me."

Pia stood up. "Come, boy," she said to Marie. "Goodbye, Mrs. Benedict. Remember what I told you."

On the way back to the camp at the mouth of the river, Pia stopped suddenly and said, as though summarizing a complex debate with herself, "So you see, parrot, how the lives of others, especially the rich, always seem less complicated than our own until we come to know them well."

"What do you mean, Pia?"

"I mean Rachel Benedict's lonely. Couldn't you tell? That may be an opportunity for you. A big opportunity."

A few minutes later she spoke again, for the second and last time before they reached the camp.

"That Captain," she said musingly, more to herself than to Marie. "He has some great and terrible secret in his past. Before we leave, I'd like to ferret it out."

That evening around the fire, Pia's older sons told her about their transaction with the Captain. He had taken them to a quarry on Kingdom Mountain, high above the Big House, where he had showed them a perpendicular vein of black granite flecked with silver mica. It was about ten feet wide by sixty feet high, and he had asked them whether they could remove it intact and carve it into a family monument in the shape of an obelisk.

"What did you say?" Pia asked.

"We told him we could," Ernest said.

Pia looked at Robert, who shrugged. "It certainly won't be easy, but I think we can probably do what he wants. Why not? He'll pay well."

Pia was instantly furious. This was too much like steady work, she shouted, and steady work always led to complacency of the worst kind. What if they decided to settle down here? Where would she be then with her feet that drove her half mad with itching if they stayed even three days in the same place? Traveling with some rundown one-horse medicine show, running a creaking wheel of fortune and guessing weights and ages, that was where.

"How much did you ask for?" she said suddenly.

"A dollar a day for us two. Half that for Ethan."

"Did he agree to pay it?"

"Without demurring."

"Asses! He would have given you two dollars a day apiece."

To reassert her control over the family, Pia went to Hell's Gate early the next morning with the intention of negotiating her son's rate upward. She took Marie, who except for her blue eyes was indistinguishable from one of the gypsy's own grandchildren. They went into the Captain's private office overlooking the lumberyard, and there, without preamble, Pia demanded and won two dollars a day for each of her three sons.

The next morning the gypsies and Marie walked up the riding path beside the brook on Kingdom Mountain to the foot of the hanging meadow. There the Captain had dammed the brook to form a small pond, whose overflow turned a wooden waterwheel with an inscription at its base that said, *The wheel will never turn with water that has passed.*

"I see this Benedict is a philosopher!" Pia said approvingly. "What a strange man he is, parrot. What can have driven him here to this forsaken corner of nowhere, I wonder?"

The quarry was at the top of the meadow, just below the steep uppermost slope of the mountain. It was more than one hundred feet deep and about two hundred feet in diameter. From it had come the foundation blocks for the factory and other buildings in Hell's Gate, but it had not been worked for a decade and it was half full of water, aquamarine and opaque, that had seeped out of springs in the walls. The runoff formed the headwaters of the brook, which wound leisurely through the meadows, here and there vanishing underground for a distance, before starting its long fall down the mountain.

The gypsies set up camp at the head of the meadow, and the men went to work immediately. First they siphoned out the pit, since they were uncomfortable working around water, even though it would help break a long fall. They spent the rest of the spring drilling out the rectangular block, using no blasting powder because they were afraid of fragmenting the vein of shiny dark granite along some hidden fault line.

Pia, in the meantime, had been commissioned to sketch Abie's portrait and the Captain's. Abie's had gone well. She had drawn him in his baseball uniform, leaning on a bat, and had captured perfectly his expression of arrogant confidence and even the ring of lighter hair around the crown of his head, which made it appear as though the sun were reflecting brightly off his hair on even the darkest day.

The Captain's likeness had been much more difficult to represent; no matter how many times she tried, his left eye persisted in gazing off into some private distance, though in fact he looked steadily at her the entire time. But when she finally gave up and presented him with the best of a dozen imperfect sketches, he seemed very pleased to hang it on the wall of his office behind his desk, across from Abie's portrait, and he appeared not to notice the discrepancy in the eyes at all.

"It's that secret of his that's responsible for my failure," Pia confided to Marie in great frustration after refusing to accept a penny for the portrait. "If I knew that, I'd at least know what he's looking at with that watch eye, and then I could get him right. I'm dying of curiosity, but I can't find a soul, not even his wife, who'll talk about it."

"Why don't you ask him?" Marie inquired.

Pia snorted. "You've got a lot to learn," she said. "Can't you just hear him telling the great secret of his life to a prying gypsy? I'm fairly sure it's something he feels guilty about, though. Otherwise his wife would talk about it if he wouldn't."

In the days that followed, Pia's conviction that the Captain was haunted by some terrible memory grew to the point where she began to wake up in the middle of the night thinking about it. Driven by a curiosity as consuming as she believed his secret to be, she stopped eating regularly and could not carry on the simplest conversation without introducing her obsession. Day in and day out she speculated on its nature, until finally one afternoon when she was pumping Rachel for all she was worth over tea at the Big House, and Rachel was being as polite and uncooperative as ever, Pia set down her cup and saucer with a clatter and announced calmly, "I understand."

Rachel smiled at the emaciated gypsy woman, who had lost ten pounds in the past week alone, and whose sunken eyes appeared to be looking out of two black craters.

"I don't know why it's taken so long," Pia said. "You see, Mrs. Benedict, it's been staring me in the face for a month. The past is as unknowable as the future, all the books that have been written about it notwithstanding. Pass me that tray of little cakes, will you, Mario? I could eat a horse."

During the next two weeks Pia did not mention the Captain's secret once. She gained back all the weight she had lost and a few pounds besides; and except for her itching feet, which were really beginning to drive her to distraction, she seemed as content as ever, which is to say dissatisfied with everything and everyone nearly all the time.

In late May, to Pia's relief, her sons began to carve out the obelisk. By June it was ready to inscribe. Although he was not a religious man, the Captain asked Ned Baxter to suggest a suitable epitaph from the Bible to go under his name and was pleased with Ned's choice. It was from Proverbs, and both apt and to the point: *Seest thou a man diligent in his business? He shall stand before kings.*

When the obelisk was finished, it was fifty-five feet high and tapered to a slender, elegant spire. Leaning against the rock wall from which it had been freed, it rested on a ledge just over the aquamarine water, which had gradually seeped back into the pit again.

On the morning of Independence Day the Captain sent Ned Baxter to haul the monument out of the pit. The gypsies and Marie stood nearby to watch. Working carefully and methodically, Ned ran a new two-inch steel cable from the spool of the old steam winch bolted to the solid rock at the quarry's edge out through a gigantic spruce boom looming over the pit. He wound the end securely around the obelisk, which he had first swathed like a mummy with clean wiping rags from the finishing room of the factory. As he started the engine, the gypsies began to straggle up to the edge of the quarry, where they stood talking quietly, affecting little interest.

The swaddled obelisk straightened out away from the wall. Coal-black smoke poured out of the winch. The engine strained as the great stone swung off the ledge and began to ascend. The steam engine shook and seemed to be pulling up out of its moorings.

The obelisk dangled partway up the wall, twisting slowly a quarter of a revolution in each direction; the engine could not lift it an inch higher.

"Quick, set it back down again," the Captain said.

But before Ned could reverse the winch there was a terrific vibrating crack, as though a bolt of lightning had struck directly in their midst. The gigantic spruce boom snapped like a stick of dry kindling, and the obelisk plummeted to the ledge below. There it broke entirely in two and the upper half toppled off into the water and sank out of sight.

Late that afternoon Pia sat beside the waterwheel at the foot of the meadow. The shadow of the mountain lay over the town far below. Nearby, Marie splashed in the pond with the bear.

Pia sighed. The accident at the quarry had seemed to sadden her for some reason, and she looked years older than she had two or three months ago.

"Parrot," she said in a somber voice, "the trouble with being curious by nature is that you're quite apt to find out that you didn't really want to know what you thought you did."

Marie stopped playing. "What do you mean, Pia?"

"It's like this," Pia said earnestly. "For a long time I was dying of curiosity to learn Captain Benedict's great secret—whatever it was that drove him to come here and barricade himself and his family in this wasteland. I pumped his wife, pumped the villagers, I finally even took your suggestion and asked him outright: nothing. I lost sleep, couldn't eat solid food; I thought I might go mad. I was pretty certain I'd get at it when I painted his portrait, but it was like painting the portrait of a statue, except for the left eye, and that seemed to be looking at the future rather than the past. Then I concluded that you couldn't divine the meaning of the past anyway, but that was just an excuse for my lack of success. The fact is, I was trying too hard to figure out what was obvious all the time, though I didn't realize it until this morning when the obelisk fell.

"While everyone else was gaping down at that foolish broken monument, I was watching Benedict. I suspected that he'd be angry; I was hoping he would be, since I wanted to see what he was like when he lost some of that infuriating self-possession. But he merely shrugged his shoulders and got on his horse and rode back down the mountain. That's when I realized the nature of his secret. It was as though I'd been hit by a thunderbolt. 'You fool,' I thought to myself. 'You meddling old fool. Why didn't you have sense enough at your age to leave things alone?' "

"What is the secret then, Pia?"

"I don't know. I don't want to know. I wouldn't listen if he tried to tell me. All I know, parrot, is its nature, which has nothing to do with any of the things I suspected—remorse, guilt, pride—but some enormous sorrow."

"Sorrow? How did you divine that?"

"Divining had nothing to do with it. I just used common sense. I knew he must be disappointed when that idiotic needle was smashed in two. He had to be. And when he didn't show it, but just shrugged, I understood that he was used to dealing with disappointment. I don't mean failure; any successful person can deal with that because you have to, many times, in order to be successful. But the carved stone meant a great deal to him and yet he was able to shrug off his disappointment because he's obviously had a good deal of practice. Whatever the secret is, and it doesn't matter at all, it's rooted in grief, which I'm positive he's had to deal with every day of his life since coming here; and so has she, for that matter."

"You mean Mrs. Benedict?"

"Certainly. You can see it in her eyes, hear it in her voice every time she speaks. In her case I supposed it was the awful isolation of this place from most of the things in the world that an intelligent woman like her would value. But now I don't think so. It's his great sorrow that she shares—and sorrow, parrot, is and must be a private thing that even a so-called gypsy, who's supposed to show people their true reflection, shouldn't tamper with. Ever. Remember that!"

Marie nodded solemnly, as she always did when Pia told her something important, and after a minute resumed playing with the bear. The gypsy shook her head in disgust over her own obtuseness and then put the entire matter out of her head and concentrated on the waterwheel.

" 'The wheel will never turn with water that has passed,' " Pia quoted musingly.

"What does it signify, Pia?"

Pia laughed. "No more than that a person should always be forward-looking, now that I think of it. And that reminds me of a certain matter I want to discuss with you. Come up here on dry land and pay attention."

Brown as a gypsy, Marie sat in the grass at Pia's feet to let the sunshine dry her off while she listened.

"Soon, young parrot," Pia said in her harsh, cheerful voice, "each month for about seven days you'll bleed some blood from here, between your legs. It's nothing to be alarmed over, but during that time you'll have to be especially careful to keep yourself clean. A soft clean cloth folded once or twice and placed so is usually sufficient. Are you listening?"

"Yes, certainly, Pia," Marie said, though she was not at all sure that such a strange thing would ever happen to her.

"Good. This is important."

The gypsy went on to explain that Marie's breasts would develop soon, and their purpose. "Some hair will appear beneath your arms," she said, "and on your legs and between them, where you'll place the cloth each month."

She looked at Marie steadily.

"Let nothing else come there until you love a man who loves you in return. Do you understand?"

Marie shook her head. "How will I know when that time arrives?"

"You'll know."

"Will you tell me?"

"No, I won't need to. And besides, I won't be there."

"Why not, Pia? I don't understand."

Pia scratched one foot steadily with the other, looking off over the far mountains with her smoky eyes.

"Parrot, I said some weeks ago that this Captain owed you something. Now I believe I know what. He owes you a home."

"No! My home is with you."

The gypsy shook her head. "I wish it were, but it's not. To us, one place is about the same as another as long as the family stays together. But for you, there may yet be something better in store than tramping from place to place. Now listen again. I have some final instructions."

After Pia finished telling Marie what to do, she took a package wrapped in brown paper out of her knapsack and handed it to her to open. Inside were a bright red dress with white lace trim around the sleeves and collar, a pair of high white stockings, and a pair of sandals.

When Marie had put on the new clothes Pia nodded with satisfaction. "Now, watch," she said.

From her pack she withdrew a cheap hand mirror, which she rapped sharply against the base of the waterwheel. It shattered into several pieces. "Bad luck?" she said. "No, I don't believe that nonsense." She picked up the largest shard of glass and turned it over. Its backing was as depthless and opaque as the big lake at night. "Look into this and tell me what you see."

"Nothing."

"Turn it over."

Marie looked at her own reflection. Her hair had grown out again and fell in dark curls to her shoulders. It was very glossy, with strong natural waves. Her face and neck above the collar were almost as dark as Pia's from the sun and wind on the mountain, and she looked considerably older now than she had a few months ago; her face was narrower, her high cheekbones more pronounced. She looked like a young woman.

"Now what do you see?"

"Myself."

"Good! That's as much of the future as you can ever know. The rest is as blank as the back of the mirror."

Marie grinned at her reflection. She touched her hair.

"No," Pia added cheerfully, "you aren't going to be any kind of great beauty. Beauty is a soft, fleeting quality, like the little golden leaves that come on the trees in the spring and then quickly turn green. It has no endurance except in rare instances like Mrs. Benedict's. Also, most beautiful women tend to look alike. You'll certainly never be beautiful. But look in the glass again, Marie. With your dark hair and skin and your fine blue eyes and your long, strong limbs, you'll be distinctive-looking and handsome, as I once was myself, and men will probably like you as well as or more than they like a beautiful woman. Moreover, you'll be able to do most of what a man can do, with one notable exception, and they'll admire your skill—if you're quiet about it—and like you all the better. Nor will most women be jealous of you. That much I can tell you.

"Parrot," she continued, "your last name doesn't fit. Blair doesn't tell a thing about you. Throughout the past two years you've stood up well. You didn't complain of being tired or cold or lonesome. You laughed and danced, and if you cried for your parents, you cried silently at night, alone on your sleeping pallet. Your name shouldn't be Blair any longer, but Blythe. Call yourself Marie Blythe from now on. You're basically a happy person, and your name ought to fit you."

She paused, gazing down on the yellow village far below. "Once again, Marie Blythe, remember these things well. First, the family is most important. Never act against it. What lies between your legs is yours to keep or give; don't give it away lightly. Be careful what you wish for because you'll very probably get it, like the foolish granite vanity of the Captain; on the other hand, never pass up an opportunity to help yourself. Never run away from a situation without remembering that you take yourself along; but if you do have to leave, don't say goodbye, and above all don't watch a person or a place out of sight. It's about the worst bad luck there is. Will you remember?"

Marie nodded. She stood up and hugged the wet bear, which tried to bite her with its decaying gums. Without speaking, she started down through the woods toward the village. Just before she went around the first bend she looked back, despite Pia's warning. The meadow was empty.

Chapter Four

At an auction years later, Marie came upon a pasteboard box containing a set of small red leather diaries. She knew immediately that they had belonged to the Captain, since she recalled seeing him make regular brief entries in identical pocket-sized books. They began about ten years before he arrived in Hell's Gate, and although most of the entries were very brief, they revealed a good deal about the man who by then had already become something of a myth throughout Kingdom County and northern Vermont. . . .

The myth was that he had come into the county penniless, from no one knew where, getting off the train in Kingdom Common with nothing to his name but the jawbone of a great blue whale and the deed to the unincorporated and still totally unsettled township of Hell's Gate: which he had somehow, no doubt in return for some dark service like dynamiting a railroad bridge or a sawmill dam, gotten from George Van Dyke, the New England lumber baron.

The facts were different. The facts, as the diaries made clear, were that Captain Benedict came from a prosperous Maine shipping family; that he had plenty of money, though neither then nor ever the millions ascribed to him by the myth; and that he had purchased the one hundred thousand acres of

wilderness comprising Hell's Gate from Van Dyke for ninety
cents an acre with money he had earned in his family's lumber
shipping business.

When Abraham Benedict stepped off the train on that mild
September afternoon in 1890—without the whale's jaw, which
he did not bring to Vermont until four years later—he was
thirty years old: a good age to undertake an enterprise of the
magnitude he had evidently already envisioned, since by then
he was old enough to have had considerable experience in the
world (he had captained his first lumber ship at twenty-one
and been around the world on it several times), yet still young
enough to believe that he could do whatever was necessary to
realize that vision: a self-contained community in one of the
last pockets of wilderness east of the Mississippi. He rented a
canoe, paddled north up the Lower Kingdom River into the
south bay of Lake Memphremagog, and shortly before dusk
put ashore near the tip of the thickly wooded peninsula between the two northernmost peaks of the Green Mountain
range. "Ten years," he wrote in his diary that night by firelight.

The myth, as it began to take shape in a line parallel to but
only occasionally coinciding exactly with the actual events,
was that he cleared the peninsula single-handedly. In fact, he
hired a gang of local loggers, under the supervision of Ned
Baxter, to cut off the timber on the future site of the town and
went back to his home in Portland for the winter. Most of the
accessible softwood, the big first-growth pines and firs and
spruces, had already been cut and warped up the lake to Canada in gigantic booms by Van Dyke's crews, but there was
hardwood timber everywhere—sugar maples and yellow and
white birches, ash and basswood, beech, wild cherry, butternut; and, near the lake, some red oak. As soon as the river and
bay froze, Ned brought in a sawmill piecemeal, which he assembled on the brook near the foot of Canada Mountain, just
across the narrows from the tip of the peninsula. That winter
he turned out a quarter of a million board feet of lumber, which
Abraham rafted to Magog, twenty-five miles away, when he

returned in the spring, living for a few months in a log house roofed with hemlock bark through which, on clear nights, he could look up at a narrow strip of stars.

The second year Ned cut a million feet of lumber, which Abraham again took north to Canada in the spring. But the Captain, as he was already called by most of his men, did not plan to raise his family in a logging settlement. It had come to his attention that good hardwood chairs were in high demand in Vermont and elsewhere. Whenever people gathered together for any length of time, they sat down. They sat to eat, to ride on trains and streetcars, to read, to attend church and school. He himself sat only rarely in those days, except to tally up the number of board feet of lumber cut in his sawmill in a given week or to make a brief entry in his diary. *(23 April 1892: Today the ice went out of the lake. It rains tonight.)* But he knew from talking with Ned Baxter, who before he was hired by the Captain had worked for ten years at the American Heritage chair factory in the Common, that there was a nearly unlimited market for all the chairs and settees he could manufacture. First, however, he would have to devise a way to get them to the railhead.

"Can we drive a spur track up through that swamp along the river?" he asked Ned.

The logging foreman thought a minute. "That shouldn't be impossible."

"Nothing's impossible," the Captain said.

"A good many things are impossible," Ned told his employer quietly. "But a railroad from Kingdom Common isn't one of them. We'll need more than a few dozen loggers to do it, though."

There was a myth about the railroad too, to the effect that it was laid by a thousand Irish immigrants (in fact there were no more than three hundred) whom Abraham brought down the river through the swamp on several tandem rafts. Midway between the mouth of the river and the peninsula, as they stared with growing incredulity at the mountains rising almost sheer up out of the bay, they began to express strong reservations about working at a job they believed couldn't be done. They were a rough gang of men just off the train from Boston —that much was no myth—so they were somewhat taken aback when, according to the story, the Captain stopped the rafts over deep water, drew a pistol, and told them they had a choice. They could continue up the bay with him, he announced calmly, and work for fair wages laying the ballast and tracks; or they could go ashore immediately, he didn't say how. Ned Baxter always maintained that the gun was the only error in the mythical version of this part of the story; the Captain was in fact not brandishing a pistol or any other weapon. Ned said that the grumbling died away quickly, and the immigrants never objected to working for Abraham again.

A little less than a year later, the peninsula was linked to the rest of Kingdom County and New England by rail. Captain Benedict's diaries revealed that he had fifty thousand dollars in assistance from the Boston and Montreal line, which was eager for his business, and that the entire project cost four times that much, though he saved a substantial amount by cutting the ties at his own sawmill and bringing in ballast for the embankment with his own rafts. He paid the Irishmen fairly and gave each of them a twenty-dollar bonus for completing the spur track on schedule.

The chair factory flourished immediately, and at the Chicago World's Columbian Exposition of 1893 the Captain secured a verbal contract to supply the United States Seating Company with all the hardwood chairs and settees he could manufacture. That was the same summer that Herman Fischner and the German cabinetmakers came to the peninsula to build the Big House and the village.

The myth was that the Captain had gone to Germany to recruit them, but actually he had traveled west to Michigan, to the furniture manufacturing city of Grand Rapids, to locate the man who had made a remarkable rolltop desk that had won a gold medal in the furniture exhibition in Chicago. Conversing with Fischner in his own language, Abraham learned that he was dissatisfied with his situation in Grand Rapids. He and half a dozen other cabinetmakers from the Black Forest region of Germany had been induced to come there by promises of high wages, comfortable houses, and a share in the profits of the factory that would employ them, but after eight years in America they were still working for apprentice pay and living in shabby row houses.

"I think I can help," Abraham said. "How would you like to make furniture for twice what you're earning here, in a beautiful place that will remind you of home?"

"I would," the cabinetmaker said, and a week later he and five of his neighbors got off the train in Hell's Gate. They looked at the long two-story factory, the bark-sheathed log houses clustered at the end of the peninsula, the soaring mountains, just starting to turn color for fall. "It's very beautiful," Fischner said. "Like Germany. But where are the good houses you said we'd live in?"

"You're going to build them," the Captain said equably. "You're going to build them just like your houses in Germany. Then you're going to go back to Grand Rapids for your families."

As time passed and Hell's Gate grew from a sawdust pile in the wilderness to a unique and prosperous village, the myth concerning the Captain grew too. He was worth a million dollars; he was worth five million. He had a mistress in Montreal, another in Boston. Perhaps he contributed to some of these legends by being close-mouthed about his past, dressing always in a blue captain's coat and admitting no close friends to his family, whom he did not bring to Hell's Gate until the fall of 1894, when the Big House was completed.

In the spring of 1895, the Captain began work on his most ambitious and remarkable project, a vast natural park which eventually encompassed most of the eastern slope of Kingdom Mountain above the Big House. With the assistance of Ned Baxter, he designed two one-way carriage drives from his house to the hay meadow on the mountain and proceeded to spend thousands of dollars each year in the construction of bridges, dams, lawns, flower beds, and rustic cabins, while leaving the wild beauty of the mountainside untouched. Anyone in Hell's Gate could walk in the park at any time, but neat yellow signs posted at intervals prohibited anyone from "cutting, picking, or mutilating any flowers, vines, shrubs, plants, or trees" growing there; the Captain strictly adhered to his own rule, cutting no logs in the park, which he dedicated to his wife and deeded in perpetuity to the people of Hell's Gate.

As the factory grew, Abraham began hiring more day laborers from the Common, whom he transported to and from his village each day by train. Most of these men worked assembling and caning chairs or with the logging crew on the mountains, and from the start they were paid considerably less than Abraham's more skilled machine operators and less than half the wages of the German cabinetmakers. Gradually this discrepancy in pay became an issue with the day workers, and one January day in 1899 a Commoner named Forrest Hill angrily barged into Abraham's office and slammed down on his desk a petition demanding higher pay for the day workers and threatening a strike if this demand was not met immediately.

The factory owner read the petition carefully, put it in his top drawer, and walked up to the chair room, where he calmly informed the men that they could work for the wages he paid or find jobs elsewhere. Forrest Hill was furious. A big rough-spoken man who stood an inch over six feet and weighed two hundred and forty pounds, he had considerable influence over the day laborers, for the simple reason that most of them were afraid of him. Of the sixty or so men in the chair room and on the mountain, nearly fifty walked off the job, and the remaining ten were bullied into quitting within the next few days.

The Captain did not seem perturbed. On the morning following the walkout, when the factory train pulled into Hell's Gate nearly empty, he asked Ned Baxter to meet with him in his office. "Ned," he said, "I'd like you to have several hundred handbills printed up in French, advertising jobs in Hell's Gate. Have them printed on yellow paper with a sketch of the village. Then take a carpentry crew across the bridge and build some plain tight houses."

Early one morning in the fall of 1899, about six months after the Canadians arrived in Hell's Gate, Ned Baxter discovered a piece of paper nailed to the main entrance of the factory. It was addressed to Captain Abraham Benedict and it announced in large printed words, most of which were badly misspelled, that unless the "Canuck strike brakers" returned to Canada within a week, they would be burned out, along with the factory and the village. It was signed with three scrawled K's.

The Ku Klux Klan is not ordinarily thought of as having been active in northern New England, but from time to time as late as the 1930s, night riders even as far north as Kingdom County crusaded under that banner against Catholics, and against French-Canadian Catholics in particular, usually on the pretext that their unwillingness to speak English exclusively and to become naturalized immediately was unpatriotic. For the most part, Vermont Klansmen confined their depredations to burning a cross just out of shotgun range in some backcountry French tenant's barnyard, or hanging the effigy of a priest at midnight in the dark graveyard of an empty parish church. But because of the aborted strike, which Forrest Hill was now said to blame entirely on the Canadians, Ned was very concerned about the threat, which he immediately took to his employer.

The Captain glanced at the paper, then threw it into his office stove, advising Ned to notify the Canadians on his crew to be on the lookout, without frightening them, and to come to the factory office or Big House immediately if anyone appeared in Little Canada without business there. Abraham himself did not seem in any way alarmed, and after an uneventful week passed, and then another, Ned turned his thoughts to other matters.

In Hell's Gate and throughout Kingdom County, the night before Halloween was and still is today known as Cabbage Night. For generations, youthful pranksters have been given mild license on the evening of October 30 to avenge themselves against the adult population in general by heaving rotten cabbages and pumpkins into dooryards, chalking caricatures on porches, and hooting from house to house with various homemade noisemakers until an hour or so after dark.

Ned Baxter, who viewed this night of frivolity skeptically and did not want his family involved in any of the scrapes that sometimes resulted, took his son duck hunting that evening. Ned Jr. was ten and had just received his first gun; the shooting was excellent, and they stayed in Ned's blind in a small cove on the east side of the bay, about a quarter of a mile below the sawmill, until dusk. Just at twilight, a late-flying flock of goldeneyes came in from the north, and the man and boy sat watching silently, their guns across their laps, until it was too dark to see the birds on the water. Then the moon rose, a great orange Halloween moon, and they watched for a while longer.

Ned sighed happily. "That was something, wasn't it, Neddy," he said.

Ned Jr. nodded. He was a quiet boy, like his father, and like Ned he loved the woods and the lake and the brooks that ran off the mountains into it. Almost since the time he had started walking, his father had taken him hunting and fishing with him, and he was proud of the boy's ability to handle a fly rod and, now, a gun. Ned Jr. was a good student too, in contrast to Abie Benedict, who had little interest in either school or the woods and this very minute was running wild up in the village. Ned's single criticism of the Captain, in fact, was that he did not control his own son better, and this is what he was puzzling over as he and his son waded toward shore.

Just as they entered the tall marsh grass, Ned heard the click of oarlocks from down the bay. Ned Jr. raised his head; he had heard it too.

The boat came around the south point of the cove. It was

quite distinct in the moonlight; Ned could see the outline of five men. They were wearing white hoods and talking loudly, as though they had been drinking. It was a long boat, and there were two rowers. Several gun barrels jutted out over its sides, glinting in the moonlight.

"Quick," Ned whispered to his son. "Run up to the Big House as fast as you can and tell the Captain that the KKK has come to burn the village."

Ned Jr. was off like a shot, racing up the path along the edge of the cove. He was already one of the fastest runners in the village, and in less than five minutes he had reached the hulking dark cone of sawdust beside the sawmill and was scrambling up the embankment below the covered bridge. He pounded across the bridge and sprinted down the long street. He passed the dark factory; passed Early Kinneson, the storekeeper, standing vigil on his porch steps with a bucket of water intended for juvenile marauders; he passed Abie Benedict, taunting Early from the safety of the street. Abie called to him, but Ned kept running. Something soft and wet splattered against the back of his head. He did not turn or slacken pace. He raced up the hill, past the darkened schoolhouse, under the whale's jaw, and up the drive toward the Big House, where for the first time in his life he did not stop to knock but burst through the door.

Abraham was sitting in his shirt sleeves in the library, reading. Ned Jr. ran past the open library door, whirled, turned back, and half stumbled into the room. He had just wind enough left to deliver his message. "Quick, Captain Benedict. Ghosts in white sheets—they've come to burn the town!"

No one person, including Ned Jr., witnessed everything the Captain did during the next five minutes; the account of his actions, as pieced together first on the village street, repeated in kitchens and parlors lighted long past midnight, and then refined some evenings later on the porch steps into part of the myth, was necessarily a composite one. Ned Jr. saw him get out of his armchair and put on his blue coat. The boy was certain of that detail, since he had never before seen the Captain in his shirt sleeves. He said that the Captain did not seem to hurry, though he wasted no time, either, and was already buttoning the coat and moving toward the parlor when he told Ned to go around to the stable and get his mare for him and not to bother with the saddle.

The Benedict housekeeper, Wyalia Kinneson, saw him remove the harpoon from the iron brackets over the fireplace mantel, but she could add no more than that because as she started back toward the dining room where she stood open-mouthed at the sideboard holding a tray of Haviland dishes from supper, she promptly fainted. She did not, she claimed, even remember the sound of the breaking china, which brought Rachel hurrying from her bedroom to the top of the stairs.

"What's wrong, Abraham?" she called down. "Did Abie break a window?"

Then she saw Wyalia and the broken dishes, and the Captain standing over her with the harpoon, and her hand shot to her mouth.

"Mrs. Kinneson had a start, that's all," he called up in a calm voice. "Perhaps you could get her some smelling salts. I have to step downstreet for a few minutes."

Later Rachel told Ned Baxter's wife, Ellen, that it was almost as though he was apologizing to her for having to go out again, since he had returned just fifteen minutes ago from checking on things at the factory, and did not like to be away from the house after eight o'clock in the evening. She confirmed Ned Jr.'s report that her husband did not seem especially hurried, though by the time she reached the bottom of the stairs he was outside, where young Ned was waiting under the portico with the mare.

He thanked the boy courteously, mounted, and from inside the house Rachel heard the hoofbeats going down the drive. She still thought Abie had been into some mischief until she revived Wyalia, who had heard enough of Ned Jr.'s report to sit bolt upright and state quite calmly that the town was on fire and they were all as good as dead, before fainting again. This time Rachel let the housekeeper lie where she had collapsed, in the shards of the expensive china, and ran to the door herself, expecting to see flames. But all she glimpsed was a boy whom she mistook for her own running fast down the drive.

"Abie!" she called. "Come back here!"

The boy kept running.

What was happening below in the factory yard, in the meantime, took place so quickly that no one except Ned Sr. and the Captain, neither of whom ever discussed the episode, was ever certain of the sequence of events. But Ned Jr. was the next person to arrive, and what he told later was the closest thing to an eyewitness account.

The Captain was sitting on his mare about twenty feet from the main entrance of the factory, Ned Jr. said. A crude cross of two planks nailed together and soaked in turpentine lay burning on the ground between the Captain and four hooded figures, who stood facing him with their hands high over their heads. Behind them, his shotgun leveled at their backs, stood Ned Sr. Near the factory entrance a torch lay sputtering.

The Captain glanced at Ned Jr., who was panting hard. "Pick up that torch and bring it here, will you please, Neddy?" he said calmly. "It's too close to the building."

The boy nodded mechanically. He trotted across the yard, passed behind his father, standing silently with the gun pointed at the four men in hoods, and picked up the torch. In its light, he saw something white above his head. He looked up and almost dropped the torch in his astonishment.

Impaled to the factory door like his own scrawled ultimatum, with his boots dangling several inches above the ground and the long wooden handle of the harpoon projecting from between his shoulders, was the body of Forrest Hill.

Rachel Benedict was as delighted by the arrival of the Canadians as she was dismayed, soon afterward, by their aloofness. Like the wives of the German cabinetmakers, and, for that matter, the wives of the foremen and machine operators who lived in the thirty yellow houses, the French-Canadian women were ill at ease with the beautiful, well-educated wife of their husbands' employer, who, as Pia had told Marie, had been lonesome since the day she first set foot in Hell's Gate.

Still, especially in the early years, she was charmed by the Big House and the village, which was nearly as remarkable for what it was not as for what it was. It was not, for example, a railroad town, though it had its own railroad with its own private train that came and went twice a day, six days a week. But no trains passed through the village, which was literally the end of the line, and the depot was used mostly to store paint, machine parts, and crates of furniture.

Nor was it a horse-and-buggy town. The only horse was Abraham's Morgan mare, which he rode in the park on Kingdom Mountain once each day except in the worst weather, and the only buggy belonged to Rachel: a fancy Upland Flyer with a red leather dash and two brass lamps. Because it was not a horse-and-buggy town, Hell's Gate had no feed store, no livery stable, and no harness shop, and the only place for the village men to loaf was the company store or, in fishing season, the walkway of the covered bridge; but since all the men in the village were employed sixty hours a week at the factory, no one had much time for loafing anyway.

Kingdom Common, ten miles to the south, was a trading center for farmers, but no farmers came to Hell's Gate. Hell's Gate had no trolleys, no horse cars, no street lamps, and only one street. It had a fine silver cornet band consisting of four German cabinetmakers and two machine operators, and later, when Abie was in his teens, a town baseball team that once won forty-six consecutive games. The schoolhouse was the largest gathering place, so there were no traveling minstrel shows or plays and no temperance lectures or travelogues, though the Captain always ran a special train to the Common when a Shakespearean troupe or circus or Chautauqua came there. And since there was no way for them to reach Hell's

Gate, the train being used only for day workers at the factory, villagers, and special guests, there were no peddlers: no ragmen, scissors grinders, horse traders, yeastmen, or patent medicine hawkers, all of whom came regularly to the Common and most other turn-of-the-century rural towns in northern New England.

Hell's Gate had no saloon, though most of the German families brewed their own strong dark beer, and the Canadians made delicious wines from dandelions, potatoes, turnips, and every kind of edible berry that grew on the mountains.

There were no churches either. The Germans held their own Lutheran prayer meetings in one another's houses, some of the foremen and machine operators went to church in the Common on a Sunday morning train specially provided for that purpose, and a priest continued to visit the Canadians off and on for many years. (The Captain and Rachel did not go to church themselves, and had not since coming to Kingdom County.) Nor were there many secular celebrations in which the entire village participated. The Canadians visited the Big House on Christmas Eve, the rest of the people on Christmas Day afternoon. Children hung flower baskets on one another's front doors on May Day, planted small trees in the park on Arbor Day, and played pranks on adults on Cabbage Night and April Fool's Day. The Canadians celebrated New Year's with a feast and general exchange of gifts; the Germans kept mainly to themselves and saved more scrip than anyone else.

Hell's Gate was a quiet, tolerant, and attractive place to live, remote from the clamor and tumult of the rest of rural America. Every day in the Boston newspaper (which itself arrived a day late) there were grim and lurid accounts of farmers going under and committing suicide, country wives going insane and murdering their husbands and children, hired girls drinking Paris green, whole armies of tramps invading railroad towns. In Hell's Gate there was none of this. There was no poverty, no prostitution, and no police protection because there was no crime. Yet although Rachel appreciated the village's unique qualities, her loneliness increased every year. Even her friendship with Ellen Baxter was somewhat constrained by Ellen's job as the Captain's auditor and stenographer.

The park was a great source of pleasure to Rachel. Soon after it was completed, however, a premature arthritic condition limited her walking excursions there to dry sunny days in the summer. She hoped in time to become better friends with the villagers, but after a few mutually embarrassing attempts to entertain the village women at her home and three or four even more awkward goodwill visits to the Canadians, she turned most of her attention toward her husband and son. What she needed, however, was a companion, an intellectual and social equal with whom she could converse freely, as she could not with a young boy, however precocious, or even always with her husband; for although Abraham was devoted to her, he had his vision to occupy him, and he was one of those constitutionally active persons who are always busy with some large or small project and cannot completely understand how anyone else finds time to be lonely.

Early one evening in the summer of 1903, Rachel sat on the love seat at the head of the stairs reading a light travel account of India. The Captain was taking his after-supper ride in the park, Abie was off somewhere playing ball, and she found herself hoping that Pia would stop by to visit, as the gypsy had been in the habit of doing in the late afternoon or early evening two or three times a week. Pia's visits had become great events to look forward to, and from time to time Rachel looked hopefully out the landing window.

After half an hour she closed the book and stood up to go for a walk. Just as she started to turn toward the stairs, she caught a glimpse of someone coming up the drive.

It was not Pia, as she'd thought at first, but a young girl she did not recognize. The girl was pretty, with dark curly hair, and looked a year or so younger than Abie; she was dressed like a gypsy, in a bright red dress and gold earrings. Yet so far as she knew, the gypsies had no young girl traveling with them.

Strangers of any age were unusual in Hell's Gate, and as she hurried downstairs, Rachel was both pleased by the prospect of variety in her evening and slightly apprehensive that something might be wrong.

She reached the door just as her visitor knocked, twice, not loud.

"Mrs. Benedict."

"Yes?"

Already something about the girl's blue eyes and solemn manner had struck her as familiar, though later she did not know whether they reminded her of Mario the gypsy boy or the little Canadian girl who had vanished with her sick mother more than two years ago.

"I'm Marie, Mrs. Benedict. I've come to see about that opportunity you offered me when I lived across the bridge."

It would not be accurate to say that at the instant Rachel recognized Marie Blythe (*née* Blair; the girl gravely recounted her entire history to Rachel later that evening) she made up her mind to take her not only into her household but also into her family, as a sort of surrogate daughter. But certainly even then she was inclined by her own needs and wishes to do more than apprentice her to the housekeeper—and for more reasons than one, since although Early Kinneson's sister-in-law Wyalia was a superb cook and domestic manager, she was also the meanest and most hated individual in Hell's Gate.

Mrs. Kinneson was a small, red-faced woman of an indeterminable age between forty-five and sixty. Her husband, John Trinity Kinneson, had mysteriously disappeared from the face of the earth ten years ago, leaving her alone and without any way to support herself. At Early's recommendation, she had been hired when the family moved into the Big House, and she had remained ever since. She had never been known to say a good word about anyone but the Captain, of whom she was as afraid as everyone else was of her, and during the years she had spent with the Benedicts, she had gone through more than a dozen hired girls, whom she despised both as a class and as individuals.

If a hired girl was unfortunate enough to be pretty, Mrs. Kinneson despised her even more. The most recent girl, an attractive eighteen-year-old from the Common named Mattie Pierce, had not lasted a month. One morning a week before Marie's arrival the housekeeper had surprised the Pierce girl and Abie kissing in the pantry and discharged her on the spot. When Abie angrily promised to pay her back, she laughed in his face and ordered him out of the kitchen.

"This is Mrs. B's grandmother's Haviland china, gypsy," she told Marie grimly two minutes after Rachel brought her into the kitchen and introduced her as the new hired girl. "Do you know what Haviland is? No. Gypsies wouldn't know such things. This is your sterling silver jam spoon come down from Mrs. B.'s Great-aunt Sophie on her mother's side. It goes on the jam tray—never, never in the jam. These are your sterling napkin rings from the Gloucester branch of Mrs. B's family. They go to the left of the place setting with the napkins rolled up in them, so. Do you know left from right, gypsy?"

Marie would begin at the head of the table and distribute the china with its wonderful hand-painted pictures of men and women cocking up hay near cottages with steep yellow straw roofs and blue smoke curling out of the chimneys. Next she set the gleaming silverware at each place. Finally the crystal.

The housekeeper watched silently, with heavy disapproval. Then without explanation she would say, "Back in the sideboard with everything, gypsy."

A second week passed before Marie set the table the first time to Wyalia's satisfaction, and more than half of a third week went by before she did it again.

"Sweep the kitchen, gypsy."

For this job the housekeeper provided an old broom with a broken handle that did not come up to Marie's waist. The bristles were worn and bent and left a long, ragged streak of sweepings in her wake; but when she went back and swept up the streak, she would leave another, and so on, sometimes for an hour, until Wyalia came in and swept the floor herself with a new broom.

Marie put the old broom in the dust closet.

"Gypsy."

She looked at the housekeeper.

"Never, never stand a broom on its bristles."

Marie turned the broom upside down.

"Scrub the double boiler," Wyalia said.

The copper double boiler on the back of the stove was used for cooking oatmeal, which Marie made in the evenings for the following day's breakfast. It took her at least half an hour to scrub it clean and smooth, and the smell of oatmeal was to gag her for years afterward.

The housekeeper bullied Marie in proportion to her increasing proficiency at her work. Over the years she had acquired a plentiful stock of esoteric tortures. "This is the French burn, gypsy, for girls who don't roll up their sleeves whilst doing up dishes." She would seize Marie's wrist and, with an expert plumber's motion repeated a dozen times, twist it until she winced. "This is the Dutch rub for girls that won't wear their caps"—scouring Marie's scalp thirty or so times with her fist. She knew all the most vulnerable and sensitive spots to pinch, and frequently pinched Marie's ear or chin or the tender part of her upper arm until tears came to her eyes.

Since Wyalia was too lazy to do anything herself that she could make her apprentices do, Marie learned a good deal about cooking and managing a household. Both Rachel and the Captain went out of their way to make her feel at home, and, to her relief, Abie had been sent away to a summer camp after the episode with Mattie Pierce. But the housekeeper made Marie's existence so miserable that, like all of her predecessors, she began to dread each new morning.

Matters came to a head one day in late August. Marie had already made up her mind to begin looking for another place if the gypsies didn't return that fall and take her back with them, but as she rose in the darkness before dawn and smelled the fresh scent of grass cut the day before, she was not thinking about the gypsies or about leaving the Big House, but that it was Saturday and she would have an entire half day off to walk on the mountain or along the bay. She was especially eager to get away from the house for part of that day because Abie had returned from camp the night before, as self-assured as when he had left and three inches taller, and she was shy about being around him.

As she had done each morning for several weeks, she lighted the lantern on her dressing stand and washed her hands and face thoroughly in a porcelain basin. She pulled her arms out of the sleeves of her nightgown and, standing in the warm tent of the gown, put on her drawers, underwaist, long-ribbed black stockings, petticoat, and dark blue maid's uniform and lace collar. Then she brushed her hair, taking more care with it than usual, picked up the lantern, and went down the steep back stairs to the kitchen.

She built a fire in the wood-burning range, then went down cellar with the lamp and a market basket and selected ten potatoes from the bin. Marie liked to peel potatoes in the early morning when she was alone in the kitchen, paring each one carefully and dropping it into a bucket of cold water. This was her favorite part of the day, before Wyalia came in to cook the Captain's breakfast, her face already splotched from the first brandy of the morning, her mouth full of criticism: The fire was too big or too small; Marie had peeled too many potatoes or too few; the lantern wick was too low or too high.

The housekeeper was in an especially bad mood that day, as she was apt to be on Marie's half-holidays, and immediately began issuing abrupt directions, one on the heels of the other, in order to cram as much work into the morning as possible. As soon as she finished the dishes, Marie had to carry out the ashes from the wood range. Next she wound each of the Captain's clocks. Then, since it was a breezy day and the dew had already dried on the grass, she had to roll up the blue Persian library rug, carry it out on the lawn, and sweep each side for a full half hour. So far, Marie's only piece of good luck was that Abie had not yet gotten up. Her worst job, however, was still to come.

Once a week, on Saturday morning, Marie had to polish each piece of Rachel's silverware. There were one hundred and twenty-eight pieces in all, each monogrammed at the base of its handle with a handsome cursive *B*. Marie hated this job more than any other, even scrubbing the oatmeal boiler, because it seemed interminable. Today it was worse than usual because she knew she couldn't finish before eleven, when it would be time to begin setting the table for the large noon dinner. She was determined to have the entire afternoon to herself, however, and although she had polished only about half of the silverware, immediately after dinner—through which Abie had continued to sleep—she asked Rachel for permission to go walking.

"Of course, dear," Rachel told her. "Saturday afternoons are always yours to do with as you please."

Five minutes later Marie had changed to a wash dress and was on her way back down the stairs, but as she went past the hallway to the kitchen a hand reached out and grabbed her ear.

"Where do you suppose you're off to, gypsy?"

"Mrs. Benedict said I could have the afternoon to go on the mountain."

"Mrs. Benedict?" the housekeeper said incredulously, as though she had never heard the name of her employer. "What does she know of domestic management? Is Mrs. B to polish the silver, crippled as her hands are with arthritis? I misdoubt it. I shall Mrs. B you if you ever go above my head again. Come up!"

She gave a vicious yank on Marie's ear, pulling her onto her toes.

"Come up, gypsy. Your posture is atrocious. Mr. Kinneson stopped *his* back, and for all I know he's in the state penitentiary."

The housekeeper thrust her face so close that the smell of

brandy on her breath was almost overpowering. "You, girl, will be sent to the penitentiary, never, never, never to see your thieving gypsy friends again."

Without thinking, Marie lashed out with her open hand, catching the housekeeper hard on the side of the head. The blow drove her back several feet and she sat down—she did not fall, Marie was certain of that—on the bottom step of the stairs and stared at Marie stupidly.

Marie was as surprised as Wyalia. She stared back for several seconds, and then she heard laughing from the head of the stairs. Standing on the landing in just his pajama bottoms and looking down at her was Abie Benedict.

Marie whirled and ran out the door, down the drive, and up the lower road into the park. She continued running until she reached the waterwheel at the foot of the hanging meadow, and there she sat down, near where she had talked for the last time with Pia, and began to cry.

Gradually Marie became aware of the rapid *clap-clap-clap* of the waterwheel. For the hundredth time, she wondered why Pia had sent her to the Big House. So far, the only opportunity she had found in her situation was the opportunity to get away from it temporarily on Saturday afternoons. Yet the more she considered her dilemma, the more convinced she became that it would be senseless to run away before spring, when the gypsies would surely return. At the least, she should try to get a good character recommendation from the Benedicts to take with her; so although she was still angry, as well as apprehensive about what would happen when she returned, she decided to go back to the village.

When she arrived she discovered that Wyalia was indisposed, as she often was on Saturday evenings after drinking all afternoon, so Marie cooked supper. That was fine with her. She liked to cook, especially when the housekeeper was out of the kitchen, and she thought that by the following morning

Wyalia might very well have forgotten what had happened earlier in the day. Apparently Abie had said nothing about the trouble; the Captain and Rachel were as friendly to her as usual.

For dessert that night Marie served a maple pudding she'd learned to make years ago at home. It turned out especially well, and she was very pleased because she wanted to impress Abie.

"Marie, dear," Rachel said, "where are the dessert spoons?"

"I thought I put them out," she said.

"These are coffee spoons," Rachel said, not critically. "The dessert spoons are a little deeper."

Marie picked up a spoon and saw that she was right. "I guess I was in too big a hurry," she said. "I'll switch them."

"These are fine for tonight, dear. Don't bother to change them. I think you've learned very quickly."

"Gypsies catch on early to everything," Abie said, grinning.

Marie couldn't help grinning back at him, but the Captain gave him a stern look, and he resumed eating.

"I can tell you where the dessert spoons aren't." Wyalia Kinneson stood in the hallway that led to the kitchen. Her face was blotched from brandy. Her high quarrelsome voice was shaking slightly, and more than slightly slurred. "I can tell you where they aren't," she repeated. "They aren't in the silver box."

The Captain looked at her. "Why aren't they in the silver box?"

"Because the girl didn't put them back after polishing them. She went straight to her room with them. By and by she slipped back down, sneaking and stooping her back and trying to maneuver her way out around me. When I tried to stop her, she knocked me down savagely and run out the door."

The Captain stood up. He walked over to the sideboard, opened the silver box, and looked inside. Then he looked at Marie. "Is this true, Marie?"

"No."

Wyalia Kinneson pointed a quivering finger at her. "Are you calling me a liar, gypsy? Don't you dare call me a liar." Now she was screaming. "You stole them! You stole them and hid them abovestairs, and no doubt you've already spirited as many as you could up to your thieving gypsy friends in the woods." She rounded on the Captain. "Search her room! Unless you think I'm a liar too, search her room!"

"Come, Marie," he said gravely.

She was dazed by the housekeeper's sudden attack. The next thing she knew she was standing in her room watching as the Captain searched her washstand and dresser and bed. One by one, he removed four dessert spoons from beneath Marie's mattress.

"I didn't take them."

The Captain sat down on her bed and looked at her gravely. "Marie, do you understand that taking something that doesn't belong to you is always wrong?"

"Yes."

"I'll ask you again then. Did you take the spoons?"

"No."

He looked at her. She was crying now but she looked straight back at him, and for a time neither of them spoke.

"All right." He stood up. "Nothing more will be said until the rest of the spoons are found."

They returned to the dining room, where he silently replaced the four spoons in the box.

"Do you still think I be lying?" Wyalia Kinneson said.

"I never thought anyone was lying," Mr. Benedict told her. "Twelve spoons are still missing. Nothing more will be said until they turn up."

"They won't turn up. They've been spirited out and passed along. Next it'll be the tea service."

"Mrs. Kinneson, I said that we will drop this matter now."

"No, we won't," Abie said.

Marie looked at him in astonishment. She had never before heard anyone contradict the Captain. Abie grinned. "I know who took the spoons," he said.

"Be careful, Abie," Rachel said quickly. "Name no names."

Abie continued to grin. "I will be careful, and I'm going to name names. Wyalia Kinneson took them. She took them this afternoon after Marie went out. I was just coming downstairs and I saw the whole thing. It was very entertaining. They got into a scuffle and Marie shoved her away, and to get even old Wy hid the spoons and said Marie took them."

The Captain looked at Wyalia Kinneson, who promptly fainted.

"Abie, why on earth didn't you speak up sooner?" Rachel said while the Captain carried Wyalia to her room.

"I wanted to see what that girl would do," Abie said, eating his dessert.

A minute later the Captain returned with the missing spoons.

"Marie, I'd like to apologize to you," he said. "I apologize for my own suspicions and for the false accusations Mrs. Kinneson made. You won't have to work for her any longer. I've already informed her that she'll have to find a new situation."

Marie took a deep breath. "Mr. Benedict, you and Mrs. Benedict have been very good to me. But I can't stay on in any case."

Now the Captain was surprised. "Why do you say that, Marie?"

"Because whether Mrs. Kinneson leaves or whether she stays, I'll never be trusted here again. I know I won't be. I wasn't trusted this time, and I won't be next time."

He looked at her kindly. "Come into the library, Marie. I'd like to speak to you privately."

He asked her to sit at the long library table, and he sat down across from her.

"Now, Marie. Was that you speaking in the dining room, or was it your pride?"

At first she wasn't sure how to answer. Then she said, "Well, maybe it was my pride. My pride's part of me."

"Yes. But there is good pride and harmful pride."

"No doubt," she said. "But I won't be suspected of being a

thief. I know you didn't believe me, Captain Benedict. I know you didn't."

"I wanted to believe you. That's why I said we'd wait until we found the missing spoons." He thought a minute. "We want you to stay, Marie. I think a great deal of you, and so does Mrs. Benedict. We both want you to stay and be part of the household."

She started to shake her head, but he held up his hand.

"Don't give me an answer now. Sleep on it. I always sleep on an important decision if I can. What is it the Canadians say? 'The morning's wiser than the evening.' Let's talk again in the morning."

Lying in bed that night, Marie thought about Pia's advice not to leave a place without considering that she would take herself along. As young as she was, she knew that if she did leave, she would take her pride with her. She realized too that the Captain was right; some pride was harmful. Yet she was still determined to leave the Big House and Hell's Gate the next day.

Whimpering over the stove at dawn while Marie sat at the kitchen table peeling potatoes, Wyalia Kinneson didn't even have her pride left. "I'm sure I don't know what to do," she said with a sob. "I don't have a place on earth to go to."

"Don't you have any folks?"

"Only Mr. K, and he's no doubt in the penitentiary."

"His back must be pretty bad," Marie said, abstracted by her own thoughts.

"It's the county home for Wyalia Kinneson. I hope you're satisfied, gypsy."

Marie stood up; Wyalia sprang back. "Don't you touch me!"

Suddenly Marie realized that the housekeeper was actually afraid of her and probably had been since the day she had first come to the Big House. She looked at Wyalia, cowering beside the stove; she no longer seemed very formidable—just a frightened old woman with nowhere to go.

"Why did you make up that story about me?" Marie said. "You didn't need to do that."

"I never made up no stories in my life," Wyalia said, bursting into tears. "I never made up no stories nor stole nothing that didn't belong to me. You had the whole thing planned, you and that wicked boy. Slipping and stooping and spying and maneuvering, making me think you stole them spoons and then planting them in my room to have me discharged. I suppose you'll be moving up to housekeeper now that I'm out of the way."

"I don't want your job," Marie said. "And I never went near your room. Why don't you just admit that you took them? Maybe Captain Benedict would change his mind if you'd tell the truth about it."

"I *am* telling the truth!" Wyalia sobbed, and ran out of the kitchen weeping hard.

Marie was more confused than ever. She couldn't understand why the housekeeper would continue to lie about the spoons when it was so obvious that she had stolen them, had even been seen doing it. Yet she couldn't help feeling some concern for her. Where on earth would the woman go without a job or friends or close relatives?

"Well, Marie," the Captain said, looking up and smiling as she brought his coffee into the library, where he had been writing in his diary. "It's good to see you. Is the morning wiser than the evening?"

She set the coffee down on the table. "Captain Benedict," she told him, "I want you to know that I respect you and Mrs. Benedict a great deal. I'm grateful for what you've done for me. But if you mean have I changed my mind, no. I haven't."

She hesitated. She almost didn't broach the next subject, but she couldn't bring herself to leave until she did.

"Before I go I want to ask you not to do something."

He looked at her kindly, but shrewdly now too.

"Please don't let Mrs. Kinneson go," she blurted. "I don't like her and I won't pretend to, but she's getting old and her husband's sick and I don't want to lie awake nights wondering what's become of her."

"I don't want to lie awake nights wondering what's become

of you," the Captain said quickly. "Marie, ordinarily I don't make bargains, but I'll make one with you now. I'll retain Wyalia Kinneson if you'll agree to stay too."

Now she could see that she had backed herself into a corner, but she made one last attempt to get out. "I can't work for that woman again. I can't and I won't."

"I don't expect you to," he said. "From now on you'll be working directly for Mrs. Benedict."

She looked at him dumbly.

"She and I discussed the matter last night," he continued. "Rachel isn't strong, Marie. I don't mean she's seriously ill. But the arthritis bothers her so much on some days that it's difficult for her to get around and do things for herself. She needs more help, especially in the morning. You've been doing more and more for her recently, and you couldn't keep that up and handle your old job at the same time anyway. I'll reinstate Mrs. Kinneson immediately if you accept this offer."

Marie was very excited. This new job might lead to the opportunity Pia had spoken of.

But even as she smiled and nodded, even as she and the Captain shook hands to seal the bargain, she was remembering how Abie had grinned at her the day before at the dinner table.

Marie liked working for Rachel Benedict. In good weather, when Rachel's arthritis didn't bother her, they walked together on the broad, sloping lawns around the Big House and in the park. Rachel taught her the English names of the trees and late-blooming wildflowers, and on rainy fall days they spent whole mornings together in the glass conservatory on the south side of the house, potting geraniums and begonias to be set out the following spring. In the afternoons Rachel read aloud to her on the love seat at the head of the stairs and talked with her as she would with a close friend.

The gypsies did not return, and although she continued to miss them, Marie felt increasingly at home in the Big House.

She had no further trouble with Wyalia, who had replaced her with Yolande Bonaventure, a big, strapping, somewhat slow-witted Canadian girl from the settlement across the bridge who paid no attention at all to the housekeeper's bullying but simply plodded through her duties from one day to the next like one of her father's oxen. The Captain was unfailingly kind to Marie and always had time to ask how her day had gone and whether she needed anything.

With Abie, however, Marie never knew what to expect from one day to the next. Sometimes he would ask her in a condescending way to shag fly balls for him in the hanging meadow or stand against the rear wall of the factory with a bat while he practiced his pitching (an experience she found terrifying, though she didn't say so). At other times he acted extremely resentful of her presence in the house, called her a dirty little gypsy, and threatened to have her discharged or sent back to the kitchen. Once she bumped into him by mistake as they passed in the upper hallway, and without any warning he punched her hard in the stomach, causing her to lose her breath for nearly a minute. On another occasion, when she declined his invitation to play ball because she was on her way to rub Rachel's aching arms and legs with witch hazel, he spit on the front of her dress.

One morning in late September, when Abie had stayed home from the Common Academy (where he was now attending high school), complaining of a headache, Wyalia Kinneson burst through the cellar doorway. "Rats!" she shrieked. "In the molasses barrel!"

Marie got a lantern and went hurriedly down the stairs. Abie came casually along behind her, holding half a slice of buttered toast.

The rats, six of them, were trapped in a molasses keg Marie had emptied the day before and left open, standing upright, near the bottom of the stairs. She had no idea how they had gotten into the keg, but once inside they had not been able to climb up the slick sides. As Marie peered down at them, they scurried around the sticky bottom, chittering frantically.

Abie looked at the trapped animals and chittered back at them in an uncanny imitation of their cries.

"Watch this," he said, and flipped a piece of toast crust into the barrel.

Instantly the rats devoured it. Then they began racing around the bottom of the barrel again. From time to time one would leap high up the side, but not high enough to clear the rim.

"I wonder how they ever got down in there," Abie said, in a way that made Marie suspect he had put them there himself. Then she remembered that he had pointedly asked Wyalia for a pitcher of molasses for his pancakes when he sat down at the table a few minutes ago.

"Well," he said briskly, "we can't have this, can we, Marie? Go get Tom."

Tom was Rachel's ancient housecat; a great gray village patriarch who had not been known to catch so much as a mouse for years. Although Marie was not at all sure that he would be a match for six fierce, trapped rats, she was excited to be a part of Abie's scheme, and ran upstairs for the cat, which as usual was sleeping on the inglenook bench in the hallway.

"Give him here," Abie said when she reappeared. "It's time you started earning your keep, my boy," he told Tom, dropping him into the barrel.

In less than a second the swirling rats closed in on the pet cat, which for the first time Marie could remember seemed to come fully awake. He quickly dispatched two of his attackers, but the other four clung savagely to his throat and sides and belly and would have killed him if Marie hadn't reached in and yanked him out. Two rats came along, dropping onto the floor and scurrying into the darkness. Tom ran howling upstairs to safety.

Marie was horrified, at least as much by her own part in the cruelty as by the terrible fight between the animals. Abie merely laughed.

"Go get me a bucket of water," he said.

When Marie returned with the water he took it from her and dumped it into the barrel. She looked at him inquiringly.

"Get another one," he told her.

After the fourth bucket, the two remaining live rats were swimming in the gluey water in the bottom of the barrel. Abie had Marie get another bucketful to be sure they couldn't touch bottom. Then he settled his elbows on the rim of the barrel to watch.

At first the rats swam around the sides of the barrel very quickly; but when they realized that they would soon exhaust themselves, they slowed down into a methodical, steady circling. From time to time they raised their sharp-featured heads, like miniature otters looking for a bank to crawl out on.

After a few minutes Marie said, "Let's get a shovel and bang them over the head. That way they'll die fast."

"No. I want to see how long they keep going. Rats are great survivors, Marie. They're quite a bit like people in that way. Maybe they'll figure out how to get out. You've heard the story of the rat that fell into the cream churn and swam until he made butter?"

"They aren't going to make butter out of that mess. They're just going to drown. I'm getting a shovel."

"No, you're not. They're going to drown, and I intend to see how long it takes. How can you possibly have any feelings for a rat?"

"You just said they were like people in some ways."

He grinned. "A lot of people aren't even as smart as rats." He spoke abstractedly. The rats had slowed down, and from time to time the smaller of the pair rested its paws on the other.

A short while later, the smaller rat crawled up on the other one's back. As the stronger animal tired, its circles became tighter. It began to create a little swirling vortex in the center of the barrel. Then the little rat slid off and started to go under, but the big one picked it up by the back of the neck and treaded water until it was just barely able to hold its head up.

Marie reached down and lifted the rats up out of the greasy water. Before she set them on the floor, one of them bit her three times on the hand, drawing blood each time.

"That's just what you deserve, you interfering little bitch!" Abie shouted as she ran upstairs holding her hand. "I'll kill you! Wait and see if I don't. And first I'll have you turned out of your job here."

Throughout the day Marie waited to be discharged; but Abie said nothing to his parents about the episode, and the following day he asked Marie to play catch with him as though nothing had happened.

Abie continued to miss one or two days of school a week for the rest of the fall, complaining of chronic headaches and stomach pains. One afternoon in early October when Rachel was napping, he asked Marie to walk along the track with him to the causeway at the mouth of the river. It was still very warm, and Abie wanted to go swimming.

"You ought not to do that right after being sick," Marie told him as he started to undress.

He grinned at her. "What makes you think I've really been sick?"

"You said you were. I heard you tell your mother Monday that you had an awful headache."

Abie kicked off his shoes. He sat down on the sandy bank of the causeway and pulled off his socks.

"Thinking about school gave me a headache," he said. "Come on, Marie, take your clothes off—or are you afraid?"

"The water's colder than it looks. You go ahead if you want to. I'll look for turtles."

Abie shrugged. "Suit yourself," he said shortly.

He stepped out of his trousers, took three running steps, and dived in. Marie watched him for a minute as he moved quickly out into the bay. He did not act sick, but she couldn't imagine why he would feign illness to avoid going to school, which she would have given nearly anything to do.

There were a few turtles out sunning themselves on the sand, but they were too wary to catch. As soon as she approached one of them, it would scurry down to the water, moving much faster than she'd realized a turtle could. After a while she sat down in the sun herself. A few minutes later Abie joined her.

"Where's your turtle?"

She shook her head. "They're too smart for me. They run into the water."

"Why don't you take off your clothes and go in after them?" he said teasingly.

"They bury themselves in the muck on the bottom. It wouldn't do any good."

He thought for a minute. "I'll catch one for you if you'll do something for me."

"What?"

"Not much. Just a small thing I want done."

"All right. How do you intend to catch it?"

"You'll see," he said. "By tomorrow you'll have your precious turtle."

That evening the Captain told Abie that if he was well enough to go gallivanting over the countryside with Marie, he was well enough to go to school. Rachel agreed; but the following morning after his father left for work Abie refused to eat any breakfast, claiming the headache had returned. After a brief argument, his mother allowed him to stay home, with the provision that he remain in bed. At one o'clock, when Rachel went up to her room to rest, Abie borrowed his father's power launch without permission and headed down the bay with Marie.

It was a gray day, warm but threatening rain, and Abie gunned the speedboat fast over the dark water.

"You aren't sick at all, are you?" Marie shouted to him.

"I'm sick of being told what to do," he shouted back. "Why should I go to school when I already know more than my teachers? Besides, they're harder on me than on the others because Father's told them to be. He said so himself, and I hate him for it."

"You shouldn't say that. That's wrong. You don't mean it, and you shouldn't say it."

"Don't tell me what's right or wrong or what I mean or don't mean. I mean everything I say."

As they approached the reedy south end of the bay Abie eased back on the throttle. "For instance, Marie," he continued in an ordinary speaking tone, "Wyalia Kinneson found out that I mean what I say. I said I'd get even with her for firing Mattie Pierce, and I did."

Marie looked at him inquiringly. "How?"

"Stop and think. You don't really suppose she'd risk her place for a few pieces of silverware, do you? As stupid as she is, she isn't that stupid. She never touched those spoons."

"How did she know they were gone?"

"I told her—after hiding a few in your room and the rest in hers."

Marie was astonished, but Abie merely laughed and asked her whether the morning was wiser than the evening, in a voice so much like his father's it made chills run down her back.

At the mouth of the river, he produced a bicycle basket, some heavy twine, and a coiled clothesline. To each corner of the basket he fastened a two-foot length of twine, which he gathered together at the loose ends and tied to the clothesline. Then he dropped the basket over the side of the launch, paid out line until it reached the bottom, and began to troll it slowly back and forth across the cove until a vibration on the rope told him that the basket had scooped something up off the mucky bottom. The first time he pulled it in, there was a rock in the bottom; on the next pass, however, he dredged up two snapping turtles.

Marie was delighted. She kept the smaller, which was not much larger than her hand but very lively and fierce, snapping and hissing at her fingers every time she touched it. Abie wanted to try for some more but just then it began to rain hard, so they headed back up the bay, returned the Captain's launch to the boathouse, and were home and wearing dry clothes before anyone knew they'd been gone.

Marie put her new pet in an apple box under her bed. After two or three days it stopped trying to nip her, but it refused to eat and spent every waking minute trying to scrabble up the sides of the box, so she decided to take it back to the causeway and release it before winter.

Abie, in the meantime, had caught a miserable head cold from his soaking and spent three days in martyred seclusion in his room, where he was waited on hand and foot by his mother; whenever his father stopped by to see how he was, he acted at death's door.

A few evenings later, he appeared in Marie's room and asked her how her turtle was. Then he told her casually that she could do the favor for him and, to her surprise, asked her to let him see her naked. Marie was approaching puberty and becoming self-conscious about her body; although she found Abie's request titillating, she flatly refused to take off her clothes.

"You might wish you had," he said after a pause. "I spent the better part of a week in bed because of you."

"I didn't know what you were going to ask. If I had, I wouldn't have agreed to it."

"You made a bargain."

"Well, I shouldn't have. I learned something."

Abie picked up the turtle, which continued to move its legs in the air.

"He's not happy here anyway," Marie said. "He won't eat, and all he does is try to get away. I'm going to put him back in the bay while he still has time to get bedded down in the mud for winter. I'm afraid he'll die if I keep him penned up here much longer."

Abie shrugged. "He won't die," he said. "You can't kill these things if you try. Keep it a few more days, and if it still won't eat I'll take it back where we got it and let it go for you."

He replaced the turtle and left, and she did not see him again until the next afternoon, when they met at the head of the stairs.

"How's your turtle?" he asked. "Has he eaten anything yet?"

She told him she was on her way to see, and Abie said he'd come along with her.

Together they walked down the hall to Marie's room. She opened the door and stepped inside. The apple box was under her bed where she'd left it, but the turtle was missing. She looked at Abie.

"Did you let him go?"

He smiled.

"Where is he?" she demanded.

"Not very far from here."

She frowned. "I want that turtle. He's mine. Where is he?"

Abie was looking at something behind her.

"Look on your nightstand," he said.

She turned and looked at the top of her nightstand. At first she saw nothing unusual. The white porcelain wash basin with blue cornflowers sat beside the white porcelain pitcher with pink roses. Her towel and washcloth hung on the rack above them.

"Look in the basin."

The turtle was sitting in the porcelain basin. As Marie stepped closer Abie reached down and removed its upper shell as casually as lifting a lid off a sugar bowl. Inside the bottom shell the animal's dismembered parts were stacked in a neat pile, on top of which lay its small red heart, still pulsing slowly.

"I told you you couldn't kill these things," Abie said nonchalantly. "And I told you I mean what I say."

With a terrible cry Marie turned and leaped for him, but he was in the hall, on his way toward the stairs, laughing as he ran.

One evening in early winter as Marie was sitting with the Benedicts in the parlor after supper, Rachel asked her what she would like for Christmas.

"I don't know," Marie said. "A pair of stockings?"

"No," Rachel said, "we want you to pick something special, something you've always wanted."

"All right," Marie said promptly. "I'd like a sled."

Rachel and Abraham nodded, but Abie looked angry.

"Why should she get anything for Christmas?" he said. "She's just a servant girl. Nothing more."

Immediately the Captain stood up. "You come with me," he told his son.

Five minutes later they came out of the library together and Abie apologized to Marie for his remark; but as he did he looked at her in such a hateful way that she thought he would have killed her on the spot if he could have.

On Christmas morning Marie received a red and gold sled with metal runners. That afternoon, after the family dinner, the Captain ordered Abie to take Marie sliding with him. Although neither one of them was happy with this arrangement, they silently pulled their sleds up through the park to the edge of the woods above the quarry. It was a cold, brilliantly clear day after a mild night, and the deep snow on the mountain was covered by a hard crust.

"We'll have to be careful," Marie said as they stood looking down at the village, far below.

"I'm always careful," he said.

"You don't need to be so cross," she told him. "I was just reminding myself. This crust is slick as glare ice in places."

"Well, if that new sled's too fast for you, I'll ride it down and you can take mine. Here, switch."

Abie's sled was three years old. It had been in several crack-ups, and once he had left it outside for most of a summer so that the runners were now rusty, the paint faded. Besides, Marie liked her own new sled better than anything anyone had given her since her father made her the red dancing clogs years ago. She did not want to relinquish it so soon, especially since she knew that in the mood he was in Abie might very well deliberately wreck it. She shook her head and held tight to her rope.

"No, thanks. I'll drag my feet if I need to slow down."

He shrugged. "All right," he said indifferently. "It's your neck. Go ahead."

She lay down on her new sled, racing-style. Braking with the toes of her boots, she started slowly down the meadow. The first hundred yards or so sloped quite gently, and after a few seconds Marie lifted her feet and gained speed. Fifty yards below her was a fork where the meadow road veered to the left and a short path led down to the quarry. As she approached the fork in the road, still accelerating, Marie shifted her weight left, away from the granite pit.

There was a terrific jolt, a clash of colliding wood and metal. Although she knew immediately that Abie had run into her from behind, for a moment she did not realize that he had knocked her off course onto the steep path to the quarry. Her sled had spun entirely around. It was now moving backward, skidding out of control down over the frozen crust. When she managed to get it turned, the edge of the pit was not far below her.

Instantly she rolled off the sled. To her horror it careered straight down into the quarry, where, a moment later, she heard it shatter on the ice a hundred feet below. She began to pound at the crust with her mittens. She tried to drive in her heels, as she had once done high on Canada Mountain when pursuing the deer, but the crust was as solid as granite; spinning slowly, her arms and legs flung out like those of a person falling from a great height, Marie slid toward the lip of the quarry. She pulled off her mittens and clawed at the crust with her nails, but couldn't find any purchase.

At the last moment she reached out and grabbed the bottom of a birch sapling no bigger than her arm. She was so close to the edge that her feet and part of her legs hung out over it. When she looked down she could see the remains of her sled, on the ice far below. She clung to the small birch and shouted for help.

By the time Abie finally appeared, a minute or so later, her hands were going numb.

"Abie!" she shouted. "Quick, give me your hand."

He stopped a few feet away, by the donkey steam engine

Ned Baxter had used to try to raise the Captain's monument.

"Why should I?" he said. "You didn't give me your sled. Why should I give you a hand?"

She could not believe what she heard. He was looking at her quite dispassionately, the way he had looked at the drowning rats in the molasses barrel.

"Hang on a while longer," he said. "I might change my mind. I might decide to help you. You can't ever tell."

"Abie! For God's sake give me your hand!"

She scrabbled at the crust with one hand without being able to make the slightest impression.

"Your fingers are turning white," Abie said. He squatted down beside the donkey engine. "Hang on," he said encouragingly.

"I can't." She did not have strength enough left to shout. "I'm slipping."

"Hang on with your eyelids then," he said nonchalantly. "I'm slowly changing my mind. Will you take off all your clothes for me tonight if I pull you up here?"

"Give me your hand—I'll do anything!"

He shook his head. "No, you won't. You say you will, but you won't. You said you would before and then you didn't."

"I will. I swear it."

"Will you tell Father you wrecked your sled yourself?"

"Yes."

"All right," he said agreeably, and reached out and pulled her up beside him.

She began to cry.

Abie laughed. "Come on, Marie," he said impatiently. "You don't suppose I really meant to let you fall in there, do you? I'll give you a ride down the mountain on my sled."

In fact, Marie had no idea what Abie had meant to do, and she was so confused that when he did come to her room that night, although she cried, she let him undress her and look at her in the lantern light.

"You aren't good for much yet, are you?" he said after a

minute, with a mean laugh. "Who wants to do anything with skinny little crying you, anyway?"

As spring approached, Marie's situation at the Big House improved somewhat. Although Abie continued to badger her whenever he could, his father insisted that he attend school regularly, headaches or no. At the same time Abraham began to take a stronger interest in Marie himself as he realized how valuable she was to his wife. Whenever he went away on business he bought her a new doll and, though she did not play with dolls at thirteen and in fact had never played with dolls, her room was soon crowded with wax dolls, wooden dolls, cloth dolls, shell dolls, and china dolls of every imaginable size and nationality.

Only once during Marie's time at the Big House did the Captain speak sharply to her. It was during the spring of 1904, about eight months after she had started work at the Big House, when he noticed her carrying a scuttle of live coals from the kitchen stove upstairs to start Rachel's fire one chilly morning.

"Marie!" he said. "Put those back where you got them and don't ever take fire through the house again. Don't you know you could burn us all to cinders that way?"

Marie told him she was sorry and hurried back to the kitchen. She had seen the Captain angry two or three times, but she had never before seen him act alarmed; for the rest of the morning she was deeply chagrined by her heedlessness.

After lunch, as Marie sat on the love seat at the head of the stairs, still humiliated, Rachel came out of her room, sat down beside her, and asked what was wrong. She listened kindly as Marie related the incident and then explained that Abraham had not meant to be abrupt with her, but had always insisted that everyone in Hell's Gate exercise utmost caution around fire. "One careless accident could destroy everything he's worked so carefully to build up," she said. "Do you understand now why he was upset?"

Marie nodded, but by now she was crying. Rachel put her arm around the girl's shoulders and let her sob for a while. Then she gave Marie her handkerchief and asked her if she could say what was wrong.

Marie shook her head. "I don't know, Mrs. Benedict," she said. "I just don't seem to fit in anywhere. I didn't fit in when I lived across the bridge in Little Canada, and I didn't fit in with the gypsies, and it's plain I don't belong here either. Sometimes I just feel like crying and can't help myself. Sometimes I even cry for no reason at all."

"I know how you feel," Rachel said quietly.

"You do?"

"Yes indeed. I've cried many times for no good reason, Marie. Would you like me to tell you about one of those times?"

Marie nodded.

"All right," Rachel said. "It will have to be a secret between just us two, though, since I've never told this story to anyone else. It was the first time I ever saw Hell's Gate."

"You cried then?" Marie said incredulously.

"I did, and I've felt terrible about it ever since. You see, Marie, Abie and I didn't come here until several years after Abraham cleared the peninsula. He'd even had the Big House built, and from all he'd told me about it, and about the mountains and lake, I was sure it must be a very beautiful place. But for some reason the morning we got on the train in Portland I felt terribly sad. Of course I'd been on much longer journeys, twice around the world as a girl on my father's ship and once with Abraham, the year we were married. Yet I'd never been on a stranger one, Marie, for behind us, in the car we'd rented for our belongings, was the jawbone of a blue whale."

Rachel sighed.

"In Portland it was lilac time, nearly summer. But as we traveled up into the wooded hills of Maine, we moved back into spring. The hills were yellow with new buds, the rivers were full to the brim. The second spring should have made me happy, and I should have been happy to be coming to a new home, but as we traveled north, passing through one little paper-mill town after another, I began to cry."

Marie nodded. "I understand that, Mrs. Benedict. You were frightened by that jaw. I was too the first time I saw it—I thought it was the legs of a werewolf."

Rachel smiled and patted Marie's hand. "That must have been partly it, dear. The worst thing was, I couldn't seem to stop. Abie was very small, and after a while he started to cry too. Finally his father took him and hummed him to sleep, but I continued to weep like a little girl, despite myself, and each time I thought I had myself under control the tears would start in again, do what I might.

"In the late afternoon, as the train crossed the height of land and started down into Kingdom County, we caught our first glimpse of the twin peaks of Hell's Gate, far to the north. Abraham pointed, and I saw the late snow still lingering on their tops, and thought that in less than one day we had passed from early summer back into late winter again, as though we'd spent the day climbing one of those high Asian mountains where it's always summer at the foot and winter at the top. And though I tried not to let Abraham notice, I was still weeping.

"The following morning we came up the bay on a lumber raft, to which Abraham had lashed the jawbone upright with a piece of canvas in it for a sail, so that we were sitting literally in the jaws of the whale, and he pointed again. 'It's for you,' he said. 'It's yours.' I looked and saw the house, this house. But my first glimpse of it was blurred because by then I was crying again, since I had never seen such a desolate and forlorn-looking place in all my life."

During the following weeks Marie thought frequently about the story Rachel had told her. She believed she understood Rachel's loneliness much better than the Captain's purpose in bringing the whale's jaw to Hell's Gate, though she was sure that the jaw had something to do with the secret part of his past Pia had mentioned. What that secret might be, however, she could not imagine. Rachel never mentioned the jaw or her first trip to Hell's Gate to her again, but after that day Marie felt that there was a deeper understanding between them; and if Rachel was never quite the surrogate mother Pia had been to her, she was certainly far more than an employer.

Nevertheless, Marie still felt the uncomfortable ambiguities of her position in the household—neither daughter nor servant nor guest—and Rachel, understanding the girl's predicament, realized that she must do everything possible to make her independent, especially when the gypsies did not return for her that summer, as she feared they might.

"We really have to send Marie to school this fall," she told her husband as the new school year approached; but with the arrival of fall Abraham decided to take the entire household to the exposition in St. Louis.

During the spring and summer of 1904, Herman Fischner had designed and built a large flattop desk. It was made of solid bird's-eye maple cut high on Canada Mountain, where conditions were exactly right to produce the small dark oval "eyes" so admired and sought-after in maple paneling and furniture. The desk was five feet long by three feet wide. It contained a shallow center drawer running its entire length and a double pedestal with three deep drawers on each side. Although it was much less ornate than the factory's rolltop desks, Abraham believed that it was more practical for modern offices, and it had an elegant simplicity that greatly appealed to him. Soon after it was completed he wrote to the Exhibit Committee at St. Louis to enter it in the furniture display at the Palace of Manufactured Products.

They left in late August in Abraham's new private rail car, which had been custom-built for him by the Wagner Palace Car Company in Schenectady, New York. It was nearly as long as a freight car and divided into three sleeping compartments, a kitchen with a deep nickel sink and hot and cold running water, a parlor, a dining area, an office, and a bathroom with a flush toilet and a short tub on legs cast in the shape of lions' heads. It was paneled throughout with Canada Mountain bird's-eye maple, which Abraham had shipped to Schenectady the previous winter to be installed. It was equipped with electric lamps (the first Marie had ever seen), powered by current generated from its own running wheels, and rode on the most advanced suspension system in the world.

Marie loved the train ride west and the three weeks they spent at the exposition. Sometimes with Rachel, more often on their own, she and Abie explored the vast palaces of Machinery, Electricity, and Forestry, Fish, and Game. As long as he could do exactly as he chose, Abie was fine company, and in the evenings at their hotel they flirted together mildly, sneaking in and out of one another's rooms late at night without being quite sure what they would do once they were there, except that it was exciting for both of them. They spent days on the mile-long amusement area called the Pike while Rachel walked in the vast formal gardens with Abraham, who sent Ned Baxter a postcard with a colored illustration of a floral clock and a characteristic message: *The exposition seems well laid out but the city itself is not. I know how busy you must be with orders, etc., and hope to be home to be of some help by the end of September. The heat here is terrific until past midnight.* To Herman Fischner he wrote in German: *Congratulations! Your fine new desk has won a gold medal. I have had several requests for identical ones already, and expect to proceed full-scale with this new line upon my return.*

During the next decade the Hell's Gate firm received thousands of orders for flattop maple desks, both bird's-eye and plain, from insurance companies and private and municipal offices and banks throughout New England and as far away as Seattle, Los Angeles, and Mexico City. For the gold-medal desk the Captain declined an offer of five hundred dollars from his friend the mayor of Chicago, who ordered thousands of settees from Hell's Gate each year for the city streetcars and parks. He presented the medal to the local historical society in the Common, where it is still displayed today in a case in the basement of the library; but from St. Louis he brought back to Kingdom County a far more interesting legacy than an inscribed piece of metal confirming what everyone in Hell's Gate knew already, and that was a large tank containing two dozen California rainbow trout from the Palace of Forestry, Fish, and Game.

To support the fish, which weighed from five to eight pounds apiece and ran well over twenty inches in length, the water in the tank had to be changed four times a day. A few miles south of Chicago, however, Abraham's train was delayed for three hours by a freight derailment. Although it was late September by then, the afternoon was as hot as an afternoon in August, and before the track ahead was cleared, some of the big fish began to turn on their sides and come to the top. They weren't dead yet, but after another hour or so in stale water they would be.

Abraham did not panic. He dispatched a crewman to walk cross lots to the nearest town and telegraph a short message to Chicago. As soon as the track was clear, he sent word forward to the engineer to put on all possible steam, and as the train raced over the tracks toward the great city he sat relaxed in the parlor listening to Scott Joplin's "Maple Leaf Rag" on the Aeolian Vocalian phonograph he'd bought Rachel at the Palace of Manufactured Products. Meanwhile, more of the trout bellied over and drifted toward the surface, like played-out hooked fish after a long fight.

At almost exactly the same moment that the train pulled into Chicago's Union Station, there was a loud clanging on the street outside. Its bells ringing wildly, a horse-drawn tanker personally dispatched by the mayor came hurtling down the cobbled pavement. Streetcars veered aside. Carriages ran up over the curbs onto the sidewalks, and pedestrians rushed into the doorways of buildings. The tanker came clattering to a halt in front of the station. Two men in black rubber coats and red

helmets began furiously working the hand pump while other
men in identical outfits rushed through the crowded station
with a heavy hose in their arms. They ran up a flight of marble
stairs, through a door onto the long boarding platform, and
stood knee-deep in the cloud of steam from the St. Louis Flyer.
"Where are those damn fish?" one of them shouted. "Where
are those goddamn trout?"

Ned Baxter and Herman Fischner and a dozen or so other
village men came over to the Hell's Gate station two evenings
later to greet the Benedicts and have a look at the gold medal,
but the first order of business was to transfer the trout in milk
cans from the tank to Lake Memphremagog. The special tanker
had arrived with its cargo of fresh lake water in time to resusci-
tate all but two of them, which Marie had baked that night for
dinner, and there was still just enough light left for Ned to see
that the transplants from California were handsome fish with
wide crimson bands running along their silvery sides. But the
factory foreman was not impressed. When the fish slid out of
the milk cans, hung finning near the surface for a moment, then
dispersed leisurely into the cold depths of their new home, Ned
said quietly, "I don't know what they are, Abraham, but they
aren't trout. Trout have speckles and square tails."

As the rainbow trout flourished and established themselves
in the big lake and its tributaries, the story of their trip from
St. Louis became part of the myth, with men on the steps of
the company store at first claiming that the tanker was drawn
by eight, then ten, and finally twelve white horses with red
plumes, when in fact there were only six and they were dun-
colored and undecorated. Over the years, though, as the villagers told and retold how Abraham had ridden fast into the
faraway city, while ever-increasing numbers of horses came
charging to meet him with sparks flying from their hooves as
though to prevent another such conflagration as the famous
one caused by Mrs. O'Leary's cow, the anecdote began to

assume the transcendent realness of the man himself—who, if he did not quite measure up to the myths that had evolved from his achievements, transcended them all in his dedication to the vision that had brought him to Kingdom County that warm afternoon in the early fall of 1890.

As long as he lived in Hell's Gate, Abraham Benedict worked tirelessly to improve his principality in the wilderness, augmenting it with German craftsmen and Canadian laborers, with California trout and whatever else he considered worthwhile from the world on the other side of the mountains; protecting it fiercely—ruthlessly, if necessary—from what he perceived as the dangers of that world: unions, taxation (as an unincorporated township, or gore, Hell's Gate never levied local taxes, which the Captain believed would have been like taxing himself), written contracts, even money.

Chapter Five

In the summer of 1899, a few months after the Canadians came
to Hell's Gate, Abie Benedict had climbed up the outside of the
covered bridge where Marie had hidden and walked along the
edge of the metal roof to a point midway between the tip of
the peninsula and the great faded heap of sawdust beside the
east shore of the narrows. He waved to the men in the lumberyard, and then he dived fifty feet into the channel below. He
surfaced, swam to shore, and before the yard crew knew what
he was going to do, he repeated his performance; and he would
have repeated it again if Ned Baxter hadn't collared him and
marched him into his father's office, where he stood grinning
and dripping like a seal while the Captain, trying not to smile,
combed him out in front of his foreman.

"That Benedict boy's growing up as wild as a yellow bum-
blebee," Ned grumbled to Ellen that evening at supper.

Few villagers would have disagreed with him. At ten, Abie
could be nearly as mischievously ingenious as Peck's Bad Boy,
whose exploits the Captain read out loud to his son from
George Peck's syndicated column in the Boston paper.

By the time he was twelve Abie had become a minor legend
himself, at least among the other boys of the village, by riding
the steel rods under the factory train to the Common and back,

skating all the way up the lake to Magog with a bedsheet for a sail one windy day in November when the ice was only a couple of inches thick, and throwing a baseball over the rooftops across the entire width of the peninsula, a distance of more than three hundred feet. Tall and athletic, an excellent mimic and actor, he always had half a dozen pranks and projects going, though never for very long at a time; displayed a cavalier disregard for schoolwork and chores; and was, in the opinion of the villagers, a typical spoiled only child. Yet for years the worst that either of his parents could say of their son, and this only to each other, was that he was lazy. Rachel softened even this stricture by pointing out accurately that he worked hard enough at anything that interested him.

As Abie grew older, the Captain frequently wished that school interested him more. He himself had been an excellent student, especially adept in mathematics and languages, but he did not spend much time remonstrating with his son, whose instincts he considered sound, or much time with him at all. Abraham was too busy for hunting and fishing, the principal recreations of most of the village men and their sons, and except to read him George Peck's column and to take him to Boston once or twice a summer to see the Red Stockings (it was after watching Cy Young pitch that Abie threw the ball across the peninsula), he allowed the boy to go pretty much his own way. There was a saying in the village that Abie would be a man before his mother, but most of the villagers liked him for his youthful egalitarianism (he liked to joke with the men on the company store steps) and his spirit of derring-do—as they would probably have liked a wild son of the local minister, if there had been one.

Between Abie's junior and senior years in high school, however, at the beginning of the summer of 1905, Abraham decided at last that his son should do something with his vacation besides play baseball and to Abie's astonishment put him to work as a messenger boy at the factory.

Of course the myth had it that young Abie Benedict hated

everything about the factory from the day he went to work there running errands for his father, but in fact he rather enjoyed it at first. He quickly discovered certain out-of-the-way corners where he could linger for a while undetected to sneak a cigarette, and he knew after a week which men would stop for a few minutes to visit with him about their work. As he told Marie one evening, he liked to "get them going" about their jobs on the pretext of learning the business from the ground up. Some, like Gilbert Chamberlain, the boiler-room engineer, would run on for twenty minutes or longer if prompted by just the right questions; and although Abie never concentrated on trying to understand Gil's technical explanations of how the great Corliss reciprocating steam engine furnished power for the factory's hundred-and-ten-foot drive shaft, he liked listening to the man's deep, slow, rhythmic voice and he liked the mystery and excitement of the boiler room—which Gil kept as clean and shiny as a battleship's engine room—with its giant black flywheel and twenty-four-inch double-leather reddish belt and yellow brass valves and nozzles and gauges.

Abie liked to wander through the lumberyard inhaling the heady scent of a million board feet of seasoning hardwood. He liked to loiter in the doorway of the blacksmith shop watching Jim Wynne fit a red-hot iron shoe to the smoking hoof of a big workhorse, plunge it into a pail of water to cool, and then nail it in place. He liked visiting the cabinet room, a comparatively clean and light place, cool in the summer and warm in winter, where, under Herman Fischner's supervision, half a dozen cabinetmakers who spoke to each other infrequently and then in German worked on the flattop desks that by the summer of 1905 had become the factory's specialty. Even the razzle-dazzle din on the rough-mill floor appealed to him—the screeching planers and growling molders and rasping, whining ripsaws—though there was too much noise there to stay and visit, and besides, his father could look out through a long double-plate window built into the inside wall of his office and see the entire floor from his desk.

Best of all, Abie liked taking messages to the finishing room, where Deacon Quinn, the lay preacher, who Ned Baxter said was the best finish and touch-up man in Kingdom County and probably in New England, performed the final operation on each desk. Deacon Quinn was a gruff, sarcastic man—he was the first person in the village to state that Abie would be a man before his mother—but he took enormous pride in his work and liked performing for a spectator. After cleaning each desk top thoroughly with cotton waste, he applied a coat of wood filler, which acted as a base for the finish. He removed any surplus filler with sea grass, let it harden for twenty-four hours, and applied a coat of orange shellac, which he sanded to a glassy finish. At twenty-four-hour intervals he gave each desk three coats of varnish, rubbing the final coat with pumice stone and oil until it attained a transparent semigloss quality that greatly enhanced the beauty of the bird's-eyes ingrained in the maple. Abie loved to sneak into the finishing room and run his hand over the satiny top of a completed desk, partly to get a rise out of the Deacon, but partly because he genuinely admired the lovely finished surface. Except for the color and the bird's-eyes, it was like the lake on a quiet summer evening in the shadow of Kingdom Mountain. Then Deacon Quinn would holler that he would shellac Abie if he didn't clear out, and Abie would grin and drift off on some other invented errand.

One of Abbie's pastimes during his first weeks at the factory was playing tricks on the workmen, particularly a somewhat slow-witted man called Wheeler Mason, who lived with his mother at the foot of School Hill. Wheeler was not fast enough to run a machine or strong enough to work out in the lumberyard. A short, slight man with wispy, colorless hair, he pushed a box wheelbarrow from machine to machine on the mill floor, picking up scrap lumber which he took to the boiler room and fed into the furnace.

Wheeler rarely brought a regular lunch to work but came with a couple of bread-and-lard sandwiches and a stone jug of tea, which he set on the steampipe from the boiler to keep warm until noon. Soon after the whistle blew for work to begin, Abie would find an excuse to visit the steam pipe and remove Wheeler's jug. Toward the end of the morning he would return and replace it, then arrange to be on hand to witness Wheeler's unfailing consternation to discover that his tea was cold while everyone else's was still piping hot.

Connected to many of the machines on the mill floor was a sawdust collector, a slender vacuum tube that sucked up flying sawdust and small bits of wood and fed them into a large pipe the men called the Grand Trunk, which emptied into the furnace. Instigated by two or three mill-floor bullies, Abie loved to wait until Ned Baxter went out to the lumberyard and then creep up behind Wheeler as he trundled his barrow along unsuspectingly, snatch off his cloth cap, and toss it into a nearby dust pipe. Wheeler would stop and stamp his feet and swear and inveigh against all boys everywhere, whom he tended with good reason to regard as his mortal enemies; then at the end of the day he'd plod over to the company store and buy another cap, only to have it go merrily along the way of the others a few days later. When someone asked him why he didn't report Abie to Ned, he would grin feebly and say he didn't want to be a bother to anyone.

In fact, Wheeler was terrified of calling attention to himself in any way at all because of an episode that had taken place some years ago, when he had been discovered trying to set fire to a neighbor's woodshed, apparently for no other reason than to see it burn. He had been sent to the state asylum in Waterbury for a year and reportedly cured of his fascination for fire, and from a sense of obligation to Wheeler's father, who had fallen off a lumber raft just after ice-out and died of exposure some years ago, the Captain had permitted him to return to Hell's Gate upon the condition that if he were ever seen with a match, lighted or unlighted, he would be sent away and locked up permanently. Wheeler's greatest fear was that he might incur the Captain's displeasure again, so he was a docile and ideal target for Abie's practical jokes.

After a month or so, Abie lost interest in tormenting this terrified little man, as he had earlier lost interest in tormenting the housekeeper and Marie. When a planer named Cass Ladue suggested that he lure Wheeler up to the finishing room some noon hour so that he and two others could dunk the cleanup man in the large, shallow tank of reddish preservative into which settees were dipped before they were shellacked, Abie refused to be part of the scheme and warned Wheeler to steer clear of that floor. Wheeler was endlessly grateful to him, but when Ladue and his friends found out what had happened, they waited until a day when the Captain was away from Hell's Gate on business and then got Abie alone one noon in the finishing room and pitched him into the tank instead. Although he scrambled out so fast that only his clothes and hands were stained, he was furious and swore to have the bullies discharged as soon as his father returned.

When the Captain learned what had happened, however, he merely told Abie that sooner or later most boys who came to work at the factory got painted with stain as an initiation, and though he disapproved of the practice he did not consider it worth making an issue of. Abie vowed to his mother and Marie that he would get even with all of them, including his father; but the greatest damage had been to his pride, and when Wheeler thanked him profusely for taking the dunking in his place, he began to see himself as a sort of martyred hero and quickly got over his anger.

Late one afternoon in July, the Captain sent his son with Rachel's Upland Flyer and the Morgan mare to deliver a message to some men haying the high meadows. Abie was in a hurry to go swimming, so instead of coming back on the high return drive, which was somewhat more roundabout, he took the one-way lower drive by the brook, met an empty hay wagon coming up the mountain, and had a wreck. Neither the horses nor the drivers were much hurt, but the buggy was smashed beyond repair, and for the first time in his life the Captain was genuinely angry with his son for more than just a few minutes. "Abie, that's a poor example to set for the village," he told the boy that night in the library. "If I can't trust you to take messages for me, you'll have to do something else. Starting tomorrow morning at seven o'clock, you're to go to work for Ned on the mill floor."

Ned Baxter was a compact, quiet man not much more than five and a half feet tall. Even on the rough-mill floor he rarely raised his voice, and he had the rare ability to keep many jobs going simultaneously without appearing hurried, though like Abraham he was always busy, and except in the Common Methodist Church on Sunday morning he was hardly ever seen in repose. Invariably, it seemed, he was moving, usually with something in his hand: a replacement belt for a machine, a wrench, a batch of yellow scrip to pass out on Saturday when the six o'clock afternoon whistle blew. He was one of those serene, undriven, yet enormously energetic persons who thrive on work, though he loved to fish and hunt too and spent many evenings and Sunday afternoons with Ned Jr., high on the slopes of Canada or Kingdom Mountain. It was said throughout Hell's Gate that he had an eye only a little less precise than a Stanley rule and at a quick glance could tell within a hundred feet the number of board feet in a large pile of lumber, or even a pile of unmilled logs. He liked to say, quietly, that he gave a dollar and ten cents' worth of work for a dollar's pay, which the Captain considered a very conservative estimate. But Ned Baxter was a conservative man: thoughtful, loyal to the factory, equally competent with wood, machinery, and men. Ned was not, in his employer's opinion, indispensable. The Captain did not believe that in a well-run business anyone was indispensable. But the owner of the Benedict Company took great pride in his ability to select exactly the right man for any job, and everyone who knew him agreed that Ned Baxter was the ideal number-two man for the furniture factory.

One of Ned's main accomplishments was the outstanding safety record of the areas he supervised. Of course there had been numerous minor accidents in the lumberyard and a few major ones in the woods and on the mill floor. Besides Claude Blair's tragedy, and Clifton Mason's accident on the lake, a number of factory workers had lost fingers or parts of fingers on the ripsaw and trim saws. Joe Marshall from the Common had lost a hand in a planer, and Ned himself had once gouged his thumb badly on the whirling knives of a jointer. During the first decade of the factory's operations, machines had probably clipped fingers and hands thirty times; but serious cuts were infrequent because Ned, like the Captain, knew where to station which men, and if a man liked to hurry, Ned sent him upstairs to assemble settees, away from the dangerous machines on the mill floor.

Except to tail a safe machine or to push lumber dollies from one machine to the next, Ned preferred not to use boys on the mill floor at all. Ned Jr. worked summers in the yard, which is where Ned wanted to put Abie; but the Captain, who in nine instances out of ten followed his foreman's suggestions, insisted that the boy learn to operate a machine on the mill floor. Reluctantly, Ned assigned Abie to a drill press.

On the first morning Ned took him from machine to machine, explaining each one and concluding in each case with the admonition, "This rig bites, my boy. It bites off careless boys' fingers"—as though, Abie thought, an important secondary function of the machinery on the mill floor was to maim boys. In fact, Ned was no stricter and no less strict with him than with any other boy who came to work for him; but because Abie despised the tedium of his job, and Ned was his boss, Abie despised the foreman too, whom he had always considered something of an old woman.

Operating the drill was not a complex job, nor was it a sinecure. Every minute Abie drilled the holes for eight chair legs. In the course of a ten-hour day he drilled the holes for forty-eight hundred legs. In his first week on the job he drilled leg holes for more than seven thousand chairs, and by the end of the week he was drilling holes half the night in his sleep as well. Again he complained bitterly to his father, who told him he'd made his own bed and now he'd have to sleep in it until school started. Abie then appealed to Rachel; she advised him to weather the job out as a means of regaining his father's good graces. When Marie agreed with her, he decided to take his emancipation into his own hands and at the same time punish them all for being so unsympathetic.

Just inside the main doors of the factory stood a chalkboard on a three-legged easel. On this the Captain often wrote messages to his workers: changes in pay rates, new policies, congratulations to especially efficient floors or individuals. Ned used the slate too, to show the number of consecutive days in which there had been no accidents resulting in lost working time. Each morning after his daily meeting with the Captain, and before the workers arrived, he erased the previous day's figure and neatly chalked up the new tally in bright blue chalk. When an accident occurred he wrote a large "0" on the board in vivid and recriminatory red.

Nothing bothered Ned Baxter so much as having to start the count from scratch again, since he took personal responsibility for all injuries in his areas; on the other hand, nothing gave him more satisfaction than setting a new record for accident-free days. It was not principally the bonus that he and his men received from the Captain that he looked forward to, but the sense of pride and accomplishment he felt whenever the old record, written in green in the upper right corner of the slate, was broken. In July of 1905, when Abie went to work on the drill, the standing record in green, set two years ago, was 238. Two weeks later, on the day Abie made up his mind to go through with his plan, Ned wrote 237 ACCIDENT FREE DAYS in large blue letters, followed by: TWO DAYS TO GO—BE CAREFUL!

At about ten thirty that morning, as Marie was watering the two large urns of red geraniums on the stone pillars at the foot of the drive, she heard a shriek from the bottom of the hill. It was followed closely by another and another; then Abie Benedict came charging up the hill.

"I've been cut!" he screamed as he tore past her up the drive. "That goddamn drill of Father's punched a hole through my thumb!"

"Rachel, I tell you he did it deliberately," Abraham said that noon. "Ned watched the entire episode. He saw Abie put the end of his thumb under the drill, and before Ned could stop him he'd nipped it so that he could quit his job and spoil Ned's safety record into the bargain. That's how lazy and spiteful he is."

"I don't disbelieve Mr. Baxter, Abraham. I just think he must be mistaken. No boy would run the risk of losing a thumb merely to avoid a few weeks of summer work."

"Don't you see that risks don't faze him? I've seen him do any number of fool things for the sheer love of a risk. He's no coward. It's not risks he's afraid of, it's work. There's no way in the world that a man can get hurt on that drill unless he holds the leg too near the end, and Abie didn't have a leg against the guide to begin with."

"That's just it, Abraham," Rachel said soothingly. "Abie isn't a man yet. He's as big as most men, and that's misleading, because he's still really just a boy."

Abraham folded his napkin and replaced it beside his untouched plate. "I won't go against your wishes, Rachel. If you don't want him to go back, I won't insist. But I'll tell you this much. You're right: Abie is still a boy, as he amply demonstrated this morning; and if we aren't careful, he may be one forever."

At the head of the staircase, crouched listening on the love seat with his bandaged thumb throbbing, Abie turned to Marie and grinned triumphantly.

The Big House was quiet. The Captain was at work, the housekeeper was in the village shopping, and Rachel was napping. Marie sat on the love seat and looked glumly out at the rain. Sprawled out bored on the end of the seat, Abie looked at Marie. At fourteen, she was already nearly as tall as his mother, with long slender arms and legs and the darkest hair he had ever seen and—depending on the light—blue or slate-colored eyes that looked at nearly everything in a grave and appraising way. In the elegant blue dress Rachel had ordered for her from Worth of the Rue de la Paix in Paris, where she bought her own clothes, Marie looked as though she had never lived anywhere but the Big House.

Certainly life had been much easier for her there in the past year. Although she still waited on Rachel and the Captain, they now regarded her almost as part of the family and treated her accordingly. Abie had been so busy with his baseball team (undefeated in two years), several different girl friends, and, until recently, his summer job that he had paid next to no attention to her at all. Almost perversely, however, she sensed that some of her increasing loneliness recently was the result of his apparent indifference toward her.

"This rain is awful," Marie said, and to Abie's surprise she suddenly turned her head away and began to cry.

It was the fourth time in the past week that she had burst into tears for no apparent reason, though for some months, since about the time her menstrual periods had started, she had felt unaccountably irritable or melancholy for days at a time. At other times she would feel inexplicably happy. But for the past several days, since the long summer rain had set in, she had been impatiently expectant, without knowing what she was waiting for, with intervals of crying, particularly at bedtime and again early in the morning.

She had been crying earlier that morning when she took a cup of coffee into the library to the Captain, who was making his daily entry in his diary. "Marie," he said, looking up briefly, "you ought to start keeping a diary. Everyone should."

Not bothering to point out that she couldn't write anything but her name, she had returned to the kitchen, where she put on bacon and eggs for Rachel's breakfast; and although she managed to get through the rest of the morning and dinner, once she had started to cry on the love seat beside Abie, she could not stop for a long time, and the more he tried to find out what was wrong the harder she cried. At first she turned her head away and held herself as rigid as her sobbing would permit, but finally she let him put his arm around her and cried with her head against his shoulder for a long time.

When her weeping finally subsided, he stood up and pulled her to her feet too. "Come on, Marie," he said, "we've been cooped up here by the rain until we're both at sixes and sevens. Let's go berrying."

Marie grinned at him. "Abie Benedict, the red berries are gone by and the blue ones aren't on yet. There might be a few black ones, but you don't know a blackberry from a black bear."

"Come on," he said, laughing, "we'll just go for a ramble on the mountain, then. The rain's letting up."

As they walked between the pillars at the foot of the drive and turned up the lower road into the park, the geraniums in the big urns glistened wetly. The woods dripped steadily, and the brook was high and loud from the rain. Marie's spirits began to pick up. She had felt better almost as soon as she'd permitted Abie to hold her, and when Abie took her hand in his she smiled at him and didn't pull it away. They walked along together hand in hand, not trying to talk over the roaring brook.

They did not stop until they reached the falls at the foot of the high meadow, where Abraham had dammed up the small pond with the waterwheel. In the spring, some of the rainbow trout from St. Louis had come up to this pool out of the lake, to the great satisfaction of many of the villagers, including Ned Baxter, who erroneously supposed that they were trying to return to California and would never be seen again. In fact the fish were simply spawning, and afterward most of them went back down to the lake again. A few, however, had remained in the pool below the dam, where the water was several degrees colder than the deepest part of Memphremagog, and full of oxygen and food washed over the falls. The remaining fish were very easily spooked and impossible to catch in the clear water, even if Abraham had allowed anyone to fish for them.

"Would you like to learn a trick, Abie? Watch, I'll show you."

Rolling up the sleeves of her blue dress and pulling off her shoes and stockings, Marie waded out to a large pink granite rock in the churning pool below the dam. Very slowly, she put her hand and arm into the water and reached far in under the rock. The cold spray stung her face as she felt cautiously along the gravel bottom until her fingertips touched something smooth and slightly yielding. She slid her hand along the smooth surface, felt the fish's gills fanning, clamped down with her hand, and lifted a thrashing rainbow trout up out of the pool. It was a male, about twenty inches long, with a brilliant slash of crimson running along each side. As Marie held it high over her head, a last, thin snowy thread of milt trickled out of its vent and down over its tail.

"He's eager to return to work," she shouted to Abie over the falls and slid the trout back into the water. She cradled it upright between her hands, facing the current, until its gills were fanning evenly again. Then she withdrew her hands and the fish darted under the rock.

Abie took off his shoes and socks and waded out beside her. "Wouldn't the old Captain have a fit if he saw us doing this?" he shouted.

Marie nodded and grinned. "Go ahead and try it. I think I felt another one lying back in under there beside him. No doubt that's the female."

"What do I do?"

"Move your hand over the bottom. When you feel the fish, tickle her belly. She'll mistake your hand for the male fish and turn partway on her side. Run your fingers up to her gills and lift her out. Be careful not to squeeze her too hard, though, or you'll hurt her."

Abie looked at Marie. It was still misting a little, and the light rain and the spray from the waterfall made her hair shine. She had put her mouth close to his face to shout over the falls, and her face, glowing in the rain, nearly touched his. With one hand she held her elegant Paris dress above her knees, revealing one long slender dark thigh.

"Like this?" Abie said, sliding his hand up her thigh.

She looked at him; she smiled; then they were kissing in the brook and then they were kissing in last year's wet leaves beside the brook and pulling at one another's clothes by the roaring falls. They made love hurriedly the first time, then more leisurely in the wet meadow and more leisurely still in the woods near the granite quarry. Sometime during the afternoon the rain ended, and as they walked back down through the meadow in the late afternoon the sun broke through and shone brightly on the yellow village far below and the blue lake between the mountains, whose tops were still concealed by the mist.

"Look what we made it do, Abie," Marie said happily. "We made the sun come out. Look at the town and the lake. Aren't they lovely?"

Abie stopped and pulled Marie down beside him in the glistening grass. "I can see mountains any time I want to," he said. "Now I'd rather see you."

For the rest of the month they made love at every opportunity, and they found opportunities every day. They walked up the mountain into the park and made love by the spawning pool at the foot of the dam and in the meadow. They rowed out to an island five miles north of the village, on the Canadian line, where they spent whole afternoons together. After dark they met in each other's rooms, and in the new roundhouse Abraham had built at the tip of the peninsula, afterward running fast for the door shouting "Echo!" to the Minotaur they pretended lived under the turntable, who boomed back, "Echo! Echo! Echo!" Once they spent half the night together in Abraham's private rail car, which Abie said was as elegant as a Boston fancy-house, then had to explain what a fancy-house was. Marie listened gravely, then said, "Well, Abie, you'll never have to pay me anything. That much is certain."

"Marie, I'd like to ask you a question."

It was foliage time again, late September, and Rachel and Marie were sitting together on the love seat, looking off over the village at the bright colors on Canada Mountain. For nearly a month, since Abie had left for a new school in New Hampshire, Marie had been quiet and dejected.

"You needn't answer if you don't wish to," Rachel said. "But I'm quite certain I know the answer already. Tell me if you will, have you and Abie been keeping company?"

Marie nodded, looking at the mountain, whose colors were running together as once again she started to cry.

"That's all right, dear," Rachel said, taking the girl's hand. "Now tell me this. Has Abie made you promises?"

"No," Marie said quietly.

It hadn't occurred to her that Abie might make her promises, though she realized after a moment that Rachel must be referring to marriage, which had never once crossed her mind until now.

Pia's verse on marriage occurred to her, and she smiled; at that moment she was certain that she would never marry anyone, and she told Rachel so.

Rachel patted Marie's hand. "I'll just say one more thing, Marie. Please do be careful of expectations that don't match. I mean yours and Abie's. You're both very young, and when Abie comes home for Christmas he'll undoubtedly have new interests, and by that time so will you. I've been thinking. How would you like to learn now to read and write? I could teach you in the afternoons if you'd like. It's something I should have done long ago."

Marie nodded, but she was not thinking about learning to read, which would have delighted her a few months ago. She was thinking that Abie would not be home for three months and that when he did come he would have new friends and might not still love her.

Because she was so worried, Marie couldn't concentrate on her lessons. After a few unproductive sessions, Rachel wisely suspended them and began reading aloud to her again, and for a couple of hours in the early afternoon, as she sat listening, Marie was able to forget her sadness. Rachel's arthritis still bothered her too much to walk outside, but several times a week Marie got out for a tramp through the woods or along the bay or lake; although she rarely felt much better after these excursions, at least she did not feel worse, which she supposed was the best she could expect until Christmas.

The Captain went out of his way to speak kindly to Marie too, but he was certain that he had done the right thing by separating her and his son temporarily, and confident that a little time would do more than anything else to improve her spirits. He was also confident that sending Abie to St. Mark's had been the right decision, though to do so had cost him a donation of ten thousand dollars toward the construction of a new woodworking shop for the school.

At Christmas Abie brought home a friend, a polite dark-haired boy named Charlie Pike. Although he greeted Marie with great affection, hugging and kissing her in front of Charlie and both his parents, she was badly disappointed when he and his friend spent nearly every waking moment of the first few days of the vacation together, skating and skiing and riding Abie's two-runner bobsled at breakneck speeds down Kingdom Mountain into the village street.

Late on Christmas Eve, long after the Canadians had gone home, while Marie lay crying in bed wishing her parents were still alive, Abie slipped into her room, sat down on the edge of her bed, and hastily asked her to do a favor for him.

"I thought you'd never ask," she said, sitting up and starting to unbutton her nightgown.

But to her surprise he reached out and stopped her.

"No, not that kind. Not yet, at least. Listen, Marie, I have a small problem. I promised Charlie I'd find a girl to go with him over vacation, but all the village girls are prudes or afraid of city boys, damn them. Can he go with you tomorrow night?"

"Go where with me?"

"Here. I want you to let him come here with you. The way you do me."

"Certainly not! What do you think I am, Abie Benedict? I'd never do such a thing, and you ought not to ask."

"What's wrong? Don't you like Charlie?"

"Of course I like him. He's your friend, isn't he? But I'm not going to bed with him."

"Not even if I promise to come afterward?"

"Abie, I said no. I'll do anything with you that you want me to, but I'll never do that. Don't ask me again."

"I thought you cared for me."

"I care for you too much to think of doing such a thing as that."

He looked at her in his calculating way. Then he shrugged, stood up, and started for the door.

"Abie!" she whispered fiercely. "Abie! Don't you love me any longer?"

"I'm not sure."

She was pulling at his arm, trying to keep him from leaving. "What is it? What have I done?"

"It's something you might do," he said.

"What might I do? I'd never do anything to hurt you."

"You might get pregnant."

"No." She shook her head, laughing and crying at the same time. "No, Abie. Is that all you're upset about? I promise I won't get pregnant."

"You can't promise that, you little fool. You don't have any way to know."

"Abie, please. Please. I won't get pregnant, I just know it." Again she pulled him toward her. "I know!"

Something about her desperation had aroused him, and he was no longer moving toward the door, but when she flung herself at him and pulled him down beside her, he was actually alarmed by her abandonment, which overpowered his own desire and incorporated it into hers. Yet when their lovemaking ended and she began to cry again, partly in happiness and partly from fear that he still might not love her, he warned her once more not to become pregnant and told her in a fierce whisper that if she did, he would take her to a place where no one would ever find her and from which she would never return.

Although she did not really believe him, she was astonished that he could say such a thing immediately after making love to her. She continued to cry, and, after repeating his threat in a more casual way, he got up and left.

After that Abie did not come to her room again, and during the day he and Marie avoided each other. When the boys returned to New Hampshire to spend New Year's with the Pike family, Marie was relieved, though she still believed she loved him, in part because she was reaching that age when she needed to love someone as much as she needed to be loved herself; so in February when she first suspected and then in March when she knew for certain that she was indeed pregnant, she was nearly as happy as she had been when she was with Abie every day and night.

One afternoon in late April when the ice on the bay was starting to turn dark, Marie and Rachel sat on the love seat watching it snow. The flakes were large and wet, the kind of snow that melts as it falls and melts some of the snow it falls on, like the huge flakes that had built up on Marie's wooden shoes the day she and her parents set out for the States. Now for the first time, remembering herself as a child, she thought not just of having a baby but of having a girl or boy of her own. And the thought pleased her so much she turned to Rachel, who was still holding *Wuthering Heights* open on her lap, and said solemnly and happily, "Mrs. Benedict, I've got some news for you. I'm going to have a baby."

Although Rachel was startled by the suddenness of this announcement, she did not seem to be surprised.

"When is this going to happen, Marie?" she asked after a moment.

"Late summer, I think. I thought I should tell you."

Outside the window the spring snow continued to fall thickly, obscuring the village, closing the Big House off to itself. The Captain was at work. Abie was away at school. Mrs. Kinneson was asleep on the inglenook bench. It was a good time to talk.

Rachel took Marie's hand. "I begged you not to raise your hopes, dear."

"I'm obliged to you. I never did. I never dared hope for such a wonderful thing as this to happen. If I'd dared to, it probably wouldn't have. I just hope now that Abie isn't mad. He said he'd take me out and kill me if I got pregnant."

"He shouldn't say things like that, even in jest," Rachel said. "Young Mr. Abie is just as responsible for what's happened as you are. More so, because he's older and should know better."

Even as she spoke, Rachel realized that what she had said was not entirely just; she too had suspected what was going on between the boy and girl and done next to nothing to stop it.

"Marie, do you understand that Abie can't marry you? That he has his education to complete, and his father would never allow such a thing?"

"Of course," Marie said promptly. "I wouldn't allow it myself. Such a foolish idea never entered my mind, Mrs. Benedict. For one thing, I'm far too stubborn to be married, and I know it. What if I wanted to go to school myself some day, or just walk on the mountain, and Abie forbade me to do it because we were married? I'd go anyway, and then he probably would kill me. I don't ever expect to be married. But having a baby is something else, no matter what he thinks, and I hope it makes him love me better. It's going to be hard to wait, though. Wasn't it hard for you to wait when you had Abie?"

Rachel had to smile, but at the same time, she was afraid that the course of action she had followed by making Marie nearly a part of the family had been extremely ill-considered. Like many essentially unselfish individuals, the wife of Captain Abraham Benedict often accused herself when family difficulties arose. She had always had a much greater tendency toward self-criticism and introspection than either her son or her husband, and, characteristically, she blamed herself for what had happened now. During the following days she racked her brain for a solution, though she was careful not to show her concern in Abraham's presence.

One day about a week later Ellen Baxter mentioned to her that some gypsies had been seen in Pond in the Sky, twenty miles away, and Rachel found herself wondering whether it might be best for Marie to return to Pia. Thinking of Pia reminded her of the conversation in which the gypsy woman had asked her if she wanted another child. Until now she had always assumed that Marie was meant to fill that emptiness in her life. Suddenly a different possibility occurred to her, and at the same time she saw a wonderful resolution of the entire dilemma, if she could only persuade her husband to agree to it.

That evening she broke the news of Marie's pregnancy to him, then made her proposal. As she had expected, he was extremely displeased at first, displeased with Abie mainly; but to her enormous relief he agreed, though somewhat reluctantly, that her solution was probably the only reasonable one.

"I'll take care of it," he said quietly. "Just wait a few days before you tell Marie, if you will."

Taking care of things was one of the Captain's specialties, and everyone in Hell's Gate knew it and, for the most part, benefited from it. He took care of his family. He took care of the factory's business, personally handling all contracts and, through his foremen, all dealings with his workers. He took care of the village and saw to it that the villagers cared for their homes, offering a prize of ten dollars in scrip for the most-improved yard at the end of each August and not hesitating to rebuke privately anyone who began to let the appearance of his house or yard slide. He took care of the houses himself by having them painted every summer; and when, on the morning after Rachel told him Marie was pregnant, the gypsies showed up (this time without Pia, who was back in Barre with a bad case of shingles) with two large crates containing housepaint for the Canadians, he good-naturedly let his tenants across the bridge go ahead and paint their battened houses: salmon pink and grape purple and French chartreuse and most other wild pastel colors imaginable and some that would have to be seen to be imagined.

"If I was boss of this village you can bet them Frogs would be scraping off paint between now and Christmas," Early Kinneson said in his high querulous voice that night at the store, just as Ned Baxter walked in to buy some leader material for the approaching fishing season.

"That's one of several reasons you ain't boss of the village, Early," Ned said quietly, to the delight of the five or six men gathered there.

So although he could be ruthless if he thought ruthlessness was necessary to protect his town or family, the Captain was not intolerant or inflexible, and in time the gaudy houses across the bridge became one more minor part of the myth. True, he did not claim to understand the gypsies. And though he was not humorless, he had no appreciation at all for the ironies that seemed more than anything else to inform their lives with significance and vitality: the library clock that Ethan caused to run backward; the American chestnuts they had planted on School Hill that turned out to be horse chestnuts; the red and yellow devil's paintbrushes they introduced for color in the upper meadow in Kingdom Mountain, which proliferated so fast they soon overran the hay. It was simply that his great plan, his vision, had no room and he had no time for ironies. Yet he tolerated and even encouraged the gypsies' visits.

It was not tolerance that this remarkable man lacked, or insight, or even self-knowledge, though unlike his wife he rarely questioned a decision once he had made it; and he had no doubt at all that he was making the right decision when he wrote to Abie that once again he had disappointed his parents through heedless and irresponsible behavior by "taking advantage of the affections of a child." Then he explained that he and Rachel had decided to adopt the baby, and raise it as their own.

Rachel had been ill. Her arthritis always bothered her more in the late fall and early spring, and she had been bedridden for nearly a week. Then one day the weather turned suddenly warmer, and in the early evening just after supper she was able to walk out to the love seat and sit beside Marie for a short while. This seemed to be a good time to broach her plan to the girl.

"Marie," she said, "I have something exciting to tell you. Can you guess what it is?"

Marie thought for a minute. "Are you pregnant too?" she said gravely.

"No," Rachel replied, laughing. "But it's almost as good. Abraham and I have decided that you should keep your baby."

Now Marie laughed. "I should hope so, Mrs. Benedict. I certainly don't intend to throw it out with the bath water."

Rachel patted her knee. "And we want you to know that we intend to give your child our name."

"Give it your name?"

She nodded. "We'd like to adopt your baby, Marie." Quickly she added, "Of course you'll still be the real mother, and right here to help bring it up. This way, you'll never have to worry about your child's not having a name or a home."

"Pardon me, Mrs. Benedict," Marie said, "but I intend to give the baby my own name and bring it up myself. If Abie wants to help, that's all right too, though I doubt he will, at least until it's old enough to throw a ball, and then only if it's a boy. You don't need to worry. I'll do a good job. But my baby isn't up for adoption."

"Marie, it would still be your child. No one would forget that. But it would be so much easier for the baby this way. Don't you think we'd be good to it? Heaven knows we've waited long enough for one! Think of what's best for the baby, dear, and I'm sure you'll agree."

"I *am* thinking of what's best for the baby!" Marie had never raised her voice to Rachel or the Captain before. "I won't let you do that, Mrs. Benedict! This baby may be all I ever have in the world, and nobody's going to take it away from me. Nobody!" Before she could stop herself, before she knew what she was going to say, Marie heard herself shouting, "You planned this, didn't you? You planned it from the first day I came here. You wanted me to have a baby because you couldn't have any more yourself, then when I did you planned to take it away from me and pretend it belonged to you!"

"Marie!" Rachel said. "Marie, I never . . ."

But the girl had run downstairs and Rachel could not continue anyway. To her horror, it seemed to her that somehow Marie, in her anger, had unveiled a terrible truth.

Although Abraham Benedict was in no way a superstitious man, and laughed to himself over Ned Baxter's periodic assertion that factory accidents, like deaths, were usually spaced in sets of three, he could not stop thinking that when bad luck did arrive, it seemed to come with a vengeance. Reflecting on this as he took his horseback constitutional in the park that evening, he supposed that Marie's pregnancy had probably been inevitable, or close to it. At least it was inevitable that at seventeen Abie would try to sleep with the girl, and everything else followed logically. That was bad enough, he thought. Then there had been Rachel's idea to adopt the baby, which seemed reasonable enough at first but now, a week later, looked more and more like a Pandora's box.

The main difficulty with the adoption scheme, he realized, was the question of succession. Even though the baby would be legitimatized as a Benedict, the Captain had no idea what proportion of his estate, if any, to accord to this individual. Nor was he certain how the baby's family status would affect Marie, or, for that matter, precisely what her present status was. Despite what Rachel had said, it was not inconceivable to him that Abie might in fact someday marry her—the Captain was no snob, and though he did not understand Marie any better than he understood most women, he recognized and admired many of her qualities—but if Abie married someone else instead, Abraham didn't see how Marie and her child could continue to remain in the village.

As he was apt to do when something bothered him, he reined in his mare near the quarry at the head of the meadow and stood for a time looking down at the wavy underwater image of the great, broken obelisk. To another man, the shattered monument might have represented personal failure, or at least the failure of men in general to do all they set out to do. It might also have suggested the folly of such an essentially useless project. To Abraham, however, the broken monument remained primarily a broken monument, a mistake from the start, no doubt, but only that. Yet as he gazed down at it, he could not help thinking again about the dilemma of who would inherit Hell's Gate after Abie, and his own haste in agreeing to adopt an illegitimate child, however much it meant to Rachel.

He did not expect to find a solution in the quarry, only to think for a while, so after a few minutes he remounted and rode back down to the factory to read his mail, which Stanwood Gregory picked up in the Common on the late afternoon train run and delivered to the office each evening as soon as he returned to Hell's Gate. As usual, Stan handed him a fat packet. It included the Boston newspaper; three business letters, which he glanced at, then put in his desk to answer the following morning; a note from his friend and customer George Peck, the author of the *Peck's Bad Boy* series and the former governor of Wisconsin; and a telegram from the headmaster of St. Mark's informing him that Abie and Charlie Pike had left the school the day before, with Charlie's substantial savings from the local bank, and neither had been seen since.

Several days earlier the ice had gone out of the lake in a hard rain accompanied by a warm south wind, which had continued to gust off and on since; and although there was still plenty of snow on the mountains, it was a very warm, springlike evening. The silver cornet band was having its first outdoors practice, and some boys were playing catch in the schoolyard. Wearing only the sweater and wool dress in which she had run out of the Big House, Marie wandered down the hill along the street. She passed the Captain, walking fast up the street with a piece of paper in his hand. Ned Baxter came down the other side of the street with an armful of brush for his pea vines to climb on and said good evening quietly. Early Kinneson stared at her from the steps of the store, but she did not see any of them, though she couldn't help noticing the band members, now playing "After the Ball."

A couple of cabinetmakers fishing off the walkway of the covered bridge, leaning their forearms on the sill of the long window, half turned and glanced at her as she walked past them. One of them said something in German. The other nodded and they began to reel in. A pigeon nesting in the beams overhead made its low trill, and Marie remembered how as a small child she had climbed up onto the shelf over the window and hidden there all day, too frightened and humiliated to come down. Now the shelf seemed hardly wide enough for a pigeon, much less a girl.

She came out of the bridge and passed the sawmill yard where she had gone on the spruce root with her mother to collect discarded slabs. She walked up the path where they had dragged the sledge, the path her father had walked each morning on his way to work. She remembered Claude Blair's talk of opportunities, and her mother's taking her to see the snow geese. She stopped near a house painted lavender with bright yellow trim. The door was open to let in the warm air, and Marie could smell meat frying. Inside the house a child cried, a woman's voice said something in French, and suddenly Marie realized she was standing on the edge of her old dooryard and looking into the house where she had lived with her parents.

Cautiously she worked her way around to the rear of the house, past a recently spaded garden patch, still smelling of fresh dirt, and up the slope to the giant black spruce. There beneath the tree she began to search through last year's dead milkweed and goldenrod stems.

She found the marker in a patch of blackberry canes that had grown up untended, but it had toppled over onto the ground face up, and the indentations were so weathered and faint that she could neither see them in the settling dusk nor trace them with her fingertips. As she started to right the marker, four or five garter snakes slid fast out from under it, so she gently let it back down in the blackberry canes.

When she stood up, a woman with a baby in her arms was staring at her from the edge of the garden. She said something sharply in French and Marie started to reply, but she had not spoken French for so long she could not think immediately of the words she wanted, so she turned and went rapidly toward the woods, through the sharp blackberry thorns that ripped her stockings and tore at her legs, and then she was running down through the trees until she came out on the back side of the lumberyard. She paused, then began to run again, through the yard between the high piles of seasoning lumber where she and Abie had taken off their clothes and played hide and seek on hot summer nights, waylaying and leaping onto each other from the lumber, rolling over and over in the dirt and sawdust. She began to cry; then she was crying hard and running back across the bridge, empty now, and between the empty station platform and the roundhouse to the spur track. She did not stop until she was half a mile below the village. She was still crying, but as soon as she caught her breath she began to run again, since she now knew exactly where she was going and had known since the moment she came out into the lumber-yard and thought of Abie, though she had no idea where St. Mark's was. She was just sure that if she followed the tracks far enough she was bound to find it, and find him, and he would know what to do. It was full dark and the spring frogs in the marsh were singing for rain so loudly she barely heard her own sobbing breath as she ran south between the mountain and the bay.

Marie had walked the tracks in the daytime a hundred times or more. When she was younger her stride had just matched the spaces between the ties; now her legs were much longer, yet not long enough to take two ties at a step, even when she was running. She fell the first time on the approach to a low trestle over a backwater where she and her mother had come one spring to grapple pickerel. Her knee hit one of the rails hard, but she was on her feet and moving immediately, trotting over the invisible backwater below the trestle, then running flat out, with her second wind. She ran three miles before falling again, on the causeway near the mouth of the river. This time her feet got tangled beneath her and she blundered over one of the rails, hitting hard on her shoulder and rolling to the foot of the embankment.

The first contraction came as she tried to get up, so sudden and powerful and irresistible that she did not believe it was inside her, but thought she must have landed on a stake that had punctured her abdomen. She could not even catch her breath to scream. When it passed she felt herself, brought her hand away warm and wet, and was certain she had fallen on some kind of stake or pointed rod or stump, though she could not see or feel any near where she was sitting, with her back against the embankment.

The second contraction was so hard she thought whatever she had fallen on must have broken off inside her. She was quite sure that she was dying, and years later, when she remembered how she had believed she was bleeding to death at the foot of the railroad embankment, she was surprised by the matter-of-fact way this thought had occurred to her. The pain passed again and she could feel the wet warmth on the sand beneath her. Still she had no idea what was happening to her.

The third time it came she screamed and then each time it came she screamed again, though the frogs were singing so loudly and there were so many of them in the swamp that her screams could not have been heard a hundred yards away even if anyone had been nearby to hear them. Automatically she began to pant like a dog between the spasms.

As the contractions came faster and closer together it seemed to Marie that the pain and the singing of the frogs were connected, and that if she could scream loud enough to make the frogs stop, the pain would stop too. She managed to take off her sweater and shove it between her legs; for a time she thought the bleeding had stopped, until she felt the warm wetness seeping through the sweater. It did not once occur to her that the baby was coming, because her own mother had given birth to Marie's two younger sisters almost casually, both times working right up to the last hour, then walking the cabin floor silently with Claude's assistance, back and forth, back and forth, until the moment came to lie down and have the babies.

Around midnight the pains and the bleeding stopped for a time. Marie slept briefly, and when she woke up the moon had risen and there was a pale halo around it so she knew that the singing frogs had been successful and it was going to rain, though maybe not before morning. She was thirsty, but she was afraid that if she stood up she would begin to bleed again. She sat still with her back against the sand embankment, looking out over the bay.

The moon went behind a cloud, and when it came out again Marie saw a turtle coming up from the edge of the water. As she watched, it climbed up the railroad bank and began to dig in the sand with its back claws and tail. It scooped out a hole as deep as a soup bowl, then tilted itself at a steep angle and began laying eggs in the sand at the bottom of the hole. Soon other turtles were emerging from the bay and digging nests all along the embankment. Some were no larger around than dessert plates and others were bigger than the tops of apple barrels and weighed fifty or sixty pounds. They paid no attention to Marie or to each other but came and laid their eggs and went back to the water, while she watched as fascinated as though she had strolled out from the village just to watch the turtles.

It took each turtle about twenty minutes to lay her eggs and another five or ten minutes to fill in the hole, and Marie was so absorbed in watching the margin of the bay for more turtles that she did not see the first skunk until it had nearly finished rifling one nest and was already looking around between bites for another. Two more skunks appeared, then another, taking care to stay well away from the turtles until they headed back to the water, then going immediately to the nests and beginning to dig. A pair of raccoons appeared and began digging too. Then a fast shadow passed over the sand and there was a single cry and a terrific scurrying as the skunks ran up the embankment, and Marie saw a huge owl turn and rise and fly silently for the swamp with something dark and limp in its claws. When she looked along the embankment the skunks were gone, though the raccoons were still digging. A warm breeze came up from the southeast, and a few minutes later the pains started in again.

This time there were only ten or twelve, so close together Marie had almost no time between to rest, and then the baby was coming. It was a boy, followed almost immediately by the afterbirth, and it was born dead but perfectly formed; Marie counted the fingers and toes twice to be certain before wrapping it in the sweater. Although she was still bleeding and felt very weak, she carried her sweater to a knoll back in the woods, where, using a stick and her hands, she dug a grave about three feet deep. She buried the baby wrapped up in the sweater, piling as many stones as she could find on the grave so that the skunks would not dig it up, though carrying the stones made her bleed more.

"This will have to suffice for you," she said out loud when she was through. "But maybe you don't need a great monument, or even a cedar slab, since you weren't ever completed."

She went back to the track and started walking south. She was no longer crying and no longer heading for St. Mark's, only away from Hell's Gate. After a while it began to rain, and it was still raining at dawn when she walked through the Common.

Chapter Six

"Tea's on, miss."

She was sleeping on a pile of empty potato sacks in a boxcar on a siding a few miles north of Pond in the Sky, about twenty miles east of Kingdom Common, when someone stuck his head through the door and lifted a crownless hat and spoke to her in a cheery resonant orator's voice that could not have been more in contrast with his diminutive size and shabby appearance. She was startled, but only for a moment, since at first she actually mistook him for a small boy. By the time she was fully awake, he had leaped up into the car and she realized that he was a man, though how old she had no idea. His hands and feet were tiny, and the features of his filthy, oval, somewhat pointed face were as fine as those of a small child.

His name, he told her over the tea, was John—just John would do, for the time being—and he was a "sort of railroad man" and a part-time logger. Just now he was on his way to Portland to put in a few days shoveling grain off the cars from Montreal, and if Marie wanted to come with him he would be charmed—that was the word he used—to show her the sights of the city. Had she ever seen the ocean? Then it was settled, unless of course she had a prior engagement.

On he jabbered, like a talkative pet crow, so that although Marie was still weak from her miscarriage two nights ago, and still in some pain, she could not help smiling at the voluble little man serving her spruce tea from a sooty tin kettle with manners that would pass muster at the Big House. Yes, she said solemnly when he finally stopped for a breath, she would very much like to go with him. She did not add that she had no place else to go, but she didn't need to. He had surmised that much at dawn when he discovered her asleep in the boxcar. They shook hands formally, and their partnership began.

On the way to Portland, sitting with their legs dangling out of the open door of an empty newsprint car in which a brakeman allowed them to ride for a penny a mile, Just John told her stories about his travels. It seemed to Marie that he had been everywhere and done every kind of work imaginable. He had picked lettuce in California, apples in Washington, potatoes in Idaho. He had worked in the gold fields of Alaska, where he had been frostbitten and lost three toes on his left foot, which he showed her with boyish pride. He had doctored in Montana, set himself up to practice law in a mining town in Colorado, and worked as an advance man for the Miles Orton Circus. Once, in Alabama, he had even taught school for part of a term, until it came to the attention of the board of trustees that he could not read or write twenty words, a revelation which very nearly resulted in a tarring and feathering. He had ridden all the major railroads in America and half of the "little lines," first as a newsboy and then, when it occurred to him that he liked riding trains better than working on them, as a tramp. He loved all trains, especially those on the Grand Trunk, and apart from his travels he seemed to have no home or family or friends.

It was easy to earn enough to live on in Portland by working a few hours a day at odd jobs. John shoveled wheat for a morning now and then; Marie swept out day coaches. She liked the ocean, but before long John developed itchy feet and they went back north for the haying season, working for farmers by the day and sleeping in tramp rooms in stifling attics or in barns or out in the woods.

From the start, John treated Marie like a favorite daughter.

He seemed to have no sexual interest in her or anyone else, and one day he confided that he had been "impotent with women" since an unfortunate early marriage with a "lady of spirit" whose first name, though he doubted Marie would believe it, was Wyalia. So although she did not tell him then or later, Marie realized that without even trying she had solved the mystery of John Trinity Kinneson's disappearance—he had fled matrimony with Wyalia to become a railroad tramp. It had not, she thought, been a bad decision.

As fall came on, they went up to Aroostook County in northern Maine to pick potatoes. From there they traveled even farther north to a pulp camp on the Allagash, where John got a job as an axman and she helped the cook, until he was fired for drinking too much peppermint extract and passing out one morning at breakfast; after which Marie did the cooking by herself.

She and John slept in separate bunks in a drafty shack where the camp boss did his bookwork. Every morning she was up two hours before dawn. Her first job was to go into a lean-to off the cookhouse, where great sides of frozen beef hung on hooks from the rafters, and hack off meat to thaw out for the following day. Next she would bring in four ten-quart buckets of potatoes, which were kept frozen in fifty-pound sacks against the outside wall of the lean-to, and pour cold water over them to draw out the frost. She spent the next hour baking, and then she got breakfast—and so her routine went until eight or nine at night. The camp boss did not allow the men to visit at mealtimes, but often they drifted back into the cookhouse after supper or on Sundays and joked and talked with her, just to be around a woman. Many of them were French, and Marie's own French returned to her quickly.

Until about Christmas, John was the best-liked man in camp. He was constantly laughing, joking, singing, and telling stories, and he could walk on his hands on the packed snow, and throw handsprings backwards, and fight like a gamecock; and sometimes he would jump and crow like a fighting rooster for sheer exuberance. He was good with an ax too, though too much of a talker to be very productive; as the big snows of January set in and the work grew harder, he spent more time building great roaring fires to get warm by and less time cutting, and the camp boss would have fired him a dozen times over if he hadn't been afraid of losing Marie as well.

The boss's name was Jigger Johnson, and he was considered to be one of the best foremen and river drivers in New England. He was not a big man, though he towered above John Trinity, but he was famous for announcing when he first took over a camp in the fall that he could "work harder, eat more, drink longer, and fight dirtier than any son of a bitch in the United States, Canada, or Prince Edward Island." What he said was probably true, yet he always treated Marie with great respect, and saw that his crew did. He taught her how to drive the camp pung that carried the crew's lunch out to where they were working, and toward the end of the winter he often took her with him nights on the sprinkler sled that kept the log roads icy and easy to skid logs over, and on the big snow roller that packed down the snow.

Marie liked going out in the woods at night with Jigger, who didn't talk much at first but would stop the horses from time to time to show her a pair of snowshoe rabbits jumping over each other in a moonlit clearing, or a place where a moose had stripped the bark off a stand of young hardwoods. He taught her to drive the huge logging horses too, but as their excursions together became more frequent, John grew so jealous that one afternoon in March he quit the crew and demanded that Marie quit with him. Although she hated to leave the camp and her job and her new friend Jigger Johnson, she reluctantly went down the tote road after the irate and frustrated little tramp— in part because she was not yet ready to be intimate with another man and in that respect she was safe with John.

Again they rode the trains John loved. He took her to visit small spur lines the way another man might take her to meet old friends. Sometimes they rode roped to the top of a boxcar, wearing goggles to protect their eyes from the hot cinders that streamed back from the engine. Sometimes they rode "blind," on the platform at the front of the baggage car behind the tender. When they had to, they rode the steel rods under the cars, though that was dangerous because you could fall asleep and roll off under the wheels, and some brakemen would even lower an iron bar attached to a long rope under the moving cars to dislodge tramps. Just once Marie saw that terrible jittering bar coming toward her, bouncing up off the cinders and ties into the frame almost directly below her back, missing her by less than a foot; after that she refused to ride the rods again.

One night in the summer of 1907 they went to sleep in an empty potato car, which an hour later was shunted onto a siding and locked up. They spent nearly two days inside the car in the hot dark without water, cutting their way through the door with John's penknife, and came within a few hours of dying of dehydration. That fall they had another close call. Heading back to Portland after the potato harvest, they were overtaken by an October blizzard, which they waited out under a blowdown for nearly five days before a plow train came along. By this time Marie had begun to think seriously about leaving John, but she did not quite know how.

It was April 1908, and she and John Kinneson had been together for nearly two years. She was seventeen and looked older, and she was cooking again, this time for the Nulhegan River crew of George Van Dyke's Connecticut Valley Lumber Company, back in Kingdom County. John was working on the drive, though not as a river driver, since he had somehow persuaded Van Dyke's Nulhegan foreman, Frank Roby, that he was an experienced engineer and had devised a method of bringing down the logs quicker and safer than ever before.

Running southeast out of the vast tract of uninhabited forest and swampland known as the Wenlock Woods, the Nulhegan is a rocky, narrow, and very fast river. In the summer it is hardly deep enough in places to float a canoe, but for two or three weeks in the spring, after the ice has gone out, it becomes a whitewater torrent which loggers always hated to drive because of the notorious jams that invariably built up in its sharp bends. John's idea was to erect half a dozen small log dams on feeder streams and then open the gates of those dams just as the drive was coming down, discharging enough water to float even the biggest butt-end spruces; but there was an adage among New England rivermen that if something could go wrong on the Nulhegan it would, and what went wrong in the spring of 1908 was that the small river, already tumultuous from snow runoff and rain, could not contain the terrific rush of water pouring in from John's dams on the tributaries. It promptly went over its banks, flooding beaver meadows and woods on both sides for a mile or more and stranding logs in some of the most inaccessible backwater bogs in New England. Frank Roby and his crew were furious. There was serious talk of throwing John into the river, and he and Marie had to leave camp without supper and without their pay.

It was very cold and drizzling a sleety rain, and by the time they reached the Grand Trunk tracks, five miles south of the lumber camp, it was dusk and they were soaking wet. Bloomfield, where the Nulhegan empties into the Connecticut, was only three miles to the east, but John wanted to put as much distance between himself and the angry rivermen as possible before stopping and insisted that they head west up the tracks toward Pond in the Sky. He was still wearing his calked boots, which bit deep into the slick wooden ties, while Marie slipped and slid along in her gum rubbers.

On into the darkness they slogged. The rain turned to sleet, which fell faster and faster, and they were nearly abreast of the flickering light before they saw it. Four or five shadowy figures were sitting around a sputtering fire on the edge of the cut through the woods.

"Good evening to you, gentlemen," John called out in a bold voice. "I see you're just out of the lumber camps like ourselves. Who's got a hot bite to eat and a drink for a story?"

"I know your story and I don't care to hear it repeated," a gruff voice replied.

"I shall tell you a story, by the Jesus," a second voice said. "We come down to the Wenlock station to load pulp on the cars this forenoon, and it turned out some sapheaded son of a bitch hung the entire drive back in the swamps and now there's no Christly pulp to load."

"That's a damned crying shame," John said, moving in toward the fire. "I guess these are hard times for you and me and poor people everywhere. I and my daughter here have certainly had our own share of misfortune. Sarah passed away last fall, then a week later I lost my job at the shipyards, and now we're going up to a place called Pond in the Sky to live with a cousin and look for work ourselves."

"What's that you say?" the man with the gruff voice said. "Is that a woman you've got there?"

"No, by God, it's a lady," John said. "Fallen onto hard times, yes, but a lady nonetheless, like Sarah, rest her soul."

The gruff man was holding a flat bottle in his hand. "Well there, Jack, I'll tell you what. I'll give you the rest of this whiskey if you'll give me the use of the highborn lady for the night."

"My daughter isn't for sale," John said flatly.

He began to edge back away from the fire toward the tracks, but by then the man with the whiskey bottle had stood up and grabbed Marie's arm.

"I want this woman and I intend to have her," he said.

"I'll tell you what, brother," John said quickly, getting out a pack of cards. "I'll play you a card game of your choice. If I win, you give me the bottle. If you win, take the girl and be damned."

The man gave a derisive laugh. "I know you card sharps and I won't fall for that. I'll fight you for her."

Marie was terrified. She knew John was a fighter; she'd seen him outlast two loggers in a go-round over a dispute in a game of high-low-jack one slow Sunday afternoon in Jigger Johnson's pulp camp two winters ago. But the man who had challenged him was well over six feet tall, with shoulders as broad as an ax handle is long, and his hand was so large it encircled her upper arm completely.

"What'll it be then, my bucko?" John said cheerily, seeing that he had no choice. "Catch as catch can, or the Marquis of Queensbury?"

The big man stared at John Trinity Kinneson incredulously. Then suddenly he shoved Marie back toward the woods, picked up a dead limb intended for the fire, and struck John in the side of the head with it, knocking him to his knees like a stunned ox.

"Stomp him, Hiram," a man growled. "Give him a dose of logger's smallpox."

To Marie's horror the man proceeded to leap at John, driving both his calked boots into the little tramp's face. Then they were rolling back and forth through the fire, with sparks flying and men scrambling to get out of the way. Somehow John Trinity managed to pin the bigger man briefly. Grasping his hair in one hand, he jammed his other thumb into his antagonist's right eye socket and with a rapid twist tore his entire eye out of his head.

Jumping to his feet, John held the eye up to the firelight and began to jeer at Hiram, who gave a great roar and groped frantically around the fire with blood pouring off his face. "Keep the whore," he screamed, "but for Christ's sake give me back my eye."

"Certainly," John said in his politest voice and made as though to hand it back, but instead he tossed it into the fire, and then he and Marie were running down the tracks in the dark.

John had been badly injured himself, since Hiram had landed full along the side of his face with his nailed boots, but they continued to run until they were sure no one was following. Then Marie led him away from the tracks into the woods, where he passed out in a blowdown, as insensible as one of his own hung logs. Marie sat down beside him, too tired even to cry. By this time the sleet was changing to snow, but she was crying too hard to notice.

Moving had become a habit for Marie. Moving kept her from thinking about Abie and her baby and Hell's Gate, and when she was on the move she did not worry about the future and what would eventually become of her. John's face began to heal, but he had lost his high spirits in the fight in the Wenlock Woods, and for some reason he was never the same after that. He told fewer stories, sang less, drank more, and refused to work for longer than a day or two at a time. He began to dream of falling off a freight and being used as a medical corpse, as dead tramps without homes or identification sometimes were if their bodies were discovered soon enough. Haunted by this macabre anxiety, he'd wake up screaming for Marie to haul him out of the vat of preserving fluid that such bodies were reportedly kept in. One hot afternoon outside Berlin, New Hampshire, they came upon the severed, decomposing trunk and head of a man who had probably slipped off the rods or been knocked off by a brakeman, and John couldn't sleep for a week afterward. For half a dollar or a bottle he'd go off in the woods and let other tramps abuse him, and much of the time he sulked, wearing a perpetually aggrieved expression enhanced by his disfigurement.

By the summer of 1909, Marie was supporting both herself and John, who now refused to work at all. She took care of an elderly woman with thirty pet cats. She took care of a madwoman whose family kept her in a cage made of cedar poles. She picked potatoes until her back was bent like a barrel hoop, wired balsam boughs together for grave blankets, and worked as a short-order cook at county fairs.

On the day she turned eighteen the man who guessed weights and ages at the Fryeburg Fair estimated that she was twenty-nine years old.

They could not find a job in a logging camp that winter, for no foreman wanted to take on a man who wouldn't work. During November and December they squatted in a boxcar on an abandoned siding near Bloomfield, and Marie earned a little money selling Christmas wreaths. After the holidays they went over to Pond in the Sky, where she hoped to find work cutting ice for the refrigerator cars.

They arrived in the evening with twelve dollars and some change, enough for meals and lodging at the Pond House for three days if they were careful. Since it was too late to check in at the railroad station where the hiring for the ice-cutting crews was done, they went directly to the hotel, where Marie wanted nothing so much as a bath, a hot meal, and a good night's sleep.

Located midway between Portland and Montreal on the Grand Trunk Railway, Pond in the Sky was a booming town during the early years of this century, with twenty trains a day passing through, three mechanic crews to service them around the clock, a gigantic roundhouse with twelve stalls, half a dozen restaurants and boardinghouses, and three hotels including the Pond House, which was always busy. The only available room on the winter night they arrived was on the fourth floor, which had only one bathroom, so Marie had to wait more than an hour to take her bath. In the meantime John, who hadn't washed in months, went downstairs and lost every penny she'd earned making wreaths in a poker game with two well-dressed French salesmen from Montreal.

"Come here," he said when Marie finally found him at a corner table in the barroom. "I owe these gentlemen twelve or thirteen dollars. Get it out and give it to me and I'll win it back."

"Don't involve me in your gambling, John," Marie said gravely. "I've told you that many times."

John had cadged a few drinks from the salesmen, which always made him reckless. "I'll tell you what, friends," he said. "I'll put up the little woman here against the twelve dollars I owe you."

One of the men glanced at Marie in her men's clothes, spat

on the floor, and shook his head, and at exactly that moment she decided to leave John Trinity. What physical danger and the degradation of supporting a man who wouldn't work and a hundred other hardships and indignities had failed to do, that salesman's shake of the head accomplished. Not that she would have considered going with him anyway; she would not have. Yet she still had pride enough to be deeply hurt by his contempt and deeply outraged by John's proposal.

"Well, John," she said angrily, "I'm glad to know that I'm worth twelve dollars at least, for there have been times recently when I would have sworn I wasn't worth that. But I'm afraid I'll have to decline your generous invitation to be the stake of the game. Here's the twelve dollars. Take it and pay your debt. And if you come near my room or bother me ever again, I'll have a sheriff after you before you have time to turn around twice."

She slammed the money onto the table, spun around, and returned to her room, where she put a chair against the door and went to bed without eating, too tired and upset to care. To her great relief John never appeared, but continued to sponge drinks and gamble with money he didn't have, making a greater and greater nuisance of himself until the hotel proprietor had a couple of men carry him out and throw him into an empty boxcar on a southbound freight. Marie never saw or heard of him again.

"Mister, can you use another hand on the ice?"

It was dawn, and already the pond was covered with men and teams. Marie had located the foreman in the stable near the freight yard, giving a tongue-lashing to a man trying to harness a team of horses and not having much luck.

He turned around angrily. "I need a driver is what I need. All the experienced drivers are up in the lumber camps, and these Irishers the railroad brung up from Boston don't know a bridle from a whiffletree—why, Matthew, Mark, Luke, and John! It's Marie. How be you, girl?"

"Better than nothing, Jigger," Marie said, smiling. "Do you want me to harness those horses for you?"

Without waiting for a reply she buckled the heavy working harnesses onto the two horses, just as Jigger had taught her to do the year she cooked for him and drove the camp pung, and for the rest of the winter she cut ice on Pond in the Sky. She began work each day at first light by hitching her horses to a wooden plow and scraping off any snow that had fallen onto the ice during the night. When the pond was clear of snow, she hitched onto a steel plow and began dividing the ice into grids four feet long by two feet wide. Jigger showed her how to make the first cut just an inch deep and then to go over the same furrow again and again until she was down nearly a foot. While she went on to make another grid, sawyers with iron-handled hand saws cut through the furrows to the water below. Men called tampers filled the spaces cut between the ice with snow so they wouldn't freeze over again; then the sawyers made a channel to the conveyor chains leading up into the icehouse, and floats of ice cakes weighing five to six hundred pounds apiece were shoved through the open water to the chain by the tampers, using wooden pickaroons with double steel points.

When she was on the ice, Marie dressed in long flannel underwear, a pair of flannel pajamas, wool pants, overalls, two shirts, three pairs of men's wool stockings, a lined sheep coat, a knitted wool face mask, and India-rubber gumboots. Yet if she stopped moving for two minutes she got cold. Twice the temperature dropped to forty-five below zero, and often when it was twenty below or lower the wind blew hard. But she liked the long regular hours and the men she worked with and she especially liked the horses, a gelding and a mare no longer good for woods work but careful and patient on the ice. At the end of her second week on the job she bought several spools of different-colored ribbon, blue and pink and bright yellow, and decorated their working harnesses; and to the vast amusement of Jigger, she braided their manes and bought each of them a brass tail band, which she kept polished like the brass balls on top of the parlor stove at the Big House.

For the first time since she'd worked in Jigger's logging camp she earned good wages. Some weeks she worked overtime and made thirty to thirty-five dollars, from which she was able to save at least ten dollars each week. She ate prodigiously, slept well, and felt better than she had ever felt in her life. The gray film on her skin disappeared and her teeth tightened up, and she bought two skirts and three blouses at the dry-goods store.

In late February there was a thaw. Two horses went through the soft ice, sinking before anyone could get to them, so Jigger pulled the teams and men off the pond for three days, until it froze hard again; during those days off, he and Marie began to spend time together. The following Saturday night they went to a square dance at the Pond Pavilion, and before Marie knew exactly how it had happened they were lovers.

In April when the ice went out, Jigger went to work for George Van Dyke on the Connecticut River log drive. He got Marie a job cooking on the Mary Anne, a caravan of four tremendous freight wagons painted bright blue with gilt trim, like circus wagons. Each wagon was pulled by eight horses, and they followed the drive with supplies and food from First Lake in northern New Hampshire to Mount Holyoke, Massachusetts, a distance of nearly three hundred miles. One wagon carried a tent as large as a circus tent, where Jigger's river drivers ate in four shifts of fifty to sixty men at each sitting. For a month Marie slept no more than three or four hours a night. She was second cookee, in charge of baking, and her hours were longer than anyone's except Jigger's and the head cook's, because she had to bake the beans and bread and pies and cookies each night for the following day; also, she drove one of the wagons, sometimes falling asleep with the reins in her hands while the horses plodded on through the mud to the next campsite, ten or fifteen miles down the river.

Jigger was first foreman of the drive under Frank Roby, the walking boss. He was a great favorite with both the crew and George Van Dyke because he was always the first man to go out on a jam with a lighted stick of dynamite in his teeth or ride a log through Seven Mile Falls on a dare. When the drive ended, Van Dyke offered him an easy summer job tending a fire tower in the Wenlock Woods between Pond in the Sky and the Canadian line. Jigger was terrifically excited because his boss had told him that if he'd man the tower in the summers and work for him each spring on the drive, he could buy some land in Wenlock and homestead it.

"There's a small pond of maybe thirty acres at the foot of the tower mountain," Jigger told Marie. "It don't have a name so far as I know. Ten, twelve years ago when we logged it in there we just called it Pond Number Four. The Yellow Branch of the Nulhegan rises up out of it, and it's a pretty place. The trapping along the pond and river should be prime." He thought for a minute. "Marie, I'm forty, maybe forty-one years old, and I never owned nothing but a pair of Bass calk boots and an ax and the clothes on my back. It's time I settled down and owned something. I'd like to ask you to come with me."

She thought for a minute. "Jigger, I know this isn't any of my business, but would you mind telling me how much Mr. Van Dyke wants for that land?"

"Two thousand dollars will buy the old log camp, or whatever's left of it, plus the pond and fifty acres. That's more than enough for a couple of horses and a cow if we want. I've got five hundred now, and by next spring when I sell the furs I expect to have another five hundred."

She looked at him in the solemn manner he had come to expect, and said, "Well, I'll tell you what, Jigger. I've got a little money saved up myself. About two hundred dollars, I think. I'll put that with yours. Then you and I will go up to Pond Number Four—which is no name for a pond, and I intend to change it as soon as it belongs to us clear and free—and make a life for ourselves."

"Hoo!" Jigger shouted. "That's it, we're on our way! Only you keep that money of yours, girl, and do what you want with it. I reckon Van Dyke can wait till spring for the next payment."

They outfitted themselves in Pond in the Sky, where Jigger had credit, and on the last day of May they set off down the tracks for Joe Roby's Wenlock station on a flatbed with the same two horses Marie had driven on the ice and their gear and supplies. "You've heard of the old pioneers going up in the mountains with just a rifle and an ax?" Jigger had told Marie when she objected to buying so much on credit. "I'll tell you something: They weren't homesteaders. We need logging tools and hand tools, horse liniment and spare horseshoes, flour, sugar, salt, bug dope—the bugs up there will carry you off, they're so thick this time of year—ammunition, fishhooks, blankets, dishes, knives, forks, tea and coffee, yeast, pepper, salt pork—and that's just a beginning."

They reached the pond with their first load about five in the afternoon, and as they came out onto the south edge and looked across at the tower mountain Marie saw that it was a lovely place. It was set in a basin at the foot of the mountain, and drained off into the headwaters of the river through a decaying old dam. It had no visible inlet but was fed by underwater springs. The trees around the edge had been killed by high water backed up by the dam, and most of the big firs and spruces had been cut off the mountain, but there was plenty of hardwood, and a clearing where the horses could graze on wild hay near the dilapidated log camp.

"Jigger," she announced that evening after supper, "I was wrong. This spot is so pretty it doesn't need any different name. I want to thank you for bringing me here to Pond Number Four."

"You know how to do that, Marie," Jigger said, following her inside to their bedrolls, which she had spread out on balsam fir tips. "Do you ever know how to do that!"

The next four years were among the busiest and happiest of Marie's life. The first summer was especially active. It rained a good deal during June and part of July, so they did not need to spend much time in the tower and were able to make excellent progress with their house. It was a log house built from cedar trees they cut themselves and chinked with mud from the pond. The rafters and roof boards came from the cook's shack off the back of the lumber camp, which they converted into a stable. The house sat on a knoll overlooking the pond, with the mountain at its back to keep off the north wind. It consisted of a single room, like Marie's old house on the St. Francis, but twice as large and much better built, with a good-sized root cellar with a trapdoor entrance from the house and a bulkhead entrance at the rear.

Jigger was always up before daylight, banging the lids of the cookstove and singing one of his logging songs at the top of his voice, so Marie couldn't have slept even if she'd wanted to. At dawn she went down to the pond to wash, and then she liked to pole an old raft around for a few minutes and catch two or three brook trout for breakfast. The fish ran from half a pound to a pound and a half apiece and were so wild they struck a hook baited with a strip of red flannel. There were two families of beavers, which learned to come up to the house for handouts, and an otter that kept its distance but sometimes dived off the old dam while Marie and Jigger watched, and a mated pair of loons with a nest at the end of a point on the west side of the pond.

Just before the raspberries came on, the wet weather ended, and after that Jigger was very conscientious about watching for fires. He was fond of saying grimly that there was nothing this side of hell so terrible as a raging big forest fire, and from the middle of July until the October rains they spelled each other every day in the high rickety wooden tower on the mountaintop, where Marie could sit contentedly for hours on end, gazing out over the unending woods and ponds and rivers that lay below her like a vast green and blue map. On fair days she could see a hundred miles in every direction: far down the Presidential Range in New Hampshire, far up into Canada, and all the way to Mount Mansfield in western Vermont. It was

exhilarating to watch an electrical storm from the mountaintop, and she loved to watch the hawks soaring and learned
from Jigger how to tell them apart by the shape of their wings
and the way they hunted. In August a pair of fish hawks visited
the pond, and when they dived for a trout, slamming into the
water from terrific heights, the echo would reverberate off the
mountainside like a gunshot.

They spotted about ten fires that summer, all small and all
along the Grand Trunk between Bloomfield and Pond in the
Sky, set by live cinders from the locomotives. Instead of a
telegraph or telephone line they had a system of flags to indi-
cate where the fire was: red, green, and yellow, which they ran
up on a pole on top of the tower for Joe Roby down at the
railhead to see. Joe would then wire Pond in the Sky for a gang
of men to come out on a handcar and put it out or, if it was
nearby, extinguish it himself. Jigger and Marie also had a good
system for relieving each other. When they got bored, they'd
hang one of Jigger's red flannel undershirts from the bottom of
the platform, and then the other would come up and take over.
Sometimes they'd watch for a while together, but not often, so
they rarely got tired of each other's company and were nearly
always glad to be together at the end of the day.

Of all the things they did together—making love, fishing in
front of the house in the evening, going berrying—Marie liked
their long talks in bed best. Companionable as any affectionate
long-married couple, they often visited far on into the night,
talking about anything and everything. Jigger was full of stories about his past. He loved to tell Marie how he had gone into
Frank Roby's lumber camp on Paul's Stream as bull cook at
fourteen and worked his way up to second foreman within
four years. He recounted story after story about the big drive
on the Connecticut—how when the Mary Anne was a raft
instead of four blue wagons it had come apart against the
bridge in Colebrook; how five men had been killed in the
spring of 1901 when the three-mile jam below North Stratford
went out; how a dozen other men he'd known well had been

killed on the river or in the woods—until it seemed to Marie that most of his closest friends were dead. It was a constant wonder to her that he had not been killed himself.

"I've done some things I wish I hadn't," he told her. "But I've never jumped from a runaway team or a jam in the river. That's what I'm proudest of in my life." He thought for a minute. Then he said, "The closest call I ever had wasn't with horses or on the river. It was in a fire. It was the dry summer of '94, and I and Frank Roby was cruising timber up to the head of Chesuncook Lake, off over in the State of Maine. Well, we got caught in there somehow in a big forest fire, and mister, don't you think we wasn't scared! We got right into a river with just our noses poking out and watched a whole mountain burn like a farmer's haystack. The flames was shooting two, three hundred foot into the sky, and what was worse, you could see the reflection of that blazing mountain upside down in the tower of smoke it sent up. I never see nothing that bad before and I never hope to again. Scared! You don't know what scared is until you see such a sight as that. I ain't lying. There was that mountain, Marie, a-burning up in the sky like the Second Coming."

As interested as Marie was in Jigger's history, he seemed even more interested in hers. "Tell about that Christly needle," he'd say out of the blue, and she would tell him how the gypsies had carved the obelisk for Captain Benedict, which never failed to exasperate Jigger as much as it intrigued him because he was certain that he could have devised a way to lift the monument out of the quarry without breaking it. He called Abie Benedict a cowardly little piss-ant for not marrying Marie; then a minute later he laughed and said he ought to be grateful to young Benedict because, if it hadn't been for him, she would never have gone on the road. He pestered Marie to tell him in detail what she and young Benedict had done together, and when she laughed and told him that they had done what two people of the opposite sex could do and then some, he wanted to know *what*, exactly, with the same unabashed interest with which he looked at the provocative pictures of gun molls in the *Police Gazette.*

He was endlessly fascinated by Hell's Gate and the factory, the Big House and the park, and most of all by Abraham Benedict himself. "He puts me in the mind of old Van Dyke," Jigger said. "I and that Captain of yours would hit it off fine, Marie. I'd like to shake his hand sometime."

In the fall Jigger shot a moose for them to eat that winter. Also, he insisted on showing Marie how to use his rifle, though since killing the deer with her ax as a girl she had not been interested in hunting. In November, when the pond started to freeze, they laid out their trapline. That first winter they set out a hundred traps and caught more than seven hundred muskrats and eighty-four minks. (Marie made Jigger promise not to trap her pet beavers or the otter, which he somewhat reluctantly agreed not to do.) In the spring they boarded the horses for a month at Joe Roby's while they worked on the Connecticut drive again. When they returned to Pond Number Four, Jigger began to clear some land to grow more hay on.

That was the summer Marie thought she was pregnant again. Jigger took her to Pond in the Sky to consult a shrewd country practitioner who more than once had sewed him back together after a fight or logging accident, and after examining Marie carefully, the doctor asked her whether she had ever had a miscarriage. When she replied that she had, he nodded and looked at her gravely. "You're not pregnant," he said, "and I don't think you're going to get pregnant." He explained that when she had lost the baby something deep inside her had been twisted out of place and that it was unlikely that she would be able to carry a child long even if she became pregnant.

Although Jigger gallantly insisted that the real trouble was that he must have been kicked "where the sun don't shine" one time too many, Marie suspected that the doctor was right. It was a serious disappointment to her, and for several months she was despondent. In desperation Jigger bought her a wedding ring and asked her to marry him. She was touched, but wore the ring only on her right hand.

"If we got married, we'd no doubt begin to quarrel," she told him. "We're much better off just as we are, Jigger. Did you ever hear the old verse about marriage? The gypsies taught it to me:

> "Ice cream is a very strange thing,
> And so are codfish balls.
> But the people that people marry
> Are the strangest thing of all."

"I didn't know codfish had balls," Jigger said angrily; yet he seemed pleased that she wore the ring at all, and she suspected that he distrusted the idea of marriage nearly as much as she did.

As winter approached, her good spirits gradually returned, though the thought of being unable to have a child troubled her off and on for many years and probably accounted in part for her aversion to marriage.

The winter of 1913–14 was especially fierce. Some days the wind blew so hard Jigger couldn't get out to check his trapline. Since he had no patience with inactivity of any kind, he would pace back and forth across the floor and drive Marie to distraction with his frequent trips to the door to see if the storm had let up. She felt the oppressiveness of cabin fever herself and began to snap at him over small things. For the first time in her life she had trouble sleeping. Sometimes at night when the wind was right and she heard a train whistle come floating up from the Grand Trunk, she wondered whether this remote and isolated life with a man twice her age was right for her; and one day it occurred to her that although she loved Jigger deeply, in many ways he reminded her more of her father than of a lover her own age, like Abie Benedict. They were both relieved when at last, in late February, the weather started to break.

Early in March while she was ice fishing Marie heard the mating call of a jay. That was the first sign of spring. The next day she saw a crow picking at the frozen trout heads she'd left on the ice, and that afternoon she started her cabbage and tomato seeds in a narrow wooden box Jigger had made to fit onto the south windowsill. Just as she planted the last of the seeds, she glanced up and saw three men advancing across the pond on snowshoes.

She was surprised, since these were the first people she and Jigger had seen since fall, when a few hunters had stopped by. They came up and the tallest asked politely for Mr. Johnson. He had long gray hair that hung nearly to his shoulders and long yellow teeth, like a horse.

"Well, Mr. Johnson is still out on his trapline, boys," Marie said. "But if you'd like to come in and wait, the teakettle's on and I'm just about to mix up a batch of ginger cookies."

"Don't you have nothing with a little more kick to it than tea and cookies?" a man with enormous shoulders said in a gruff voice. "I'm cold, by the Jesus!"

The tall man had been admiring the pelts stretched out on the outside wall of the house. Turning back to Marie, he smiled. "Don't you pay any attention to Hiram, miss. Old Hi is always cold, when it comes to that. Ain't you now, Hi?"

The broad-shouldered man shrugged, pulled his wool hat with earflaps lower, and walked past Marie into the house. Something about the way he had spoken seemed familiar, but she did not place him until they were seated around the table. "Take off your cap, Hi," the gray-haired man said as Marie approached with the tea. "Don't you know it ain't considered good manners to wear a dirty old hat inside a house?"

The big man lifted the earflaps of his hat, at the same time pulling it a little lower over his forehead—but not far enough to conceal the glass eye that started a good inch out of his head; and instantly Marie knew that she was serving tea to the man who had tried to rape her on the Grand Trunk the night after John had hung the drive on the Nulhegan.

The last thing in the world she wanted to do was to show her fright. She was quite sure the man with the glass eye didn't recognize her. It had been very dark and sleeting hard and he had been drunk. He was not drunk now, however. He was stone sober and so were the other two: a short, grinning Frenchman named Tuque and the tall lean man, whom the others called Preacher.

While Marie baked her cookies, Preacher made a little small talk, asking how the trapping had been and how long she and Jigger had lived there. Several times she glanced out the window, and when Jigger finally appeared she was greatly relieved. Although she met him at the door with a meaning look, mouthing the words, "Watch out," he did not seem concerned. He visited with the men about the hard winter and without quite asking found out that they were timber cruising for George Van Dyke. The man called Preacher said he also worked as a traveling evangelist, distributing tracts and Bibles to logging crews and preaching to those who would listen. "Have you been born again, my daughter?" he said suddenly to Marie, grinning hideously with his yellow horse teeth.

"Well, no," she said uncomfortably, "I haven't. It's enough of a job just to be born once, I suppose."

"Except a man be born again, he cannot see the kingdom," Preacher said, and Hiram burst into a loud laugh.

"Never mind that hogwash," Jigger said. "I don't imagine you come clear up here to give us a Sunday school lesson. What was it you boys said you wanted?"

"We didn't say," Hiram said, but Preacher quickly asked Jigger if he wanted to sell his furs.

Periodically Tuque made an irrelevant remark in French or laughed crazily, like a loon, at some private joke. Once he leaned across the table and said in French to Preacher, "Greenwood told us not to bother with nothing but the wom—"

The tall man shook his head in warning. "Be patient," he said in French. "You'll have your fun soon enough, my little friend."

Hiram, in the meantime, sat picking his teeth and scowling. From time to time he seemed to look fixedly at Marie with his glass eye.

The three men stayed on for supper, which Preacher praised lavishly, although in her nervousness Marie had forgotten to add ginger to the cookies. When the meal was over the men discussed the furs again, but did not make an offer.

"Well, gentlemen," Jigger said after an hour or so, pushing back his chair and standing up. "It's getting late. Now this cabin's small, else I'd offer you accommodations here, but you're welcome to bunk in the old camp next door if you don't mind sleeping with the horses."

Tuque and Hiram looked at the Preacher, who nodded, and after thanking Marie again for the meal he got up and put on his sheep coat and went outside with a lighted lantern Jigger had given him; the other two followed. As soon as they were through the door, Jigger closed it. "Those bastards intend to steal our furs," he said to Marie. "Timber cruising for George Van Dyke! They're nothing but common thieves."

"Yes, Jigger," Marie said.

"Well, I don't intend to let them."

"No, Jigger. But I must warn you. That big man who kept looking at me after supper—he's the one John Trinity fought that night I told you about."

"Be he now?" Jigger said with interest. He looked around the curtain at the window to the right of the door. "They're out there in the dooryard still, confabulating with each other. Maybe I ought to run them off with the rifle right now."

He took his deer rifle down from the pegs over the door and checked the clip to make sure it was loaded, and the next moment Preacher called out in a loud ringing voice, "Jigger Johnson! Open the door, Jigger Johnson."

Jigger opened the door a crack.

"You listen here, Jigger," Preacher shouted. "We want that woman in there with you. You send her out, and we'll leave you and your furs be."

Jigger and Marie looked at each other, equally astonished.

"We want that woman," Preacher shouted again. "We intend to have her too. You may not know this, Jigger, but that woman in there with you's a murderess. Three years ago she married Hi's brother that was gatekeeper up at Eagle Lake dam and slit his throat whilst he was sleeping. When Hi got too close to the truth of the matter she took out his eye with a hot poker and then cut and run. No doubt she plans to serve you the same some night—you send her out here so we can take her back over to stand trial in Maine, and we won't harm you."

"Go to hell in your grandmother's handbasket," Jigger said coolly. "That's the biggest cock-and-bull story I've heard in all my life. If you aren't off these premises in fifteen seconds I'll drop you in your tracks like a buck deer. Now, shove!"

As Marie watched from the window, Preacher took a long horse pistol out of his coat pocket. "Look out!" she shouted, and just as the tall man fired, Jigger slammed the door and bolted it.

"Marie," he said, "I've got a small job of work to attend to here tonight. I want you to get your coat and boots on and take your snowshoes and go down cellar. When I give the word, skin out through the bulkhead as quiet as you can. Strike straight up into the woods behind the house, and then and not until then put on your snowshoes. Circle out round the dam, cross the ice on the river down by the second bend, and cut for Joe Roby's. It's a pleasant enough night and you should be there within an hour. Tell Joe to wire down to Pond for the sheriff and bring him back up here as quick as possible. You stay with Joe's wife at Wenlock."

Marie shook her head. "No, Jigger. You and I aren't married and I don't have to do what you say. I intend to stay here and help you."

He looked at her, looking gravely back at him. She did not speak stubbornly or raise her voice. She simply wasn't going to obey him. That was that. There was another shot from outside, and the window shattered. "Put out the lantern,

Marie," Jigger said. He was smiling grimly, and as frightened as she was of the three men outside, Marie would not have changed places with them at that moment for anything.

"You send that woman out straightaway, Jigger, or we'll burn you out," Preacher yelled.

Jigger fired twice out the broken window. "That box of shells on the shelf over the stove," he said to Marie in a low voice. "If you can see your way clear to crawl over and fetch them without being married, I'd be grateful to you."

Marie got the shells.

"Do you need a marriage license to fire this gun?" he said.

"No, Jigger."

"Good. Now listen sharp. Fire every minute or so, but don't empty the clip. After you've shot three times, take it out and reload it. That way you won't be caught with an empty clip if they rush you. I'm going out the bulkhead and slide in behind them. If they fire the house, get out the back way and run like hell for Wenlock."

Without waiting for her to answer, Jigger gave her the gun and the box of ammunition and was gone.

Two more shots came from dooryard, one following the other immediately. Marie fired back. She counted to sixty and fired again, then reloaded the clip. She fired, counted, fired. This went on for about five minutes, with Preacher firing back at the house at frequent intervals. Then it was still for a time, and Marie did not fire any more shots because there were only four bullets left in the ammunition box.

When she saw the man he was already running toward the house, the birchbark torch soaked in kerosene held over his head, firing as he came. Jigger shouted and Preacher spun around and fired twice, then came on toward the house, running across the snow with the torch, his long hair streaming backward. Just as he drew back his arm to fling it Marie fired, and then she fired twice more, and he collapsed in the snow.

"Jigger!" she shouted as she ran outside. "Jigger, where are you?"

"I'm all right," he called back from the edge of the dooryard. "It's just my leg that's hit a little."

"Where are the other two?"

"Where they won't steal no furs, I'll assure you of that." She was shaking badly as she bent over him, and she thought she was going to be sick, or maybe cry, but he squeezed her hand and told her again that he was all right. Then he said, "I ain't telling you what to do as though we was married, Marie, but if I might venture a suggestion you could just kick some snow over that firebrand on the doorstoop. If you don't mind, of course."

When she returned, still shaking, he grinned at her, and then he fainted.

Jigger had been shot an inch below the knee, and his lower left leg was broken. Marie cut out the bullet with his hunting knife and made two splints from a long birch pole. She dragged the three bodies down to the outlet below the dam and dumped them in, and then despite herself she was sick in the woods, though she did not see how she and Jigger had had any other choice than to do what they did. Hiram and Tuque had their throats slit, and the Preacher had been shot in the chest at nearly point-blank range. Why had these three men wanted to kill her? Neither she nor Jigger had the slightest idea.

Jigger was up stumbling around on a pair of homemade crutches within a week. Not knowing what to do with himself while Marie ran the trapline, he'd stand on one leg in the melting snow in the dooryard, like an exasperated heron, watching for her to return an hour before she was due. He chopped kindling enough to last three years and watered Marie's tomato sets until they turned yellow. He did some of the cooking and baking, though by his own admission he was the worst cook in the world. Finally, in the last week of April, he took off the splints and began to limp around the dooryard with the help of a stick. Every day he went farther, and by the time the ice started to turn soft and dark he was able to put his full weight on the leg, though he still walked with a noticeable hitch.

Marie wanted Jigger to wait until he'd been back on his feet for two or three weeks before taking the furs into Pond in the Sky. Jigger said they would bring a much higher price if he could get them to town before ice-out, and he was impatient to make the final payment on their homestead, so one sunny morning in early May when the ice was covered with an inch of meltwater he roped the furs on the pung behind the two old horses, planning to drive down to the railhead at Wenlock and then go in to Pond in the Sky on the noon train. At the same time Marie started around the pond through the woods on snowshoes to meet him and the team below the dam.

As she walked along the steep slope above the northeast side of the pond, she looked down from time to time to watch the team sloshing through the water on the ice. She had decorated them to celebrate going to town, and the red and yellow and blue ribbons fluttered in the soft breeze. The sun gleamed on their tail bands and on the bright trunks of the birch trees on the mountain, and Marie was very happy to be on her way to town after the hard winter.

The snow in the woods was still deep, and in places she had to go out around drifts concealing blowdowns. In one place she climbed a hundred feet or so up the mountainside to circumvent a gigantic fallen hemlock. Just as she went out around the uprooted base of the tree and started back down through a thick stand of reddish birch saplings, Jigger shouted and the horses began to scream.

She was running down the slope and the horses were screaming steadily, but the birches were too dense for her to see what was happening until she reached the edge of the pond. They had broken through the ice about three quarters of the way across, though apparently Jigger had been able to cut the traces to the pung because the heads of the horses were still in sight, and he was in the water with them, holding their bridles up and trying to swim toward the opposite shore. He was talking to them quietly as they reared and plunged in their harness, and his firm voice carried across the pond as though he were much closer.

Marie started out onto the water on the ice and fell. She scrambled up and fell again, unable to run through the water in her snowshoes. As she stood up the second time the horses rolled completely over, and then they rolled again, and went under. One of Jigger's arms shot straight up, whether in some sort of desperate signal or farewell she never knew; then there was just the flat dark water.

For minute after minute Marie stood on the ice in her snowshoes, hoping that somehow Jigger would come up and knowing that he would not, that he was tangled in the harness deep below the surface with his horses. At last she turned, waded to shore, and went back to the house, though she could not remember how she had gotten there, and later she had no idea how long she sat at the table, staring blankly at the open door. When she finally stood up again and went into the yard, the sun had gone down and the skin of water on the pond had started to freeze around the edges.

Chapter Seven

Marie had been wonderfully happy on Pond Number Four with Jigger Johnson, but she couldn't bear to stay there alone. She took down the curtains and rolled up the rugs. She crated her dishes and bedding and Jigger's traps and tools, rafted everything down to the railhead at Wenlock, and asked Joe Roby to sell her things for the best price he could get. Before the last trip she climbed up on the cabin roof and removed the cedar shingles and the roof boards, since it was against the law to leave the roof on an unoccupied building in the woods, where a hunter or fisherman might go in and build a fire and set the woods on fire through carelessness. She stacked the boards neatly beside the cabin and put the nails in a paper sack, which she delivered to George Van Dyke's Pond in the Sky office on the twenty-first of May. "Tell Mr. Van Dyke that Jigger Johnson went through the ice with his team," she said to the clerk. "Tell him he could have jumped clear, but didn't." Then she went over to Bull Francis's Pond House to apply for a job.

Between them, Bull Francis and Canadian National owned nearly every business in Pond in the Sky. Canadian National owned the railroad and roundhouse and ice business, and Bull owned everything else, including three hotels, two restaurants, the livery stable and feed store, and a considerable amount of stumpage and cleared acreage in and around the Wenlock Woods and north to the Canadian line. He was not quite a lumber baron like George Van Dyke, but he was both wealthy and powerful, a big bluff man with magisterial side-whiskers who had gotten himself elected justice of the peace and was widely disliked and distrusted, and yet respected to a degree, in the sort of grudging way ruthlessly successful men often are.

One of Bull Francis's recent innovations at the Pond House was a great gilded cage suspended by a log chain from an eight-by-eight beam in the barroom ceiling. Inside this contraption, girls in brightly colored, scanty costumes would dance to a player piano each night from nine o'clock until one or two in the morning. These girls were a strong attraction to the railroaders, loggers, and salesmen who came through the town, and at any one time Bull kept four or five of them. They were city girls, for the most part, and came and went so fast that even the regular patrons at the Pond House had trouble keeping track of them.

"Missy, how are you at dancing?" Bull asked Marie the day she appeared in his office.

"Mr. Francis, I've been dancing since I was three years old. I can dance in that cage and never sway it more than a little yellow canary. You let me try it and see for yourself."

That night and every night from then on, Marie danced in the barroom of Bull Francis's Pond House. During the day she helped in the kitchen, earning her board and thirty dollars a week, most of which she saved, thinking she might like to go west. She got along fine during her shifts in the cage, and although at first the ragtime on the player piano ran through her head day and night, after a few weeks she hardly heard it, even when she danced.

Because of her long curly dark hair and blue eyes, her slim figure and long legs and solemn pleasure in dancing, she quickly became a favorite among the customers. The only serious problem she had during her first months as a cage dancer was that, being confined, she was an easy target for bullies and drunks. Some of the other dancers had ugly scars where men had bitten them or butted out cigarettes on their bare legs; what to Marie was more horrifying still, some of the girls permitted men to do these things to them for money. One girl showed her a long ugly scar on her thigh and claimed that Bull Francis himself had come to her room with a razor and offered her fifty dollars to let him cut her, and certainly the hotel owner made no attempt to stop similar sadistic practices in the barroom when the girls were dancing, though these usually took place after regular closing hours when only a few very drunken men stayed on.

One hot night in July Marie felt a terrific pain on the back of her left heel. She whirled around and saw a drunk reaching through the cage with a twenty-dollar bill in one hand and a lighted cigar in the other. Without pausing she drew back her burned foot and kicked out two of his teeth. After that she had no more trouble with drunks, though the scar on her heel remained: a small white oval to remind her of her days as a dancehall girl.

It was a hard time for Marie, during which she often cried herself to sleep at night thinking of Jigger. She did not have any close friends among the other dancers, sad girls who in some instances were addicted to liquor or laudanum. She was not surprised to learn that some of them preferred women lovers, although most also made extra money by entertaining men in their rooms after the bar closed. Several times she was on the verge of leaving, but did not really have any idea where to go.

One evening in October, Bull assembled his dancers in the kitchen. "Ladies," he said sarcastically, "I've arranged to give the boys up to the Wenlock camp a good time this Saturday night. I'm going to run a special railway car up there, and any of you who are on it will make an extra twenty-five dollars that night."

A couple of the girls laughed and clapped and the rest

seemed indifferent; Marie was the only one who didn't want to go. "Mr. Francis," she said as the others drifted out to the barroom, "I don't intend to go up to Wenlock or to any other place for that purpose. What the rest of the girls do is their business, but I won't be on that pleasure excursion."

"Fine," Bull Francis said curtly. "I need someone to work here that night anyway. Does that suit your high principles?"

"That suits me," Marie said.

Later that night, while she was taking a breather between performances, Bull beckoned her over to his table near the player piano. He was sitting with a well-dressed stranger, a dark slender man with slick hair smelling strongly of clove-scented barbershop tonic. The stranger paid little attention to her, but Bull asked her a curious question.

"Missy," he said, "what's your last name, anyway?"

She told him, and he nodded and dismissed her with an offhanded gesture, telling her she could take the rest of the night off if she liked.

She was surprised by his agreeableness, but as she looked at him she saw that the whites of his eyes were still red with anger, and if he hadn't owed her a week's pay, she probably would have taken her savings and gone west on the spot.

At ten o'clock Saturday night she would have gone even without her savings; but by then it was too late, since at nine forty-five two of Bull's constables had come into the barroom, arrested her for soliciting customers, and escorted her to the town jail.

The jail in Pond in the Sky was in the basement of the brick railroad station, which also housed the town offices, including Bull Francis's office as justice of the peace. It was a cold, drafty place with five cells, reserved mainly for loggers who had had too much to drink. Marie spent the first night shivering and crying, but the next morning a constable came in and told her to get a grip on herself. "I thought you knew," he said. "Bull always pulls one or two raids on his girls every year in order to satisfy the church ladies and deacons, and then he bails them out and gives them a ticket to Boston or wherever the next day."

But the following morning Bull Francis sentenced Marie to six months in jail for solicitation, something she had never done or thought of doing.

Going to jail was the worst experience of her life. When someone thought to bring her any, the food was terrible— four-day-old bread and half-raw potatoes and cold leftovers from the dining room of the Pond House. The one stool at the end of the basement had been plugged for years so she had to use an old ten-quart canner. There was no hot water except what she heated herself on a coal stove which would barely have heated a small bedroom, much less a sixty-by-forty-foot basement. Bull Francis let her out of her cell during the day to tend the stove, but he kept the large metal door to the stairs locked at all times, and the windows were barred and too small to squeeze through anyway. There was a supply closet next to the door, and using a solution of cleaning lye and hot water she kept the basement immaculate, cleaning for several hours a day because she had nothing better to do. "Marie," she would say to herself to keep her spirits up, "you must have the cleanest jail in all New England." Mainly, though, she felt dejected, and bitterly disillusioned with her old friends from the railroad and lumber camps who had flocked in to see her dance but would not walk across the street to visit her in jail. And when she asked Bull for her savings, which he'd been holding for her in the hotel safe, he laughed in her face.

Early one morning she was awakened by someone's racking cough and wondered why Bull would put a person that sick in jail until, sitting up and coming fully awake, she realized that the cough was her own. She pressed her handkerchief to her mouth, coughed hard, and brought the handkerchief away red. Instantly she remembered seeing the bright spots of blood in the snow where her mother had coughed and spat as they walked to work long ago in Hell's Gate, and for the first time since she had gone to jail she was badly frightened.

That was the morning the Chinese man arrived with his hands bound and a log chain locked to his ankles. He'd been picked up trying to cross the border from Canada and was wearing a black suit and coat and thin black shoes, and he was solemn and quiet and looked dignified and self-possessed even in chains. Marie had never seen a Chinese person and was very interested in him, and so was most of the rest of the town. All day Bull Francis let a steady stream of spectators in. He charged ten cents apiece for men and women and a nickel for children to troop down into the basement and gape at the new prisoner, and many came back again with friends and relatives.

One woman who had been in three times already pointed down at Marie and said in a scandalized voice, "Look, there's the fallen woman." Another offered to pray with her, though most people paid no attention to Marie at all but couldn't stare at the Chinese man long enough. A small boy called him "chinka chinka Chinaman" and poked at him with a stick until his mother said, "Watch your step, Bobby. If that yellow man catches hold of your stick, he'll lam you with it." But the Chinese man just stood in his chains, as still as the porcelain Chinaman on Rachel Benedict's parlor shelf, looking at the boy and his mother. He ate nothing all day and either couldn't or wouldn't speak English.

During the next week Marie tried to make friends with the man. She encouraged him to eat, which he refused to do until his chains were removed, and then he ate only very small amounts and only once a day. By then, however, she was seriously worried about her own health, since she was spitting blood every time she coughed and her breathing was becoming labored.

"Bull Francis," she said, "you have to let me see a doctor, or you're going to have me on your conscience for the rest of your life."

"Well," he said, picking his teeth with a matchstick, "if you was to come down to the storeroom with me for a little fun this evening, we might be able to arrange parole. And if you left town to see a doctor, I don't suppose anyone here would look too hard for you."

"I'll take my chances here, thank you. But I still need to see a doctor."

"How's our Chinaman today?" Bull said. "Has he decided to eat yet?"

"Maybe enough to stay alive," Marie said. "You did a terrible thing, putting him up on display that way. You'll have him on your conscience too now."

"How can a Chinaman be on anyone's conscience?" Bull said. "Think over that offer I made, missy. It's your ticket to Canady or wherever. You ought to at least get where you can see a doctor. That's a nasty-sounding cough, if I do say so."

On Christmas Eve there was a snowstorm, with a gale wind off the frozen lake, and it was colder than Marie thought it could be and still snow so hard. She was running low on coal but doubted that Bull would replenish the supply until after Christmas, because he'd announced that he intended to go on a two-day drunk to celebrate the holidays. That morning he had forgotten to unlock her cell, and she had not eaten or had anything to drink all day. As evening approached she lapsed into a fever, dreaming again that she was back in Canada, walking between the two receding dark lines with her parents. In the middle of the evening she woke up wringing wet and shivering. Upstairs Bull was moving around in his office. She could hear him banging the stove, banking it in preparation to begin his celebrations.

"Bull!" she shouted. "Bull Francis, come down here."

Over and over she shouted his name until finally she heard him clumping down the stairs. He opened the heavy door, and in the dim night light Marie could see that he had been shaving; there was still shaving soap on his face and he was holding his open razor. "It's cold down here," he said. "Can't you prisoners keep a fire going any better than this?"

"Bull, come over here. I've been thinking about your proposition."

"Have you now?" He spoke sarcastically, as always. He walked down to her cell, not very steadily, so Marie knew that he'd already started drinking. Remembering what the cage dancer had told her about Bull's disfiguring her with a razor, she knew also that she would have to be very careful.

She waited until he stood just outside the door of the cell. Very deliberately, looking him solemnly in the face, she unbuttoned her shirt.

Bull hesitated, then closed his razor and put it in his back pocket. He fumbled with his key ring. After dropping the keys twice, he managed to get the cell door unlocked. Marie could smell the sweetish odor of whiskey and knew he'd been drinking all afternoon, and she believed that she could break past him and be up the stairs and into the street before he knew what had happened. But with a man like Bull Francis she had to be as certain as possible.

"The storeroom," she said, glancing at the Chinese man, who had been watching them intently.

Bull nodded and they went down to the supply room, where Marie lighted a lantern.

"Shut the door," she said gravely.

Bull shut the door.

Marie stood with her back to the shelf containing the cleaning supplies. Slowly, with a solemnity that could be interpreted as provocative, she unbuttoned her pants and slid them partway down her thighs. She took off her shirt, lifted her hands above her head, and threw her hair back onto the shelf.

"Say, now," Bull said. "You ain't trying to trick old Bull, be you? Bull don't like his screwing standing up, missy."

"You ought to try it sometime," Marie said. "How do you know what you've been missing?"

"You got nice smooth legs," Bull said drunkenly.

He reached in his back pocket and took out his razor. As he opened it, Marie watched his face. Her arms were still uplifted, her hands behind her head, concealed by her hair. She moved her right hand back until it touched the bottle of cleaning lye. With her left hand she removed the lid. Bull Francis stepped toward her with the open razor in his hand. He bent his head toward her breasts and she flung the entire contents of the lye bottle into his face.

For a second he looked surprised. Then he dropped the razor. His hands shot up to his eyes. He stumbled wildly around the room, crashing against the walls. Marie tore the key ring off his belt loop, grabbed her shirt, and got into the corridor, slamming the door behind her. She ran fast up the stairs into Bull's office, where she put on his warm sheep coat and boots. Just before she was ready to leave she remembered the man locked in his cell below. She returned to the foot of the stairs and threw the keys down to him, and ten seconds later she was out of the building.

The wind was blowing hard off the ice, whipping the snow into her face, stinging her eyes. Drifts were piling up in the street. The temperature was well below zero.

She bucked her way through several drifts and crossed over the eight sets of railroad tracks on a high wooden footbridge leading to the upper part of the village. She remembered where the doctor lived from the time she had visited him with Jigger, but his wife met her at the door and told her that he had been called up to Wenlock, where there had been a bad derailment on the Grand Trunk, and might not be back until morning.

She did not dare go to the hotel to wait, but the lights were on at the Catholic Church, where a Christmas Eve service was being conducted. Marie slipped inside and sat down in a back pew. It was warm in the church and there were Christmas candles in the tall colored windows and the priest was reading the Christmas story from the Bible. When he finished, the people in the church stood up to sing. The organ began to play, and Marie thought she had never heard such a wonderful sound; just as Father Boisvert had told her long ago when she was a small girl in Hell's Gate, it sounded like a thousand violins; yet as she listened, Marie could not help thinking of how differently the events of her life had turned out from the way she had once planned, and how hard it had been since Jigger's death to maintain even a little faith in anything at all.

After the singing, everyone sat down and the priest gave a short Christmas message in which he said that the meaning of Jesus' life was that he loved everyone, especially the poor and sick, and although his mother and father had been turned away from shelter the cold night he was born, he had never once turned anyone away himself. When the service was over Marie lingered in the warm church, listening to the organ postlude. She looked at a great bank of candles on tiered shelves to her right. Some were lighted and some weren't; she wondered why.

After the priest and most of the people had left, a man in a black suit came down the aisle and stood by the door. She asked him about the candles, and he told her that people paid to burn them for the souls of the dead.

"How much does it cost to light one?" she said.

"The little ones are ten cents. They burn twenty-four hours. The big ones burn a week, or at least they're supposed to; they cost two bits."

"I don't have two bits," Marie said. "Or ten cents either for that matter."

The man in the dark suit, who was the sexton and impatient to go home, fished in his pocket and gave Marie a dime, which she dropped in a small metal box with a slot in it. Then she lighted a small candle and said, "This is for Jigger Johnson."

She stood looking at the candle without much conviction that it could help Jigger. She thought of his bones rolling around under the thick ice on Pond Number Four and doubted that a whole churchful of candles would do him much good. Still, lighting a candle couldn't hurt him, and the church was a pleasant place to be on a stormy night. She thought if she explained that she was ill and waiting for the doctor, the man who had given her the dime would let her wait there, but he shook his head and said he was sorry, she'd have to leave now, because it was time for him to button up the church for the night.

"I didn't suppose you ever buttoned up the church," Marie said.

"We never did until just lately," the man said. "But with all the tramps that come through Pond these days, it got so we was running a free hotel here. We had to start locking the doors, which as you say is a shame because now the townspeople that might come in at any time to light a candle or say a prayer have to suffer for it."

"Maybe if I could speak with your priest?"

"Father's gone home for the night," the sexton said with some satisfaction. "Look, I'd like to help you, but I can't go against church regulations. Why don't you go over and set by the stove in the railroad station? They're open all night, and it'll be warmer there than here. Here. Take this and buy yourself a hot drink. Merry Christmas!"

Outside in the wind Marie immediately began coughing again. She could see a lighted Christmas tree through one of the station windows, but she did not dare go inside for fear of being recognized. She thought that someone had probably discovered Bull Francis by now, and she wanted to find a place where no one could find her. Then she thought of the stable by the lake where the horses that worked on the pond were kept.

The wind was blowing so hard that at times she couldn't see the lights from the station or the Pond House, and it took her ten minutes to get through the drifts in the street to the stable. It was not very warm inside, but at least she was out of the wind. She borrowed a blanket from a horse and lay down on the straw in an empty stall. She had always liked the smell of the stable, and she lay thinking that there were worse places to spend Christmas Eve and jail was one of them. After a while she fell asleep, and for the first time since being arrested she slept through until morning without waking up.

It was still storming at dawn on Christmas Day when she made her way up to the doctor's house. He had just gotten in and was as brusque and kind as ever, insisting that Marie join him and his wife for coffee and rolls before he examined her. As they ate he told them about the derailment, in which no one had sustained so much as a scratch though the man who had reported the accident to him had said at least a dozen trainmen and passengers had been killed. "When I got back into town, though, all hell had let out for recess," he continued. "It seems that about midnight Johnny Bingham over at the station noticed that the door to Bull Francis's office was open. The light was on inside but Bull wasn't there, so Johnny went poking around looking for him. He found him too. Bull was downstairs in the jail chained to the bars with both his ears clipped off, and that poor devil of a Chinaman he had on display over there was gone. As soon as the storm lets up they're going to scour the countryside for him, but I guess they won't find much. There were three freights through last night, and if that man isn't back in Canada by now I'm greatly mistaken."

The doctor finished his coffee and turned to Marie. "All right, young woman, come along and let me listen to that cough. It sounds ugly, all right. What have you been doing with yourself, working out on the ice without warm clothing?"

He examined her quickly, listening to her chest for only a few seconds. Then he said to her, in a voice that was no longer brusque or kind, but merely flat and factual, "We have to get you some immediate attention, my girl. You've got one of the worst cases of galloping consumption I've come across in years."

It sat on a low knoll between the railroad tracks and the Connecticut River, a few miles south of the Canadian line, a long brick building of four stories. Once, when sheep raising was in its heyday in Kingdom County, it had been a woolen mill, but for the past twenty years it had been used as a state tuberculosis sanatorium for indigent patients. Supposedly the mountain air was a curative, but squatting beside the river as it did, the sanatorium was a dank cold place, resembling a prison more than a hospital, and the vast majority of its patients grew worse instead of better.

There were four floors: A, B, C, and D. The kitchen, dining room, and staff offices were on A. Women patients able to walk down to A to eat were quartered on B, ambulatory men on C, and the sickest patients of both sexes on D, the uppermost floor. There were about two hundred patients at any given time. There was a nurse on each floor during the day and an aide on each floor at night and a part-time doctor from across the river in New Hampshire who dropped by two or three times a week to clap a stethoscope to the chest of new patients, X-ray them and assign them to a bed, and sign the certificates of those who had died since his last visit. Since very few bodies were claimed by relatives, most were disposed of in a crematorium at one end of the building. The doctor wore a gauze mask from the time he arrived until he left, half an hour or at most an hour later, and all he ever prescribed, besides an opium painkiller for dying patients, was "plenty of fresh air and rest." Since the fresh air blew in around the rags stuffed in the broken panes of the high windows, and there was nothing for the patients to do all day but lie on their cots or wander up and down the floors, his single order was easy to carry out.

"These look like a Canadian blizzard," he said when he saw Marie's X-rays. "This woman needs plenty of fresh air and rest." Without further comment he assigned her to a bed on Floor D.

The next morning a stocky woman with a beefy face appeared at Marie's bedside with a towel, a pair of scissors, and a paper bag. "I got to clip your hair," she said. "Set up."

Marie was exceptionally proud of her hair, which was still curly and very dark, though much less shiny since her illness. She felt too weak to sit up, but she looked steadily at the woman and said, "If you touch my hair I'll throw those scissors through your head."

"I guess you won't," the woman said, seizing her by the back of the neck like a cat.

Marie struggled with what little strength she had left, but the woman cut off her wind with one arm and then proceeded to shear her like a sheep. Along with her hair Marie lost her spirit to keep going. That day she succumbed to the fever she had fought off for weeks, and when she woke up three nights later and remembered who and where she was she was genuinely surprised that she was still alive. She was thirsty, but the aide had gone out, and the water pitcher was at the far end of the room.

Years later, when she had time and inclination to think about the course of her history, she had no doubt that the hour after she woke up from the three-day delirium at the sanatorium was among the most important in her life. She had no visionary dream, heard no mysterious voices. It was not a religious or hallucinatory experience, but much more ordinary than that. She simply knew in that hour of lucidness that her life was probably in her own hands, and she felt two opposite and nearly equal inclinations. One was to lie back and let events run their course, which would be the same as letting go and dying. The other was to get up, if possible, and get a drink for herself and refuse to give in—to go on fighting the fever and the infection and the seductive prospect of an end to all pain and difficulties forever—and this inclination was slightly more powerful, though she lay still, gathering resolve and strength, for at least another hour before sitting up and then standing up and then walking, one short step at a time, to the end of the room for a drink.

The walk back seemed even longer, but she made it, and a month later she walked down the stairs to Floor B. She had lost twenty pounds. Her teeth were loose and bleeding. She had a livid bedsore on her left thigh. But she was no longer coughing blood and the fever had been gone for two weeks, though it took her half an hour to descend thirty steps and another fifteen minutes to walk twenty feet to an empty bed.

One day she woke up at dawn to the rumbling of the spring

log drive going by. She walked to the window and looked out at the river, which was a seething brown mass of logs from bank to bank for as far as she could see in both directions, and for the first time since Jigger's death she was able to think of him without wanting to cry. The following day she went outside for a few minutes. The cold spring air smelled delicious, and the next day was warmer and sunny and she went across the railroad tracks to the woods and picked a bouquet of wild violets and painted trillium. Everything delighted her that spring: the woods flowers, the dark earth in the cook's kitchen garden, the sunshine on the sooty bricks of the sanatorium, the reflection of the building in the river. Remembering Father Boisvert's advice, she borrowed a fish pole from the cook and caught a mess of trout. In June she went to work in the kitchen as the cook's assistant and moved into a small room on the ground floor.

Again, as she had done so often in the past, Marie peeled potatoes, made bread, set and cleared tables, and washed dishes. In addition to her room and board she earned only fifteen dollars a week, but she was able to save nearly all her wages. In August she was offered the housekeeper's job on Floors B and C, where for twenty dollars a week she scrubbed floors, washed walls, changed bedding, emptied bedpans. From time to time she helped wash and feed bedridden patients, which she liked doing so much she began spending most of her off-duty time on the wards.

Just after Christmas she was promoted to the night aide position on Floor C. Although she was frustrated and baffled by the despair of most of the patients, she worked hard to do what she could for them, and as she became immersed in her job it occurred to her that without really trying she had at last found a purpose in her life beyond just getting by from one day to the next.

Late in the winter of 1916 a new doctor came to work at the sanatorium. On the day he arrived he walked through the entire building and spoke to each patient and staff member. He was a young man, only a year or two older than Marie, with light hair and a serious, friendly smile, and in some ways he reminded her of Abie Benedict.

"How do you do?" he said. "I'm Philbrook Jamieson."

"My name is Marie Blythe," she said, putting out her hand. "I am very pleased to meet you, Dr. Jamieson."

He had a warm, firm handshake and Marie could not stop thinking how much he resembled Abie, though Dr. Jamieson's eyes were blue, not brown, and she could not really be sure what Abie would look like now after ten years.

"You're the nurse Jane Kinney told me about," he said.

"I'm just an aide," Marie said. "Not a real nurse like Nurse Kinney."

"From now on you're a nurse," Dr. Jamieson said briskly. "See Jane Kinney for a uniform."

The new doctor turned out to be a Canadian from the province of Ontario. He had served his internship at a private sanatorium in Toronto where some of the patients had actually recovered, and under his direction the treatment at the Vermont sanatorium immediately improved. He encouraged everyone who could to take outdoor exercise every day. He varied and improved the patients' diets. He continued to go through the building speaking to each patient every morning, as Captain Benedict had walked through his factory daily to greet his workers. Before he had been there a month, morale began to pick up.

Thinking of the Captain reminded Marie how he had painted the village annually. "Dr. Jamieson," she said one morning when he came through her ward, "a great number of the people here have given up. A coat of paint works wonders for anyone's spirits. I'd like your authorization to paint B and C."

Dr. Jamieson smiled at her formal manner. "By all means," he said. "You have my authorization."

She bought ten gallons of light yellow paint and painted the walls on the two wards. She bought five gallons of ship-deck gray and painted the floors, which still showed lighter where the looms had been bolted down. Then she replaced all the broken windows.

In the self-contained world of the institution, Marie felt happier than she had been since she had lived on Pond Number Four with Jigger Johnson. She was twenty-five years old. She weighed her usual hundred and fifteen pounds. Her hair, which she kept pinned up when working, hung halfway down her back when loose and was again thick and shiny. Her teeth had reseated themselves, as they had after her travels with John Trinity. Depending on the light, her eyes were gray or blue against her smooth dark skin and dark hair. She was well liked by both the patients and staff for her cheerfulness, her energy and willingness to be helpful, and her direct way of speaking.

As she came to know him, Philbrook Jamieson reminded her both of Abie and of a younger Abraham Benedict, a man wholly dedicated to his work. He began asking her to go walking with him after supper, and sometimes she helped him in his laboratory, where he worked every evening. One spring night he was examining saliva specimens under a microscope and Marie was transferring specimens from bottles to slides. It was well after midnight, and the third consecutive night they had worked late together. Outside the open window of the office the logs were going downriver again, grinding against each other and grumbling like steady heat thunder on an August night; and the passing logs reminded Marie of passing time, how fast it went by, like the logs on the river.

"Dr. Jamieson," she said quietly, "I'm ready for bed."

He was drawing what he saw in the microscope. Without looking up he said, "All right, Marie, go ahead, I'll see you in the morning. I may sit up for another ten minutes or so. Thanks again."

"Don't thank me yet," she said.

He looked up, and she was standing naked in front of him, smiling.

From then on they slept together nearly every night.

One afternoon in May, the nurse on Floor D quit and Dr. Jamieson asked Marie if she would take the job. In those days few nurses received their training in school, but served apprenticeships in hospitals, more or less the way Marie had been doing. Marie felt that she had learned enough while assisting Nurse Kinney on the lower floors to take over D. She knew too that almost anything she did there would be an improvement. If the previous nurse had felt like it, she had poured a glass of water for a patient; if not, she hadn't.

"When would you like me to start?"

"Tomorrow."

The next morning she went upstairs and announced that she was the new nurse. "Please don't hesitate to ask me if you need anything," she said. "That's what I'm here for."

From the men's side of the room someone passed gas loudly, and someone else laughed.

Immediately Marie said, "That's the first time I've ever heard a laugh on this floor. Now let me tell you something. Some of you could get well if only you knew it, and then you'd have the last laugh on this place. But you've got to help yourselves more than you have up until now."

"There ain't any help for the dead," a woman's voice said.

"You're not dead, my friend," Marie said angrily. "Do you want to know something? Not three years ago I was a patient on this very floor myself. My X-rays looked like a big snowstorm. Now, as you can plainly see, I'm well again. And some of you can be too. But you have to want to."

"Well," the same voice replied, "I don't want to."

"Suit yourself," Marie said, and walked down the corridor between the rows of beds and opened the window.

Every day from then on Marie worked on Floor D from

dawn until dark or afterward, painting the walls and floors, changing each patient's bed linen every three days, washing the sheets herself at night if necessary. She washed her patients and washed their hair, which was never cropped off again. She made sure that they ate as much as they could and that no one went thirsty.

Yet while her patients were certainly more comfortable, only a few seemed to want to improve, and the mortality rate at the sanatorium in 1916 ran even higher than in the trenches in France.

In early April of 1917, when the logs were once again going down the Connecticut, America entered the war that to this day in Kingdom County is known as the Global Conflict. Partly because Marie was so absorbed in her work and her new love life, and in part because nothing outside the hospital was quite real to her any longer, the fighting seemed like fighting in a war long ago. When the war did come to the sanatorium, it came as a total surprise to her. Everything seemed to happen at once. One morning the lieutenant governor of Vermont appeared in Dr. Jamieson's office and informed him that some of the patients would be transferred to a hospital in Burlington so that part of the sanatorium could be used for recuperating soldiers, especially those whose lungs had been damaged by chlorine gas.

"What's chlorine gas?" Marie asked Dr. Jamieson that night.

"It's a poison," he explained. "When you inhale it, it burns out the lining of your lungs. Both sides are using the stuff, damn them."

Marie thought for a while. It was difficult for her to imagine men killing each other with poison gas, or with anything else for that matter, though she herself had shot the man called Preacher on Pond Number Four. "Where are you going to put the soldiers?" she asked the doctor.

"Well, Marie, I'm thinking about putting them with you on D and reassigning the patients there to B and C."

From the start she liked working with the soldiers. Most of them were younger than she was and so grateful to be home that they laughed and joked constantly. Some did not recover, and those, instead of being cremated, were buried beneath neat white crosses beyond the railroad tracks, but most eventually were well enough to go home. Closing D had also lowered the death rate among the TB patients, so that Dr. Jamieson was able to spend more time with the soldiers.

He was both deeply intrigued and deeply frustrated by the gas cases. Night after night, he studied damaged lung tissue under his microscope, sometimes working through until dawn. "I can't help thinking that if I could catch these cases sooner I could cure more of them," he told Marie.

"No doubt you could," she told him. "But if you don't let up a little, you're going to get sick yourself. I think you're overtired, but fortunately I have the cure for that."

He smiled, but it was another hour before he stopped work for the night, and then he fell asleep as soon as he lay down, and she couldn't bring herself to wake him. The trouble with being in love with such a single-minded man, she realized, was that his work must always come before anything else; so she was not completely surprised when, a few days before Christmas, Philbrook Jamieson told her that he had asked to be sent to France in order to work with gas victims at the front.

He left on the train the morning after Christmas. Marie, who hated farewells, did not see him off. But although she wept at night for many weeks, and could not help being resentful of him for leaving, she still believed that he had done the right thing, and neither then nor later did she regret a minute of their time together: working twelve and fourteen and sixteen hours a day, walking together along the river or in the woods, snatching an hour or half an hour to make love, though even their love had come to seem a part of their work together.

Dr. Jamieson's replacement was a fine-looking army colonel of about forty, who had been gassed in France himself. Though not a doctor, Colonel Stanley was an excellent administrator interested in the welfare of all the patients. He was very decisive in his dealings, and favorably impressed by Marie's energy and commitment to her work and by her good looks. Twice he asked her out to dinner in Colebrook, across the river in New

Hampshire; both times she declined, explaining that she already had a friend. He had a number of short-lived and casual affairs with other nurses and seemed to respect Marie for being loyal to one man.

Punctually, once each week, Philbrook Jamieson wrote to her. He wrote long, cheerful letters, which a young nurse named Maggie Price read to her in the evening. Mainly he talked about his work, especially about his theory that if he could flush out gassed lungs immediately with a neutralizing chemical, he could save more soldiers. In April he wrote that he would be spending some time in the trenches to test his idea and might not be able to write again for a few weeks.

Spring had come to be an ambiguous time for Marie. She had lost her mother and her baby in the spring. Jigger had gone through the ice as spring was approaching. Although she loved the first warm rains and the big log drive and the yellow patches of sand on the railroad embankment where the snow first melted, she was also apprehensive of this time of year, so when Colonel Stanley asked to see her in his office early one morning in May she could not help feeling anxious.

"Marie, I know you and Dr. Jamieson were very close," he said.

For a moment she thought that he was going to ask her to dinner again. But as she looked at him she saw from his expression that it was not that.

There is no good way to tell a person the kind of news Colonel Stanley had to tell Marie. Knowing this, he simply handed her the letter. When she continued to stare at him, he said sadly, "He was gassed. I'm terribly sorry, Marie. He was buried three days ago in France."

She put a white cross in the military cemetery and went about her duties. There was nothing else she could do unless she left the hospital, and since her work was now the only important part of her life, she did not want to leave. Besides, the soldiers were a link to Philbrook, so she spent nearly every waking hour with them. As the summer progressed, however, she began to show signs of nervous fatigue, including sleeplessness and loss of appetite.

Late one evening in early October, Colonel Stanley called her into his office and asked her to read some new army regulations to him since he had a headache. He pointed to a Morris chair. "Sit down, Marie. I suppose I ought to know what these say, though I doubt they say much. They never do."

Marie looked at the regulations. They were written in very small print and full of unfamiliar words. "I'd like to, Colonel. But I'm afraid I can't."

"You can't?"

"I can't read well enough," she said, though it hurt her pride terribly to admit this.

"Well, they'll keep until I can get to them," he said casually. "You ought to learn how to read though, Marie. As ambitious as you are, not knowing how to read will hold you back."

"I intend to. Just the minute I have a chance, that's the first thing I intend to do."

She was nearly crying, and the Colonel, who for some time had been aware that she was overworking, said kindly, "Marie, how long has it been since you've had a vacation?"

"A vacation? I haven't ever had such a thing as a vacation in my life, Colonel Stanley."

"Well, just as soon as I can find a temporary replacement for you, you're going to have one. You've been working too hard."

The idea of leaving her job for any reason, even a brief vacation, terrified her, so she worked even harder. Somehow she held on through the rest of the month, but for the first time since the days immediately following Jigger's death she felt close to hopeless; though the grueling routine of her job continued to wear her down, she knew it was all that kept her from total despair.

One cold gray afternoon after Marie had sat up for two consecutive nights with a dying soldier, the cook came running up to the ward where she was working and began talking in an excited voice. He said that just after lunch a very old man had appeared at the rear door of the kitchen and asked for something to eat. The cook had felt sorry for him because he was at least seventy, he thought, and barefooted except for some rags wrapped around his feet.

"I asked him in, but he wouldn't come," he told Marie. "So I inquired who he was, where he was from. But he just shook his head and smiled and said he'd appreciate a bite to eat and then he'd be on his way. I told him to wait a minute, and went to get a plate of food, and when I got back he'd dropped in his tracks on the doorstep. Well, sir! I was scared he'd died right there, but I picked him up and got him inside and laid him out on the lid of the woodbox with an apron under his head, and then I see he was still breathing. He didn't weigh much, but he had on a heavy old wool coat buttoned all the way up the front, clear to the throat. I began to open it up to give him air, and I'll be damned if he didn't have a preacher's collar on under it. No shirt or undershirt. Just that collar. Can you come down and see to him?"

Marie nodded and hurried downstairs to the kitchen, where the elderly man was lying unconscious on the woodbox.

"I don't suppose he's a real preacher," the cook said. "Just some poor old homeless codger off the tracks looking for a handout."

Marie did not reply for a moment. Then she said softly, "He's a real preacher."

"He is?"

Nodding her head slowly, she said more to herself than the cook, "He's a preacher, all right. His name is Father Peter Boisvert, and he's the priest who taught me my catechism."

Just then Father Boisvert opened his eyes, and although he was too weak to talk, Marie knew that he remembered her too because as she knelt beside the woodbox and took his hand, he winked one eye in recognition and smiled.

Two days later, Father Boisvert felt strong enough to tell Marie the rest of his story.

Soon after she left Hell's Gate the first time, with the gyp-sies, he had been retired from active duty as a traveling priest, partly because of his age and partly because nearly every Ver-mont community with a sizable population of French Canadi-ans had by then acquired its own parish and resident priest. He told Marie that he had not liked living like a monk in the home for retired priests in Burlington, and had managed to avoid going crazy or just giving up and letting old age overtake and kill him only by going fishing or taking a long walk nearly every day. Sometimes, he said, he would walk as far as twenty miles between breakfast and supper.

After a few months he began to take a blanket rolled up in a tarpaulin, and a small canvas sack with some bread and maybe a cold sausage and some beer, and be gone for two or three days at a time, trudging up and down the Green Moun-tain range more or less at random, stopping to fish a brook or pond when he felt like it, spreading out his tarpaulin and sleeping when he was tired. He stayed remarkably healthy, looked, acted, and felt like a man of sixty in good shape instead of the octogenarian he actually was, visited with dozens of farmers and lumberers and boys and girls along the back roads he sought out, used the nursing skills that he had learned during the Civil War to assist both animals and people, and enjoyed his retirement as few persons do. Although he con-tinued to make the priests' home in Burlington his headquar-ters, he paid little attention to any of the place's routines or regulations, and except for a few close friends there, no one was unhappy when he deducted thirty years from his age and joined the International Red Cross in 1914, to go to France.

He was already eighty-four, an age when dates and times and places meant something different to him than they once had, so he was somewhat vague about exactly where he had been stationed, except that for approximately two years he had worked at a large hospital near Paris, then transferred to a field hospital near the Somme, and from there, despite his age, to duty in the trenches, where his medical and spiritual services were in equal demand.

One night after a fierce German assault there was a three-hour cease-fire, and medical personnel from both sides were allowed to go out into the no-man's-land between the trenches to retrieve their dead and wounded. Father Boisvert, who as a Red Cross representative had helped arrange the truce, assisted both the Germans and the Allies and lost track of time, and found himself on the eastern side of the lines when the shelling began again. He was more surprised than concerned, and the Germans were delighted to have him, even temporarily, because of the terrific shortage of trained medical workers in their trenches. Father Boisvert was as ready to help them as to help anyone else, but within a week the division he was with was shipped to the Eastern Front, he thought as a punishment, and took him along with them.

They traveled by trucks, mainly, but there were some days of marching too, which did not bother him because he had always been a great walker and even at eighty-six could keep up with nearly anyone. Someone else usually carried the medical supplies for him, and he suffered much less from fatigue than hunger. For weeks there was hardly anything to eat except potatoes, and sometimes not many of them, since the retreating Russians were burning their own crops as they withdrew. Once or twice Father Boisvert was so light-headed from not eating that he imagined he was a child again, walking through the burning fields of southern Quebec.

One night as they were trudging through a tall beech woods along the side of a ridge that might have been a ridge in Quebec, they were ambushed. The German commander ordered his men to take cover behind the trees and fire back. In the skirmish, Father Boisvert became separated from the men he had been traveling with.

The priest was not especially worried for his safety. His Red Cross armband was sewed to the sleeve of his overcoat, and under his coat was his priest's collar, which would safeguard him with the Russians even more than the armband. But it was a bitter night, with two feet of snow on the ground and more falling steadily, and he needed to find shelter. Heading down the slope of the ridge, away from the firing, which had by then become intermittent since the Germans were retreating fast, he did not see the farmhouse in the clearing in the beeches until he was within six or eight feet of it and the sentry was holding a bayonet against his chest. Fifteen seconds later he was inside the building, surrounded by the Russian officers who had converted it into a command outpost, though all he cared about at the time was that it was warm, and there was food on the table. He could not remember being so hungry since the day nearly eighty years ago that he had walked up to the door of the monastery and refused to tell his name.

The Russians were in even more desperate need of medical assistance than the Germans, and as they continued their retreat through the mountains—the ambush had only been an attempt to slow down their pursuers—they provided him with a horse, warm clothing, and as much food as they had themselves. Several of the officers had been educated by French tutors, and the commander of the battalion spoke good English and became a particular friend. He was distantly related to the Czar, a connection that he had always found useful until he arrived in Moscow with his decimated battalion and Peter a week after the Revolution broke out and was immediately put aboard a trainload of captured German prisoners destined for the work camps in Siberia.

Because of his Red Cross affiliation, Peter could probably have arranged to be sent back to America, but by then he had no intention of deserting his new friends, who needed his help more now than ever, and so, in the general confusion, he was allowed to accompany the prison train east out of Moscow late that winter as a sort of voluntary medical trustee. After a few days, however, the Bolshevist guards made no distinction between the priest and any of the other prisoners, political or military. This was the hardest part of his travels, he said, and the hardest time to maintain some small amount of faith in something since the day he had realized that old age had very nearly crept up on him at the priests' home and started walking to keep out ahead of it. To make matters worse, his friend the Czar's relative was shot to death by a Bolshevist sergeant during the second week of the trip, leaving Peter at the mercy of the other prisoners; he did not even dare reveal to them that he was a priest for fear the guards would learn his identity, as they had his friend's, and kill him on the spot.

On the train went, into the vast interior of Asian Russia, past the charred remains of great estates and tiny villages, through forests of birch and fir, by great frozen rivers. Since nearly every other train on the track had precedence over theirs, they often sat on a siding for days on end. Father Boisvert lost track of the seasons, and when the snow began to go he could not remember whether it was early spring or late fall until he saw peasants breaking ground with oxen and other peasants walking behind and planting what looked like potatoes.

As a boy in Quebec he had planted potatoes behind his father's oxen, and now, thinking of his father's farm, it occurred to him that at last he wanted to go home but was moving farther away with every mile. Until then, he said, he had not known that it was actually possible to die almost as suddenly from despair as from a gunshot wound, which is what the despair felt like. It was not that he minded the thought of dying so much (though he did not wish to die) as that he did not want to die of despair—and here he looked carefully at Marie, who was being held intact only by the work she continued to prosecute sixteen and eighteen and twenty hours a day, in order not to think of Dr. Jamieson.

He had tried, he said, to think of something, however small, in which to place a little faith. Then an interesting idea came to him. There were, he suddenly realized, two ways to get home. One was by going back the way he had come, which now seemed impossible. The other was to continue heading due east—so, in a very real sense, every mile he traveled away from where he had been was also a mile traveled toward where he wished to go.

"That gave me a little faith, Marie," he said. "That was all I needed; the next day I made up my mind to escape."

By that time, he explained, half the prisoners had died and most of the rest had given up all hope altogether and required very little vigilance on the part of the guards because, as Father Boisvert had believed at first, they assumed they were too far into the country to get anywhere if they did escape. A great hopelessness and malaise had settled over the entire prison train, which now sat on sidings for a week at a time, so that even the guards suspected that it was lost, as the country itself was clearly lost, and began allowing those prisoners who were strong enough to go into the countryside on foraging excursions.

One morning Father Boisvert did not return from one of these trips. He and several other men had been assigned to go off along the shore of a huge lake, maybe Lake Baikal, in search of edible greens, and he had gone farther than any of the others, and simply kept on going, in a direction roughly parallel to the tracks, which he struck again that evening at dusk. The lakeshore was marshy, so he stayed near the embankment or on the ties and continued walking east through the cut in the firs. Later he found an empty woodcutter's hut, where he slept until dawn, when he resumed walking. Around noon he heard a train approaching and moved away from the tracks into the woods until it had passed. Maybe it was the prison train; he had no idea.

He had found a fish line and a hook in the logger's hut, which he used to catch a few fish resembling small pike, but since he had no way to cook them and was not desperate enough to eat them raw, he lived mainly on greens. He had not eaten much for years anyway, and when he came to a village he had no trouble getting a little soup for himself in exchange for hearing a confession, since by now he was back in Imperial territory where most the villagers did not yet know a revolution was going on and supposed that the violent fighting for control of the railroad was between the Czar's troops and unruly Tatars. Now, again, Father Boisvert could ride the train sometimes, where the track had not been blown up and locomotives and carriages were still available. He was heading for Vladivostok, still fifteen hundred miles away. When there were no trains, he continued to walk.

The greatest danger, he said, was not posed by the Bolshevists or the government troops, but the homeless men and women who flocked to the tracks by the thousands and tens of thousands: starving house serfs from burned estates, roving bandits, fleeing noblemen with small bands of retainers, any of whom might murder a man, even a priest, for a piece of bread or his clothes. He gave his coat to a Tatar woman and his boots had worn out weeks ago. To protect his feet from the ballast along the railway, he wound rags around them.

Although he was in excellent condition for a man nearly ninety years old, or almost any man, the natural depressions and loneliness of old age tormented him, and he no longer seemed able to walk them off, as he had at the priests' home. There were days when he was quite sure that he would never reach Vladivostok, much less America, and his faith seemed to have abandoned him entirely. At those times, he said, he simply counted his steps, counting one hundred or five hundred or one thousand steps, then starting again, to ward off despair. On other days he surprised himself by feeling, for no particularly good reason, that he might very well reach home before winter.

He came into a town where the railroad was operating again, and managed to squeeze aboard a troop train heading for Vladivostok along the southern route, through Manchuria. He slept most of the way and was not sure whether he dreamed that the train was attacked by men on horseback wearing white paint on their faces and shooting arrows, or whether this really had happened.

In Vladivostok, almost two years after he had blundered into the Germans' trenches on the Somme, he walked into the Red Cross office and identified himself. Although no one there believed his story, the officials put him on the next ship out to Vancouver, where he immediately boarded a train east. He had arrived in Montreal two weeks ago, and without hesitating started walking east, through the country where he had been born and past the same fields he had once walked through in heavy smoke as a boy and again as a young man going south to the States, until he had come to Kingdom County and the sanatorium. And there, once again, as he had long ago at the monastery as a boy of eight, he had refused to identify himself, this time for fear someone would send him back to the home for retired priests.

"But I thought you wanted to go home," Marie said. "You said you wanted to go home, and you did, but you didn't even stop."

Father Boisvert, who was tired after recounting his adventures, smiled. "The truth is," he said conspiratorily, "I can't seem to stop walking. I might revisit some of the places I saw in the South, during the war. I think I've still got time to get there before winter comes on, and if I don't I'll get a pair of boots from the Red Cross. They owe me a pair."

He continued to smile.

"But what about you, Marie? You look as though you've been through a lot recently. Do you want to tell me about it?"

She was silent, thinking of Philbrook Jamieson.

"Have you lost someone?" he said shrewdly.

She nodded.

"Have you kept a little faith, however small, in something?"

She thought. "My work, I suppose."

He shook his head. "Something besides work. Say—in fishing."

She grinned and, if only to please her old mentor, nodded.

"Good," he said, and then he shut his eyes and fell asleep in his chair, breathing lightly and easily.

In the morning, she was not particularly surprised to discover that he was gone again.

Marie had been genuinely delighted to see Father Boisvert again, and she knew he was absolutely right about the matter of maintaining some faith. Yet it was one thing to agree with his advice and another to follow it, and if she did not feel quite so desperate as before, she was still unable to commit herself to anything beyond work for its own sake.

Early November of 1918 was a bleak time at the hospital. It would drizzle for a day or two, then turn cold, then drizzle again. The sun had not been out for more than an hour at a time for days. Everything was some dispiriting shade of gray: the sky, the river, the mountains, Marie's thoughts. To make matters worse, everyone was constantly on edge because of rumors that the war would end. Each day the war was supposed to end, but didn't, and the constant disappointment and constant bad weather made it a very difficult time.

On November 11, late in the afternoon, twenty-six new soldiers arrived unexpectedly and unannounced, except by a flighty young aide named Sadie Begin, who ran onto Marie's ward calling, "Nurse Blythe, you won't believe it. It's a whole carload of darkies!"

"Darkies? What do you mean, Sadie?"

"Colored soldiers, Nurse Blythe. Why, they're as black as your boot. I'm afraid to go near them. I'd sooner see old Kaiser Bill himself a-coming for me."

Marie hurried down to the tracks, where she was greeted by a strange scene. Not only were the new soldiers black, not a single one could walk. They had been placed on stretchers on the platform and were lined up like corpses in the drizzling rain.

"What's wrong with these men?" she asked a white sergeant.

"I'll tell you what's wrong with them," he said bitterly. "Their battalion spent three weeks standing in trench water up to their butts. Some of them lost one foot and some two. Some just have a bad case of trench foot and can't walk."

"Good God!" Marie said. "Get them into that door over there. Get them in out of the rain or they'll have more than trench foot, they'll have pneumonia. Hurry as fast as you can. I'll get some help from the staff."

For a few minutes her fatigue disappeared. Since the hospital was crowded, she assigned the new soldiers to Floors C and D at random, wherever there was an empty cot. Like most of the wounded men on the wards, they laughed about their condition, but Marie was furiously angry to think how they had been neglected and in the worst possible frame of mind when out of nowhere Colonel Stanley appeared on C, where she was quartering the last of the black soldiers, and roared, "Who admitted these colored men?"

She looked at him with astonishment. She'd never heard him raise his voice before. "I did," she said. "I admit all the soldiers, Colonel."

"Well, you just readmit them, every man jack," he shouted. "I want them quartered together, not mixed in with the other patients like this. I don't care who you have to move to do it, but do it."

Marie stepped close to the Colonel. He was somewhat taller than middle height, but even in her low-heeled nursing shoes she was only two or three inches shorter. "With all respect," she said in a quiet, angry voice. "I won't do that. What they have isn't catching."

"You'll catch a ticket home if you don't follow orders this second," he shouted. "We'll set up field tents if we have to. We'll do whatever's necessary. But I never have had, nor will I ever have, colored and white in together. Get them off this ward!"

Marie was never able to explain to herself exactly why she refused to carry out his order. Nor could she understand the Colonel's prejudice, since he had once mentioned to her that in France the black regiments often got the most dangerous duty and had conducted themselves bravely. Certainly everyone's nerves were bad, and that might have accounted in part for his display of temper and her stubbornness, but she never regretted her reply.

"Colonel, I won't obey that order."

He looked at her. She looked back at him, and when he saw that she meant what she said, he turned away and repeated the order to Maggie Price and then told Marie to come to his office in fifteen minutes.

She had no doubt at all that she was going to lose her job. She put her few possessions in a paper bag. She changed out of her uniform into her single off-duty dress. She put on her raincoat, got her handbag, and went to meet with Colonel Stanley.

"Nurse Blythe, you don't administer this hospital. I do."

She looked at him steadily. "I know that."

"I believe in an old saying: 'One ship, one captain.' Do you know what that means?"

She nodded, looking at him.

"Then you also know you can't work here any longer." He held out an envelope. "This is your last week's pay, plus an extra two weeks, along with a brief letter of character saying you did a good job here."

"Then why are you sending me down the road?"

"Because you were insubordinate. Because you accorded too much authority to yourself. Because I won't have a woman who can't even read telling me how to conduct my business."

"I wasn't telling you how to run your business. You were telling me how to run mine."

As she spoke, Marie did not take her eyes off the Colonel once. She stared at him hard the entire time, until finally he looked away, as he had looked away the day he informed her that Dr. Jamieson had died in France. Only then, when he averted his eyes, did she pick up the envelope; but instead of putting it in her handbag with the rest of her savings, she opened it up, counted out the one week's pay she was owed, and put the envelope with the rest of the money and the letter of reference back on his desk. Without speaking again, she turned and left his office, walked down the corridor to the door, and went out into the darkness.

It was raining harder now, but the night was quite warm. She crossed the tracks and went up the slope into the military cemetery, but in the dark and rain she could not tell for sure which cross was which, so she sat down and began to cry.

She did not know how long the bell had been ringing when at last she could cry no more and stood up and started down the tracks and heard it. At first there was only one, faint beyond the hills across the river; but as she walked south along the tracks another joined it, and then another, pealing out in the night, though it was some minutes before she realized that an armistice had been declared and the war was over.

Chapter Eight

Everything looked exactly the same to Marie. The double row of yellow houses, the factory, the Big House, even the cluster of battened houses across the narrows, faded again to a weathered uniform gray, like boulders that had broken off the cliffs high above and come crashing down at random—all of them looked just as they had looked when she had seen them for the first time as a girl of eight. And curiously, as Marie rode north along the bay on the morning factory train, watching the village emerge from the dawn mist, she herself did not feel much different than she had felt that morning nearly twenty years ago when she rode into Hell's Gate in the cattle car. She could feel her heart beating faster as the train neared the town.

"Please tell Captain Benedict that Marie Blythe wants to see him about a job," she said a few minutes later to Ellen Baxter—who, like the village, looked just the same way she had always looked.

Ellen stared at Marie for a moment in surprise, then asked her to sit down and went into the Captain's private office and shut the door behind her.

A minute passed. And another. Then the door opened and Ellen said, "Mr. Benedict will see you now."

As she stepped through the doorway, Marie saw at a glance

that the Captain's office was as unchanged as the rest of the village. The mill floor was visible through the long window in the inner wall, the portrait of the Captain with one eye watching whoever came into the room and one looking off into the distance still hung above the big gold medal desk, which was as uncluttered and shiny as ever. But the man sitting behind it was not Captain Benedict. This man was young, with light hair and brown eyes, and he was not wearing a blue coat, or any coat at all for that matter, but a white shirt and a sober gray tie; and although he had filled out, and his face was fuller than she had remembered (but also strangely drawn in a way she did not remember at all), she recognized him immediately.

"Abie!"

"Marie."

It was not quite a question. She had given Ellen her name, so she knew Abie could not have been taken totally by surprise when she came through the door, yet he appeared to be even more astonished than she was, and so confused that when at last she stepped across the room and held out her hand he took it without rising.

"Why, Abie," she said before she had a chance to think. "Your hand's cold. Are you sick?"

Only then did he smile.

"You're as outspoken as ever, Marie," he said. But although he was smiling, and his teeth were still white and perfect and the halo of lighter hair still shone around the crown of his head, his eyes looked worried, reminding her of the eyes of soldiers at the hospital who knew they were not recuperating quickly enough. "Well. Sit down, Marie."

She sat in the single chair the Captain had always kept across from the big desk for guests, then continued to look around the room.

Abie spoke again, more naturally this time. "He's not here, Marie."

"Oh! I'm sorry, I just expected—"

"I know. Even the people who have been here the entire time

can't believe it. I can't believe it myself. But it's true. There was an accident this past July. Nobody knows exactly how it happened, but he was riding his horse in the park, near the old quarry, and somehow he was thrown. One minute he was alive and riding and as much in charge of things as ever. The next he was gone."

"Good God! I'm sorry, Abie. I'm so sorry."

Abie shook his head, as though he still couldn't assimilate his father's death. "I had just gotten home from Europe. I wasn't planning to stay long, but after the accident somebody had to carry on the business, so here I am, just where I said I'd never be."

"What about your mother, Abie? How did she take it?"

"Well, that surprised me nearly as much as the accident itself. I thought she'd just pine away after he died. That was my biggest worry; but she didn't. Much the opposite. She packed a few things, not many, turned over her interest in the business to me, and went west to Arizona with my father's remains, where they'd been going winters for her health for half a dozen years or so. I can't say she's happy, really—but she didn't crumple up." He spread his hands and shrugged. "It just goes to show you how unpredictable people are. But what about you, Marie? Where have you been? What have you been doing all this time?"

Quickly Marie summarized her travels away from the village. When she told Abie that she had lost the baby, he looked out the window in the factory yard with no expression on his face; she had no idea what he was thinking. She did not mention Jigger Johnson or Philbrook Jamieson, though she described her nursing work in some detail. Midway through her account Abie got out a cigarette and lighted it. When she stopped talking he continued to smoke on for a time silently, looking out the window.

"You haven't said why you decided to come back," he said finally.

Marie nodded. "I knew you were going to ask that question,

Abie. I wish I could tell you. My feet just headed this way, I guess. It was time to come home."

Abie frowned. "Things have changed in Hell's Gate, Marie. It's not just my father's death." He made an encompassing gesture with his hand. "In more ways than one, the war brought an end to a certain era in this village. I think my father saw the change coming and knew he couldn't do anything to stop it, though whether that had anything to do with his death I can't say. Mother thinks it might have.

"Of course, the old boy loved to say that everything changed and change was the one constant you could count on. But up until the war broke out, he was always the chief agent of any important changes in Hell's Gate. Then too, I suppose he must have felt that he'd accomplished everything he wanted to accomplish here. As long as some part of his little domain remained unrealized, he was interested in it. But he was already bored when he bought the ranch in Arizona, and there wasn't a lot he needed to do there. Here in Hell's Gate, the park was his last project—discounting me, that is."

Abie paused to light another cigarette. "I was a project that never worked out," he said.

Marie looked at him across the polished desk. He was as good-looking as ever, she thought, yet there was something about his eyes that went beyond mere worry and something in his voice beyond just self-pity, something akin to a deep and implacable resentment she had encountered only once or twice before, in badly wounded soldiers.

"You said you were in Europe, Abie?"

He nodded. "Twice. Once with Charlie Pike after we ran away from St. Mark's. Then again during the war."

"Well, begin at the beginning. Do you have time? I didn't know that you ran away from St. Mark's or were in the war either."

He laughed. "I've got time. This place runs itself, Marie, or very nearly so. I've been looking for things to do, like my father toward the end."

From his top drawer Abie removed a small silver bell, like a doorbell, which he set on the desk top and tapped lightly. A moment later Ellen Baxter opened the door.

"Ellen," he said, "would you please bring us each a cup of coffee? We'll be visiting for a while."

Marie was surprised by the bell, which seemed a peculiar affectation, and certainly one the Captain would never have indulged himself in or approved of. Ellen brought in their coffee on a tray and went back to the outer office, shutting the door behind her. Without rising, Abie poured a cup for Marie and one for himself.

"Charlie Pike," he said, shaking his head. "I haven't thought of him in a long time. Charlie loved Europe, loved everything about it. He enjoyed that trip as much as I was bored by it. I hardly cared where we went; I didn't travel so much as I drifted. Sometimes I'd stay in our room and sleep all day or get on a train and ride to the end of the line and back without knowing where I'd been. I was at loose ends from the day I got there.

"You see, Marie, when my father wrote that letter with the news about the baby, and adopting it and so forth, I was so confused and mad—mad at myself, mostly, though I didn't know it at the time—that I decided to show everybody what I thought of them and just disappear for a while. As it turned out I didn't show anybody anything. Father hired a detective who kept him informed about our whereabouts, and by the time we got back you were gone and the whole thing had blown over anyway."

"What did you do after you came home, Abie?"

"Oh, I went back to St. Mark's for a term, and graduated, and then I went to Dartmouth, just as Father intended for me to do. I followed the plan he'd laid out for me. To tell the truth, that was pretty much a waste too; I drifted through Dartmouth about the same way I'd drifted through Europe. The only part I really liked was playing ball; that was fine, and in the back of my mind I planned on playing professionally afterward. I had some offers too, including a chance to try out for the Red Sox; but that didn't come about either because the day after I graduated he whisked me off to Portland to open a sales office, which I knew even then was a waste of time and money. My duties there seemed to consist mainly of serving as a sort of long-distance clerk to my father. I went to lunch with customers, saw a lot of ball games in Boston, pitched summers for a local semi-pro team. The fact is that Father didn't need or want anybody else to handle sales for him, and I certainly didn't want to. It cost him considerably more to operate the office than I ever brought in."

"I don't understand, Abie. Why didn't you tell him how you felt? Why didn't you just go play baseball anyway?"

Abie shrugged. "I should have. But for one thing, by then he had me half convinced that that would have been as frivolous as he seemed to think. And for another, I guess I didn't dare. He was a very strong-willed man, Marie. You know that. I don't know what he would have done if I'd defied him outright, disowned me or what. I didn't want to take that chance."

"Maybe you should have. I don't think he would have disowned you."

Abie looked at her sharply. "You don't? Well, I'm not so sure. At any rate, this charade went on for three or four years, until finally even Father had to admit that it wasn't working. Ever the optimist, though, another scheme occurred to him. Somehow he fixed on the idea that I liked to travel, maybe because I'd run off to Europe that time. So without even consulting me he bought a Pierce Arrow and put a sample rocking cradle Herman Fischner had made in the back seat and packed me off on a cross-country tour to promote baby cradles and Benedict furniture in general.

"As you can imagine, I wasn't exactly ecstatic over the prospects of this odyssey. At least in Portland I could play ball five or six months a year. But I'd learned a long time ago that usually it's easier to nod your head at the right places and go along with the tide, so I nodded and in the summer of 1914 I headed out. Father had provided me with an itinerary of places to visit—and places to stay and places to eat and sights to see and other sights to avoid as not worth seeing—and at first I followed it religiously because it was the easy thing to do. I went to Buffalo and Indianapolis, Chicago, Kansas City, Denver. But after a couple of months a curious thing happened."

Abie looked at Marie expectantly, almost as though she were telling the story and about to divulge something interesting.

"What was that?"

"Well, about halfway through the trip I began to deviate from the itinerary. Not all at once. Not even intentionally, at first. But in between the planned stops I began to find myself in smaller places—not villages like Hell's Gate, but not big cities either, places where I knew ahead of time I'd be in no great danger of finding customers for Herman's cradles."

"You mean to say you weren't trying to sell them?"

"Evidently not. After all, I didn't want to disappoint him." Abie gestured backward with his thumb toward the picture of the Captain on the wall behind the desk. "What would he have done if I'd actually succeeded at something?"

"I can't believe he wouldn't have been proud of you. I'm sure he would have been."

"You always were willing to give him the benefit of the doubt, Marie. But maybe that's because he didn't expect as much from you. He didn't even expect you to go to school. Just to keep Mother company."

"Your father was always good to me, Abie."

"Oh, he was good to everybody. He was the next thing to a saint—just ask anybody in Hell's Gate."

He lighted another cigarette. "Well, I drove from place to place, and after a while I tore up the itinerary and threw the pieces in a hotel wastebasket. I kept my ball glove and bat in the front seat beside me, and if I saw a gang of kids playing in a lot I'd stop and play with them. I played with a few town teams too, Sunday afternoons. Once I was offered a job in the office of a meat-packing plant in Texas so I could pitch for the company team—a light job, the manager kept saying. He didn't know I could probably have bought his company three times over, and I never told him.

"I didn't sell a single cradle on the whole trip. The closest I came was one evening up in northern Washington. A wholesaler, a German who by coincidence was from the same Black Forest town as Herm Fischner, took me out to dinner. 'My boy,' he said, 'I might place a small order with you. But truthfully, I'm not much interested in baby furniture.' I began to laugh, and once I was started, I couldn't seem to stop. I laughed so hard the poor man was embarrassed for me. When I finally got my breath back I said, 'Truthfully, my friend, neither am I.' He probably thought I was drunk, but I wasn't. I'd just suddenly realized how absurd the whole trip was and how absurd my whole life had been up to that point. Quite a bit later that night I gave the cradle to the German's stenographer, who may very well have had a good use for it nine months later, and started south. I intended to take that office job in Texas, get my arm in shape over the winter, and then try out for the Red Sox."

"Good for you! Did you?"

"No. The next morning Canada entered the war. The papers were full of it. I'd just ordered breakfast at a little roadside eating spot, and I didn't even wait for it to come. I left a dollar bill at my place and walked out and got behind the wheel and drove straight to Vancouver to enlist. I guess I thought that if I was going to make a break it might as well be a total break. I was half afraid Father would hunt me down in Texas anyway, to tell you the truth, and I thought I could always play ball after the war was over—no one believed then it would last more than a few months. Besides, they needed pilots desperately, and I was eager to fly.

"I pushed that Pierce Arrow just as hard as she'd go, and the engine blew as I was coming into the outskirts of the city. It occurred to me that I hadn't put in any oil since Denver, but at that point I couldn't have cared any less. In fact, I was amused. I pulled over to the side of the street, got out, and left it there for somebody else to worry about. An hour later I'd enlisted in the Royal Canadian Air Force, and three months from that day I was flying over Germany."

Abie reached into his desk drawer and took out a snapshot of himself, which he handed across the desk to her. In the photograph he was standing beside a bi-winged airplane. He was holding his flying helmet and goggles loosely in one hand and pointing with the other at two fist-sized holes in the upper wing above his head, and he was smiling.

Marie was oddly touched, though less by the scene itself (she had seen dozens of similar ones at the hospital) than by the memories it evoked. Abie looked youthful and unworried, and his jaunty grin as he pointed at the bullet holes reminded her of how he had always loved risks—how he'd dived off the roof of the covered bridge into the lake and skated up the lake on skim ice with a bedsheet sail and, later, come boldly into the ring to fight her when she had been disguised as a gypsy boy. She imagined him high up in the air in the flimsy-looking biplane, being shot at and enjoying it.

"That's a fine picture of you, Abie," she said, handing it back to him across the desk.

He shrugged and grinned at her, and for a moment it seemed as though they had never been separated but were teenagers again, exchanging secrets on the love seat in the Big House. In fact, Abie seemed as ready to confide in her as ever; and yet from time to time as he spoke he looked at her with a brief, searching intentness, as though he was still not entirely sure she was who she said she was.

"Well," he said, replacing the photograph, "to make a long story short, I flew over France for a couple of years, then volunteered to train pilots for Russia, which was just developing an air force. That was even more exciting than shooting at the German nobility. We were flying French training planes put together mainly from spare parts, and for practice we'd go in after German ships in dry dock at Constantinople, which is how I finally got shot down. I drifted around in the Black Sea for the better part of a day before the English picked me up. Then I went to an English hospital, and after that I came home."

Marie shook her head in wonder. "Abie, as I came into the village this morning nothing seemed any different. Now it seems that *everything*'s different. Your father's dead. Your mother's out west. You've been off to war and become a hero and now you're the big boss—the boy who hated the factory so much he cut himself deliberately in order not to have to work here! But what about the factory? Do you still make desks and chairs?"

"That hasn't changed any. We still make office furniture. We've even got a new line of folding chairs, much to Ned Baxter's disgust. We make them up in lots for United States Seating."

"How are the Baxters, Abie? When I first spoke to Mrs. Baxter I don't think she recognized me."

Abie looked sober. "Well, they're all right. You know Uncle Ned; he's solid as the Rock of Gibraltar. But in July, Ned Jr. was killed in France. They don't talk about it much, but you can tell it's always on their minds."

He shook his head. "It hardly seems right, does it, that he should be the one to get killed? Armand St. Onge lost a boy too. So did Heinrich Michler and John Moon. And there are still five or six other local boys scattered here and there. Now that Armistice has been declared they should be back soon, though whether they'll stay is anybody's guess. A number of young people have left already. Herman Fischner's oldest son is teaching down at the state university. The Morse boy is studying medicine in Boston. Three of the Canadian families cashed in their scrip and bought played-out farms up in Lord Hollow and are trying to bring them back. Armand St. Onge did even better for himself. He lied about his age and joined the Canadian forces about the time I did, got to be a master sergeant, and was wounded in the chest on the Somme. On the transport coming home he made a small fortune playing poker, and two weeks ago he bought the Common Hotel."

Abie had been speaking hurriedly for the past minute or so and looking out the window, as though for an overdue visitor. When he looked back at her, Marie was struck again by a certain apprehensiveness in his glance. But almost immediately he turned away and said, "Where are you headed from here, Marie?"

"Abie, I know it must be hard for you to see me show up out of the blue this way. If you're still angry with me for what happened twelve years ago, I wouldn't blame you. It was foolish to get pregnant, and I take my full share of the blame—and I'm sorry for the trouble and unhappiness I caused you. I'm sorry too that I ran off like a fool and lost the baby."

He waved his hand, as though to say that was water over the dam; yet at the same time he looked at her closely.

In her uneasiness she blurted out, "I want to stay here in Hell's Gate, Abie. I want to work here if I can. There's something I've put off doing for a long time, that I've got to do now or I never will. But to get started I need a job. That's why I came here to the factory this morning. To see about a job."

Abie hesitated. "Well, Marie. There might be an opening on the night crew. They're mainly women from the Common on that shift. It's unskilled work on the folding chair contract, and they're a pretty rough bunch. Even Bill Kane, my night foreman, says so. Isn't there some other way I can help you? This plan of yours. Give me some idea of what it is, how I can be of assistance."

"I won't do that, Abie. This is something I have to do completely on my own. That way, if it doesn't work out, it'll be my responsibility. Besides, I'm just superstitious enough to believe that if I tell anyone ahead of time it's less apt to work. As for the women on the night shift, they won't bother me. I've worked with some pretty hard customers before, and I've always gotten along."

Except for the muffled roar of the machinery on the mill

floor, the office was quiet. Abie smoked silently, frowning out
the window. From the wall behind him the portrait of the
Captain looked on calmly with one eye.

"Well," he said reluctantly. "When would you want to
begin?"

"Tonight," she said. "I'll take the rest of the day to find a
place to board and get settled in, and I'll be there tonight."

She stood up, expecting Abie to stand too, but still he remained seated, looking wryly at Pia's portrait of himself as a
boy in his pale yellow baseball uniform with black piping,
hanging across from the portrait of the Captain.

"Abie, I have to ask you a question. After you came home
from the war and put things in order, didn't you still want to
play ball?"

"Yes," he said. "I did."

"Do you still?"

"Yes," he said, looking at the portrait.

"Couldn't Ned manage things here for a while?"

"Yes."

She looked at him, puzzled. "Well, why don't you then?
Good Lord, you're still a young man."

Abie turned his head toward her slowly, but now his eyes
seemed to be looking into some private distance of their own.
Placing his hands on the edge of his desk and leaning forward,
he pushed himself to his feet. He bent over and picked up a
crutch, which had been out of sight beside his chair. When he
came around the desk, he was dragging his left leg behind him
and his shoe was twisted at a sharp angle to the leg. Supporting
himself on his right leg and his crutch, he extended his hand,
which was now hot and damp.

"Good luck on your job, Marie," he said.

Chapter Nine

Marie's fingers trembled as she buttoned her high shoes in the early gray light. She had gotten in from work less than four hours ago and slept badly, and she could gladly have returned to bed until noon; but she had already waited a week and she was afraid that if she waited any longer she would never follow through with her plan. As she brushed her hair in the half-light of the upstairs room she rented at the Baxters, her hands shaking hard now, she was not sure that she could go through with it anyway, but she had been determined to try since the night she left the sanatorium.

"Today's the big day, Marie," Ned Baxter said to her a few minutes later in the kitchen.

"Today's the big day," she said.

"You'd better eat a good hot breakfast," Ellen said.

Marie shook her head. "Just a cup of coffee, thanks. My stomach feels like a butter churn this morning, Mrs. Baxter."

"You'll do fine," Ellen said, patting her on the shoulder. "I'm not worried about you one bit."

Ned grinned and made a short hammer motion with his fist. "Hit them hard, girl," he said to her, then headed out the door for the factory.

Marie managed to grin, but as she did her lips quivered. She could not remember being so nervous ever before in her life.

She left the house with her dinner pail at six thirty, though Ned and Ellen had assured her that seven would be early enough. It was December now, and she shivered all the way down the street through the dusting of snow that had fallen overnight. At the foot of the hill she paused and took several deep breaths. Then she started up the path under the bare horse chestnut trees the gypsies had brought to the village years ago. Partway up the hill she paused by the iron gate of the small cemetery across from the school to watch the factory train come up the track between the frozen bay and the foot of Kingdom Mountain. She was still shivering. Her teeth chattered; she had to fight the impulse to run back down the hill to the Baxters.

The train pulled into the village. The day workers got off and went across the street to the factory, where they stood singly or in small groups until the second whistle blew and Ned opened the big front doors of the mill floor. Foremen and cabinetmakers came out of the yellow houses along the street and walked toward the factory. Across the bridge, the Canadian drovers headed up Canada Mountain with their teams; except for the fact that the drovers used horses now instead of oxen, it could have been 1900 as easily as 1918, though the village still seemed strangely empty and unfamiliar to Marie without Captain Benedict. Her stomach rolled and churned, and she looked around for something else to take her mind off her nervousness.

Across the gravel street in the schoolyard stood a set of wooden swings. As Marie looked at them it occurred to her that she had never swung in her life. She glanced up and down the hill. Seeing no one, she went across and sat down on the middle swing. She smiled to herself to think how a grown woman must look, sitting on a set of children's swings. Tentatively at first, then with more confidence, she began to move. Recalling how children she had seen swinging kicked their feet, she kicked her feet hard several times—and ten seconds later she was bent over in the dead milkweeds and mullein stalks behind the school, losing her coffee as she had once lost the milk Rachel Benedict made her drink as a girl.

"Hello! Are you ill?"

Marie spun around and saw a woman looking at her with concern. She was a rather stout, friendly-looking woman approaching middle age, with dark hair and eyes.

"I felt a little queasy, I guess," Marie said sheepishly. "I was trying to swing."

"That's all right," the woman said, coming up to Marie and offering her handkerchief. "I'm apt to feel queasy in the morning myself." She smiled. "The truth is, I drink way too much coffee. I love it, the stronger the better, and I always drink three or four cups, and then I have to run to the toilet half a dozen times a morning and all my students titter like jay birds because they know I drink more coffee than I ought to. But I keep right on doing it, and I imagine I always will."

She spoke rapidly, cheerfully, and while she talked on about her coffee drinking she looked shrewdly at Marie.

"I'm sorry," she said, laughing. "I got talking so fast I forgot my manners. My name's Margaret Simpson. I'm the teacher here—when I'm not running to the toilet, that is."

Marie smiled. "My name's Marie Blythe, Miss Simpson. I'm pleased to meet you."

"Well, you've got a good strong grip, Marie Blythe. I like that. My father always told me, shake hands the same way you grab a plumber's wrench, as though you meant business."

Despite her embarrassment, Marie smiled again. Already she liked this talkative woman who was so cheery and forthcoming.

"Miss Simpson, I've been waiting here for half an hour to speak to you."

Margaret Simpson nodded. She looked at Marie kindly, not hurrying her.

"I'm twenty-seven years old. I can do my sums, and sight-read a little—not much. I know how to write my name after a fashion, but I haven't even mastered all the letters, and the truth of the matter is I'm scared to death of trying to learn and not being able to. But I have to ask you, and if I don't now I never will. Can I go to school to you?"

"Of course," Margaret said in a businesslike voice. "Of course you can. I'd be very pleased to have you come to my school, Miss Blythe. When would you like to start?"

"Today. I want to start today, and begin right at the beginning, and learn as much as I'm capable of learning, which at twenty-seven may not be very much—that is, if you don't mind having a twenty-seven-year-old with a very nervous stomach for a pupil."

"Not if you don't mind having a forty-one-year-old with a very nervous stomach for a teacher," Margaret said, grinning. "Come in, Marie Blythe. Welcome to the Hell's Gate Village School!"

Except for a few times when she and John Trinity had sneaked into a schoolhouse at night to sleep, Marie had never been inside a school before. The smells of chalk dust and textbooks and polished wood were both exciting and frightening to her, but Margaret showed her where to put her coat and where the books and supplies were kept with such a friendly and businesslike manner that she began to feel at home almost immediately.

"Marie Blythe, can you build a fire?"

Marie nodded.

"Well, I can too, but half the time it doesn't catch and the other half I forget to open the damper and the school fills up with smoke. I wonder if you'd do me a favor?"

"I'd be glad to make the fire every morning," Marie said.

Margaret laughed. "Well, that's good of you. But right now, how about just showing me how to make one? I grew up in cities, you see, and I've lived in cities most of my life. If you'll show me how to build a good fire, I'll be eternally grateful to you."

Marie suspected that the teacher knew very well how to

build a fire and was just trying to make her feel useful, but she was touched by the gesture anyway and immediately went about showing Margaret how to make a tent of small kindling around crumpled newspaper sheets, then add larger sticks gradually, until the stove was roaring.

"There!" Margaret said with satisfaction. "I learned something. I've wanted to know how to do that for three months.

"I'll tell you, Marie—you don't mind if I call you Marie? Half my students call me Margaret—no, I won't tell you, I *can't* tell you how delighted I am to find a single woman in this town to talk to. You can't imagine how lonesome it's been here; or maybe you can, but whether you can or not it has been. I came in late August, loved the place, still do, it's different from anywhere I've ever been, but there isn't a soul to talk to—I mean really talk to. They're all married with families and concerns of their own. . . . Listen to me complain. I've got my house and garden, and naturally there's plenty to keep me busy, correcting papers and planning lessons and so forth—I never taught in a grade school, so that's all new—but believe me, it's good to find another woman who isn't so bogged down peeling potatoes and washing out her husband's long johns to think of improving herself. You're not married, are you?"

Marie shook her head, grinning with delight at Margaret's candor.

"Well, I'm not either, but I wish I were sometimes." She paused and smiled mischievously. Then she said, "I'll tell you a secret. I came up here from the city partly to find a man. And now I see they're all spoken for!"

When school began, Margaret took Marie around the room and introduced her to each student. There were thirty in all, the boys on one side of the center aisle, the girls on the other. The smallest students sat at the front of the room, the biggest at the back. After the introductions, Margaret handed her a slate and a piece of chalk and said she could sit in back with the big girls, where Gretchen Fischner, Herman's daughter, would help her learn her letters.

"Pardon me, Miss Simpson," Marie said. "But I'd feel a great deal better starting right up with the youngest scholars."

Some of the students laughed out loud, but Margaret looked at them sternly and told Marie that if she'd be more comfortable sitting on the first bench, that was fine. She seated Marie beside Gretchen's younger sister, Heide, and asked Heide to write out the alphabet for Marie to copy.

The little girl was patient, but by the middle of the morning Marie's forehead was dripping sweat and her right hand was shaking from pressing down too hard on the slate.

"Don't fight it, Marie," Margaret whispered to her. "Take your time. It'll come, and when it does, it'll come fast."

"I've taken nearly thirty years already," Marie said, nearly in tears. "I don't want to take another thirty just learning these letters. Look here. My C and G still look like two twins you can't tell apart. And half the time I can't remember which way to make a B or an S or an R."

"Just go slowly," Margaret whispered. "You can't expect to learn everything in one day. Look how long it's taken me to get what I told you I wanted, and I still don't have it! Now I'll be back in a minute; I have to get rid of some more coffee!"

The small children nearby giggled, and Marie, supposing they were laughing at her, didn't blame them. She knew how comical it must be to them to see a grown woman bending over her slate with her long legs tucked up nearly to her chin, trying to form letters most of them had known how to make before starting school. Heide had even had to show her how to hold the chalk, bending her thumb and first two fingers around it and guiding her hand across the slate.

At noon most of the children went home for dinner. Marie stayed at school and ate lunch with Margaret, which turned out to be a mistake because before she had finished her first sandwich she was throwing up again in the dead weeds behind the building.

As she came back into the yard, now actually crying from shame and exasperation, she met Clayton Not Slayton Kane and his brother Slayton Not Clayton, Bill Kane's sons. Clayton Not Slayton and Slayton Not Clayton were big boys, sixteen and fifteen years old, but they had never progressed farther in school than the seventh bench. For the past several years they had started at the seventh bench in September and finished there in June. Although they could barely read their own names, they knew much of the Barnes *National Seventh Reader* by heart from going over it so often with so many different teachers.

As Marie came out of the weeds, the Kane boys began to snicker.

"What are you two laughing at?" Marie said sharply.

"We wasn't laughing at nothing," Slayton Not Clayton said.

"Certainly we was laughing at something," Clayton Not Slayton said. "We was laughing at a good joke."

Marie didn't want to get into a fight on her first day of school, but Ellen Baxter had warned her that the Kane brothers were notorious bullies, as mean as they were dumb, and she knew that if she didn't confront them immediately they'd make every day of school miserable for her.

"Haw," Clayton said.

"Haw, haw," Slayton said.

"I'd be glad to learn why you were laughing," Marie said. "Tell me the joke."

"It ain't a joke for women," Clayton said.

"That's all right," Marie said. "So long as you weren't laughing at me. That wouldn't be wise."

"We ain't afraid of you," Clayton said.

"You don't have any reason to be. Nor I of you."

She went back into the schoolhouse, feeling much better for standing up to the Kane boys. That afternoon just before school let out for the day she wrote the letters A through H without a mistake, and as she went down the hill to get ready to go to work at four o'clock she was as excited as she could remember being. She knew that going to school would not be easy, but with the help of her new friend Margaret Simpson she believed she could do it successfully.

"Don't ever say what you'll never do," Pia had said.

Marie knew now, heading across the street from the Baxters to the factory, what the gypsy woman had meant. Many times as a girl and young woman she had promised herself that, whatever else she might do, she would never work in the factory. Yet here she was, not by necessity but by choice, working ten hours a night, six nights a week, in order to go to school and learn the alphabet with six-year-olds during the daytime. As Pia had also said, life was unpredictable. The future was as blank as the back of a mirror and no one, not even a gypsy, could predict it or should try to.

The whistle gave a long blast. Although it was not quite four o'clock, it was nearly dark and bitterly cold, and the lighted factory looked warm, almost inviting. Marie walked quickly through the front doors, past the day shift filing out. She crossed the rough-mill floor and went up the wooden stairs to the machine floor. She nodded to Durwood Baxter, the machine-floor foreman. Durwood, who was more aloof than his brother Ned, was the only foreman who did not live in Hell's Gate. He had a house in the Common and commuted to work with the day laborers.

Marie worked in the finishing room, off the west end of the machine floor. She put her lunch pail on the high windowsill nearest her work station, got her cans of varnish and brushes from the long counter on the opposite wall, and nodded to the small, hatchet-faced woman at the next work station. The woman pointedly looked away. Marie was irritated and made up her mind not to bother greeting her again.

Compared with many of Marie's other jobs, varnishing folding chairs was easy. The chairs were brought on dollies from the machine floor into the finishing room, where a huge woman known throughout Hell's Gate as Madame Laframboise, or Madame Raspberry, dipped them individually into the large tank of reddish preservative by the door where Abie Benedict had been stained the summer he first went to work in the factory. After dipping the chairs, Madame Raspberry hung them up on a moving rail under the low ceiling, where they dried in a matter of minutes. As the stained chairs traveled slowly down the assembly line, the women reached up and removed them, applied a coat of varnish, then hung them up again to pass on into the shipping room. Brushing with short, rapid strokes, a good varnisher could complete a chair every three minutes.

At first Marie had tried to use her brush like a paintbrush, but after Bill Kane showed her how to slap the varnish on quickly by flipping her wrist like a fly fisherman setting the hook in a trout, she progressed quickly. Now, three weeks after starting, she had no trouble varnishing twenty chairs an hour.

As long as the women on the line met their quota, Bill Kane let them visit while they worked. There was no noisy machinery in the finishing room, and often Marie could overhear snatches of half a dozen different conversations going on simultaneously. Most of the women were young, in their late teens or early twenties, and they talked mainly about saving money, getting married, and making homes for themselves. Except for Madame Raspberry, they were all from the Common. Marie had little interest in the affairs of that village, and no one talked with her anyway, so she worked silently, repeating the alphabet to herself or thinking about other concerns of her own.

Tonight she was puzzling over two recent conversations she'd had with Abie Benedict. Twice since she'd started work, once the night after she began and again two nights ago, he had returned to his office after supper and asked to see her there. The first time he had inquired how her job was going; after pausing to light a cigarette, he casually asked whether during her travels she had ever happened to spend any time in Montreal. She told him no, aware that he was watching her carefully through the cigarette smoke hanging between them. He nodded—she could not tell whether he believed her—and after a moment she excused herself and returned to work.

The second time Abie had called her in was on the night after she had started school. Again he asked to see her after the shift had started—an interruption that distressed her because she disliked falling behind in her work and knew that his attention made the other women on the shift jealous—and began by congratulating her on enrolling in school. Then he caught her totally by surprise by suggesting that she stop work altogether and let him help her further her education at a better school outside Hell's Gate, under easier circumstances. When she demurred, he became jovially insistent, though with an undertone of irritation. But she was unwilling to accept his assistance. For one thing, she did not wish to leave Hell's Gate. For another, she was reluctant to obligate herself to him more than she already had.

"Well, Marie," he said when she declined his offer. "I see you're still as proud as ever. You always did want to do everything the hard way."

Although he had shrugged and dropped the matter, she knew he was angry; to make matters worse, when she went back to the finishing room, several of the other women on the night shift had given her unmistakably hostile looks, and the hatchet-faced woman had asked her how much extra scrip she made on her trips to the boss's office.

School, on the other hand, was going better. She had already memorized the alphabet and she was partway through the *National First Reader,* which she had begun bringing to work with her to study during her lunch break. Now, as she whisked her brush over one chair after another, she put Abie Benedict's troubling behavior firmly out of her mind and concentrated on repeating the alphabet to herself, visualizing the letters she had first encountered many years ago on the crude cedar marker of her brothers and sisters.

At break time, she got her lunch and book and sat down to read and eat near the door leading into the machine room.

"You, girlie. Mr. Abie wants to see you."

Marie was so absorbed in her story that she started. Madame Raspberry, the huge chair-dipper, was standing over her, grinning.

Marie thought quickly. Then she said, "Tell Mr. Benedict I'll see him after work. I have to finish this right now."

Madame Raspberry looked at her incuriously and then waddled off to report to Abie. Meanwhile the hatchet-faced woman said to the women eating nearby, "It must be her time of the month. Otherwise she'd be in there like a bitch in heat."

Marie looked up from her book. She stared at the small, mean-mouthed woman from the Common, who glanced back, then said something to her friends in a lower voice. Marie caught the word tramp. She stood up, gathered her things together, and moved to the opposite side of the room. A few minutes later Madame Raspberry reappeared and began talking and laughing with the other women, who looked her way from time to time. Marie took one of Ned Baxter's twenty-ounce apples out of her lunch pail, then put it back, too upset to eat it. To her relief Bill Kane came in a minute later, and it was time to return to work.

When the shift ended, she cleaned her brush and put it to soak in a can of turpentine. She cleaned her hands with a rag dipped in turpentine, deliberately waiting until all the commuting women had left to catch the train for the Common. Then she got her lunch bucket and started for the door.

"You, girlie."

Madame Raspberry stood squarely in Marie's path. She had been standing in the shadows near the staining tank, and Marie had not seen her until she stepped out in front of her.

"Excuse me," Marie said. "It's quitting time."

"We ain't going to quit yet, you and me," Madame Raspberry said. "We got some unfinished business to tend to."

Marie looked up at Madame Raspberry. She was a mountain of a woman, well over six feet tall. Ned Baxter had said that when Harlan Smith, the commission sales auctioneer in the Common, gave her fifty cents to step on his grain scales, she had tipped them at a quarter of a ton. Although she was as French as yellow pea soup, as the Hell's Gate saying went, she had not come to the States with Marie and her parents, but appeared a few years later in a small blue rowboat, barely large enough to hold her, from no one ever knew where. Unable to speak a word of English, she had gone to live with the Bonaventure family. She was an expert angler and an inveterate forager. Many times the children had tried to discover her secret berry patches, but although she was as slow on cleared land as one of the turtles she loved to catch and eat, in the woods she could move with remarkable speed and silence, and no matter how stealthily the children followed her she would always dip majestically under a knoll or slip into a stand of softwoods, only to reappear two or three hours later with a heaping pailful of blueberries or raspberries or whatever else was in season.

"You ain't been baptized yet," she said to Marie now, grinning and running a tongue as thick as a blood sausage over her lips. "Time for your bath, girl."

"What do you mean?" Marie said.

"You know what I mean. You going into that tank!"

Marie stepped back, alarmed. The stain was as impermeable as red ink; you could scrub until your skin came off and still not remove it. If Madame Raspberry threw her into the tank, she would not be able to return to school or work for weeks.

"Madame Raspberry," she said quickly. "What did those women promise you to put me in the tank?"

"Never mind who promised what. You going into the tank."

"I'm not going into that tank. Not now or any other time. I won't be stained or have my clothes stained."

"Take them off, then. Because you going right in, by the Jesus." As Madame Raspberry spoke, she spread out her huge hands and started toward her. Working her hands like a person trying to corner a cat, she said, "Here, kitty."

Marie began to back up.

"Here, kitty, kitty, kitty."

Marie moved slowly backward, taking one step at a time. If she could decoy Madame into the middle of the room, she could feint one way and dodge the other, away from her clutching hands, and beat her to the door. But with surprising cunning Madame had already worked around so that she was angling Marie back toward the staining tank.

She was moving in fast. The rancid odor of her sweat was overpowering. Her tongue flicked out and in eagerly, like a lizard's.

Marie could go no farther. She felt the metal rim of the tank pressing against her back.

"Madame Raspberry, if you lay a hand on me I'll do something terrible to you."

The big woman paused, her arms outstretched. "What that?" she said.

"I'll bite off your left ear."

"Jesus!" Madame said, deeply impressed. "You really do that?"

Very solemnly, Marie nodded once.

Madame took a step back. Unconsciously she raised her hand to her ear and tugged it, as though to confirm to herself that it was still there. Then she shrugged. "All right. You don't have to go in the tank then." She turned and started toward the door, waddling majestically. Suddenly she paused. With her back still to Marie, as though turning her gigantic bulk again was too complicated a procedure, she said, "Say. What become of that big yellow apple I see you put back in your dinner pail at break?"

Grinning to herself, Marie reached into her dinner pail for the apple and handed it to Madame Raspberry. A minute later she was outside in the street, breathing in great lungfuls of the cold mountain air as she headed toward the Baxter house.

Everyone in the village agreed that the school was extremely fortunate to have acquired Margaret Simpson. A native of Boston, she had worked her way through college, gone on to acquire a master's degree in English literature, and taught at several private schools and at Vassar College. She was endlessly curious about life in Hell's Gate and equally at home discussing the intricacies of the Corliss steam engine at the factory with Gil Chamberlain and the best way to can cowslips with Gertrude Fischner. Like Ned Baxter, she was always busy with some project or other—planting a hydrangea or a yellow rosebush on her lawn, papering the dining room of the teacher's house, holding a winter carnival with sliding parties and a snow sculpturing contest in the hanging meadow on Kingdom Mountain, taking her students on the train to see the state legislature in session.

Often on Sunday afternoons Marie visited her for extra help, and as Margaret had predicted on the day they met, the two women quickly became good friends. Just why she had come to Hell's Gate remained a mystery to most of the villagers, but she confided to Marie in a laughing but serious way that, having failed to find a husband at the exclusive schools where she had previously taught, she had decided to try for one in an entirely different neck of the woods.

Because they were so different from her own background, she loved to hear the stories of Marie's life on the Grand Trunk and in the lumber camps, on the big log drives and at the sanatorium, and she helped Marie see for the first time how valuable many of those experiences had been to her. She was the first close woman friend Marie had ever had, and as the year progressed they became more like two sisters than a teacher and her student, talking and laughing together before and after school and on almost every Sunday and teasing one another about Margaret's determination to land a husband and Marie's to avoid marriage at all costs.

Although they were old enough to be her parents, Ned and Ellen Baxter were good friends to Marie too. She slept in Ned Jr.'s room, used many of his old schoolbooks, and knew that to a certain degree she helped fill the terrible gap in their lives caused by his death. Marie respected the Baxters as much as anyone she had ever known—quiet, kind, terrifically hard-working people who despite their great loss went on bravely, though Ned especially seemed lonely at times. He and his son had been inseparable, fishing and hunting together, playing ball, working together on the mill floor, where Ned Jr. ran the cut-off saw summers to save money for his books and clothes.

Ned had also been close to the Captain—the only really close friend the Captain had ever had, so far as anyone in Hell's Gate knew—and more than once since Marie had come to the Baxters to board, she had heard him say that the village would never be the same without Abraham Benedict. It was not that Ned disliked Abie, he was quick to say, or that he expected Abie to fill the Captain's shoes. So far, Abie had treated him with respect, followed his recommendations, come to work early each morning no matter how late he'd been up the night before, and hitched his way through the entire factory every day, greeting each man as his father had. Yet Ellen especially worried about him, fretted over his drawn, almost haunted appearance, scolded him mildly for not taking better care of himself (he had discharged Wyalia Kinneson, who was now keeping house for her brother-in-law Early), and disapproved of his weekend parties at the Big House, at which he entertained customers and friends from the war. Sometimes these affairs began on Thursday or Friday and ran straight through Saturday and Sunday into the first part of the work week. Although Abie rarely drank much himself, he was apt to act disconsolate and disinterested in his job for days after his friends left. Ellen thought his war injury probably bothered him more than he admitted, and both Baxters agreed that what Abie needed was a wife and family of his own. Marie suspected that they wished she would set her cap for him and provide him with both.

Her own feelings toward Abie remained ambivalent. After the night of the incident with Madame Raspberry—now Marie's best friend in the varnishing room—he had not called her away from her work again. Twice he met her on the street and inquired how her job and schoolwork were progressing, each time reiterating his offer to help her. But during these conversations she sensed that he was abstracted by some other unspoken consideration, and after Christmas, to her relief, they did not see each other except to speak in passing for a number of months. At about the same time, the all-night parties at the Big House ceased altogether, and Abie began spending most weekends away from Hell's Gate, leaving on Friday evening on the factory train and usually not appearing again until Monday morning, when he would get off the northbound train in the Common, from where no one had any idea, and ride up to the village on the morning factory train, tired but in good spirits.

Marie was as curious as anyone else in the village about Abie's mysterious excursions—in March he was gone for five consecutive days without any explanation—but she did not have much time to dwell on them. Although school was never really easy for her, she had moved steadily through one book after another. Getting along on five or six hours of sleep a night, she sometimes drowsed at her desk, especially when the mild late-winter sun came in through the tall windows. Yet this was not the kind of anxious, enervated exhaustion she had felt at the sanatorium after Dr. Jamieson's death, when she had worked so incessantly just to stay busy, but the solid, healthy weariness that results from steady accomplishment. By ice-out, she was halfway through her seventh reader, and one sunny morning in early May, Margaret told her that she could move to the eighth-grade bench that afternoon.

Marie was so pleased, and it was such a fine spring day, that at noon, instead of staying inside and studying as usual, she volunteered to be the fox in a game of chasing the fox that some of the children had gotten up. She was given a headstart of about a hundred yards, and then a dozen or so boys and girls started out after her, trying to overtake her before she could circle back to the school. She headed up the low road on Kingdom Mountain along the brook, cut through the bottom of the hanging meadow overlooking the village, and returned on the

upper drive, supposing she had easily outdistanced everyone.
But just as she reached the park gates above the Big House,
Clayton and Slayton Kane jumped out of the woods in front
of her.

Marie suspected that the Kane boys had played unfairly by
lying in wait for her the entire time, but she didn't care. "Well,
boys," she said, "You caught me. You'll be the foxes tomorrow, I imagine."

"I imagine we won't," Clayton Not Slayton said. "We ain't
playing none of your fool kid games, Marie Blythe. You listen
here to me. If you pass us by on the seventh bench this afternoon, I and Slayton intend to whip you till you can't stand up."

"Plus strip you and tie you to a tree," Slayton Not Clayton
added. "Just the way Mr.—"

Clayton rounded on his brother. "Shut up," he said. "You
keep your mouth shut."

"Boys," Marie said, "if you'd buckle down to your work,
I've no doubt that you could go on to the eighth bench yourselves. But I'll tell you something. Whether you do or whether
you don't, I'm going to be sitting there by the close of school
today."

But she did not move up that afternoon. It was very warm
inside the schoolhouse, and she was so tired from studying
days and working nights and then running hard that she fell
asleep with her head on her desk in the sunshine. Since it was
Friday afternoon, which Margaret usually spent reading aloud
to the whole school, she let Marie sleep until dismissal time.

The following Monday morning Marie was promoted to the
eighth bench. It was another warm day, after a clear weekend
over which most of the villagers had gotten their gardens in.
At noon the students started a game of one old cat in the
schoolyard. Again they asked her to play with them, but she
was so excited to have received her new books that she stayed
inside to look at them, and she stayed late again after school
to complete her geography lesson.

"Marie," Margaret said after the other students had left, "do you know you can graduate from the eighth grade this June if you keep going at this rate? You're setting the whole school on fire with your progress."

"Do you really think so?" Marie asked. "I want in the worst way to do it, but with all the written exercises in these new books, I don't see how I'll have time to finish everything between now and the middle of next month."

"Don't bother to write those exercises out. Just spend class time reading them over, and when you're ready I'll give you the eighth-grade syllabus book to study for the exam."

Marie thanked her friend. Then, since it was already quarter of four, she took her books and headed quickly across the schoolyard, down a shortcut through the cemetery, and along the lake toward the factory. The poplars were starting to come out in the sudden mild weather, and as she hurried along their strong minty fragrance reminded her of the spring day she had first set out for the States with her parents.

It was a beautiful day, one of the handful of really good spring days villagers could expect in Hell's Gate, where winter hung on so long that summer sometimes seemed to come immediately afterward, with no spring at all. The sky was a soft spring blue. The great expanse of water to Marie's left, running far into Canada between tall mountains, was nearly the same color. The far mountains were bluer still.

"Marie Blythe!"

Clayton Not Slayton Kane was standing in the path in front of her, holding a stick.

"We warned you not to pass us on by," he said. "Now you're going to get a good thrashing with a hardhack stick."

There was a crash behind her and Slayton Not Clayton dropped out of a poplar tree like an ape. He was holding a coil of rope and grinning. "That's not all you're going to get," he said. "We warned you."

Marie was annoyed without being frightened in the least. "Boys," she said, "it's a grand day to give someone a licking, and if you persist in this nonsense I'll give you both one free.

Then I'll tell your father what you've been up to, and he'll lick you again. Step aside, Clayton. I don't intend to be late for work."

"You're going to be late," Clayton said, brandishing the stick.

"You're never going to get there," Slayton said, maneuvering in behind her with the rope. "We're going to tie you up and see what you look like naked, Marie Blythe. Then we're going to sell tickets to see you for five cents apiece."

"Clayton, if you try to clip me with that hardhack stick I'll have to hurt you and your brother. I don't want to do that."

Clayton made a wild cut and Marie ducked. As the stick whistled by above her it caught Slayton cleanly in the side of the head and knocked him off his feet. He howled, jumped up, and belted his brother with his fist. Marie stepped back out of the way, and the two Kane boys began to pummel one another fiercely.

Marie shook her head and started for the factory. She grinned to herself; then she began to laugh. Just as she came into the factory yard the whistle blew, which meant that she would have to work at least until break time in her school dress, but she was laughing so hard she didn't care. One way or another, she was going to graduate from the Hell's Gate school that spring.

She was not laughing the following Sunday afternoon, though, when Ned Baxter came into the kitchen from digging a trench for an asparagus bed and found her sitting at the table with her eighth-grade arithmetic book. She was bent over the book with her face in her hands, and it was obvious from her rigid shoulders that she was either crying or trying desperately not to.

"Here," Ned said gruffly, putting his hand on Marie's shoulder. "Here now. What's the matter?"

"Mr. Baxter, it's these fractions. I just can't seem to see how they work. Unless I pass the arithmetic exam I won't graduate, but the longer I look at these figures the less sense they make. They might as well be Greek, and that's the truth."

Ned thought for a minute. Then he said, "Come along with me, my girl. You need a breath of fresh air."

He took her across the bridge to the lumberyard, and there, patiently and good-humoredly, figuring with the stub of a pencil on a clear piece of spruce board, the mill floor foreman who had never gotten past the third grade showed her how to add and subtract fractions as they applied to lumber.

This small event was typical of the way Ned and Ellen Baxter had helped Marie all winter and spring. They were more like parents to her than people she boarded with—not in the ambiguous, strangely possessive, yet strangely detached way the Benedicts had been, but affectionately and, she believed, disinterestedly. She knew that the Baxters liked her for herself, for who she was rather than who or what she might become, and she felt closer to them than she had ever felt to Abie's parents. A month ago she had written a simple letter of condolence to Abie's mother, expressing her sympathy over the Captain's death, and Rachel had duly written back to express her great relief that Marie was well and back home in Hell's Gate again and going to school at last. Yet even that letter seemed faintly guarded, as though Rachel herself might not be quite sure of Marie's motives in returning. Of her own life in Arizona, she said next to nothing, and Marie concluded with some sadness and more relief that whatever her relationship with the Benedicts had once been, it was now over.

Almost before Marie knew it, the county eighth-grade examination was less than a week away. She studied incessantly, drank coffee by the quart, thought about nothing else. She worked the night before the exam, then came home and studied and got only two hours of sleep, but she felt alert and fresh as she rode the factory train to the Common at dawn with Margaret and the three other eighth-grade students from Hell's Gate.

The examination was held in the Common Academy, a solid red-brick building overlooking the long green with the statue of Ethan Allen, which Marie had seen from between the slats of the cattle car on her first day in the States and mistaken for a live soldier. Students who had arrived early looked at Marie as she walked into the examination room. She quickly found a seat and sat down. A moment later someone tapped her shoulder. She turned around, and a girl in pigtails in the seat behind her said in a loud whisper, "Can I ask you a question?"

Marie nodded.

"How old are you, anyway?" the girl whispered loudly.

Marie grinned. "Twenty-eight," she whispered.

"My lord!" the girl said. "Have you been in school all this time?"

"Not quite. I started late."

The pigtailed girl stared at Marie with her mouth open. Then she wheeled around to share her discovery with the girl behind her.

At eight o'clock Margaret and a teacher from Kingdom Common handed out the first part of the exam. It smelled strongly of fresh ink and consisted of thirty questions on English grammar, which Marie answered in five minutes. Thinking she must have gone too fast and made some errors, she checked her answers carefully. They all seemed fine; she had learned grammar from Rachel Benedict at an early age and had rarely made a grammatical error in her speech even before starting school, since to Rachel good grammar was as important as good manners.

The second part of the exam was arithmetic, including fractions, decimals, and word problems. This section was more difficult for Marie, but she finished in plenty of time to check her answers and then went on to spelling and geography.

At noon she and several of the other candidates ate their lunch under the elm trees on the common, and Marie told how she had seen the statue for the first time, which made the girls laugh. Then they walked around the village until quarter of one, when they returned to the Academy.

The entire afternoon session was reserved for essay writing. The teachers handed out a blue copy book with lined pages to each student, and at exactly one o'clock Margaret wrote the essay topic on the blackboard: *My First Day of School.*

She smiled slightly at Marie, who grinned back. Not only was she going to write a good essay, she was going to have fun doing it. She spent ten minutes jotting down an outline on the back cover of the blue composition book, then began to write. When Margaret announced that it was time to stop, it did not seem that more than half an hour could have gone by, but it was already three o'clock.

All Margaret Simpson's eighth-grade students passed the exam with a good grade. The two highest marks were Gretchen's 96 and Marie's 89; but although Marie was certain that she'd written an excellent essay, Margaret said nothing to her about it until three days before commencement, when she asked Marie if she would consider reading it at the ceremony.

Commencement evening was warm and clear. The scent of the faded lilacs still lingered in the air as Marie walked up the hill to the school with Ned and Ellen. She was so excited about graduating that she could hardly concentrate on staying upright in her new high-heeled shoes, and she had trouble paying attention to Herman Fischner, who as president of the school board gave a short talk congratulating the graduates and wishing them well before handing out the diplomas.

There were some recitations, and then it was time for her to read her essay. Somewhat to her own surprise, she read calmly and distinctly, and although many of the people in the crowded schoolroom laughed at her comical descriptions of how on that first dreadful day of school she had leaped off the swing to run and be sick in the dead milkweeds and sweated over the difference between a C and a G, many villagers shook her hand afterward and said she had shown remarkable perseverance to stick it out and get her diploma. To Marie the diploma was doubly precious because it signified that, as well as an education, she had at last attained a certain respectability in her home town.

After the ceremony, Margaret invited the graduating students and their parents to her house for ice cream and cake. Marie stopped by briefly with the Baxters but felt uneasy, because she had not missed a work night since starting at the factory and she had promised Bill Kane that she would be in by ten. At nine forty-five she returned to her room at the Baxters and changed her clothes. Ten minutes later she was at her workbench in the finishing room.

At eleven, when the shift broke to eat, Marie gave Madame Raspberry a piece of the commencement cake from her dinner pail. Nodding approvingly, the big woman broke it neatly in two. One half she ate slowly and daintily, as she ate everything. The other she set aside to eat later at home.

When they finished eating Marie got out her diploma, which she'd brought to show her friend. Madame Raspberry reached out and took the heavy gilt-edged certificate. She looked at it with great curiosity, turning it sideways, checking the back, holding it up to the overhead light bulb to see if it was translucent. Suddenly an enlightened smile spread over her face. Picking up her leftover cake, she wrapped it neatly in the diploma and put it into her lunch bucket.

"Well, Marie," she said as Bill Kane appeared, "it getting to be that time, I guess."

Marie started to say something, but Madame was already heading toward her staining tank, majestic as a ship in full sail.

Marie smiled to herself and picked up her varnish brush. Graduation, she thought, was behind her.

Chapter Ten

For the first time since returning home, Marie had time to relax and enjoy village life. During the past school year she had been increasingly convinced that coming home had been the right decision; now, as she settled into a less hectic routine of working at the factory, gardening, and helping Ellen with the meals and housework, she became aware of a serenity and quiet satisfaction that she had not enjoyed since the years on Pond Number Four with Jigger Johnson. She began to fish again, going up Canada Mountain early in the morning for brook trout as she had once done with Father Boisvert. She and Madame Laframboise went strawberrying, and she spent a Saturday shopping in the Common, where she bought some new clothes.

The summer of 1919 was a flourishing time in general for Hell's Gate. Although the years immediately following the end of the war were not generally prosperous ones in Kingdom County or most of the rest of northern New England, everyone in the remote mountain village on Lake Memphremagog seemed well off, from Abie Benedict to Wheeler Mason, the slow-witted clean-up man on the mill floor. Besides acquiring the lucrative new contract for folding chairs, the factory had maintained throughout the war its large bread-and-butter agreements with the United States Seating Company and New England Life Insurance. Every month more orders for custom woodworking jobs for new banks, department stores, and municipal offices arrived than Herman Fischner's cabinetmakers could handle. Not only had the business not disintegrated under Abie's first year of management; it had grown considerably larger. And the same villagers who a year ago had predicted the downfall of the factory within a matter of months were now saying that it had been long past time for a change at the top.

"One year may not mean much," Ned told Ellen and Marie one noon a few days after commencement. "But things have never gone better at the factory. Abie seems to have the knack of making money without half trying, and as they used to say of his father, when the boss makes money, we all make money."

"He certainly seems to get along with the men," Ellen said.

Ned agreed. "He leaves them pretty much alone to do their work, the way Abraham always did. He leaves Herman and Durwood and me alone too. If I have any complaint against Abie these days, it's that he isn't around enough, though where he goes when he's away is a mystery. But I'll tell you, it's a hundred times better this way than having someone looking over your shoulder every fifteen minutes. That's the one thing I couldn't abide. Abie's still Abie, but most of his uneven edges got sanded off in the war and the few that are left a good woman would smooth out in short order—the way Ellen did mine, Marie. I used to be an awful rig before she took charge of me!"

Marie laughed, unable to imagine that Ned was ever any different from the Ned she knew. But she had to agree with his assessment of Abie, who on the following day invited everyone in the village to a Fourth of July picnic in the meadow on Kingdom Mountain, where he announced his intention to modernize Hell's Gate. He began implementing his plan immediately by directing the factory carpentry crew to build a spacious social hall beside the store, which contained a kitchen, a game room, a library with subscriptions to a dozen magazines, and a meeting room large enough to hold twice the entire population of the village. On the north side of the peninsula, behind the factory, he put in a large public dock and boathouse. He tore down the old railroad station where Marie and her family had eaten their first meal in the States and replaced it with a new one, with telegraph communications to the Common and the world beyond. He brought electricity into the homes of all of the villagers who wanted it (most did), and continued to maintain the park on Kingdom Mountain in excellent condition.

Nor was this all. Even before the social hall was completed he arranged for a series of Chautauqua lectures to be held there in the fall. On Friday evenings he ran a special shopping train to the Common. And in haying time, he called Ned Baxter into his office and revealed his most ambitious project of all, disclosing at the same time, to Ned's complete surprise, the purpose of his frequent trips away from the village.

"He intends," Ned told Ellen and Marie that noon in a voice that was simultaneously bemused and incredulous and grim, "to build a hotel up on the mountain."

"Which mountain?" Ellen said.

"Kingdom Mountain. He's going to put it up at the head of the big meadow, overlooking the village."

"I don't understand. What kind of hotel? Why does Hell's Gate need a hotel? Who on earth would stay there?"

Ned nodded grimly. "That's what I said. And he didn't even wait for me to finish before he told me. A resort hotel."

Ellen and Marie looked at Ned, still not quite comprehending.

"A resort hotel?"

"Yes. That's where he's been spending those long weekends you supposed he was off courting and I supposed he was in Montreal catting. Visiting resort hotels. To see how they work."

Ellen laughed incredulously. "Ned, however they work elsewhere, one couldn't possibly work here. Why there isn't even a road into—"

Ned held up his hand. "Not yet there isn't. That's coming too, no doubt, though he went so far as to tell me that the railroad might actually be a 'selling point,' as he put it. Oh, he'd thought of all the possible objections I could raise, raised most of them himself, in fact, before I had a chance. 'Don't worry, Uncle Ned,' he told me, 'I'm not proposing to put up a rival to the Mount Washington House—just a modest building of a hundred or so rooms but with all the outdoor and indoor activities anyone could want, from fishing to shuffleboard to golf."

"Golf?" Marie said. "Golf in Hell's Gate?"

"Golf is the least of it, my girl. Why, there's to be tennis, and excursions on the lake, and skiing and bobsledding in the wintertime, and nature walks in the summer, and I don't know what all. Horseback riding trails. He mentioned horseback riding trails, I believe, before I lost track."

Ned shook his head, as though to clear it. "Well, sir! I just sat there with my mouth wide open and Abie going on faster and faster, and every so often looking over his shoulder at that picture of his father and then looking away like a man coming out of the woods after dark who thinks something, maybe a big cat or a bear or something worse, is following him—except that Abie didn't look scared but had a sort of a smirk on his face, like the day I caught him jumping off the top of the bridge and took him to his father. Maybe if he'd gotten the tanning he deserved right then and there this wouldn't be happening, though I don't know about that either. He acted almost like a man possessed. And when he finally saw that nothing he said was going to make me jump up and turn handsprings over the idea he began to get mad.

" 'Abie,' I said, 'you've got to give me more than three seconds to get used to this proposal. Some of us thought you were off courting a wife all this time; this is quite a jolt, you know.'

"Then he laughed and said, 'Hell, Uncle Ned, I can get one of them'—I suppose he meant a wife—'I can get one of them anytime I want without leaving Hell's Gate.'

"I wanted to ask him why he didn't then, if that was the case, and let this other alone, but I knew better. By then I knew better than to ask him anything."

"My heavens!" Ellen said. "Abie's certainly well off, but I don't believe he's well off enough to undertake this venture. Where on earth is he ever going to come up with the capital to finance such a scheme? And who's going to do the work for him? It would take a crew of a hundred men, wouldn't it?

Ned stood up, leaving his meal untouched. "I'm damned if I know," he said, and went out to the garden.

It was the first time Marie had ever heard him swear.

Although the village disapproved of Abie's resort project at first, its curiosity was even greater than its disapproval as, early in August, the first architects began to arrive. By the time surveyors appeared, just a week later, most of Hell's Gate was resigned to the idea, and a number of natives, including Marie, had changed their minds and decided that it might very well be good for the village.

What pleased her most was the apparent transformation in Abie. Now he seemed to be everywhere at once, consulting the architects and engineers, consulting the Baxters—Did Ned think the larger suites should be paneled with bird's-eye maple or birch? How much domestic help did Ellen think they'd need in the laundry?—going across the bridge to Little Canada to line up a good pastry cook, making a dozen trips a day from his office to the hotel site on the mountain in a Buick touring car driven by Jim Wynne (whose wife refused to let him wear the chauffeur's uniform Abie ordered because she thought it was demeaning, though Jim confided to Ned that he would have liked to).

Unlike his father, who never seemed to hurry, Abie now

hurried all day long, swinging himself along on his crutch faster than most men could walk, always out in front of his engineers on the mountain. Once when the Buick's engine got wet and wouldn't start he hitched his entire way up the mountain, and Jim, accompanying him with some papers, had to trot to keep up.

Overnight Hell's Gate was changed from a sedate little village, as well-regulated as the clocks in the Big House, into a boom town. Freshly peeled spruce poles thirty-five feet long appeared beside the railroad track, and a crew of strangers strung electrical wires between them, since the factory dynamo could not begin to generate enough power to light both the village and the Canada Mountain View House, as Abie had decided to call the hotel. Steam shovels and huge bobbing cranes rolled into town on flatbed cars and were driven up the mountain and put to work the same day. At Abie's invitation, Walter Hagen spent a week as his guest in the Big House, refining the design of the eighteen-hole championship golf course to be laid out in the hanging meadow.

The construction foreman arrived, a dour Bostonian in hiking boots and a business suit, who looked as though he had never had a full day's recreation in his life, though he had built half a dozen other large resorts in his time, mostly in Colorado and Florida. He commuted to work each day from the Common, where he rented the smallest and cheapest room on the third floor of the hotel and shared a bathroom with two elderly railroad pensioners. Since he brought no crew with him, there was widespread speculation among the after-supper talkers on the store porch that Abie would hire help from the Common and surrounding villages. This was not his plan, however, and when the workmen began to appear on the mountain, first singly and in pairs, then in small groups of three or four or five, everyone was astonished to discover that they were Chinese who apparently had come directly from their homeland, since not one of them spoke a word of English.

They lived in tents near the construction site, and although it was hard for the villagers to tell for certain, few seemed to stay in Hell's Gate more than several weeks, but moved on as soon as they had a small stake and were replaced by newcomers. The Chinese minded their own business and worked hard from sunrise to dusk, seven days a week, for a quarter of the lowest wages paid at the factory (though like the factory workers they received their pay in yellow squares of Benedict Company scrip, which they traded for currency before departing for wherever they went). The phlegmatic foreman had worked with Chinese crews in the West and spoke their language fluently, and it was generally assumed that he was responsible for getting them into the country; but how he managed to do this was a complete and, to Early Kinneson and the men on the store porch, a maddening mystery, since they did not arrive by train or boat or on foot, unless they came in the dead of night over the mountains; they just appeared mornings on the worksite with shovels, already digging, as though, Early said, they had "dug their way up from Chiny and didn't have sense enough to stop for breakfast." One day there were twenty, the next twenty-three or twenty-four, a week later thirty-two: digging, lugging lumber, wheeling concrete, working quickly and efficiently under the foreman's directions.

By blueberry time, when Abie closed the factory to paint the town, giving each worker two weeks of paid vacation for the first time in the history of the business and paying the painting crew double-time, the Baxters were the only villagers who still expressed reservations about the Mountain House. Ned wondered aloud whether, now that "every office clerk who wanted one had an automobile and a two-week vacation to tour around the countryside in it," people would still want to spend a vacation in one spot, no matter how appealing, and Ellen still worried over how Abie would pay for the venture, speculating that Rachel must be using her own nest egg to finance most of it. (Abie had not involved Ellen in the bookkeeping for the hotel, though she handled all other fiscal business for the company.)

Marie, on the other hand, was increasingly enthusiastic about the Mountain House and took advantage of the general excitement to try to put matters between herself and Abie on a better footing by stopping at his office one morning to congratulate him. At first he acted unaccountably uneasy, as usual, but when she wished him good luck with the resort he seemed pleased and asked her to sit down.

"Marie," he said, "I'll tell you something. This is the first real idea of my own that I've had since taking over here. The social hall and other little improvements were fine, but this is a way to employ more people without expanding the factory anymore—which Ned is dead set against, for fear of diluting the quality, and probably rightly so. At the same time, it's an opportunity to diversify Hell's Gate's income." He glanced over his shoulder at the portrait of the Captain. "My father always said that change was all you could depend on—he never said anything about taxes because Hell's Gate has never had any, and I guess that death wasn't on his agenda either, or at least I never heard him acknowledge it—but since things are bound to change anyway, if I can control how they do, so much the better. Despite all of Uncle Ned's grumbling about the Mountain House, I have an idea that my father just might have approved of what I'm doing, for once."

Marie had her doubts about this, but she smiled encouragingly, relieved to hear Abie speak genially about his father and optimistically about his own plans. This was a different man, she thought, from the self-pitying, uncertain war victim she'd listened to on the day she'd arrived back in the village the previous November, and once again she felt the strange, powerful attraction that Abie had held for her since that first day she had seen him as a little girl just down from Canada, when he had mocked her father and then touched her hair.

"Marie, I'm delighted that you stopped in," Abie continued. "For weeks I've wanted to talk with you, to tell you what a good job you've done here at the factory, and how much I admire your accomplishments—going to school days, getting your diploma—God knows it can't have been easy for you; I'm sure I never could have done it. And that brings me to something that's been on my mind for some time."

He paused and, for the first time since she'd stepped into the office, lighted a cigarette. "In plainest terms, Marie, I'd like to be of some real assistance to you. I've been thinking about this a great deal recently. I know you weren't treated fairly years ago at the Big House. There's no point in rehearsing all that; but I won't feel right about what happened until you let me try to give you some of the help now that you needed then."

"Abie, what happened at the Big House wasn't your fault or your parents'. I was a foolish young girl, and I got myself into a predicament I didn't know how to get out of. As far as helping me goes, you've already helped me by letting me work here while I went to school. Now that I've got some education, I can go on and help myself."

"Fine. What would you most like to do—to be, if you will? Where would you go from here if you could go anyplace and do anything at all?"

Marie thought for a minute. "I'm not sure," she said. "It's something I haven't given much thought to yet. One thing that did cross my mind a few weeks ago was going on to take some formal nurse's training. Margaret Simpson told me that the government is always looking for nurses to send out west to Indian reservations and other interesting places. She encouraged me to look into it, and probably I will."

"You should," Abie said. "And as far as the cost of your training goes, don't let that be a consideration—that's a favor you can do for me, and for my mother. Recently she hasn't been too well, Marie. Even in Arizona the arthritis keeps her from getting out much. But she feels the same way I do about wanting to help in any way we can."

"I'm sorry that your mother isn't feeling well. I wrote to her in the spring, and I'll write again today. I'll think about your offer too, Abie. It's kind of you, and I appreciate it. Margaret says that there's a way the government can pay nurses to get their training if they agree to work for the Indians for at least two years afterward, and I've got some money of my own saved up so I doubt I'd need much help. But I'll make some inquiries right away and let you know by fall."

"You can't work it out any sooner?"

"Abie, I've been working things out, and working period, since the day I arrived back in Hell's Gate. I'm going to continue to work nights this summer, if you'll let me, but I want the days for myself. I want to weed Ned's garden. I want to help Ellen put up her preserves, and do some fishing, and read some books. When fall comes, and the leaves start to turn, I'll have an answer for you."

"All right," he said. "Just don't wait too long. I know you don't want to jump into anything, but don't hold off too long. Because sometimes that doesn't pay either."

Marie went away from this interview both relieved and puzzled. Abie seemed more at ease in her presence (he had not once looked at her in that suspicious, half-incredulous way she had observed during their earlier encounters); yet he still seemed to want her to leave Hell's Gate, and although she could not imagine why he cared one way or the other, she was quite sure that this was his principal motivation for offering to help her.

But as the days grew warmer and she fell into the pleasant midsummer routines of the village, she gave little thought to the future. It was a summer of clear blue days, one after another, with only enough rain to prevent a drought, and to Marie the evenings seemed longer and the mornings more promising than they had in years. Hell's Gate seemed lighter than she remembered, especially after supper when the reflected light from the lake continued to illuminate the village long after the sun had gone behind the mountains. Although she slept very little, rarely longer than from the time her shift ended until daybreak, she felt fresh and rested in a way she had once supposed she would never feel again. Her only disappointment was that Margaret Simpson spent the summer away from Hell's Gate, traveling in the western states—searching, she wrote half facetiously, for a cowboy husband.

When Margaret returned at the end of August, she surprised everyone by asking to be released from her teaching contract. On the afternoon of the day she arrived, as hopeful and unattached as ever, she had been invited to accept a position teaching at a new state normal school for training teachers opening that fall in the Common, and although they were disappointed to see her go, the school trustees of Hell's Gate did not want to stand in her way and honored her request.

"What about you, Marie?" Margaret asked the next afternoon in her kitchen, where Marie was helping her pack for the move. "What are your plans for the fall?"

"To tell you the truth, I still haven't given them much thought," Marie said. "I suppose it's time to sit down and do that. Abie's offered again to help me go on with my schooling, and that nurse's training you and I talked about last winter interests me some; but I haven't gotten around to doing anything about it yet. In one way, I'd like to. In another, I don't want to leave Hell's Gate."

"Why not?"

"Why not?"

Margaret smiled. "Why don't you want to leave Hell's Gate?"

"I'm tired of traveling around, I suppose."

"You're sure that's it?"

Marie shrugged. "Oh, I'd leave for the right opportunity. I just want to be certain it's what I want."

Margaret nodded. "I understand that. It's easy for me to leave. This isn't my home, and I've always been a mover anyway. A year here, two there, then somewhere else. I'll say one more thing, though, Marie. Then I'll keep quiet. Try not to become too dependent on Hell's Gate. Don't mistake me, it's a wonderful place, but I don't think it's going to stay this way forever. Don't pass up too many opportunities, I guess I'm saying—you can always come back after you finish your education. And one more thing. . . ."

Margaret stopped talking and began to laugh. "Marie," she said, "do what you think best! If I were really any damn good at this matter of giving advice, I'd advise myself how to net a husband. Until I do, don't pay any attention to a word I say. I talk too much!"

Marie did not think her friend talked too much, though she talked a great deal, and very rapidly, without appearing to need to stop for breath or to think. Ideas came easily to Margaret, by the dozens, one tumbling after another, and most of them made excellent sense. Yet Marie still held off deciding what to do about her career. It seemed ironical to her that she had acquired just enough education to need more before she could put it to any good use.

The days grew shorter, the nights longer and cooler. Here and there on the mountains patches of red and yellow began to appear.

To replace Margaret, the trustees hired an eighteen-year-old girl just out of the Common Academy, who taught for three days, got homesick, and went back to her parents' farm in Lord Hollow. Next a scholarly-looking young man with a year of normal school was appointed, but he didn't last as long as his predecessor. On his second day on the job he swatted Clayton Not Slayton with a ruler for reciting the first story in the *National Seventh Reader* backwards, and that afternoon the Kane boys lay in ambush for him behind the horse chestnut trees along the cemetery. As he went by, loaded down with books and papers, they jumped out and whipped him all the way down the hill and along the street to the new train station, where he sat nursing his bruised face until six o'clock, when the factory train left with him aboard.

This excitement took place on a Friday, and by the following morning it was the main topic of conversation in the village. That afternoon Marie went to look for butternuts on Kingdom

Mountain. Sunday was Ned Baxter's fiftieth birthday, and she wanted to make him a cake with butternut frosting. On her way back, partway down the street to her house, she met Stan Gregory, who flagged her down excitedly.

"Marie! I've been looking for you all afternoon. There's a special meeting at the schoolhouse tonight at eight o'clock. Can you come?"

She said yes, then went on to the Baxters with her sack of nuts. She wondered briefly what the meeting at school was about, but Abie was always calling village meetings to announce some new project. An hour later, when she walked into the schoolroom, she was surprised to find only Stan, Bill Kane, and Herman Fischner, the three trustees.

"Come up front and sit down, Marie," Stan said genially. "We want to talk to you about a problem."

Puzzled, Marie sat down at one of the small desks in the front row.

Stan grinned. "Well, Marie, it's no secret that we've had our troubles keeping a teacher here this term. They come, but they don't seem to want to stay for one reason or another."

"That's the God's truth," Bill Kane said. "Clayton and Slayton drive them right out before they get their valises unpacked. That college boy with the spectacles weren't here three days before they landed on him. They booted his educated behind all the way down the hill to the train."

Stan winked at Marie, but Herman Fischner impatiently rapped his knuckles on the desk where he was sitting. "Come," he said in his German accent. "Let's get down to business."

"All right," Stan said, still grinning. "This is why we asked you here, Marie. Last night Herm and I went to visit Margaret Simpson about this situation and asked her to recommend someone for the job. She thought a minute; then she said she'd recommend her best student. I said no student could manage the school, but she said there was one who could. She recommended you."

"Me?" Marie was astonished. The idea of teaching school

had never occurred to her. "You mean to fill in for a few days until you can find a permanent replacement?"

Bill Kane brought his hand down on his desk with a bang. "Fill in, hell," he roared. "We want you to take this Christly school in hand!"

"Yes, we select you," Herman Fischner said. "It's all settled. Fifty dollars a month salary. Also the teacher's house and garden plot. Also your stovewood for the winter. Do you accept?"

"Well?" Stan said. "What do you think, Marie? Can you put up with those young wildcats for a while?"

Marie's mind was made up. "Yes. On one condition."

Now the trustees were surprised.

"What's that?" Herman Fischner said suspiciously.

"My condition is that the pay be raised to sixty dollars a month. I make more than that at the factory right now, and so does everyone else who works there."

Bill Kane's face turned bright red. "By God, they do!" he shouted.

He brought his hand down so hard on the little desk that the ink bottle jumped out of its well and would have smashed on the floor if Marie hadn't reached over and caught it. Stan grinned and winked at her.

"By God, you make that much now!" Bill Kane roared. "But you don't get no house throwed in. You don't get a garden plot or no long vacations off."

"You forgot the stovewood for winter, Mr. Kane," Marie said. "I don't get that now either. But those are my terms. I won't teach in the school for less than I can earn in the factory."

"Then you won't teach in the school!" Bill Kane yelled at the top of his lungs.

Stan in the meantime continued to grin. He seemed to be equally delighted by Marie's condition and Bill Kane's reaction to it. "Bill," he said, "you say you won't accept Marie's terms. Do you want to take over the job yourself?"

"No!" Bill Kane shouted. "I wouldn't do that job for any amount of money."

Realizing what he had said, Bill got even redder and pounded the desk again in exasperation.

"Bill," Stan said, "Mr. Abie left for Portland last night just before Herm and I went to see Miss Simpson. The last thing he told us was he wanted an able teacher hired and ready to go by the time he got back or he'd step in and take over running the school himself. I don't think any of us, including Mr. Abie, want that."

"Well," Bill said, "when's he coming back?"

"Tomorrow night."

The three trustees sat looking at each other. Except for the crickets out in the schoolyard, the evening was very still.

"The woman has us over a barrel," Herman Fischner said glumly. "For heaven's sake, vote for her before we have to close the school."

Bill Kane looked at Marie. She looked back at him. "There's just one thing," he said slowly. "If Clayton and Slayton get out of the traces, I want you to knock them down and make sure they stay down. Then I'll be behind you one hundred percent."

Marie smiled and nodded. She shook hands with each of the trustees, and when she shook Bill Kane's hand he nodded at her good-naturedly and said, "One hundred percent!"

As soon as it got light the next morning, Marie hurried down the street to her new house. The hydrangea bush Margaret had planted in the front yard the previous spring had put out two puffy blossoms, which were just starting to turn pink for the fall. Marie could hardly wait to begin planting her own flowers.

She fumbled with the key. "Calm down," she said aloud. "Calm down here. It's only a house."

Although Margaret had been gone only a week, the hallway smelled shut up and unfamiliar, like some long-departed tenant's old carpeting, so she left the door open to air it out. She opened the windows in the parlor and dining room and in the three upstairs bedrooms. Marie had been inside the house numerous times, but it still seemed new and strange to her.

She spent the rest of the day cleaning and moving in. At noon Gertrude Fischner stopped in with a deep dish of German potato salad, which Marie ate standing at the kitchen counter and looking out across the backyard garden patch, over the spur track and down the bay. Ellen and Ned, who had been over twice already, brought in a picnic supper of cold cuts and pickles, sharp yellow cheese, coffee, and pie. It was one of the last warm evenings of the year, and they ate sitting out on the back stoop.

"Mr. and Mrs. Baxter, you've helped me a great deal," Marie said. "I'm grateful to you."

"It seemed pretty lonely around our house until you came," Ned said. "I guess you know you'll always have a home there."

He stood up and went down to the rear of the garden, where he stood looking across the bay in the dusk.

Ellen put her arm around Marie's shoulder and gave her a hug. "Our Ned always said he'd like to be a teacher, Marie. He was going to normal school nights and working days for his father at the factory when the war broke out." She paused. In a lower voice she said, "Ned had his father's patience, and he loved books. He would have been a fine teacher. Now you're going to be a teacher, and that makes Ned very proud. It makes me proud too, of course. But it means something very special to Ned."

"Ned Jr. would have been a wonderful teacher, Mrs. Baxter. I don't know about myself. I don't doubt I can do it passably, but to tell you the truth I'm afraid I lack the necessary patience to be really good at it."

"You'll be patient," Ellen said. "Sometimes you're impatient with yourself, Marie, but not with others. You'll be a fine teacher."

Ned walked back to the stoop. "It's starting to rain," he said.

"I felt a few drops down by the garden." He held out his hand. "There's another. Well, we can use it before winter. The brooks are low."

"Oh, it'll rain all right." Marie laughed. "I just finished washing all my windows a few minutes before you arrived; that's always a certain way to bring rain."

"We'd better get back and put our own windows down," Ellen said. "All the upstairs windows are wide open, and the wind's coming up."

The Baxters told Marie good night and walked home quickly to beat the rain. By the time Marie had hurried through the house shutting her windows it was pouring, and the wind was blowing hard.

She heated a tub of water on the kitchen stove and took a stand-up bath. She laid out her school clothes for the following morning and blew out the lamp on the table. Then for a while she lay in bed listening to the rain.

After the excitement of the day, she felt somewhat let down. The rain came harder, reminding her of the rainy night—was it only last fall?—she had walked away from the sanatorium and searched for Philbrook Jamieson's cross in the cemetery. She thought of her father building the fire in the tree in the driving rain, and of how it had rained the night she lost her baby.

Eventually she fell asleep and dreamed that she was a little girl again, walking south with her parents in the rain toward the dark line on the horizon, which moved steadily ahead as they moved. She knew that they would turn and head back to the north, and the line would still be there, and again she would be trapped in the flat, treeless no-man's-land between Canada and the States. But instead she dreamed next that she was in the cattle car, stopped between the two lines. Someone was pounding on the door, trying to get in and send her back, and she was crying because she knew there was no longer a way she could get back.

She woke gasping for breath and for a moment thought she

was in the cattle car with her parents. Then she couldn't remember where she was, until the rain dripping off the eaves reminded her that it had been raining when she went to bed, and she knew she was in her own house, and someone was knocking on the front door.

He was bareheaded and his yellow hair was damp and shone in her lantern.

She smiled sleepily. "Hello, Abie. I've got some good news for you."

"I've got some news for you," he said angrily. "I want you out of this house and out of this town by tomorrow morning."

"Abie!" She was astonished, particularly since she had assumed he might have helped arrange the teaching job for her. "What are you talking about? I've just taken over the school. I can't leave now."

"You can do what I tell you to do, goddamn it. You don't run this town. Against all my better judgment I allowed myself to feel sorry for you. I gave you a job at my factory, I let you attend my school and live here in my town, where you've never caused anything but trouble. You came between me and my parents, you deliberately got yourself pregnant in order to insinuate yourself further into the family, for years you lied to my father about—"

"Abie, I never lied to your father in my life. What are you talking about?"

"You know exactly what I'm talking about, Marie Blythe. And you know why I don't want you here."

"Abie, I don't."

"I don't believe you. I don't believe you for one minute. But I'll give you the benefit of one last doubt and make my offer once more. I will make it once more and not again. So think carefully. If you'll agree to leave this town and never come back here—not in a year or two years or ten years, not ever— I'll stake you to any reasonable education or training you want, anywhere you want it."

"Abie, this is what I want, at least for the time being. To stay here in Hell's Gate and teach school. I don't want to make trouble for you, and no matter what you think I never have wanted to make trouble for you. But I don't intend to be sent down the road from a job I haven't even begun yet, just because of some terrible misunderstanding. You don't manage the school; the trustees do. They're the ones who hired me, and they're the only ones who can fire me. That's how your father set it up, and that's the way it still is."

"Don't you mention my father to me! My father doesn't run Hell's Gate any longer, and you aren't going to find me so easy to lie to. I may not manage the school, but I still own this village. This is my house, and I've ordered you out of it by morning. What you do then is up to you, but I advise you strongly to accept my offer."

"Abie, I don't want to do this. But if you put me off these premises, I'll write to your mother."

He stared at her, speechless with anger. Supporting himself with his right hand on the porch railing, he lifted his crutch, as though he might strike her; but before he could bring it down he slipped, fell on the steps, and tumbled down them into the hydrangea bush. Marie was horrified and started out onto the porch to help him. But instantly he was up, and without another word he headed fast off up the street.

She stood on the porch, trying to collect herself. She could not have been any more upset if he had actually struck her with the crutch, and her first clear thought was that it might have been better if he had; at least that way the trouble might have been resolved one way or the other. What did Abie mean by accusing her of lying to his father? Why was he so desperate to cajole or threaten or bribe her into leaving the village?

Someone was coming along the street. It was Stan Gregory, returning from the roundhouse, after bringing Abie back up from the Common. Stan, she realized, must have told him about the trustees' meeting the previous night.

Marie stepped back inside and shut the door. She walked into the kitchen and checked the clock. It was just two, but she knew there was no chance that she would get back to sleep that night, so she built a small fire in the stove, put on her teakettle, and sat down at the table to wait for the water to boil.

Whatever his reasons, Abie Benedict not only hated her as much as ever but also feared her, as he had once hated and feared his father.

Chapter Eleven

From the first morning, when she walked into her classroom to discover Clayton and Slayton preparing a lesson on human anatomy, accompanied by crude but unmistakable illustrations on the chalkboard, went briskly to the front of the room, and without breaking stride slapped them both so hard Heide Fischner heard the resounding smacks from the far side of the playground, Marie enjoyed teaching as much as any job she'd ever had. ("Who doesn't, who likes to talk?" she told Margaret a few weeks later, though in fact she did a great deal more listening than talking, hearing as many as sixty-five different recitations a day from her classes.)

Although she quickly realized that she would never be the gifted teacher Margaret was, she took a shrewd piece of advice from her ex-teacher, which was simply to do the job her own way, without comparing herself with anyone else.

At the same time that she spoke to Margaret about her teaching, she told her about the confrontation with Abie. "Something's terribly wrong," Marie said. "The trouble is, I don't have any idea what it is. He keeps saying he wants to help me advance myself, but I don't think that's really what he wants. For some reason, Abie just can't stand to have me in Hell's Gate."

"He hasn't ever entirely grown up," Margaret said. "It's a tragedy that such a bright young man seems so determined to spoil things for himself and everyone he comes into contact with—as though he's still spiting his father by hurting himself. But I don't see any way he can hurt you, Marie, if you're determined not to let him."

"I don't know, Margaret. I'm not afraid of him, exactly, but he's never been able to tolerate being crossed. As a boy he'd hold a grudge longer than anyone I've ever known and do almost anything to get even—remember how I told you about his cutting himself deliberately in order to get out of working at the factory? And that time he knocked my sled into the quarry; to this day I believe he was trying to kill me. I'm just glad he's got the Mountain House to occupy himself with. I hope he stays so busy with it he doesn't have time to think about me." She smiled. "Not that I have all that much time to think about him. I never knew teaching kept a person so busy!"

As the year progressed, week succeeding week so rapidly that Marie had little time to think of anything but her work, she became increasingly independent in her teaching, gaining confidence every day and relying more and more on her own intuition and ideas. Sometimes to stimulate interest in a book, she would read a chapter or two out loud, not just on Friday afternoon, which like Margaret she always set aside for reading to the class, but several times a week, especially on warm fall days when she knew time was dragging for her students. Partly she did this for her own delight, since she loved to read aloud the stories Rachel Benedict had read to her as a girl: *Great Expectations, Pride and Prejudice, Ivanhoe.* With the boys, *Tom Brown's School Days* and *The Hoósier Schoolboy* quickly became favorites; all the girls wanted her to read *Little Women.*

One winter afternoon after reading aloud Charles Dudley Warner's essay "A-Hunting of the Deer," Marie told her students how she had walked down a deer and killed it. Every day after that the children asked her to tell them a story, and she began using the last fifteen minutes of the day to recount tales of her experiences cooking for the great lumber drives, and about the bright blue wagons of the Mary Anne. She told how she had picked potatoes with Canadian Indians in the sandy potato fields of Aroostook County, told fortunes at fairs, watched for forest fires from the tower above Pond Number Four, and nursed tuberculosis patients and soldiers at the sanatorium.

Encouraged by her success with the reading and storytelling innovations, she decided that the time had come to make a sharp departure from a classroom tradition prevalent not only in Hell's Gate but in rural schools throughout the country. One morning in March she announced to her students that boys and girls would no longer use separate doors and sit on separate sides of the aisles. "After recess, come back in either door you want," she said, "and sit on either side of the aisle, as long as you sit near pupils in your own class."

She was more amused than surprised when, a few minutes later, the boys came in their door, the girls theirs, and the only two students to change their seats were Clayton and Slayton. The next day, though, two more boys moved over to the girls' side, and Heide Fischner, who was as bold as she was small, took her slate and books over and sat down beside Jimmy Moon.

On the following morning Heide came to school with a curt note from her father informing Marie that her presence was requested at a trustees' meeting that evening. After handing Marie the note, Heide returned to her old seat on the girls' side of the room. Marie had half expected this response.

"Listen here," Herman Fischner said to her without preliminaries. "We don't want our boys and girls mixed in together. We don't want them courting in school. Put them back where they belong."

"You listen to me, Herman Fischner. Those boys and girls are going to grow up to be men and women. They're going to be working together and living together. They need to learn how to do that, and now isn't too soon to start."

"Don't you preach to us!" Bill Kane shouted. "You work for us, girlie, not the other way around."

"Mr. Kane, when I worked for you nights at the factory, did I ever once tell you how to run the finishing room?"

"No, and it's a damn good thing you didn't. I'd have sent you down the road on the spot."

"Then why are you trying to tell me how to run my classroom?"

"That's different."

"I don't see how. Do you want that boy who hightailed it back to the normal school because he was scared of Clayton and Slayton to come back and teach for you?"

"You know we don't want him," Herman Fischner said. "Don't try to confuse us. You still work for this man, just the way you did at the factory. And for me. And for Stanwood. You do what we say."

"Whom do you work for, Herman Fischner?"

"Young Mr. Abie. You know that."

"Does he come into the cabinet room and tell you where he wants your men to sit while they do their job?"

"That's different."

Marie was tempted to quit her job on the spot. Ten years ago she probably would have. Now, though, she had another idea.

"If you want the boys and girls to do things separately, why is there just one privy?"

None of the three trustees had a ready answer.

"I want a separate privy for the girls," Marie said. "Some of them are so embarrassed to have to go to the toilet in the common privy they don't go at all until they get home."

"How do you know?" Bill Kane said.

"Because they've told me so. Now I'll make a deal with you. I won't ask you to build the second privy. Just furnish the lumber and nails and the lime. The girls and I will build it ourselves."

"Fair enough!" Bill Kane shouted, as Marie had suspected he would. "I'm behind you one hundred percent."

Herman nodded slowly. "All right," he said. "We'll supply the lumber and nails and lime. How soon do you want them?"

"This Saturday morning by eight o'clock."

On Saturday morning Marie and six of the oldest girls arrived at the school early. The lumber and other materials had been sent up the day before. She had borrowed some tools from Ned Baxter, and, working that Saturday and the next, she and her students completed the small building. Like the cabin she'd helped Jigger build on Pond Number Four, it was crude but tight. It had a sharply sloping roof shingled with long cedar shakes and a traditional half-moon window. It sat discreetly off on the southwest side of the school in a little brake of cedar trees out of sight of the boys' privy, and when it was finished Ned Baxter came up with two gallons of pale yellow paint and painted it.

"Well, Uncle Ned," Marie said proudly. "Is that front wall plumb?"

Ned looked at the privy. He shut first one eye, then the other, squinting appraisingly.

"Marie," he said with the trace of a smile, "she's plumb and a little besides, for good measure."

"Why don't you ever do anything for us boys, Miss Marie?" Jimmy Moon said the following Monday morning. He added teasingly, "We know you like the girls better anyway."

Marie smiled, partly because she suspected herself of showing favoritism at times to the boys. She thought a minute. Spring was coming, and a few days ago she had seen Jimmy and his older brother playing catch in front of their house. She had stopped to play briefly and surprised them with her ability to throw and catch a baseball.

"I'll tell you what, Jimmy. When you come back from dinner today, bring your ball and bat. We'll have a game of baseball."

Not ten minutes of the noon hour had gone by before the boy appeared in front of Marie's desk with a raveling old ball wound with black tape and a short bat his father had turned out from a piece of white ash on his lathe at the factory. From then on Marie played ball with her students at every recess. To Bill Kane's irritation, both boys and girls played, not only during the school day but often in the evenings after supper. On the first Saturday in May they played the grade school in the Common and won 21–1 with Clayton pitching and Slayton catching and Marie playing first base, where her long reach was a great advantage. Clayton, who had been throwing rocks and other hard or sharp objects at his brother for years, pitched a two-hitter.

It occurred to Marie that her students should have some music in their school. Music had been an important part of her childhood, but except for the few French Canadians left across the bridge, who still kept mainly to themselves, and the four or five Germans who still gathered to play in the silver cornet band on Sunday evenings in the summer, no one in Hell's Gate seemed to spend much time singing or dancing or playing an instrument. Partly this lack of interest in music was because Hell's Gate did not have a church of its own. As far as Marie knew, except for the unused grand piano at the Big House, the only piano in town belonged to the Fischners.

"Where can I get a cheap secondhand piano for the school, Uncle Ned?" she said, a few days after the victory over the Common grade school.

She was eating Sunday dinner with the Baxters, and as usual they had been talking about the changes that were bound to come to Hell's Gate with the Mountain House, now scheduled to be completed early that fall. (Abie had begun the excavation the previous fall, and already the earth movers and cranes were working again on the mountain, where he was now spending nearly all his time.)

"Ask Abie for one," Ned said. "I'm sure he can come up with a couple of hundred for a piano. He's already spent who knows how many times that up on the mountain."

"I'd rather not," Marie said slowly.

Ned shrugged. "See Harlan Smith then," he said. "The auctioneer at the Common Commission Sales; if he doesn't have a piano on hand, he'll no doubt know where you can find one. Abie'd probably just say he'd do it and then forget anyway."

"All right, boys, here we go, what are you going to give for her? This is a first-calf heifer out of the Walter Kittredge herd up to Lord Hollow, due to come in this month. She's registered; the papers come with her. She's from one of the best milking herds in Kingdom County, not to mention Vermont. Who'll start it off at seventy-five dollars? Seventy-five, eighty, seventy-five, boys, seventy-five dollars in gold for Spring Blossom, sired by Gallant Charging Arthur . . ."

It was the second Saturday in May, and Marie was sitting in the rickety unpainted grandstand in the depths of the Commission Sales barn in Kingdom Common, watching Harlan Smith sell cattle. The day before she had read her pupils the story of the twelve labors of Hercules, and now, as she looked around the dim run-down barn, it occurred to her that the Augean stables Hercules flushed out by diverting two rivers must have been immaculate by contrast. The aisle between the stanchions where the cows stood waiting to be auctioned, the pens where calves were packed together in a blatting mass, the center ring where Harlan Smith stood, the walls themselves—all were covered with a thick layer of manure dry enough to burn like wood chips. The windows were obscured by decades of cobwebs. Single weak bulbs on strings spaced unevenly along the fly-specked ceiling provided all the light there was. Yet the auctioneer was dressed neatly in a clean white shirt and tie, a bottle-green sport jacket, sharply pressed dress slacks, and handstitched western boots polished to a glowing ruddy copper.

Harlan Smith was a big man in his middle forties. He had thick brown hair slicked down with tonic and parted in the middle. His eyes were blue and sharp. He talked faster than any man Marie had ever heard, and his voice sounded like gravel sliding out of the back of a wagon bed. Helping him was a tiny man named Jehoshaphat Kinneson, Early's cousin, who drove the cows into and out of the ring through a gate in the high board walls. While the auctioneer raised the bids, his ringman pointed to the bidders with a red cattle cane and bobbed up and down in rhythm with Harlan's singsong gravelly voice like an orchestra leader with his baton. Occasionally Jehoshaphat repeated a bid in a gobbling imitation of the auctioneer's voice.

When the cows had all been sold, Jehoshaphat brought in a small horse named Applejack, which Harlan Smith claimed had formerly performed in a traveling circus. According to the auctioneer the circus had failed and Applejack had been sold into bondage to slave out his life in a granite quarry, from which he had nobly rescued him. It was a good story, and a pretty horse, the color of old cider, with one milky eye. At Harlan's command, it put its foot on an upended nail keg, counted to five, and bowed to the grandstand.

"Who'll start it off with thirty dollars, boys? Thirty, twenty-five, thirty dollars for Applejack the circus pony. Gentle enough for the little woman at home to ride, tame enough for the kids, smart as a whip. Count to five, Applejack, one, two, three, four, five."

"Can he pull, Smitty?" a bulky man beside Marie said. Except to open his mouth about a quarter of an inch, he did not move another muscle as he spoke.

"What do you suppose he was doing in that granite pit?" Harlan said sarcastically. "Of course he can pull. Why, he's a pulling fool, Dale. He'll win you a blue ribbon to the fair every Christly time. You can hitch Applejack to a maple tree and tell him to pull and he'll dig a hole two feet deep in the ground."

"That horse appears to be blind in one eye," the man named Dale said. This time he did not seem to open his mouth at all. Sitting still as a statue, he said, "Can he see out of that near eye?"

"I don't know of a reason in the world why he can't," the auctioneer said, smiling as though he pitied anyone who would ask such an absurd question. "Who'll start it off with twenty-five dollars? Twenty-five, twenty, fifteen, twenty dollars to save Applejack from the glue factory."

No one bid.

In a louder, irritated voice, Harlan said, "By the Jesus now, gentlemen. This horse will roll for New Hampshire and somebody's dog food tonight if you don't make an offer, and I'm not fooling. Who'll bid ten dollars? This is your last chance. Ten dollars. The truck goes down the line tonight. Who'll bid ten dollars to save this little circus star?"

A fly landed on Marie's nose; she raised her hand and swatted it away.

"Sold for ten dollars to the schoolteacher from Hell's Gate!" Harlan roared.

"I didn't bid on that horse," Marie said.

"Any motion of the hand or head's a bid, schoolteacher. You just bought yourself an ex-circus pony. Take him out, Hosh."

Gobbling like a turkey pullet, Jehoshaphat led the horse out of the ring. Marie stared after them until horse and man disappeared in the dusky nether regions of the barn. She wondered what on earth she'd do with a half-blind horse in Hell's Gate village, while in quick succession the auctioneer sold two dozen wooden sap buckets, a shoebox containing thirty or so metal spiles for tapping maple trees, a crate of one-quart Ball canning jars, a sackful of baby clothes, and a frayed harness for a working horse.

Next Jehoshaphat brought in two gray geese tied up in feed sacks with just their heads sticking out. The geese were twisting their necks in his hands and hissing like two big angry snakes as he dragged them along. Some of the men in the crowd were laughing and giving Harlan's helper facetious advice.

"Here's a pair of Toulouse geese, gentlemen," Harlan said. "Four dollars will buy you the both of them. They'll guard your dooryard when the tax lister comes around; they'll protect your wives and children whilst you're attending the commission sale. It's a mated pair now, boys. You can set the goose this summer and get rich selling young geese. There's money in geese, big money. Who's got four dollars in silver for a brace of watch-geese? Four, five, six . . ."

"Four dollars, five, six," Jehoshaphat gobbled, bobbing like a conductor.

"Fifty cents apiece, one dollar for the pair," a man in the front row said.

"For that I'll keep them myself till Thanksgiving," Harlan said angrily. "These geese are worth twice that just for watchdogs. Shut the gate, Hosh."

Jehoshaphat closed the gate to the wooden ring. Harlan Smith winked at the crowd, then bent down and deftly untied the baling twine around the mouth of each sack.

Instantly the geese burst out and started for Jehoshaphat at a dead run. Gobbling like a turkey pursued by a fox, the little man began to run around the ring. The hissing geese ran close behind him, their necks stretched out flat along the sawdust, their big orange bills snapping at his heels and ankles.

"Five dollars, six, eight, ten," Harlan called out as the laughing men in the grandstand bid higher and higher.

Jehoshaphat tried to clamber up the side of the ring. He lost his hold and fell back and the geese flailed his head and shoulders with their powerful wings.

"Twelve dollars, thirteen," Harlan called out.

Marie had seen enough. She jumped down off the grandstand and vaulted into the ring. As the geese raced by in hot pursuit of Jehoshaphat, now on his feet and running again, she grabbed first one and then the other and flung them flapping and honking over the high board walls. "You ought to be ashamed of yourself," she said to Harlan.

She walked across the ring to the gate, opened it, and went out to find her pony. Behind her the grandstand was still. So for the first time that afternoon was the big auctioneer. Then Marie heard him say, as though both surprised and impressed, "Well, I'll be goddamned!"

Applejack was tethered to a ring in the wall by the door. In the late-afternoon sunlight he was exactly the color of hard cider. He was between the size of a large pony and a small workhorse and weighed about eight hundred pounds. His right eye was a milky blue, and when she passed her hand by it he didn't blink. She moved around to the horse's good eye and stroked his smooth muzzle. When he lifted his head, she blew lightly into his nostrils to get acquainted, a trick Jigger Johnson had taught her.

"Hello, Applejack," she said.

Jehoshaphat appeared from the dark interior of the barn. Stepping shyly into the shaft of sunlight, he blinked and moved his hand in front of his face as though to make a path through the dancing dust motes. "Thank you, missus," he said.

"Jehoshaphat, how old is this horse, do you know? He's getting gray around the muzzle."

The small man shrugged. "Maybe fifteen, sixteen."

"Well, that's all right. I'm glad I bought him."

She went on conversing about the horse as she unclasped her pocketbook. But when she got out ten dollars in yellow scrip, Harlan Smith appeared.

"I'll take that," he said. "I'm the clerk of these works." He glared at her. "What do you mean by busting up my auction, schoolteacher?"

Marie looked Harlan Smith squarely in the face. "My name is Marie Blythe, mister."

"I know who you be," he growled in his deep grating voice.

"Why don't you try calling me by my name, then? My pupils don't call me teacher."

"Well, I ain't one of your pupils. What did you come in here for anyway? I'm not sure this is a respectable place for a schoolteacher. Breeding of cattle and horses and every other kind of creature goes on here all the time. Did you ever see a big stud woods horse breed a mare? It would send you back to your schoolhouse with quite an education, I believe."

"I'm not sure it's a respectable place period," Marie said. "I came here because Ned Baxter told me you might be able to help me find a piano. Is that right?"

Harlan Smith smiled sarcastically. He swept his hand back toward the interior of the barn. Three feet behind him the sunlight was snuffed out completely, as though by the odor of old manure.

"Does this look like a piano store?" he said.

"No," Marie admitted. "It doesn't at that. So I'll just take the horse I didn't know I'd bought and see if Stan Gregory will let me put him on the train and take him home."

"You hold your water a minute," Harlan said, to the amusement of several men who had stopped on their way out to listen. "I said this weren't a piano store. I never said I couldn't find you a piano. How much would such an instrument be worth to you?"

"Not too much. I was thinking about paying twenty or twenty-five dollars."

"That's too much," he snapped. "I know where I can get you a pretty good one for fifteen."

Marie grinned. Despite herself she was beginning to be amused by this bluff man with the bullying voice. "Make up your mind, mister. If you can get me a piano, say so. I've still got groceries to buy and a train to catch and a horse to get home."

"You wait a few days. I'll see what I can do about that piano," he said grimly, as though making a threat. "And you leave that horse here. I'll get him to Hell's Gate for you."

She looked at him. "All right," she said. "Now I want to ask you something. How did you know who I was?"

Harlan laughed in a self-satisfied way. "I know everybody in Kingdom County. Besides, I see you playing ball with your kids over to the Academy last week. I'll tell you something, schoolteacher. You'd hit better if you kept your back elbow up higher." He turned suddenly to his assistant, who was hanging on every word he uttered. "Ain't that right now, Hosh?"

Jehoshaphat nodded vigorously, and the men nearby

laughed and went outside. Marie patted Applejack and went across the street to do her shopping.

She wasn't at all certain that she'd see either the horse or Harlan Smith again. But in case the auctioneer did decide to deliver Applejack she whitewashed the inside walls and ceiling of the shed behind her house where she'd been keeping her gardening tools. She borrowed a wheelbarrow from Ned Baxter and brought some bedding sawdust over from the sawmill and bought some loose hay and a bag of grain from Pamphille Bonaventure, who was now head of the woods crew.

The following Wednesday after supper, when Marie was transplanting her tomato plants from the house to the garden, she glanced up at the factory train returning from its evening run. She waved to Stan Gregory, who waved back and grinned. With his gloved hand shut and his thumb pointing backwards, he made a gesture toward the rear of the train. Harlan and Jehoshaphat were standing in the open doorway of a Canadian Pacific boxcar between the second of the two Benedict passenger coaches and the caboose. Harlan frowned out at her and lifted one hand to about belt level, as though he resented having to wave. Jehoshaphat grinned. Behind them, inside the boxcar, Marie glimpsed Applejack and something bulky and dark that she thought might be her piano.

"Get a wagon, schoolteacher," the auctioneer said when she met them at the station platform.

By the time Marie returned with Ned Baxter, who helped Harlan hitch Applejack to an empty lumber wagon in the factory yard, three or four of the village men had rolled the piano down two slanted planks from the boxcar to the platform. As they maneuvered it onto the wagon bed, Marie examined it closely. It was the sorriest-looking piano she had ever seen. Most of the ivories were missing. One pedal had been snapped off. The top was gone, and there was a Rhode Island Red chicken sitting on a nest of straw in its innards.

Harlan fastened the piano to the sides of the wagon with haywire. He lifted out the hen, nest and all, and put it in a pasteboard box, which he handed to Marie as though she had extorted it from him by duress. He crooked his finger at Jehoshaphat. "Come here, little man."

"Here I come now, Smitty, here I come," Jehoshaphat gobbled as he climbed up into the wagon.

Harlan reached down and lifted up his assistant under the arms like a small child and deposited him inside the piano, where the chicken had been nesting. He handed him Applejack's reins and got down out of the wagon. He picked up the slack in one of the reins. "You stay put," he told Jehoshaphat. Then he slapped the line hard down on the horse's rump.

The wagon, with the piano wired onto its bed and Jehoshaphat standing inside it proudly holding the reins, started along the street. Jehoshaphat jabbered away happily, pretending to drive, though in fact Harlan walked beside Applejack and guided him by the bridle. Marie walked alongside the wagon. As the cavalcade progressed, other villagers joined in and still others stood in their yards to watch it pass.

The greenish gravel in the street crunched under the wheels as the wagon moved briskly along. The stout little horse had no trouble on the long level stretch between the houses. When he reached the foot of the hill going up to the school and the Big House, he leaned into the harness and plodded steadily upward. He was a strong horse, accustomed to pulling heavy loads of granite, and he did not run into any difficulty until he reached the water-bar in the road just below the cemetery.

Water-bars were commonplace throughout Kingdom County in horse-and-wagon days. They consisted of trenches three or four inches wide and two or three inches deep running at a slight slant across the steeper inclines of unpaved roads. Their purpose was to channel excess runoff water from snowbanks or hard rains from the road into the ditch. Usually they were tiled or bricked on the bottom so that they didn't wash out themselves. A wagon wheel could become lodged in a water-bar, but this happened only infrequently, since seasoned country dray horses automatically quickened their pace as they passed over one.

Applejack, however, was not a dray horse, and Harlan Smith was too busy addressing the crowd, which now numbered about twenty, to notice the trench until it was too late. He and the horse stumbled at the same instant. The wagon gave a lurch. The haywire snapped like rotten string, and out of the rear of the wagon rolled the piano, hitting the road with a terrific crescendo which signaled not the end but the beginning of what everyone agreed must have been the most remarkable performance it ever gave.

The instrument began rolling down the hill at a stately, unhurried pace. One of its casters had broken off when it landed, so it wobbled from side to side, but its weight kept it going in a fairly straight line for some distance. Despite the wild tales of the runaway piano that went round the village afterward, there was ample time for everyone to get out of the way, and no one was really in any danger of being hurt—no one, that is, but Jehoshaphat Kinneson, who was still crouching in its interior, as helpless, as Harlan said later, as "Jonas in the whale."

"Bail out! Jump, Hosh, jump!" the auctioneer shouted as the piano began to pick up speed.

But Jehoshaphat had frozen at the throttle. He could no more jump than stop the strange conveyance in which he rode, which by this time was rolling along at a fast clip. Abruptly and for no apparent reason it swung in toward the cemetery gates. Just before it entered the graveyard, Clayton Not Slayton leaped to its side and grasped one of the wooden handles on its back; while he couldn't slow it down, by sheer bull strength he was able to guide it back onto the road.

Not to be outdone by his brother, Slayton Not Clayton rushed to the keyboard side. Together, trotting like high-stepping harness racers to keep their feet out from under the wheels, the Kane boys proceeded down School Hill beside the hurtling piano, now swerving right, now left. It was their great moment of glory, and neither would have let go for anything.

"Give us a little of 'Take Me out to the Ball Game,' Hosh," Harlan shouted as he ran down the hill after the piano in the midst of the laughing, cheering crowd.

The piano rolled faster. Clayton's legs pumped hard; Slayton's legs pumped like a sprinter's. Marie was never prouder of the dedication to music of any of her pupils, even when Heide Fischner won a full music scholarship to the University of Vermont a few years later. In the end, though, the rescue attempt proved too much for them. At the foot of the hill the piano made a little uncanny sidewise jump, leaped the ditch, plowed through the grove of poplar trees where a year ago the Kane boys had waited in ambush for Marie, and plunged into the lake, where it foundered on its side just long enough for Harlan to pull out his ringman before it sank out of sight.

Sputtering and coughing, Jehoshaphat looked up at the auctioneer. "Smitty," he said when he finally got his breath, "promise me right now we'll never move no more pianos."

On the mountains above the village the maples budded out, and the mountainsides turned slowly red, then light gold, and then green. In the spring of 1920 the villagers were more aware of the progress of the new season as it climbed up the mountains (one hundred feet a day, the Hell's Gate saying went) because they spent much of their time looking upward, toward the site of Abie's grand hotel.

"We've needed change and new blood around here for years," Early Kinneson told Marie one soft evening when the June bugs were batting against the screen door of the company store.

She was on her way to an end-of-the-year meeting with the school trustees and had hurried over to pick up a box of new pen points, but she stayed long enough to tell the tall storekeeper that for once she agreed with him.

The resort seemed to bring to the village the kind of vitality Marie remembered from the early days, when the Captain's presence had been felt everywhere (as, after his death, his absence had been a nearly palpable force) and his own remarkable vitality had been transmitted to everything he touched.

Although she arrived at ten of eight, Bill Kane, Stan Gregory, and Herman Fischner were already at the school. They looked sober, and she wondered if she'd mistaken the time of the meeting and come late, but Herman shook his head. "No, no," he said. "You're early."

Marie looked at him. "Would you like me to come back a little later?"

Herman glanced at Stan. "No," Stan said. "Sit down, Marie."

Marie sat down. Herman and Stan continued to look at each other; obviously each one was waiting for the other to begin.

Finally Herman cleared his throat. "Marie, you've done a good job for us this year. We want—to thank you."

"Well, I've enjoyed it," she said. "I won't say it's all been easy, and now that the year's nearly over I realize how little I've really done compared with what I hoped to accomplish. But next year I should do better."

The three trustees looked at each other. Bill Kane's face was beet-red, and he seemed both angry and frustrated.

"All right," Herman said. "I'll tell her." For the first time he looked at Marie. "I don't like to be the one to say this, but someone has to. Yesterday we found out that according to state law a Vermont teacher has to have one year of normal school, or be enrolled in a normal school program, in order to earn a temporary teaching certificate."

"What does that mean?" Marie said.

"Goddamn it, I'll tell you what it means," Bill Kane said, as angry as she had ever seen him. "It means the Christly state has waltzed in here and said we have to send you down the road."

"Whose school is this? Yours· or the state's?"

"It's not that simple, Marie," Herman said. "I wish it were. You see, the state pays part of your salary. Well, that we could get around. But the state certifies the school as well as the teacher. If the teacher isn't certified, neither is the school. Then the diplomas mean nothing: the children can't take the eighth-grade examinations, or go on to high school, or anything."

"This doesn't make any sense at all," Marie said angrily. "A few months ago you asked me to take this school in hand, and I did. I established good order where there was no order. More than that. If I didn't know enough about a subject to teach it, I got a book and learned what I needed to know. You've said you're satisfied with my work. The parents of my pupils are satisfied. Everyone's satisfied but the state. All right. Who's the state? How did you find out about this? Who told you? I'll see them."

"Mr. Abie told us," Herman said. "The state told him. You'll have to see Abie."

"Why isn't he here to explain this then?"

Herman shrugged. "He's in Portland."

"He should be here," Bill Kane said angrily. "I guess he wants us to do his dirty work for him. All he did was to give us the letter from Montpelier."

Herman handed an official-looking sheet of paper to Marie, who read it slowly. It was addressed to Abraham Benedict, and it said exactly what Herman had told her. She was so angry that her hands shook and the letter trembled in her hands.

"Maybe you should go see Abie when he gets back from Portland," Herman said. "Maybe he can find some way to help you."

"Maybe," Marie said, standing up. "But I doubt it."

The following afternoon after school Marie went directly to Abie's office with the letter from the State Education Department. He was looking at some drawings of the Mountain House when she arrived, and without glancing up he waved her toward the chair across from his desk.

"No, thanks," she said. "This isn't a social visit, as you very well know." She slapped the letter down on top of the drawings. "Why didn't you tell me about this when I was hired?"

"I didn't know," he said, after looking at the letter. "If I'd known, I would have told you. Calm down, Marie. There are

always ways around these bureaucratic regulations, if you
know what they are. Anybody that's been in the service knows
that."

"Well, that's my trouble, I guess. I've never been in the
service. What ways are you talking about?"

"I think I could get a waiver for you."

"A waiver?"

"A paper from the Education Department saying that because of special circumstances you don't need to be certified
immediately."

"A paper saying I don't need a paper? What do I have to do
to get that? Secure a third paper?"

Abie smiled. "No, I don't think so." He swiveled his desk
chair around so that his back was to the window in the inner
wall looking onto the mill floor. He did not look at her but out
the outside window, as though resting his eyes. Gazing across
the factory yard, he said blandly, "You're still an attractive
woman, Marie."

"Go to hell!" she said furiously. She spun around and started
toward the door.

"Just a moment," Abie said.

For some reason, perhaps because he did not raise his voice
or even speak very sharply, she paused and half turned back
toward his desk.

"You're a proud woman, aren't you?"

She did not reply.

He continued, still speaking almost without inflection, as
though telling Ned Baxter to go ahead and order a gross of
sanding belts, as though his mind was still on the drawings on
his desk. "You are a proud woman. Why not admit it? It's
nothing to be ashamed of. I admire you for it. I always have."

She sensed that the men on the mill floor were staring in at
her through the window in the wall, though when she glanced
out onto the floor they were all bent over their machines as
usual.

She forced herself to face Abie. "The trustees will be inter-

ested in how you obtain waivers for their teacher, Abie Benedict."

He smiled. "Do you really think they'll believe you? Or care
if they do? They may wish my father were still alive and
running this town. But he's not, and they know who is. Go
ahead and tell them. I couldn't care less.

"It's fine to be proud, Marie," he said, his voice still calm and
detached and now even somewhat philosophical. "But if I can
presume to give you some advice, you're also an ambitious
woman, and it would be a shame if you were to let your pride
stand between you and your ambitions. Think it over."

"I have thought it over. The answer's no."

He shrugged. "Think it over some more. I'll leave my porch
light on tonight."

Again he waved his hand casually, dismissing her. She
started to say something else, object or swear at him again, but
he was already studying the drawings, as he had been when
she came in, so she turned and left without speaking.

Later that afternoon she rode Applejack up the low road on
Kingdom Mountain, chewed to a great muddy trough by the
heavy machinery, and tethered him to a yellow birch sapling
near the foot of the falls where many years ago she and Abie
had made love in the wet leaves. She sat down in the blowing
spray and stared into the pool. Over the rush of the falling
water and the clap of the Captain's waterwheel she could hear
the dull roaring and grinding of the machines higher up the
mountain.

Not since the night she left the sanatorium in the rain had
she felt so discouraged. For the first time she realized exactly
how much she valued her job, her house, and the life she had
made for herself in the village where Pia had said long ago her
destiny awaited her. For the fifth or sixth time since leaving the
schoolhouse the previous evening she got out the letter from
the Education Department and read it over, but the spray from

the falls blurred her vision, and she knew what it said by heart anyway, so she put it back in her handbag and stared up at the waterwheel's legend: *The wheel will never turn with water that has passed.*

A flash of color in the pool caught her eye. It flashed again halfway up the falls, crimson and silver, and she realized that one of the rainbow trout whose ancestors had come to Kingdom County from St. Louis on the fabled train trip had leaped out of the water, trying to get up into the deep spawning pools above in the meadow. It was late in the year for the trout to run—most of them had arrived a month ago and were already back in the lake—but the fish she'd glimpsed was unmistakably a rainbow and had unmistakably tried to jump the falls.

It flashed again, higher this time but still several feet below the lip of the holding pool above, and she saw that it was small, probably a first-run spawner, weighing only a pound or so. Earlier in the spring a big strong fish could fight its way up the quieter water beside the cataract; but where there had been eddies and small pothole pockets for fish to rest in last month, there was now only damp granite ledge, and if the small trout made it, it would have to be in one leap. Time and again it fell short and was washed back into the foaming pool below, and as Marie watched, silently cheering for the fish, straining upward with it each time it flashed, she gradually forgot the letter and her job and the village below.

It began to grow dusky. The intervals between the trout's attempts grew longer; it was tiring fast. Yet every two or three minutes it flashed, arched out of the water, hit the falls a few feet below the top, and was driven back. From the meadow above, the peepers began to sing, setting Marie's teeth on edge. High overhead a snipe began its evening ritual, winnowing down the sky with a shrill whistling of wings, climbing up and diving again. At the resort site at the upper end of the meadow, the machinery had fallen silent.

Still the trout kept coming, jumping, tailwalking, falling back, gathering strength somewhere in the deep churning pool below, then coming again, persistent as the snipe over the meadow, until Marie realized that despite the lateness of the season and the falling water and the approaching darkness, the fish was going to reach the pools above or beat itself to death trying.

Just before it was too dark to see, the trout made one terrific arching leap, hit the lip, and struggled there a moment. Whether it fought its way on into quiet water above or was driven back again Marie never knew. She stood up, stiff from sitting so long, and walked back to where she had left the horse; and all the way down the mountain in the darkness, toward the lights of the tiny village below, she thought about the fish.

As she passed the entranceway to the Big House, she looked up the long curved drive and saw the dark shape of Abie's new Buick sitting under the portico. As usual when he was at home, the lights were blazing in every downstairs room; and through the bow window of the library she could see him, sitting at a table, his profile toward her. He seemed to be alone, and for the briefest moment she was tempted to leave Applejack by the pillars and go up and attempt a reconciliation, perhaps even offer herself to him as a lover or confidante, whatever he wanted—but although the temptation was strong, and made stronger by her intense desire to remain in Hell's Gate, it passed almost immediately, and she kept going forward, past the pillars surmounted by the softly glowing whale's jaw, past the darkened schoolhouse, on toward the cluster of lights that had become her home. She did not yet know what she was going to do to stay in Hell's Gate, only what she would not do; but as she turned into her dooryard, she had no doubt that she would stay, and on her own terms.

The next day was Saturday, and she spent part of it with Margaret Simpson. The following Monday she mailed two letters, one to the State Education Department in Montpelier, the other to the dean of the normal school in the Common. A week passed; then she received replies to both letters on the same day. That evening she requested a meeting with Abie and the trustees, at which she read both letters aloud. The first, from the dean, certified that she had enrolled for two courses that summer and two more during the coming school year; the other was a waiver from the Education Department to continue teaching at the Hell's Gate Village School, with the requirement that she take four courses annually at a certified state normal school.

"Well, now, Mr. Abie," Bill Kane said when she finished reading. "Ain't that the best news you've heard this spring?"

Abie did not reply. Already he was pushing himself to his feet and reaching for his crutch. But just as he started out the door he turned and smiled at Marie in a way that made her wonder briefly whether it might not be wiser for her to leave Hell's Gate at once and never return.

Chapter Twelve

Marie's summer at normal school was the best time of her life since Philbrook Jamieson left for France. Every morning she rose at dawn, ate a light breakfast of fruit and coffee, worked in her garden for a short while, and then took the morning factory train to the Common for her classes. Instead of two courses she signed up for three: Introductory Rhetoric and World Literature, both taught by Margaret, and a beginning botany course from Professor John Fellows, a robust-looking middle-aged widower with four teenage sons.

The botany class met after lunch and spent most of its time walking with Professor Fellows in the woods and over his small farm a mile east of the Common, where he taught them to identify not only the plants and trees native to Kingdom County but dozens of birds and animals and insects. Marie liked this big, knowledgeable man. He looked somewhat like Abraham Benedict and had the same quiet presence. Margaret was taking the botany course too that summer, and in the late afternoons before the factory train left, she and Marie spent many hours together at her kitchen table pressing flowers and laughing and talking; but as interested as Margaret was in botany, it was clear to Marie that she was far more interested in John Fellows, and when the botanist asked her to the Midsummer's Night dance at the normal school, she was as excited as a schoolgirl.

"Pick a husband from the authors we've read, and tell why," Margaret wrote on the board for the literature class's mid-term examination on the day of the dance. After thinking for a minute, Marie chose Chaucer because he wrote so well about so many different kinds of people.

Chaucer, she thought that evening on the way back to Hell's Gate, would have enjoyed knowing the auctioneer Harlan Smith. Since the runaway piano episode he had continued to visit her one or two evenings a week, arriving in a large speed-boat with a steel hull with the words *Ice Chopper* lettered neatly across it, with which, it was widely rumored, he smuggled whiskey down from Canada when the lake was just starting to freeze in the fall, and again in the spring when the ice was just breaking up. With him on these visits Harlan usually brought some outlandish present or other that Marie never knew what to do with: a little pig (no one in Hell's Gate kept pigs, the houses were too close together); the two mated geese she'd thrown out of the ring; a white duck that laid greenish eggs— "Good for baking with, don't you think they aren't," the auctioneer told her; a sack of purple and yellow turnips. He never stayed longer than to have a piece of pie or cake and a cup of coffee, and he almost always brought along his ringman, Jehoshaphat, apparently in the capacity of a chaperone, for propriety's sake. ("This is a small town, schoolteacher, and small towns talk.") Yet frequently as Harlan rambled on about his horse deals and cattle deals and auctions—he never spoke of his alleged smuggling escapades—Marie would notice him watching her out of the tail of one blue eye in what seemed to be a calculating manner, the way he might look over a heifer about to freshen while talking to a farmer, in order to determine the highest price she might bring.

Marie began to like this unpredictable man. Although his place of business was the filthiest building she'd ever seen, Harlan himself was always immaculate, down to his square-cut clean fingernails and freshly laundered shirts. He dressed in a natty, western style and was enamored of the American West, especially the state of "Westconsin," which he supposed was the epitome of all things western, and to which he frequently threatened to strike out when one of his deals fell through or he came down with one of the innumerable small aches and pains of which he chronically complained.

A notorious hypochondriac, beset by all kinds of anxieties and phobias and always sure that he was on the brink of some obscure and fatal disease, Harlan did not subscribe to standard medical practice but consulted two or three times a week with Dr. Theloneous Rupp, a local chiropractor and seventh son of a seventh son, who claimed to be empowered with mysterious restorative abilities that resided in his fingertips.

Partly because there was little danger of choking on it, he loved to eat farmer's cheese, the sharper the better, and thought nothing of traveling to northern New Hampshire or Maine to visit remote four-corner general stores noted for especially strong varieties, which he purchased by the wheel and stashed, along with his beer, in a milk cooler behind his auction barn. The cheese kept well, but the milk from cows waiting to be auctioned had such a rank flavor he had to feed it to his hogs and cats. Although he professed to detest cats above any living creature except bees and snakes, he had at least a dozen at all times, mewing and rubbing against his polished cowboy boots and heaped up in great multicolored piles in the tilt-back swivel chair he kept in his tiny office in the commission barn —a cubbyhole whose walls were papered from ceiling to floor with girlie calendars and draped with harnesses, bridles, trace chains, and haywire, with which he could temporarily fix anything from a snapped fan belt to a broken jaw.

Of all his phobias, he was most afraid of yellow bumblebees and "gardener" snakes, though he had twenty bee and snake stories, each less probable than the last, to frighten the boys who hung around his barn—of whom he was considered to be a great corrupter, though he rarely told them anything they did not already know and was forever threatening to "flail them and whale them" if they didn't clear out of his premises. He loved ghost tales and claimed to have seen more apparitions than Marie could keep track of. Yet he would set off fearlessly up the lake on dark nights in any weather, presumably to bring a load of illegal whiskey back over the border, despite the possibility of meeting one of these specters and the much greater possibility of encountering hijackers or revenue patrols; and despite his dread of stepping on a bees' nest or snake, he made frequent expeditions to the woods, where, according to the season, he loved to forage for pennyroyal, ginseng, and spruce pitch, which he sold in large lots to Dr. Rupp to send to the Greer Patent Drug Company in Lenoir, North Carolina.

He was a good country ballplayer and still caught for the town team in the Common, and he both loved and hated the Boston Red Sox, often simultaneously.

Romance in general seemed to have played little part in Harlan's life, and when Marie recited the gypsy's verse on ice cream, codfish balls, and marriage, he nodded and said it was the God's truth. He had, he told Marie, been married and divorced three times over the years. "I traded downhill every time," he said. "Just the other day at a farm auction over to Colebrook I spotted a long-legged good-looking woman standing at the back looking into a box of cut-glass plates. 'Who can that be?' I thought to myself. 'I know her from someplace.' The next time I looked she was gone; it didn't come to me until that night that she was my second wife."

His only enduring loves, in fact, had been horse-trading and fly fishing for trout. He would spend hours and whole days, if necessary, trying to find good homes for old broken-down nags and mean killer stallions, and he tied all his own dry flies, tiny, delicate creations, seventy of which would fit easily into the palm of his hand. And although he was a big man, even bigger than Marie's father as she remembered him, he could move quickly and noiselessly through neck-high alders and drop a number eighteen Adams on the end of sixty feet of line and fifteen more feet of leader into a pocket of still water the size of a handkerchief as gently and gracefully as a bankside leaf falling into its own reflection.

In his youth he had been a boxer, climbing into crude rings at country fair and going a few rounds with other local brawlers for a winner's purse that rarely amounted to more than ten or fifteen dollars; but although he loved to talk about bareknuckle fistfights, no one could remember seeing him in one.

He knew the big lake north of Hell's Gate nearly as well as he knew the inside of his own barn, but was uneasy over deep water and awkward around boats.

One Sunday afternoon in August when the heavy machinery on the mountain was silent and the village was as still as the woods above it, Harlan appeared at Marie's door, alone this time, and offered to take her fishing. "We're going to use flies, nothing but," he said grimly, as though announcing an unpleasant but necessary duty.

Marie sat in the bow seat of the *Ice Chopper* as they roared off up the lake. At the mouth of the St. John River, Harlan cut the engine. He rigged a split bamboo fly rod with a light reel, tapered line, heavy gut leader, and gaudy red-and-white streamer fly three inches long, which Marie began to troll back and forth across the mouth of the river, forty feet behind the boat.

She was daydreaming, enjoying the warm sun and cool breeze, when her rod dipped sharply. The hard, jarring strike was nothing like the short, rapid tugging of a fish hitting live bait. Her rod tip plunged into the water and her reel clicked fast as the fish began its run. It leaped once, throwing spray two feet into the air. Then her line went slack, since she'd been so surprised she'd never set the hook. "Nice job," Harlan said sarcastically, but twenty minutes later she had another vicious, smashing strike, and this time she raised her rod tip instantly and the fish was on.

"Don't horse him!" Harlan shouted. "But don't give him no slack."

Paying no attention to his plentiful and contradictory advice, she played the fish carefully and, ten minutes later, slid it over his boat net. It was the biggest rainbow trout she had ever seen, well over twenty inches long, and from that afternoon Marie was a confirmed fly fisher.

Marie grilled the fish over a fire of hardwood coals on a strip of sand beach beside the south cove of the island five miles north of the village, where as a girl she had once come to make love with Abie. Although part of the island lay in Canada, it belonged in its entirety to the Benedict estate, and had never been inhabited year-round. It was known locally as the Indian Island, since St. Francis Indians had once come there to fish and make maple sugar.

"You're a pretty fair cook for a schoolteacher," Harlan said, dabbing fastidiously at his mouth with his snowy pocket handkerchief. He whisked a crumb off his jacket lapel as though a spider had dropped on him. "Let's go for a little walk up the hill. There's a prospect from up there worth seeing."

They followed an animal path up through scattered maples and birches and mixed softwoods, stopping from time to time to look off down the lake. Each time Marie looked at Harlan to see if he was ready to continue, he chivalrously waved her on ahead, though she suspected that he wanted her to go first to scare snakes off the path.

"There's one!" she said suddenly, halfway to the top.

"Whoa!" Harlan shouted, jumping straight up and slapping at his pants cuffs.

"It's just a little one," she said.

"I don't care how little they are, I can't abide them," he said, his hand on the .38 revolver he carried at all times.

"You don't like red squirrels?" Marie said innocently, trying not to grin.

"Red squirrels? Jesus Christ, why didn't you say so. I thought you'd stepped on a rattler."

"There aren't any rattlers this far up in the mountains."

"You can never tell," he said. "Just one is all I need to see, and it's Westconsin bound for Harlan Smith."

"I don't know, Harlan. I've read that the woods out there are swarming with them. You better check before you strike out."

They reached the top of the hill at sunset and stood quietly in an opening of evening primroses and steeplebush, admiring the view. To the north they could see far up the lake between the Canadian mountains. To the south, Hell's Gate lay like a toy village on the peninsula which jutted out from the base of Kingdom Mountain like a long, pointing finger. It was cool, nearly chilly, with the first hint of fall in the air.

"You're right, Harlan," Marie said finally. "It's a lovely prospect. I never knew what a lovely place this was. I'd like to have a house here someday."

"There are a lot of places around here you never knew about," he said. "Schoolteacher or no." Abruptly he said, "Schoolteacher, was you ever married in your travels?"

"Never," Marie said. "And I'll tell you something else. I don't ever intend to be."

"Good!" Harlan said with approval. "I wouldn't again neither. Not for all the great Benedict fortune."

"Harlan, you're always saying how rich the Benedicts are. What makes you think that? I grew up in the family. They were well off, certainly. Abie still is well off. But they aren't nearly as rich as you suppose."

"You think Benedict's building that pleasure palace on what he makes at the factory?" Harlan snorted. "The old man left him millions to play with. And all this to boot." He swung his hand and arm in a wide arc encompassing the island and the mountains on both sides of the lake.

"Well, you don't need to be so jealous. I'd rather be poor and walk on two good legs than hobble around on a crutch for the rest of my life with all the money and property in Kingdom County."

"I heard Benedict shot himself in the foot to get out of combat, and infection set in."

"That's a foolish rumor, Harlan. He was decorated five or six times. There's no love lost between Abie Benedict and me, but he never was and never will be a coward. Of that I'm sure."

Angrily Harlan changed the subject to his three ill-fated marriages, a favorite topic that seemed equally to intrigue and haunt him. Out of curiosity Marie asked if he had ever had any children.

"Certainly," he replied. "I had two girls by my first wife, big fat ones like their mother, and no doubt getting to be big fat women by this time. She took them off downcountry somewhere, and once in a while one writes for money. I never did have a son."

He looked at Marie shrewdly, and it occurred to her that perhaps he had brought her up to the hilltop to have a son with him, the way he might truck a heifer out to some farm to be bred to a prize bull, but then he changed the subject again, this time to her teaching. How, he demanded, did she manage the big boys? Did she use a "speller"? How big was it? Could she do sums in her head as fast as he could? (She couldn't.) Did she like schoolteaching better than working for a living?

On he pressed, asking questions faster than she could answer them. How long did it take to teach an ordinary pupil to read? How long did it take a lunkhead to learn? How did she go about it?

Greatly amused, Marie explained that she taught reading the way she'd been taught, by the phonetic method.

"Speak English!" Harlan said.

As she explained phonics he paced around the clearing as though getting ready to leave, but instead he asked more questions. Marie had no idea what he was driving at.

Finally, as dusk settled over the island, they started back down the path, Harlan in the lead now since any snakes had long ago gone under rocks or logs for the night. He walked quickly and did not speak again until they were quite close to the cove; then he wheeled around. "I want to ask you one more question, schoolteacher." Looking at her in the near dark, as angry as she had ever seen him, he shouted loudly enough to be heard halfway down the lake, "How much would you want to teach an old whore like me to read and write?"

"Good Lord, Harlan! A person shouldn't have to pay anything to learn how to read and write. I'll teach you gladly for the pleasure of your company."

"I guess you won't. You'll do it for pay or not at all. It's going to be work to teach me, hard work, and I'll pay and pay well. I intend to pay you a dollar an hour for every Christly hour of it we can stand. If that's not enough, I'll go higher. This is strictly a business arrangement; there won't be no pleasure in it for you or me either."

"That's a bargain then," Marie said gravely.

She put out her hand and they shook hands in the dusk. Then they started down the path again.

Just before they reached the boat Harlan turned to her again. "There's one more thing," he said. "That 'Good Lord' I heard back there. I didn't like that. I don't now nor have I ever liked to hear a swearing woman. Don't think I'm fooling because I'm not. My third wife was a swearing woman. I warned her to watch her language, but I might as well have told the rooster not to crow for all the good it did. It got worse instead of better as time went along; that woman had a ranker tongue than any cussing man I've ever heard. I had two goats at the time, and one day the nanny got into the old lady's kitchen garden and ate half a row of lettuce or so; and when she looked out and saw that goat she snatched up her broom and tore out the door and commenced to whale it, but it just stood there eating. I went out, and she give me a couple of good clips with the broom, and then the goat, and then back to me, and all the time cussing a blue streak. And it wasn't just swearing, it was vile low smut talk, to make even a commission sales auctioneer blush, and all the time belting the bejesus out of us with the broom. I don't know who she was madder at, the goat or me, but it weren't that that bothered me—I'd have been mad too if it was my garden—it was the swearing. I never heard such talk in all my life. Finally she wound down, leaning on the broom and panting, though I could tell she was getting up wind for another go at us. 'You'll have to excuse me,' I said. 'I've got to go to the barn and sweep down the cobwebs.' I took the broom out of her hand and headed for the barn, and so far as she knows I'm still sweeping cobwebs."

Harlan looked at Marie.

"So watch your language. Watch your language, school-teacher, or you'll find yourself out of a high-paying job."

Marie tutored Harlan Smith two evenings a week and every Sunday afternoon. He worked hard, and although he never did master phonetic reading, he learned how to sight-read enough to get through a newspaper or auction bill. Writing was much harder for him, until it occurred to Marie to teach him how to write by rote. He would dictate a letter to her. Studying each word he would then try to write it from memory:

> *August 12, 1920*
> *Kingdom Common, Vermont*

Buffalo Medical Supplies
River Street
Buffalo, York State

Gentlemen:
   Would you kindly send me one (1) double-reinforced truss, size extra-large, as mine busted out at the seam last week as I was loading hogs into Buster Hobb's high-backed farm truck made over from a Model A automobile which wasn't intended for such usage to begin with and a lump as big as your fist, if you are a big fellow like me, appeared on my right side? Enclosed find $5.75 to cover price of above article plus mailing.

> *Very truly yours,*
> *Harlan "Smitty" Smith*
> *Auctioneer*

As she came to know him better, Marie had to admit to herself that she not only liked the flamboyant auctioneer but in many ways admired him. Although he rarely had a good word to say about anyone, especially Abie Benedict, he had a certain cranky resilience to the setbacks of everyday life, and his invidiousness seemed to be part of his staying power. In part because he lived outside Hell's Gate and traveled constantly through northern Vermont, New Hampshire, and Maine, he was a breath of fresh air to Marie, whose life, except for normal school, was mainly confined to the small village. Until she had Harlan's visits to look forward to, she did not realize how lonely she had been since Margaret's departure; and she realized that although they were not yet lovers, and might or might not become so, he had also helped fill the emptiness that Dr. Jamieson's death had left in her life.

One of the things that intrigued her most about the paradoxical auctioneer was his night-time activities on the lake. What he did there was still a mystery to her. Like Harlan himself, she had always had a vigorous curiosity about everything, and she was determined to find out just what he was up to; but the more she pestered him about it, the more delight he took in maintaining an infuriatingly secretive air about his nocturnal adventures—until one rainy night in late August when she was studying by her kitchen window for her final exams at summer school, there was a sharp rap at the window and Harlan's voice called her outside frantically.

"Over here!" he said when she opened the back door. "Don't bring a light."

He was standing just inside the doorway of the small stable where she kept Applejack. She ran out through the rain with a dish towel over her head, and he pulled her inside fast.

"What on earth are you doing, Harlan?"

"Be quiet now and listen. I'm being followed. When I passed by the island tonight a boat come fast out of the cove and a fella hollered for me to stop. I believe it was the border patrol, but whoever it was they chased me all the way to the dock and they're going house-to-house looking for me right now. They'll be at your place any minute. Whatever you do don't let them search your property; tell them to come back with a warrant. Wait till you're certain they're gone, then let me know."

"Harlan, I'm not going to help you—"

"I ain't asking you to help me. Look."

He struck a kitchen match against his boot, cupped the flame with his hand, and held it up. In the sheltered glow of the match she saw four sets of dark eyes looking at her. And then Marie realized what Harlan had been doing on the lake, since even in the faint light of the match she could tell that the four strangers in her shed were Chinese.

"Harlan, I won't be—"

"You listen to me," he whispered, almost fiercely. "I'm responsible for these people. Do you understand that?"

"All right," she said. "All right. But for heaven's sake get them up in the loft and then get out of here fast. I'll put a lantern in my bedroom window when it's safe to come back."

Five minutes later she was standing in her doorway, talking to two men in suits and felt hats. To her relief they were not immigration authorities but revenue agents, and she was able to assure them with a perfectly clear conscience that she knew nothing about any whiskey smuggling and had seen no whiskey runners that night. An hour or so later they gave up their search and went back up the lake in their boat, and she put the lantern in her window, expecting Harlan to reappear; but he never did, and in the morning the shed was empty, and the Chinese men were working on the mountain.

She did not see the auctioneer again for three days, when he arrived for his tutoring as usual. He didn't mention the episode, and though he was clearly waiting for her to bring it up she said nothing until they had finished the lesson. Then, looking him in the eyes, she said, "Harlan, I want to know about those people. Where do you get them? How did you get started doing it? If I'm going to help you run some kind of underground railroad in reverse, you have to tell me the entire story."

"There isn't any story to tell," he said, lighting a cigar. "I pick them up in Magog and bring them down to Hell's Gate. They come out of Montreal, mainly, and only work here a month or so, until they get a small stake to move on. When they're ready to leave, I take them to the Common, where a truck picks them up. From there, they're apt to go anywhere: New York, San Francisco, Chicago, all over. All I know is every week or so I get an envelope or two in the mail from some big city or other—no letter and no return address—just five dollars or three dollars or maybe ten dollars in it, until each one is paid up."

"So Abie doesn't pay you himself?"

"No, he don't. I do business with that close-mouthed construction foreman of his. All Benedict does is employ them, and there's no law against that. What's against the law is bringing them here in the first place."

"How much do you charge?"

"Thirty dollars a head."

"How do you know when they're paid up?"

"I don't. Sometimes I can tell who's sent how much by the color or shape of the envelope, but I don't bother to keep track myself because they always do, or have so far. It's as simple as that." He sipped his coffee and thought a minute. Then he said proudly, "I've never lost one yet."

"You sound as though you like them, Harlan."

He shrugged. "I can't say I know them that well. Like I told you the other night, schoolteacher. Until they're settled here, I'm responsible for them."

She looked at him, then smiled. "Harlan," she said, "why don't you try calling me Marie. I think we've known each other long enough now."

The late summer of 1920 was full of surprises for Marie. The morning after she'd taken her last exam, having stayed over that night with Margaret, she rode up to the village with a crew of stonecutters who had come to lay up the pink granite facade of the Mountain House under the direction of two gray-haired men in business suits. With them they had brought their book-keeper, a shrunken elderly woman wearing steel-rimmed spectacles and a severe black dress. She sat in the seat in front of Marie, and as the train pulled out of the Common she looked up from a narrow black book with ruled pages in which she'd been figuring and spoke to the two men. "Make sure he has liability insurance before you put a single man up there on that mountain," she said in a harsh voice Marie had not heard for over fifteen years but recognized immediately.

"Pia!" she said, leaning forward excitedly. "I'm Marie Blythe! Do you remember me?"

"Of course I remember you," the physically diminished gypsy woman said immediately in an offended tone of voice. "Do you think I'm that far over the hill? Why did you run away, you stupid woman?" It took Marie a moment to realize that Pia was referring to her flight from Hell's Gate years ago as a pregnant fifteen-year-old. But before she could reply, Pia said, "What are you doing with yourself these days?"

Marie explained that she was teaching and going to normal school, and although Pia had already returned to her account book, in which she was rapidly adding columns of figures, she nodded abstractedly and said, "At least you've done one smart thing with your life. To get anywhere at all in the world these days you have to acquire all the schooling you can. You can't plan for the future too carefully, you know."

Marie had a dozen questions but Pia, who was almost totally unrecognizable except for her eyes, which were as gray and steady as ever, held up one emaciated hand wearily and said her head hurt from looking at numbers all day. Tersely she explained that she lived in Barre again, in a one-story modern house with her second husband, a wealthy undertaker, near retirement now, whom she had married three years ago.

"You must love him very much!" Marie said. "I mean to marry again."

"I suppose so," Pia said unenthusiastically. "Though there's no question that he likes dead people better than quick ones —he's got a hundred old jokes: his clients don't talk back to him, and so forth, and you can tell that underneath it all he's half serious. Still, he lets me do about as I please, go where I want to go when I want to go there."

Marie smiled. " 'The people that people marry,' " she said.

"I know, I know: 'Are the strangest thing of all.' Well, I proved my own point, didn't I? I never said I wouldn't remarry if I had the chance." She checked a column of figures in her book. "Security, Marie. Never underestimate its importance."

She told Marie that her two older sons, the men in the business suits, now owned the large granite quarry where their father had died from black lung. Ethan Allen had done well for himself too, and was president of a memorial stone company. "He's stuffier than my new husband," Pia said querulously. "I can hardly stand to visit him. He's joined the local lodge. His wife belongs to the D.A.R., the W.C.T.U., and the Eastern Stars. She wanted me to join the Stars, so to please her I did, and they practice more mummery there than any twenty gypsies. I'm Keeper of the East this year. Well, it's something to do evenings, and good for business contacts—but I liked Ethan a good deal better, and worried about him less, when he was doing fake rope tricks in one-horse towns like yours."

"Hell's Gate is booming, Pia," Marie said.

But the gypsy had already launched into a detailed chronicle of the myriad aches and pains that plagued her advanced years, including the inability to gain any weight. "I'm as poor as Job's turkey!" she said, holding up a sticklike arm. "I don't know whether it's more disgusting or pathetic."

She paused for breath.

"This so-called Mountain House of young Benedict's is a crazy idea," she said. "Even crazier than the old man's monument. That was over and done with fast, like an ill-advised love affair or a heart attack from overwork. The sort of temporary insanity everybody lapses into briefly during the course of a lifetime. This hotel madness'll go on for years, though, until it ruins everything. Who wants to come up here and sit on his hands for two weeks now that anybody can buy a car and travel around the country seeing sights?"

Marie laughed. "That's almost exactly what Ned Baxter said."

"Well, Benedict should have listened to him then."

As she spoke Pia rubbed one expensive high-heeled shoe against the other, and Marie was relieved to see that unlike the rest of her, the gypsy's feet had not shrunk at all. And her gray eyes were as steady as woodsmoke on a windless winter morning when, before returning for good to her ledger, she looked at Marie and said, "Get all the education you can. I've got a feeling you'll need it."

Pia spent the evening talking with Abie and left Hell's Gate immediately afterward, before Marie had a chance to see her again, but she could not stop thinking about the strange encounter with her old mentor. Never in a hundred years could she have guessed that Pia would turn into a calculating businesswoman. She wondered what unexpected twists her own life might still take. When she'd had time to think about it, she wasn't greatly surprised that Pia had praised her for acquiring an education; always the gypsy's outlook had been based on a remarkable combination of mysticism and common sense. Yet she thought that just before returning to her book Pia had looked searchingly at her, as though assessing to herself Marie's own outlook and state of affairs. She tried to imagine Ethan Allen joining clubs and selling tombstones, and couldn't.

It was a quiet private wedding, performed on the last Saturday afternoon in August by the Congregational minister from the Common in the parlor of John Fellows's farmhouse. John's oldest son, a handsome boy just turned seventeen, stood beside him, and Marie stood up with Margaret, who was giddy as a schoolgirl and immediately after the vows tossed Marie the

bridal bouquet of late-summer wildflowers John had picked
for her. Marie caught the bouquet with a look of great surprise
and everyone, including the minister, laughed. But that night
she had a vivid and unsettling dream in which she and Abie
were married on the sloping lawn of the Big House under a vast
yellow-striped canopy that imparted a lemony tint to the grass
and the people and to the icing of a three-tiered wedding cake
in the shape of the Big House. In the dream the Captain
(dressed in a blue coat that looked green under the yellow
light) gave her away, and Abie was young again and walked
without a crutch. There was a reception following the ceremony at which Armand St. Onge played his concertina and
Pamphille played his violin as they had at the first Christmas
Eve celebration in Hell's Gate. Her parents were there too, her
mother as silent and unsmiling as ever, her father boasting to
Armand that he had once said Marie would accomplish great
things, and the gypsies in their old colorful costumes were
gathered off to the side with the performing bear, which Harlan Smith, dressed as a gypsy, led on a chain. But as the sun
dropped lower and the shadows lengthened on the grass, the
Benedicts and her parents and the gypsies vanished, and Abie's
face grew gray and furrowed. The sky darkened and a flock of
sea gulls came in and perched on the rooftops of the houses and
on the factory roof, and high above the village the pink granite
facade of the Mountain House gave off a weird, unsettling
light, like the whale's jaw on damp nights in the summer. A
reception line formed between the canopy and the Big House,
and in the line Marie recognized the faces of John Trinity, Bull
Francis, and the three men who had tried to steal Jigger's furs;
but the most terrifying face of all belonged to Abie, standing
unsupported on one leg in the doorway of the house and
staring at her.

Then she was dreaming the old dream again, in which she
was trapped between the two borders, and when she woke at
dawn she was crying hard, since she was suddenly aware that
the terrible recurrent nightmare had an application to her life

she had never until now considered and that in a very real sense she had been between borders most of her life. She was, she thought, no longer a French Canadian, yet hardly a Yankee. Although she had lived as a married woman, she had never been married. She had worked as a nurse but was not one, and though she had traveled with gypsies, dressed like them, and, for a time, thought and acted like them, she was not a gypsy. Yet who and what she was she could not say, and she continued to cry for a long time, like the trapped child in the dream.

As Marie walked to her job at the school that fall, she could look up on the mountain and see the resort taking shape each day. It was a slightly curved building of six stories, with a glass-roofed rotunda and a terrace running the entire length of its facade and supporting two upper terraces on slim Greek Corinthian columns. The stonemasons worked quickly, and Ned told Marie that Abie hoped to have the Mountain House closed in by the time the lake froze; but there were all the usual unforeseen delays that accompany most large construction projects, and some besides, so that by mid-October when the first snow fell on the mountain the building was still a windowless shell. Then, with less than three weeks of the construction season left, everything seemed to go wrong at once. The glass for the three hundred and fifty windows didn't arrive. The slate roofing tiles did, but were of an inferior grade and had to be sent back to Rutland with no chance of a replacement shipment before cold weather. Finally, the inside carpentry crew from Burlington went out on strike, and although Abie immediately put a dozen cabinetmakers from the factory on the mountain project, there was not much they could do until the building was closed in, and they returned to the factory early in November. Much of the unskilled work like digging the foundation, clearing the grounds, and carrying materials up the mountain from the village had already been completed by the Chinese, who had then dispersed. Most of them had engaged Harlan to transport them to the Common, on the first stage of their journey to Chinese communities in large cities, but six men, including the four Harlan had hidden in Marie's shed, had vanished without a trace. Harlan thought they might have returned to Canada but wasn't sure; when he asked the construction foreman, the man shrugged and changed the subject.

It was an uneasy time throughout the village. Nearly everyone seemed to be on tenterhooks, waiting impatiently for the completion of the Mountain House as though for some great event that would affect all their lives deeply. Even among the project's few remaining detractors the delays engendered worry, and this worry quickly grew into a general community anxiety; twenty times a day machine operators looked up from their lathes and saws and drill presses, cabinetmakers looked up from their benches, housewives looked up from their counters and sinks toward the new railroad station in nervous anticipation of the arrival of long-overdue building materials. Also, the villagers were worried again about Abie, who once more had begun holding all-night parties at the Big House for factory customers and machine parts salesmen and his wartime friends, for whom he imported girls from Boston and Montreal whose main function he no longer even tried to conceal.

Worse yet, Abie was growing increasingly erratic in his dealings with the factory workers. Ellen Baxter told Marie that on three mornings of the week work had to be suspended on the Mountain House, he had hitched his way from floor to floor of the factory scowling at workmen and neither speaking nor nodding, but occasionally wheeling about and going back through an area he'd just inspected, as though hoping to catch the men loitering. That same week he had angrily canceled the Company's long-standing desk contract with Canadian Life Assurance over a minor misunderstanding involving the exchange rate on American currency. The following day he had just as abruptly announced an across-the-board raise of ten percent to all his employees, which Ellen did not see how the Company could afford in view of the lost contract. She also confided to Marie that for the first time since the Captain's death she was seriously worried about Ned, whose whole life revolved around the factory. Never a talkative man, he grew more and more silent at work and at home. "I don't know," Ellen said to Marie one Sunday afternoon at Christmastime. "Something, anything, just needs to happen, if you know what I mean."

Marie knew. Ridden by her own ambivalence toward the town, pulled in one direction by her need to be independent and in the opposite direction by an increasing attraction to Harlan and sexual energies she was no longer able or willing to ignore or divert to her work, fearful of what Abie might do to drive her out of Hell's Gate but without a clear idea of why he should detest her, she realized that she too was waiting for something to happen.

That spring, something finally did. But it was nothing Marie or anyone else could have anticipated, and although it resulted in a remarkable if temporary unification of people and purposes in the tiny border village, it also marked the beginning of a change not only in her own life but in the life of the community which was as unpredictable, and, ultimately, as surrounded by myth as the emergence from the wilderness of Hell's Gate three decades ago.

Although cold weather had held off somewhat longer than usual that year, when winter finally came it was relentless, and lasted far into the spring, with more snow than Marie could ever remember. There were two storms in late April, followed by another during the first week of May. In the village, the snow was level with the tops of the yellow picket fences separating the yards from the street. Gangs of shovelers worked round the clock to keep the street and factory yard and spur track clear, and the drifts on the mountains were so high all but the top story of the unfinished hotel was buried.

There was another storm out of Canada on the sixth of May, lasting until the morning of the eighth, when the sky cleared suddenly, though the wind continued to blow, whipping the light snow along over the ice on the lake and through the village so hard that lifelines had to be strung from house to house. For the first time in its history the factory was closed because of the weather.

The school had been closed for two days, and Harlan, who had rigged a pair of skis to the front of his Ford and come up for his tutoring lesson on the evening of the eighth, was snowed in. With him he'd brought Marie a package from one of the many obscure catalogue companies he dealt with, and when she opened it she was amused to discover a sheer black lace nightgown, which, to his considerable embarrassment, since he was actually a great prude, she promptly put on to model for him.

"Here," he said, turning as red as a beet and averting his head. "That's not meant to be worn in daylight hours."

"It isn't daylight," Marie said. "It's ten o'clock at night."

"Well, it's not meant to be worn in the light period. Take that right off."

"All right," she said.

"Here, now," Harlan said. "What is this, a Christly tit show?"

"It's a tutoring lesson," Marie said.

"Jesus!" Harlan said. "Now she's blowing out the lamp."

"Don't hit your head, I want you to be awake for this," Marie said, leading him into the bedroom protesting that he did not come up to Hell's Gate to take advantage of a Christly schoolteacher, and besides, he was forty-four years old and could have a heart attack at any moment.

Harlan made one more attempt to be chivalrous as she untied his necktie.

"Marie," he said, "are you sure you want to go through with this? Why, we aren't even married to each other!"

She woke up smelling coffee, and bacon frying, and she could hear the bacon sizzling and another sound she didn't recognize at first and could hardly believe when she did: it was the steady dripping of water off the eaves. She put on a robe and went to the window and pulled back the curtains. The sun was shining and the snow on the roof above her room was melting fast. Sometime during the night the deep cold had broken.

By ten o'clock the mercury in the window thermometer outside Marie's kitchen had climbed to fifty. By noon, when Harlan set out for the Common to feed and water his animals, it was sixty-four degrees and the snow was sliding off the roofs of the village houses in great cascading thuds, burying porches out of sight.

That night the temperature dropped to about fifty and a strong south wind broke up the ice on the lake and helped evaporate some of the snow runoff, but by midmorning of the next day it was well over sixty again and the humming of the factory was drowned out by the roar of the meltwater rushing off the mountains. By noon the brooks coming off Kingdom and Canada mountains were over their banks and cutting swaths fifty to sixty feet wide down the mountainsides. Boulders weighing up to a ton came tumbling down the streambeds as though hurled by giants. The lower road on Kingdom Mountain was a raging river, and the road going up School Hill from the village to the Big House was a cascade. A powerful current tore down the long street between the two rows of houses. By late afternoon Marie's cellar was full of water. Across the covered bridge, the lumber yard was partly submerged, and thousands of feet of seasoning boards were washing into the lake every hour.

At two that afternoon Abie had sent the factory train to the Common with all the day workers and most of the women and children of the village aboard, though Marie, Ellen Baxter, and two or three other women remained to help the men fighting the rising water. All the Hell's Gate men stayed on, even Early Kinneson, who, although he was terrified of drowning, couldn't bear not to be among the first to know the fate of the village and the Mountain House. Three times he tried to get up the plank sidewalk along the street to climb the mountain and view the damage at the unfinished resort, and each time he stepped in over his knee boots and retreated, so he had to be content with standing out on the store porch calling to everyone he saw that the high water would teach young Benedict a thing or two—as though the freak flood were Abie's fault. But the men were too busy moving furniture to the upper floors of their houses to pay any attention to him, and when someone told Abie what Early had said, he laughed.

If there was ever any doubt in the village about Abie's courage, his conduct during the great spring flood of 1921 dispelled it. As the Captain had said years ago on the day Marie cleaned the chimneys of the Big House and overheard his conversation with Rachel, it was never bravery that his son was lacking. Throughout the emergency he was calm and level-headed, as he had been during his war service. He did not concern himself with the Mountain House—it would have been impossible to get up the mountain anyway—but after the men had secured their own furniture he dispatched them to the mill floor of the factory to unbolt the machines and move them up to the floor above. While Ned supervised the work at the factory, Abie rowed across the bridge to make sure no one was trapped in the Canadian settlement. On the way he rescued Madame Raspberry, who had refused to go to the Common on the factory train in order to fish the high water, and had gotten trapped in the bridge's rafters.

When he returned he set up a field kitchen in the Big House, where once again Marie made coffee and peeled potatoes and prepared gigantic meals on the vast eight-burner cookstove, as she had done as a girl. Abie complimented the women, encouraged the men, and remained so composed and cheerful that later Ned said even the Captain himself could not have provided better leadership.

That night the temperature began to fall. By noon the next day the street was a street again and the water had receded into the basements of the houses. The covered bridge had not gone out, though Ned was afraid its underpinnings had been weakened. More than half the lumber in the yard had been lost, but mainly because of Abie's cool-headedness no one had been hurt and relatively little damage had been done in the factory. The next afternoon most families moved back into their homes, and the following morning Abie shrewdly insisted that business go ahead as usual, bringing the full crew back to start cleaning up the factory and sending Marie word through the trustees to go ahead and conduct school.

On the first Sunday morning in June Marie went up Kingdom Mountain to fish and saw the damage in the park and at the resort site first-hand. The lower road along the brook had been washed out entirely in most places and was littered with chunks of mortared stone from dams and fieldstone from the miles of walls built by the Captain. Parts of the steep upper drive had slid away or been buried. The dam at the foot of the meadow was gone, though miraculously the waterwheel was still intact, its paddles clapping slowly in the fallen water.

The Mountain House had not moved an inch, but the water damage to its exposed interior was extensive. The intricate fairways and raised greens of the championship golf course were a morass of mud, and the ski slope above the hotel was a raw escarpment of blue clay strewn with boulders and uprooted trees swept down from above. Marie shook her head. She did not see how Abie could possibly repair the damage, especially in view of the dwindling sales at the factory, and she could not help feeling bad for his sake; the Mountain House had meant everything to him, and although he had been away for the past week, presumably in Arizona trying to persuade his mother to put more money into the venture, she doubted that Rachel could advance more capital to her son.

That noon at her weekly dinner with the Baxters, however, she received a disquieting surprise.

"Abie's back," Ned told her shortly as she walked through the door.

"How did he make out in Arizona?"

"He wasn't in Arizona."

She looked at the mill foreman. It was obvious that he was fighting hard to maintain control of himself.

"He's been in Portland," he said. "He's arranged with a bank there to mortgage the factory for a hundred thousand dollars. He says he's going to plow every penny of it into the Mountain House and make a go of it, or sell Hell's Gate to the first paper company that comes along and makes an offer."

Chapter Thirteen

To many of the villagers, everything seemed to be going down-hill at once in the late spring of 1921, not only in Hell's Gate but all around it. To the south, in the hills surrounding the Common, places were going under nearly every week; for once Kingdom Common seemed to be in the vanguard, as one small farm and family lumbering operation and general store after another went out of business, almost a decade before the Great Depression struck the rest of the country. Harlan Smith's auction barn was full of dairy cattle, logging horses, household furniture, and grocery inventories he couldn't move, and he vowed to sell his own failing enterprise at the earliest opportunity. The railroads were struggling too. With fewer farms shipping milk, the spur track from the Common out to Lord Hollow and Pond in the Sky was abandoned, causing still more farms to go out of business. Three of the six daily freight trains through Kingdom Common on the Montreal and Boston line were discontinued. Shipping rates for the remaining freights were increased by thirty percent.

To the north of the village, there was trouble of a different kind. On Lake Memphremagog, a bloody whiskey war was being waged between two rival gangs of bootleggers: a Canadian organization operated out of Magog, at the head of the lake in Quebec, and a group of local men from the Common and nearby towns. Often on a still night Marie could hear the reverberations of gunfire carrying down over the water. Sometimes the battles were closer. In early June, one fight raged for more than two hours near Indian Island, which was used as a drop point by both factions. The next day several revenuers came to town and spent two weeks asking questions and patrolling the lake near the border. One night they chased a boat down the lake, under the covered bridge, and out into the bay, where it circled and returned safely to Canada after a great deal of shooting. But the federal officers never caught a single bootlegger and were soon reassigned to somewhere in northern Maine, and then the war resumed. By the middle of June four men from the Common had been shot. Two were killed and the other two seriously injured; most natives, including Harlan, whom the immigration authorities were watching closely, were staying off the lake altogether.

"It's gotten so an honest man can't make a living any more," Harlan complained to Marie. "The Commission Sales is going further into the red every week. Last Saturday I had to beef off fifteen first-calf registered Jersey heifers from the Nedeau place; don't you think I didn't take a terrible beating on that one. A year ago I could have gotten four times as much for them. If I could make a little extra on the lake nights, I might be able to hang on until things turn around. Now I can't even do that. There's a man over in Pond interested in the business, Marie. If I can swing it, I'm going to unload and head west to Westconsin."

Harlan had been threatening to unload and head west for as long as Marie had known him, and although she still considered his plan to be a safety valve to prevent his countless small dissatisfactions from driving him to distraction, she realized that he was more worried than usual, and not just feeling sorry for himself.

After a pause, Harlan growled, "There's one thing I'm going to do, now or later, if I don't do anything else."

"What's that?"

"I'm going to settle accounts with Benedict."

"You mean that Abie owes you money?"

"No. I told you I don't do business with him directly. What I mean, if you must know, is that I'm going to fix him. He's gone too far this time, and I'm going to settle with him."

"What's Abie ever done to you, Harlan?"

"I'll tell you what he's done. He's the son of a bitch that put the immigration boys on me."

"Did they tell you that?"

"No," Harlan said. "He did."

Marie shook her head. "I don't understand. Why would he do that after you supplied him with workers for his hotel? It doesn't make sense."

It was the first really warm evening of the year, and they were sitting out on Marie's porch in two wicker lawn chairs Harlan had brought up in the *Ice Chopper* from one of his numerous farm auctions. Harlan settled his polished cowboy boots on the porch railing. He raked a kitchen match along the floor and lit a cigar.

"It makes sense," he said, throwing the match past his boots into the budding hydrangea bush beside Marie's porch steps. "It makes sense, all right. It was two weeks ago. Two weeks ago yesterday, to be exact. It was a dark, rainy day and it looked like a dark night ahead, so I figured it was a good time to make a run to Magog to see my contact there. I didn't notice anything unusual on the way up except a couple of boys fishing in a rowboat off the mouth of the St. John. Magog didn't have anybody lined up for me to bring back over the line yet, so I started home down the lake around two o'clock in the afternoon. Everything went along good until I reached the north cove of the island. The wind was coming from the south, the way it had been since ice-out, and I could smell woodsmoke on it. That's curious, I thought. Who'd build a fire out here at this time of year? Then I saw smoke coming out of the woods near where that crazy Frenchman, Joe Canada, that squatted out there, back a dozen springs ago, built his sugar house. I figured those boys I'd seen fishing had rowed across and gone up there on the hill and set the sugar house afire, the way kids do these days whenever they find an empty building. At first I was going to let it go, but then I said no, by Jesus, next they'll torch the Commission stables, and that's my stake to go west on. So I put into the north cove. Only I was in such a rush to catch them at it I slipped getting out of the boat and went down into that cold water ass over teakettle, which didn't do much for my disposition. As soon as I got the boat hauled up I commenced to look around for a larruping stick. When one didn't come to hand I reached for my belt. 'I'll leather you until your hides come off, you little fireomaniacs,' I called up. By then I could see the sugar house, and smoke just pouring out of it. I flung open the door and jumped inside and hollered, 'All right, my lads, I've got you. Who's first on the agenda?' "

Suddenly Harlan interrupted himself.

"What are you grinning at, schoolteacher?"

"I'm not," Marie said, struggling not to laugh out loud at the thought of the auctioneer puffing up the hill sopping wet and tugging at his belt (a pantomime the boys who hung around the Commission Sales loved to provoke, though in fact Harlan had never been known to lay a hand on any of them).

"You was," Harlan said. "I'm glad you can be so amused over the spectacle of six starving Chinamen."

At first she could hardly believe him, but he nodded grimly and continued. "That's right. The four I hid in your shed the night those two revenuers chased me down the lake and two others—the same six that disappeared from here last fall, that we thought went back to Canada. Six of them, crowded together in that sugar house that isn't fit to be used for a horse hovel. They'd been there all winter, with nothing to heat the place but a home-made stove they'd rigged up from a milk can. They were burning cat spruce, of all stuff, and it smoked and stunk to high heaven. Every time they put in another piece they had to remove the stovepipe a-sticking out of the can and the whole place filled up with smoke and soot. But you haven't heard the worst of it yet. As soon as they laid eyes on me, nothing would do but they must fetch me the best food in the place. Do you want to take a guess at what that consisted of? I'll tell you: half a feed sack of rotten blue squash and a few scabby potatoes. The fiddleheads and cowslips was out by then, but they didn't have any way to know which plants was good to eat and which would poison them. They didn't even have nothing to catch fish with. They were starving."

"What on earth were they doing, squatting up there?"

"No, they were not. One of them could talk some English and he told me that Benedict sent them out there last fall to clear the island as part of his resort scheme. He wanted a little dude farm, I guess, where people who didn't like the hubbub of the hotel could go and relax, collect eggs, and so forth. So he gave these fellas a few axes and saws and enough food to last a couple of weeks and set them ashore without a boat, as much as marooning them there. Somebody was supposed to bring supplies out once a month, but they didn't show up only about half the time, and around the first of the year the supplies stopped coming altogether. By then the Chinamen would have flown the coop, struck out over the ice on foot, except that they still hadn't been paid, which Benedict evidently said they wouldn't be until they finished clearing the place. So they decided to return to Canada, but by then they was too weak to walk any distance. Soon afterward the ice went out and stranded them. By the time I arrived, they'd about made up their minds they were going to starve there.

"Well, mad doesn't begin to say how I felt, partly to think that anybody would leave people in such a fix, and partly because I'd brought them fellas down here in the first place and if it hadn't been for me none of this wouldn't have happened. It made me sick at my stomach to see those poor devils—arms like little twigs and sores on their faces and the one that could talk English apologizing, if you can believe it, because they'd run out of tea; they didn't even know enough to make tea from yellow birch. I didn't stay fifteen minutes. I didn't have the stomach for it, but I told them not to worry, I'd be back with their pay and plenty to eat and a free ride to Canada or wherever else they wanted to go. Forty minutes later I was in Benedict's office, going up one side of him and down the other. I called him everything I could think of and some things I didn't know I knew until I heard myself say them.

" 'Are you finished?' he says when I ran out of breath.

" 'Yes,' I told him.

" 'All right, Mr. Smith,' he said, as cool as a trout in January, 'here's two hundred and forty dollars, to be divided between those six men. If you want the truth, I meant to pay them eight weeks ago but simply forgot to. After they're paid, you can take them back to Canada, if that's where they want to go, and I'll pay you twenty dollars for your trouble. From then on, I'll expect you to stay off the lake at night. I neither need nor want you out there any longer, and I intend to notify the border authorities to keep their eye on you. If you think I'm fooling, I'll bring charges against you for smuggling aliens into the country. Don't think I'm not serious. I am. Now take the money and get out of here.' "

"What did you do? Did you take the money?"

"No. I paid them Chinese myself out of a little nest egg I had put aside, and returned them to Canada the next night, and saw to it they had a safe way back to Montreal. That's not all I did, either. Before I left Benedict's office I said to him, 'Mister, maybe you can abuse your help and get away with it. But you can't abuse Harlan Smith and expect not to have consequences.' "

"I hope you aren't going to do anything foolish, Harlan. Abie did a terrible thing, neglecting those men that way, but that doesn't entitle you to take matters into your own hands."

"Whose hands would I take them into then?" he said.

For a while they sat silently. From up the street they could hear the click of Ned Baxter's hoe striking stones as he cultivated his garden. High above the rooftops, chimney swifts were swooping through the dusky sky. A single heron flew over, trailing its long slender legs like a vestigial tail, heading from the cedar bog south of the bay to the big heronry on the St. John River. Harlan stood up. "To hell with Benedict and everybody else," he said. "Let's go fish off the bridge. There's a brown trout as long as your arm that lays in under them pilings, and one of these nights I'm going to snag him out of there."

Later that evening, after Harlan had returned to the Common, Marie sat in the dark at her kitchen table and thought about the story he had told her. It was hard for her to imagine Abie deliberately mistreating his Chinese employees, yet there seemed to be no other explanation for his strange behavior. She realized that the resort had become an obsession with him, and that nothing else mattered. As she reflected, it occurred to her that Abie's father had been obsessed to a degree himself, and capable of ruthless action when he felt it was necessary. But it had not been necessary, or even intelligent, to put six Chinese who hardly knew one end of an ax from another on an island, without supplies, in the middle of a huge, wild lake and tell them to clear out a farm, and she could not avoid the conclusion that something was terribly wrong with Abie Benedict. She was not really worried that Harlan would carry out his threat and harm him, but for the first time since returning to Hell's Gate, she was frightened by what Abie might do to himself, and in the process, to the village.

Gradually, other people began to focus on Abie as the direct or indirect cause of their difficulties and the general difficulties in the village. "I'll tell you," Marie heard Early Kinneson say to a group of men one night on the porch steps, "it's getting so there's no law at all up here. The bootleggers have got the run of the lake and the bay too. Young Mr. Abie better take matters in hand while he still can."

Marie looked with disgust at the storekeeper. It was one

thing for Ned Baxter to criticize Abie to her and Ellen, in the privacy of the Baxter home. For that matter, Marie had good reasons of her own for detesting many of the things Abie had done. But neither she nor the Baxters ever spoke a word against him on the street or in the store or factory, and as she listened to Early's carping insistence that Abie should "do" something, she was suddenly angry.

"He called in the G-men, didn't he?" she said suddenly. "What more do you want him to do?"

"I don't know," Early said. "I'm not in charge here, thank the Jesus. But I'll tell you this. The Captain would have did something himself. He wouldn't have gone to law for help to start with."

Marie shifted her shopping basket to her left hand, an instinct left over from the days when she half expected to have to fight her way out of every confrontation. She stared hard at Early. "Do you think Abie's a coward?"

"I didn't say that," Early said.

"Do you think so?"

Early hesitated. "No, I suppose not."

"Then why don't you tend to your store and let him run his business?" Marie said, and walked home without making her purchases, knowing that her angry defense of Abie would probably appear suspicious to the onlookers, but hardly caring.

As soon as she left, however, most of the men on the porch steps agreed that Abie was not a coward, far from it in fact, but a bona fide war hero—who, since he was doing little or nothing to prevent the whiskey traffic, must somehow be benefiting from it. From this conjecture it was only a small jump to conclude that very probably he was smuggling whiskey himself, or financing other local whiskey smugglers.

"That's it!" Early exclaimed. "It all falls into place."

"What all falls into place?" Stan Gregory said.

"That's how he's been financing that big hotel," Early replied, with as much certainty as though Abie had personally told him. "He's been running whiskey out of Canada for years."

The men on the porch were about evenly divided on this point. At the very least it was an intriguing topic to discuss, especially since Abie had recently purchased a large and powerful new yacht. One day word got back to Marie that Abie and the notorious Canadian bootleg king Jean Paul Belliveau, of Montreal and Magog, were engaged in a ruthless whiskey battle in which each had sworn to destroy the other. The following morning someone else told her with equal certainty that Belliveau and Abie were partners.

Although she could not discount either possibility, Marie doubted that these rumors had the slightest foundation in fact. So did Ned and Ellen. For one thing, none of them had ever known him to do anything illegal. Abie had many faults, which did not seem to be diminishing lately, but they believed that from his father and mother he had acquired a strict sense of honesty if nothing else. Moreover, like the Captain, Abie himself drank very little—at social events where other people were drinking he would usually order a whiskey and leave it untouched—and more than once he had worried aloud to Ned that the trouble on Memphremagog might hurt business at the Mountain House, since if the villagers were afraid to go out on the lake, he couldn't very well send his resort guests out there.

Nor did Marie and the Baxters believe that the new yacht had anything to do with whiskey running. Abie had told Ellen Baxter that he intended the yacht mainly for the use of his Mountain House guests. This explanation seemed reasonable to her, especially since that spring he had purchased a seven-passenger Cadillac to take prospective guests from the train station up the mountain to the hotel, and many expensive decorations for the building. Among these were a dozen or so original oil paintings depicting rural American scenes; expensive antique mirrors for the eighty-five bedrooms; and, to be displayed under glass in the rotunda, a collection of hunting guns from all over the world, including sixteenth-century Spanish arquebuses, long black-powder Kentucky flintlocks, and an eight-foot Chesapeake Bay punt gun once used by commercial waterfowl hunters off the coast of Maryland. Abie had proudly told Ned that punt guns would fire anything from nickels and dimes to boiler rivets and had been known to knock more than fifty ducks out of the air at once. "Go ahead and try it anytime you want," he said, but Ned thanked him drily and said he'd stick to his old twelve-gauge.

"It's not just this spending spree he's on," he told Ellen and Marie that night. "That's bad enough, granted, especially when it's all borrowed money. But whatever it is that's the matter goes way beyond that. Something's wrong with the man. One day he's as pleasant to get along with as you could want. The next he'll bite your head off for nothing. This morning I sent the carpentry crew up to the Big House to start painting, and when he found out he came onto the mill floor and right there in front of my crew he combed me out for ten minutes. He said we'd paint the town when and if he decided to, and in the meantime he wanted the men working up at that hotel. His father never spoke to me or any other man the way Abie did today; if Abraham did have something to say, he'd say it privately. I'm telling you, something's wrong. It wasn't two hours later that he came back out and told me I could use that new duck gun he bought, just as though we'd never had any words at all."

Ned was sitting at the kitchen table in his undershirt. While he spoke Ellen massaged the tight muscles in his shoulders, as she had done nightly for the past two months to try to relieve some of the terrific tension that had been building up in him since the factory had been mortgaged. "What do you mean, Ned?" she said. "Surely you don't believe those stories that are going around about his carrying whiskey."

"No, no. I don't believe that. I suppose what really bothers me is that I don't see how he could live here nearly all his life and not know that you don't hunt ducks in the summer, and on top of that imagine for a second that I'd hunt them with that cannon anyway. I don't understand him, Ellen, any better than he understands me. I never have."

"He doesn't fully understand himself, does he? It's as though no matter what the cost, he has to go ahead with that hotel to prove to himself that he can accomplish something as fine as his father did. Sometimes when I go into his office, I find him just sitting and looking at that picture the gypsy woman painted of Abraham. Just sitting there, turned around in his chair looking up at it. It gives me goose bumps to see him do that."

"He ought to take that picture down. I never liked it and I don't think he does. I could never understand why Abraham wanted it. His left eye didn't stray off like that. He looked right square in your face when he talked to you."

Ellen sighed. "Try to relax, Father. You're so knotted up your shoulders are jumping like a dog shaking off a flea. Just relax."

Ned stood up and went to the window. "I can't relax anymore. All I can do is wonder what's going to go wrong next. Today Abie told Herm Fischner he wanted him to suspend work on the latest desk order from New England Life and draw up some blueprints for beds and chairs and bureaus for that Mountain House. Herm didn't say anything at the time, he never does, but he told me later that he's afraid we're going to lose the New England contract if we aren't careful. This isn't the first time such a thing has happened. Last month a special order came in for some furniture for a bank out west. Abie pulled the men right off their desks and made New England wait until the bank order was finished. That's poor business."

"I know," Ellen said gently. "I work there too."

Ned shook his head. "I'm sorry to go over and over these things, Ellen. I know it's as hard on you as it is on anyone to see all this happening. But lately I hardly dare go to sleep at night for fear of what I'm going to wake up to the next morning."

The next day Ned saw a small, elderly woman get off the morning factory train, walk over to Abie's Cadillac, and wait for him to hobble around and open the door for her. Then they drove off up the mountain together. Nobody had the faintest idea who the stranger was or why she had come until Abie explained to Ned later that morning that it was the old gypsy woman, Pia, who had agreed on her last visit to Hell's Gate to return the following year and paint the great circular interior wall of the Mountain House rotunda with a series of tableaux representing the history of the village. She was at the resort now, he said, and would need ladders, scaffolding, several long tables for her materials, a coffee pot and coffee, and a supply of sandwiches. Also the large crates of paint and supplies she had brought with her on the train would need to be transported up the mountain. Ned made these arrangements quietly and efficiently, despite the enormous temperamentalism of the gypsy, who was nervous about painting again after a dry spell of fifteen years and shouted peremptory orders at him from the time he arrived at the hotel with the scaffolding until he left two hours later.

It was quickly apparent, however, that her artistry was as intact as ever. Working with incredible speed from dawn straight through until sunset, seven days a week, she created four remarkable scenes. Each showed Hell's Gate at a different stage of development, a different season, and a different time of day. The first tableau, on the east wall of the rotunda, depicted the peninsula before the Captain had arrived and was created mainly in shades of green, blue, and gold. It was early spring, and early in the morning, with the sun just lifting over the south shoulder of Canada Mountain and illuminating the spring snow on top of Kingdom Mountain, which shone pink in the low rays of sunshine as it had the day the Canadians arrived in 1899. Farther down the mountain, the new leaves just coming out of their buds were a lovely delicate pale yellow, and far below, the wooded peninsula lay in the green shadow of Canada Mountain, with the lake and the bay stretching off in the distance as blue as the circular expanse of blue sky visible on fair days through the skylight in the ceiling of the rotunda. Every detail seemed to be wrought with exquisite care; yet the first tableau took only a week to complete.

Even Ned was impressed enough to ask her how she could possibly work so fast and so accurately, to which she replied, with a fierce scowl: "You have to see pictures where they aren't."

On the south wall, starting just to one side of the resort's main entrance and running for nearly twenty feet to the hallway leading to the kitchen at the rear of the building, the artist created a magnificent summer scene, showing Hell's Gate as it had looked soon after the Captain's arrival. On the peninsula the trees had been cut, though stumps still jutted up here and there, and a team of horses was heaving at a stump whose roots were tilted out of the ground at a sharp angle, and you could see the sweat shining on the horses' flanks and feel the muscles in your chest tighten in sympathy with the straining animals. A cluster of cabins sheathed in rough bark had been thrown up on the tip of the peninsula, which was connected to the foot of Canada Mountain by a long bridge not yet covered over. The sawmill sat just off the far side of the bridge beside a small yellow cone of sawdust. In this scene, which was notable for its bright colors and verisimilitude, it was noon, with the sun shining down from nearly straight overhead and reflecting brilliantly on the sawdust pile and the buckles of the horses' harnesses and the axheads of the loggers and the great gleaming log saw, which you could almost hear whine as it bit through a gigantic log. In fact, the summer tableau was so real that Bill Kane said when he went close to admire it he could feel the heat of the sun and smell the hot spicy scent of pitch from the freshly cut trees and the new lumber; but before he had inhaled more than a lungful, the irascible gypsy had threatened to hurl a bucket of paint at his head and ordered him out of the hotel and off the mountain.

Because it was somewhat larger than the spring scene, the summer tableau required ten days to complete.

On the west wall of the rotunda, working high up toward the concave dome, Pia began painting in shades of red and orange, of butter yellow and crimson and burnished gold, to represent the twin mountains in the fall, at the peak of the foliage season. Far below, near the floor, she created the blue bay and, since it was now late afternoon, the inverted reflection of Kingdom Mountain stretching far into the depths of the water; and the colors of the upside-down reflected image of the mountain were as stunning as the colors of the mountain itself. In this scene the village was in its heyday, with the double row of pale yellow houses and the Big House in prime condition. Smoke was pouring out of the tall brick chimney of the factory, and the entire tableau was evocative of prosperity and well-regulated activity. Across the bay, the Canadians' houses were as multicolored as the leaves on the mountain above it, and a band of gypsies was gathered around a fire nearby. Using a complex arrangement of theater floodlamps and footlights, Pia had worked well on into the nights on the autumn tableau, finishing in just under nine days. It was a marvelous scene, with a nearly photographic faithfulness, yet as remarkable as the fall scene was, the last tableau was more remarkable still, partly because Pia insisted on doing it only at night, in absolute privacy, and covering her work in progress by day with flannel bedsheets and blankets, so it was a complete surprise to the villagers and even Abie when they saw it for the first time.

The unveiling of the north wall took place one Saturday in July, and Marie, who had been busy at normal school, was as curious as anyone else in the village to see it. In the last tableau it was evening and late fall, since the bay and a portion of the big lake were frozen; but farther north, toward Canada, the water was still open, shimmering dark under a cold white winter moon which was reflected small and dull off the ice on the bay. The wind was blowing wisps of snow across the ice, twisting like miniature cyclones, and a powdering of snow, perhaps the first of the year, lay on the rooftops of the houses in the village. High on the north shoulder of Kingdom Mountain, overlooking the peninsula, was the Mountain House, evidently completed now but strangely dark except for the glow of moonlight on its sweeping facade. In the village, most of the

windows were already darkened; yet the mosaic did not con-
vey the impression that it was especially late since there
seemed to be a narrow strip of reddish afterglow along the
western horizon. In the lingering twilight the houses were a
silvery gray, like the disused farmhouses along the county road
between the Common and Pond in the Sky. The ice was a dull
luminous white, the sky a velvet lavender, with tiny blue stars.
As lovely and mysterious as the scene was, though, it was also
somewhat disconcerting because of its air of desuetude. Marie
was tempted to risk a rebuff by asking Pia what the last tableau
meant; but when she looked for her, the gypsy was nowhere
to be seen. She had, it seemed, left Hell's Gate on the factory
train that morning.

Ned said that he disliked the man the instant he stepped off
the pontoon of the float plane and splashed up to the dry sand
on the edge of the south cove of Indian Island. Ned readily
admitted that he was prepared to dislike him, but he was still
surprised by the intensity of his own feelings, though he and
Jean Paul Belliveau had merely nodded to each other and then
the whiskey smuggler had not looked at him once again.

Everything about the man was smooth. His face was smooth
and tanned, as though he spent a good deal of time on the
water in the sunshine. His scalp shone pink and smooth
through his smoothly brushed white hair. He wore an unwrin-
kled red wool shirt, open at the throat, and light twill trousers,
neatly creased, and expensive waterproof boots buffed to a
smooth cordovan sheen that had been worked deep into the
leather. And when he spoke his mild voice was as smooth as
fancy-grade maple syrup.

"Mr. Benedict?"

Abie nodded.

"My name is Jean Belliveau, Mr. Benedict. I'm very pleased
to make your acquaintance."

Belliveau started to put out his hand, Ned said, but when he saw that Abie was not going to make any effort to balance himself on one crutch and extend his hand, the Canadian made a smooth, sweeping gesture with his outstretched arm and said, "What a beautiful spot this island is, Mr. Benedict. It must be a fine place to come on holidays. The fishing and duck hunting are very good out here?"

"I don't hunt or fish," Abie said. "You'll have to ask Mr. Baxter."

Jean Belliveau shrugged but did not look at Ned. "I still fish some," he said. "But only when my grandchildren visit from Montreal. Perch, sunfish, bullpout now and then. Those are good fish for an old man and children. I used to troll for lake trout, but not anymore. I used to hunt ducks, too: mallards, black ducks, goldeneyes, almost any duck that flew over except a fish duck. Now I'm not much interested in killing for sport. These days I'd rather look at birds through binoculars and write down their names, or just walk along the shore."

He talked on, speaking lightly and easily, in a slight French accent. He spoke about the varieties of birds that nested near Lake Memphremagog, which ones went south and which wintered over. Once, he said, many years ago, there had been a three-day line storm in the fall with the wind straight out of the east, and an exhausted puffin had been blown into the bay in front of his summer home near Magog. He had gone out and caught it and arranged for it to be shipped to Nova Scotia and released on the Atlantic coast. From the hill above the cove a white-throated sparrow whistled, and he smiled and nodded. He asked if any lady slippers grew on the island. Abie, who was grinning faintly, said he had no idea.

By then Ned had moved several yards away from them, though he could still hear their conversation clearly. He was aware that Belliveau's pilot, a dark-faced man with Indian features, was watching them intently from the plane in the cove, and he wanted to stand where he could keep his eye on both Belliveau and the Indian, though what good that would do he had no idea because he did not have a gun, and the plane, he had noted, was equipped with machine guns.

"Well, Mr. Benedict," Belliveau said affably, "we can't all be interested in the same things, and it's probably a good thing we aren't. But I asked to meet you here for a reason, and you're wondering what it is. I'd like to make you an offer."

Ned Baxter had known Abie for more than thirty years. He had known him as a small boy, an adolescent, and a man, and he believed that without ever quite understanding him, he knew him as well as any man he had ever known except the Captain. Certainly there was never the slightest doubt in Ned's mind that Abie was not courageous. Yet as long and as well as Ned had known his best friend's son, he was still amazed by Abie's answer, and by the fact that he was still grinning slightly as he spoke.

"No," he said. "I don't have any intention of selling this island. And now I've got something to tell you. From now on I want you to stay away from here and keep your people away. You're frightening the people in my town and you're hurting my business."

Belliveau smiled sympathetically. "I don't want to hurt your business, Mr. Benedict, I'd like to help it. You're jumping the gun, as they say. It isn't just the island I'd like to buy, it's your entire holdings, village, factory, and all. I'm prepared to offer you—"

"It doesn't make any difference what you're prepared to offer," Abie said. "You could offer a million dollars and it wouldn't make any difference. The answer would still be the same. I have no intention of selling Hell's Gate to anyone right now, and if I did I wouldn't sell it to you for any amount of money."

If Jean Belliveau was surprised or angry he didn't show it. He smiled. "You know, Mr. Benedict, I have no son. I have grandsons, quite young still, and three daughters. But no son. If I had been so fortunate, however, I think I would have wanted one like you."

"No, you wouldn't have, Monsieur Belliveau," Abie said. "Because if you had a son like me, sooner or later he'd tell you the same thing I'm telling you, and you'd like hearing it from him even less. Don't come here again. Don't come here at night with your plane or your boats. Don't come here in the day to botanize or look at birds. Don't send your people here during the day or at night. Don't bother me with offers to buy the town. You may run things at your end of the lake. I don't know or care. But you don't run things here. Now get back in your airplane and tell your man to take you home. I don't have anything more to say to you, and I don't want to hear anything else that you have to say."

That evening when Ned told Ellen and Marie about the meeting, he said that Jean Paul Belliveau still did not seem in any way angry, even after Abie had ordered him off the island. He had just smiled, in admiration, Ned thought, and lifted his hand and returned to the plane, which taxied in to pick him up, and then Abie and Ned had gone back to the factory.

Ellen was very upset. "Why did he take you along?" she said. "I don't understand that at all. Did he want you there to back him up?"

"No, I don't think so," Ned said. "I think he wanted a witness to come back here and say he's not involved in whiskey running. He wanted to nip that story in the bud. That's all."

"What do you think this man Belliveau will do next?" Marie asked.

Ned looked grave. "I don't know," he said. "I just don't know the answer to that, Marie."

Two nights later there was another gun battle on the lake, and dozens of shots were exchanged. Some of the flashes could be seen from the village. The next morning the revenuers came back and discovered the body of a man named Bullock, a part-time logger with no family and few friends, who had lived in an abandoned horse hovel in Lord's Hollow. His corpse had washed up onto the sand beach of the island, its back riddled with bullets. Bullock's boat was found floating bottomside up nearby; all the evidence pointed toward Canada, but except to notify the Canadian Mounted Police, who tended to regard whiskey running as an American rather than an international problem, there was not much the revenuers could do. One of them told Abie that until G-men along the Canadian border were supplied with warplanes, it was unlikely that they could stop the smuggling. "I think the best we can hope for is that this latest blowup will discourage the other fellows, the ones from Kingdom Common, and you'll have just one bunch to contend with," he said. "Unless you want to buy a plane and outfit it with guns and go up after them yourself, Mr. Benedict. Word has it that you were pretty handy in that line during the war."

For a week, though all kinds of wild rumors ran through the village, no more shots were heard from the big lake. Early Kinneson concluded that Abie was not only connected with the gang from the Common but was running it and had decided to lie low for a time. Most of the villagers, including many of those who repeated this speculation, thought it was ridiculous; but nearly everyone was glad that the whiskey war seemed to be over. It had been getting too close for comfort, and many people feared a direct retaliation against the town itself for Abie's refusal to sell out to Belliveau.

On the second Saturday in August, Harlan had to make a business trip. The deal for the Commission Sales with the man in Pond in the Sky had fallen through, as Marie had been quite sure it would, since she did not think that Harlan wanted to sell out any more than Abie did; and to keep his business afloat for another month or so, the auctioneer decided to visit a well-off uncle in Magog, at the head of the lake, to see if he could get a small loan. Besides nearly a thousand dollars in scrip, Marie still had fourteen hundred dollars in cash savings from her job at the sanatorium and offered to help him. He had indignantly told her it was against his principles to borrow money from a woman—but if she wanted to ride up the lake with him they could make a day of it and take along a picnic lunch. He raised his hand, anticipating her concern. "We'll be back long before dark," he said. "But I'm damned if I'm about to let that flying Frenchman, or Benedict either, keep me from conducting my lawful business during daylight hours."

Despite her reservations, Marie agreed that there was no reason why they or anyone else shouldn't use the lake for legitimate purposes, so she agreed to go along. They planned to leave in the middle of the morning, but there were the usual delays and complications that accompanied almost any excursion with Harlan. He had to make a sudden trip to Lord Hollow that morning to pick up a horse, which he'd been unable to catch for two hours and chased halfway to Canada, he said, before getting a rope around its neck . . . the story went on, grew more involved and less likely, and the upshot was that he had not left the Common in his *Ice Chopper* until noon.

It was a hot, humid day, more like the dog days of August than the middle of July. Neither Marie nor Harlan had much appetite, so they went straight up the lake without stopping and checked in at the Canadian customs office in Magog at two. It was a fifteen-minute walk to Harlan's uncle's place, where no one was home. They returned to the *Ice Chopper* and ate their lunch on the town dock, less than a hundred feet from the Magog Pulp and Paper Mill, whose acrid fumes made all their food taste like spoiled egg-salad sandwiches. It was still too hot to eat much anyway, so they walked up and down the main street, wiping their eyes in the smog held down by the terrific humidity.

Marie felt out of place in the French mill town. Every third house seemed to have a tiny grocery or variety shop in the front. The yards were crowded with shouting children and knickknacks of all sorts, the porches and eaves were trimmed with clashing colors that reminded her of the outlandish shades of paint the gypsies had brought to Little Canada. On a nearby street someone was playing a fiddle. It grated on her nerves like the shouting of the children in the muggy, oppressive air.

"Come on," she told Harlan impatiently. "Let's go see if that uncle's back."

He was not.

"Leave him a note," Marie said. "We're going to get a thunderstorm before evening. Maybe he'll come see you."

Harlan shook his head. "He can't come see me. He's line-bound. Two years ago he was picked up in Pond in the Sky for smuggling in whiskey, and they told him if he ever crossed back over the line again they'd lock him up for twenty years."

"This uncle of yours sounds like a hard customer."

Harlan shrugged. He lighted a cigar and sat down on the porch steps to wait. The sky grew darker. "We may have to let it blow over," he said.

They watched the storm approach, but when it had not hit after an hour they decided to return to the boat and try to outrun it before dark. If they had to, they could always put into a cove and wait for it to pass, Harlan said. All they would have to watch out for was getting caught in the middle of the lake a mile or so from shore in case it struck suddenly. Marie did not want to stay in Magog a minute longer, but when she saw the sea gulls coming in off the lake she had no doubt that rough weather was imminent. Neither she nor Harlan was a strong swimmer, and as they roared away from the dock into the choppy waves outside the concrete breakwater, she had serious misgivings about the twenty-five-mile trip ahead.

They covered the first three or four miles quickly and without any difficulty, though the bow bounced hard every time a wave quartered across its steel hull, and they both began to feel queasy. The wind was pushing the waves out of the northwest, and as the lake began to widen out, Harlan took the *Ice Chopper* into the sheltered water at the foot of the western mountains. Rather than risk crossing the wide mouth of a large cove where a river emptied into the lake between two jagged mountains, he stayed close to the marshy shoreline of the indentation.

One or two hundred yards up the river, on a knoll looking out over the water, sat a handsome half-timbered stone house surrounded by elegant lawns and shrubbery. A blue pontoon plane bobbed up and down off the end of a long dock where a small boy and a white-haired man stood throwing bread crumbs into the wind for a wheeling flock of gulls. The man waved to them and Marie waved back.

"Belliveau," Harlan shouted to her into the wind. Marie nodded and looked back at the man feeding the birds. He did not look like a murderer, as the three men who had come up to Pond Number Four had. He looked like any other grandfather out enjoying the day with his grandson. She could see him bracing himself in the gusting wind; his white hair blew wildly, and he looked frail and very happy. As they rounded the south point of the cove and headed back out into the big lake, he took the boy's hand and started up toward the stone house.

To the west and northwest, the sky was the color of Harlan's revolver barrel. Farther south, it was closer to purple than gray. The peaks of the mountains on both sides of the lake were out of sight in the low clouds, and Marie was certain that the storm would break before many more minutes, but it held off, until she began to think they might reach Hell's Gate before it hit after all. To the south, she could see Indian Island. They were making good time.

As they approached the north end of the island, the waves dropped somewhat. The lake was not calm, but the whitecaps were no longer smashing the prow of the boat and crawling up over the steel side into their laps. Suddenly the undersides of the storm clouds above them turned a much lighter blue; Marie knew that this was caused by light mixing with and reflecting off raindrops, which had already started to fall on the lake. There was a sharp snap of lightning directly overhead, followed immediately by a terrific explosion of thunder, and for the next thirty or forty seconds, as they raced for the island, the air all around them was full of electricity. Their hair stood up from the sides of their heads. The lines in their fishing rods bellied out away from the guides. A strong odor, similar to the scent of gunpowder, hung over the water, and the metal bow of the boat and the oarlocks and the lid of Harlan's tackle box glowed with a weird yellow light. Then it was raining harder than either of them had ever seen it rain, the drops hitting the water with such force that they bounced an inch back up from the surface, the wind screaming down off the mountains to the west at hurricane force, so that if they had not reached the wooded north point of the island at that moment they would not have reached it at all.

For the next six hours they huddled under a small clump of spruce trees in a torrential, unrelenting downpour that had soaked them both totally through to their skins by the time they pulled the boat out of the water. The dilapidated old sugar camp where Harlan had found the six marooned Chinese would have offered them better protection, but with the lightning cracking all around them, they did not dare climb the hill to reach it. All they could do was wait, cold and sopping wet and miserable, and hope that the tarpaulin Harlan had put over the boat's motor would keep out some of the water. The wind was shrieking, too loud for talking, and there was nothing to say anyway. For once, even Harlan was quiet.

Toward midnight the wind and rain let up enough for them to try to reach Hell's Gate. They had pulled the *Ice Chopper* out of the water onto a spit of sandy ground, and the sand had blown partway up the side facing the lake, like a snowdrift; it was a hard job to get the long, heavy, steel-hulled boat back into the water. But the engine started quickly, and they headed south along the west shore of the island, moving slowly, the boat's bright green running lights marking their progress.

A sudden flash illuminated the hill on top of the island, like a black-and-white panoramic view of a hill flashed on and immediately off a screen. A thunderous roar followed within a split second. When Marie felt the jarring impact against the prow of the *Ice Chopper,* she thought they had been struck by lightning. The boat listed hard to the left and nearly capsized. Then they heard the buzzing, above and behind them, and saw the winking red wing lights on the airplane, dipping in low over the lake.

"Jesus!" Harlan said. "He's strafing us!"

He switched off the boat's running lights, and the plane roared past twenty feet above them. Harlan snapped off three shots with his revolver, but the plane was already well beyond pistol range. He swung the *Ice Chopper* farther out into the lake and headed toward Hell's Gate at full speed. In the meantime the plane circled and started back to the north. Apparently, whoever was flying it had decided the water was still too rough to touch down.

"Here he comes," Harlan shouted. "Take the Christly wheel."

This time the plane passed between the *Ice Chopper* and the island. It was higher than before, about level with the top of the hill.

Harlan fired, and a moment later a vivid flash appeared near the plane. Instinctively, Marie ducked.

Harlan fired steadily.

And then the plane simply vanished from sight.

Marie let up on the throttle.

"Don't stop!" Harlan shouted.

She pushed the lever forward, and they roared past the south end of the island. Marie felt cold water sloshing around her ankles.

Harlan bailed silently with a minnow bucket, and fifteen minutes later, she nosed the *Ice Chopper* up onto the sandy edge of the peninsula just beyond the spur track embankment behind her house. Still Harlan had said nothing.

Only when they were in Marie's kitchen, wearing dry clothes, with a fire going in the stove and the coffee perking, did the big auctioneer speak.

"Goddamn that uncle of mine to hell and back," he said suddenly.

Marie looked at him. "What do you mean?"

"I'll tell you what I mean," he said. "If he'd been home where he should have been when we first got there, we'd have been back here by suppertime and none of this would have happened. That out there on the lake tonight was the worst experience of my life. I thought I'd been shot and struck by lightning and drowned and had a heart attack. They say a brave man don't die but only once. Well, I guess I don't qualify because I thought I died twenty times and twenty different ways tonight and then come back as my own ghost. No, sir. I'll never go to Canada to borrow money again. Go ahead and laugh," he said. "But before the summer's over, this old Smitty will be riding the range in Westconsin. I've got a little over a thousand dollars tucked away for an emergency like this, and if I have to pay somebody all of it but my train fare west to take the Commission Sales off my hands, I'm going to do it."

Marie did not pay much attention to him. On the lake she had been as terrified as Harlan, but now she wanted to try to straighten out the jumbled events and understand what had happened. She sat at the table sipping coffee and went over the sequence of the attack in her mind. First there was the flash, like lightning but not lightning; that must have been the plane firing at them, mistaking them for members of the common gang. Then the impact of the bullets against the steel hull. Then the plane which had fired at them appeared and Harlan had fired his first round of shots. After that the interval while the plane went south, seemed to be preparing to touch down, but, because even the cove was running two-foot waves, did not. The plane had reapproached them at a higher altitude, closer to the island. Harlan had fired again. Another burst of light. Then darkness.

She made a second pot of coffee. It was already starting to get gray outside the kitchen window, so she began preparing breakfast. She fixed the food methodically, paying careful attention to the details of mixing pancake batter, squeezing oranges, frying the eggs exactly the way she had once fixed them for the Captain, sunny side up with just enough bacon fat ladled over the yolks to keep them from running when she took them out of the pan.

After they had eaten, they went out through the garden to examine the damage to the *Ice Chopper*. On the way Marie noticed that her tomato plants were lying on their sides in the wet dirt, flattened by the storm. The plants looked as though they had been trampled by running animals. In the cloudburst the night before, sand and gravel had washed down off the railway embankment and covered the rear of her garden like a small avalanche.

Now in the daylight they could see that there were several deep dents, an inch or so in diameter, in the metal sheathing of Harlan's boat on the right side of the hull, and three jagged perforations just above the waterline.

"Yes, sir," Harlan said with satisfaction. "Whoever he was, he machine-gunned us, all right. If he'd aimed two inches lower, we'd have gone down on the spot. We'd be out there under eighty foot of water instead of dry and full of breakfast, Marie."

As Harlan continued to admire the damage, someone spoke to them from the top of the embankment. To Marie's surprise it was Abie Benedict, leaning on his crutch and waving cheerfully, looking better than she had seen him in a year. "Did you two hear what happened to Jean Paul Belliveau's plane in the storm last night?" he called down.

Marie had no idea what to say. Harlan gave him a hostile look, which he ignored.

"It was lost in the storm," Abie said. "Part of a blue wing washed up on the island this morning, and they're pretty sure it's his."

He paused. "Belliveau was flying it at the time," he said cheerfully, and, waving again, he limped off along the track.

Chapter Fourteen

Now that the whiskey wars were over, Abie turned his attention to the factory. Earlier that summer he had contracted with a Boston consulting firm to assess the productivity of each department. For two weeks white-shirted strangers carrying clipboards had gone briskly from floor to floor asking all kinds of questions and generally making a nuisance of themselves. Then they returned to Boston, but not before submitted sixty-five recommendations for reorganizing the business. Among these was a suggestion that the men on Durwood Baxter's machine floor switch jobs hourly in order to reduce tedium and increase production. When he read this, Durwood hit the roof. He told Abie bluntly that each man in his crew was proud of his ability to operate a particular machine better than anyone else and didn't want to be shunted about like an assembly-line worker in a box factory. Abie agreed not to implement this innovation but insisted on introducing into each department a complex cost-keeping system devised by the consultants, which resulted in Durwood's immediate resignation. Before leaving he said that he knew to the dollar what it cost to put any given job through his floor and didn't need a city man in a necktie to show him another way to find out. Hans Muhlich, the assistant cabinet-room foreman, quit over the same issue.

The new accounting system proved to be so cumbersome and impractical that Abie soon abandoned it, making Ned wonder whether he hired the efficiency team mainly to push out men like Durwood and Hans, both of whom were outspoken critics of the Mountain House. Marie agreed that this was partly the case. Yet as much as she distrusted Abie, she knew from Ned's own comments that some belt tightening would be necessary if the business was to remain solvent, especially since the folding seat contract had ended abruptly in June, just as Ned had predicted it would sooner or later, and the factory was once again relying mainly on its old bread-and-butter contract with United States Seating.

A related problem, however, was that when the lucrative government contract had first become available, the firm had cut back its work for U.S. Seating, which had been obliged to find other suppliers. To meet this difficulty, Abie shortened the work week from sixty to fifty-five hours, shutting the factory at noon on Saturday, though he still employed anyone who wanted to work Saturday afternoons rebuilding the greens and fairways on the golf course.

One concern Abie and Ned shared was replacing the lumber that had been washed away by the freak high water in the spring. More than half a million board feet had been lost, and the shortage became acute in July when a competitor of U.S. Seating recently established in Philadelphia placed a rush order with the factory for forty thousand straight-back hardwood chairs. At the time Ned was away from Hell's Gate, taking the first real vacation of his life; he and Ellen had gone west to visit Rachel Benedict for two weeks. When they returned he was astonished to discover that without waiting to consult him Abie had sent the dwindled Canadian logging crew to the park to cut the gigantic maples and yellow birch and wild cherry the Captain had years ago set aside in honor of his wife.

"What earthly good will it do him to cut those trees?" Ned said angrily. "Philadelphia wants delivery by the end of the summer. That lumber's still going to be as green as new grass then. It's just plain foolish, as I told Abie. Those boards will have to season at least a year. By then someone else will have the contract."

Marie thought he might quit and go to work at the American Heritage factory in the Common, as his brother and Hans Muhlich had, but Ned was nearly as devoted to the factory and the village as the Captain had been and had no intention of leaving. In fact, Ellen told Marie that when Rachel Benedict said that next to Hell's Gate, Arizona was the best place to live, Ned had looked at her seriously and said, "For me, there isn't any next best place to Hell's Gate, Mrs. Benedict."

A few evenings later, the Baxters asked Marie to walk up in the park with them. It was a sad scene. Except for several stands of large old hemlocks worthless for furniture, the mountainside above the low road had been clear-cut. Trees lay scattered as though a cyclone had been through; under Abie's direction the logging crew had made no attempt to pile up the brush and slash. In many places the brook was plugged almost shut by fallen limbs. None of the flood damage to the stone walls had been repaired.

Ellen shook her head. "I'm just glad Abraham isn't here to see this. It wasn't necessary."

"I don't know," Ned replied. "Anymore, I don't know what's necessary around here and what isn't."

He did not speak again until they were nearly home. Then he said quietly, "I'll tell you one thing, though. With the first good rain, I'm going to get that crew back there to clear out the brook and cut up the slash for firewood. I'll never have an easy night's sleep as long as that brush is up there where lightning or a careless match could set it on fire and burn the whole mountain down."

But the next day Abie transferred the woods crew to work on the Mountain House grounds, and nothing Ned said to him made any difference; the slash remained where it had been dropped, like a pile of gasoline-soaked rags in the corner of an old wooden building.

Despite the fact that nearly half the mortgage money was now gone, not much progress had been made on the resort hotel, which seemed to resist all of Abie's efforts to complete it. The great coal-burning furnace with its hundreds of feet of conduits was improperly installed and had to be dismantled. Water from underground springs ran into the basement, was pumped out, and reappeared a few days later. Permanent pumps were set in place, like ships' pumps. In the terrific thaw the previous spring the three new asphalt tennis courts had cracked like baked mud flats. These had to be broken up with steam hammers and resurfaced. The plots of ground sectioned out for formal perennial gardens grew up to fireweed and steeplebush. The carpenters went out on strike again and the hotel remained half finished, its sweeping pink granite facade reflecting the early-morning sunshine, a great windowless hulk open to the weather, like the hulk of a wrecked ship thrown high up on shore by a tidal wave. Again Abie engaged the Boston consulting firm that had reorganized the factory, this time to formulate a plan for completing the hotel. Once more, men in white shirts and ties flocked to the village with their clipboards and graph paper and multicolored charts, which they hung on his office walls and lectured him from by the hour. But despite their bright, hopeful chatter, many of the villagers had begun to suspect that the Mountain House was hexed, doomed to fail before it ever opened, and as Abie's borrowed capital slipped through his fingers daily with nothing but advice to show for it, he fell further and further into silent despondency.

One afternoon Ned went to the main office three times to have Abie sign a purchase order to replace a set of worn-out planer knives. Each time he found his employer asleep. The third time he woke him up, but instead of signing the requisitions Abie tossed them on top of some others on his desk and told Ned he'd get to them later.

"I guess he forgot all about it," Ned told Ellen that night. "Well, I'm sick of hounding him to do his job. He can sleep while Rome burns if he wants to. I'll do what I'm paid to do and keep my mouth shut from now on."

Ellen shook her head. "I don't know how much more of this I can stand myself," she said. "Abie maintains all the accounts for the Mountain House separately. He tries to keep them himself, but every week or ten days he calls me in to straighten them out, and they're getting to be more and more of a mess. Then there's this sleeping during working hours. I know he doesn't sleep well nights but the men can look right in and see him with his head on his desk. Yesterday Bill Kane sent Clayton and Slayton into his office with a great heavy plank when Abie was dozing. They dropped it right beside his chair with a terrible clatter just to see him jump."

Ned said nothing, but this was one of the very few times he had ever heard Ellen complain about her job, and it occurred to him that although he himself might choose to see the collapse of the factory through to the end, it would not be fair to put his wife under that strain.

Two weeks later Abie called Ned into his office one morning —he had abandoned the practice of holding regular meetings with his foremen months ago—and showed him a letter from United States Seating stating that some of the settees in the last shipment from Hell's Gate had not been sanded smooth.

"Check the next batch yourself, will you?" Abie said tiredly.

"I don't need to," Ned said. "They're right; those settees were rough in spots. It's the fault of the planer knives, though, not the sanders. Our supply of spare knives is gone and we need to order some more. The requisitions have been on your desk for days."

Immediately Abie lost his temper. "Jesus Christ!" he said. "Do you know how much a new planer costs?" ("I do," Ned told Ellen that evening, "though if he'd bothered to listen to me or read the orders he'd have known I wasn't asking for new planers, just a set of knives.")

"What do they want for settee prices, finish cabinetwork?" Abie had said, pounding his fist on his desk. "I don't intend to buy thousands of dollars worth of new machinery just so some Polack in Chicago can ride his fat ass on a streetcar to a ball game in style."

"He continued to cry poverty and berate his customers for a spell," Ned told Ellen. "So as soon as I could I ducked out. A couple of hours later he called me back in and handed me the signed requisitions for the knives. But it'll take at least three weeks to get them, and in the meantime we'll send out two more shipments of rough settees. I'll tell you something. Durwood wouldn't have let those benches go through the machine floor with the knives in that condition, and Abie knows it, whether he'll admit it or not. I'm not bragging because he's my brother, but when Abie lost Durwood, he lost a good man, worth more than all the cost systems and consultants in Boston. Things are going downhill fast around here. It's gotten to where I hate to go to work for fear of what's going to go wrong next."

"He should find a nice girl and marry her before it's too late," Ellen said. "I think he's given up hope. What he needs is something besides himself to live for."

"What he needs is a swift kick in the slats," Ned said. "And if Abraham were still here, he'd get it."

For the first time in its history, the village was not painted that year; instead, the paint crew was assigned to work on the Mountain House, and the five hundred gallons of yellow paint ordered the previous fall sat gathering dust in a room at the rear of the social hall. With the reduced orders from United States Seating and fewer cabinetmakers to handle special jobs, the factory's weekly payroll had dwindled to less than a thousand dollars in scrip, from nearly twice that amount three years ago. The work week had been shortened to five days and the crew from the Common cut in half, though Abie had promised to rehire everyone when work began on the special chair contract for the Philadelphia company. The entire village was showing signs of weakening morale in smaller and fewer gatherings at the social hall, a decreasing population as some families left for work elsewhere, and larger congregations of restless men on the store porch. Men and boys went openly to the park to poach trout, and no one but Ned Baxter seemed to care.

A few days later Abie again called Ned into his office and directed him to kiln-dry all the new lumber from trees cut in the park for two weeks at high temperatures—in accordance with a new method of rapid superheating that he'd read about in an issue of the *American Woodworking* magazine—then put through the big order from Philadelphia. Ned was astonished. But when he objected, Abie said curtly, "Just do it. Anyone who's kept up with recent developments in this business knows that lumber doesn't need to dry outside for one or two centuries, the opinion of men like my father notwithstanding."

Ned was all the more amazed when just an hour or so later he happened to overhear a machine parts salesman ask Abie how many boardfeet a pile of lumber stacked beside the saw-mill contained. Abie replied, "Oh, about ten thousand feet, I'd say. Isn't that right, Uncle Ned?"

"That's pretty close," Ned said drily. "You're just off by one small naught, Abie."

But neither the salesman nor Abie had heard, or been paying attention if they did hear; and despite Ned's continued objections, Abie insisted that the green lumber go into the kilns at two hundred and fifty degrees for two weeks. "It's like stoking up your baking oven as hot as you can get it, putting a pie in for ten minutes, and then taking it out and serving it," Ned said. "What you've got is a burnt crust and raw apples."

"Give him a chance to prove himself, Ned," Ellen said. "Maybe he did read that."

"Maybe," Ned said.

On the day the first run of lumber came out of the kiln, Ned appeared in Abie's office, where he was playing solitaire on the gold medal desk. Between his thumb and forefinger the foreman held a long sliver of wood. "This is still damp inside," he said. "It's months away from being ready to use for chairs or anything else except firing the boiler."

Abie sighed. "All right, Ned," he said. "Nobody anywhere knows lumber better than you. If you say it's not ready, it's not. That's that."

He then asked Ned to estimate how many chairs could be made from the seasoned lumber on hand in the yard and to give the figure to Ellen, who would draft a letter over his signature to the Philadelphia company proposing that Hell's Gate supply that number now and the remainder whenever Ned thought the new lumber would be ready. Ned was enormously relieved. But a week later when Abie received a letter from Philadelphia stating that the order must be shipped in its entirety by the end of August or not at all, he asked to see another sample of the kiln-dried lumber and after examining it a moment reversed his instructions and told Ned to hire back the full day crew and add a temporary night crew in the varnish room.

"Abie," Ned said quietly, "we don't have cured lumber for half that many chairs. We don't have lumber for a quarter that number."

"We've got lumber for twice that many," Abie said. "We're going to kiln-dry all that new stuff for two weeks at two hundred and sixty degrees."

"That won't make any difference. Look at this piece. Feel it. It's so green it's still oozing sap."

"It's dry as an old whore," Abie said heatedly.

In his quietest voice Ned said, "Abie, your father always listened to me. I don't believe he ever had reason to wish he hadn't."

"My father's dead, goddamn it. And before he died he spent half of every year for five years buying Indian blankets and jugs and donkeys. This is 1921, not 1911. Put through the order, Ned. Put the order through, or I'll find someone who will."

Again there was work at the factory. The day crew ran at full capacity, and Ned mustered a temporary night crew. Again the factory train ran six days a week, and on September first the new chairs were sent out in ten Benedict boxcars newly painted pale yellow for the occasion, with Abie accompanying the shipment in the Captain's private car. Before leaving he assured the factory crew that with the delivery he would consummate a large and extremely profitable agreement to become the Philadelphia chair company's chief supplier, and as the train pulled out of the village, the silver cornet band played "Stars and Stripes Forever" and brightly colored bunting flew from the locomotive that would take the cars on the first leg of the journey.

The train left for Philadelphia on Wednesday evening and was not scheduled to arrive back in Hell's Gate until the following Monday, a week before school began. That Friday Marie took her final examinations for the summer session at the normal school. This summer she had taken four courses instead of three and had been so busy with her studies she had not had much time for anything else. When Harlan asked her to go fishing with him the day after her exams, she was delighted; she hadn't been fishing more than once or twice since May.

On Saturday afternoon she packed a big picnic lunch, and at four o'clock he came by for her in his *Ice Chopper*. She thought he would probably want to fish the mouth of the St. John, but instead he went directly out to Indian Island. For a couple of hours they trolled back and forth in the mouth of the cove. It was choppy and Harlan complained of seasickness, but the fishing was good. They caught two large rainbow trout apiece. After Marie caught her second fish, Harlan headed toward the beach, near where he had asked her to teach him how to read.

Since that day they had come to the island many times, and at many different times of the year, fishing its coves, walking along the shore, climbing up the hill to look up and down the big lake. Lying as it did directly on the U.S.-Canadian border, it was a remote and beautiful place, a refuge for many kinds of water birds and wildflowers, and because of its isolation, it seemed much farther away from the village than it actually was. It was about the size of an ordinary hill farm, and had many of the same features, including a hill.

"Harlan," Marie said after they had eaten, "of all the places I've ever been, I think I like this island best. It's peaceful—no schools, no factories, nothing but the woods and the lake and us. I'd like to have a cottage out here sometime, and come and stay all summer."

"You'd best do it then, while there's still time," he said. "I'll tell you something, schoolteacher. When I was a young man, nineteen or twenty years old, I wanted in the worst way to go out to Westconsin. I planned to strike out on my twenty-first birthday. I was going to get myself a job on a ranch out there, be a regular Wild West cowboy. The day I turned twenty-one I had my valise all packed and was on my way to the station when I met old Peter Dutcher, who used to own the Commission Sales. Pete stopped me and offered me a job working for him. I told him no, I was heading west. But he pressed me on it, said he'd heard that jobs were as scarce there as here, and I'd be better off to work for him for a few months and save enough money to live on out there for a while in case I didn't land something right off. Well sir, being an auctioneer, Pete was a great talker, and I'd always looked up to him, so I let myself be persuaded to hold off on Westconsin until the next year. But right off as soon as I started work Pete commenced to groom me for his job, and then the first Mrs. Smith waltzed along, and what with that and other mistakes on my part, next year never rolled around. I was stuck. And still am today."

Harlan was quiet for a time, but Marie knew him well enough to suspect that he was almost certainly leading up to some announcement. Still, she was astonished when he said suddenly, "I sold the Commission Sales yesterday."

She looked at him and saw that he was serious.

"I sold the whole shebang, lock, stock, and barrel, for eighty-six hundred dollars. I put that with another little nest egg I've been saving from my side business, and I'm going west next week to raise horses."

Again he paused, looking down the lake. Then he said casually, "I was going to ask if you wanted to come along. Not that I'd press you on it like old Pete pressed me. But the way things are going around here, there may not be enough families left in Hell's Gate to make up a school in a few years. It might be an opportunity for both of us."

He skimmed a stone across the cove. "We'd take some time to look around, not rush into anything, until we find just what we want. I've got it all figured out. Two hundred acres ought to be plenty. That ought to provide hay and pasturage for, say, twenty horses. We wouldn't want many more. Maybe a couple of white-face cows for our own beef, but we don't want to tie ourselves down with a milker. A few laying hens if you want them, maybe a pair of ducks for baking eggs—there's no point baking with chicken eggs if you've got a spot to keep a duck. We might look for a place that's got a pond, in fact. The house wouldn't have to be too much, we could fix that up as we went along, but we'd want a good tight barn for the horses."

"Whoa!" Marie said, laughing. "Why do we need any house at all? We could just live in the barn with the horses."

"That's true," he said thoughtfully. "Then we could build what we wanted for ourselves as we had the money to do it."

He was off again, creating log houses and stone houses, renovating them entirely even before they were finished, until she cut him off again.

"Harlan, for heaven's sake, I don't want to own property. Not now, at least. Owning property's always a mistake if you can avoid it. The gypsies told me so years and years ago, and they were right. Look what owning property and trying to pay for it did to Jigger Johnson; it got him drowned. Look what it's done to Abie. Even Margaret and John are tied down more than I ever want to be. I'll tell you, I'll be happy to leave this world about the way I entered it and have enjoyed some of my best times in it, which is to say with my birthday suit and not much else."

"Stop right there," Harlan said, his face turning red. "I won't hear that sort of talk from a woman, and if you expect to come west and go halves with me then you'd better break yourself of it right now. Are you coming or not?"

Marie did not answer immediately. She stood at the edge of the lake looking far off across the water at the yellow village between the mountains. She knew that what Harlan had predicted for Hell's Gate might very well come to pass. Over the summer Ned Baxter had said much the same thing several times. Her job, which she looked forward to as she looked forward to the autumn itself; her house with its garden and flowers, its comfortable kitchen and parlor and fine view down the bay; the slow circularity of village life, which by degrees had come to provide a structure for her own life; even her closest friends—all might be gone before many more years went by. Abie had spoken to Ned again recently about getting out from under everything by selling to a paper company, and if he did, Hell's Gate would never be the same again; it would become just another reeking mill town, like Magog, at the head of the lake. Even if that did not happen, with Harlan gone her life in Kingdom County would be diminished more than she had realized until now.

Marie had never made a practice of analyzing her feelings. Most of her life she'd been too busy, first just surviving, then earning a living, then acquiring her education and living and working in the village. Like nearly all the villagers, and most country people everywhere, she tended to believe that scrutinizing one's close relationships with others was both unnecessary and unlucky. Yet she could no longer deny to herself that against all probabilities she had somehow fallen in love with this man of so many contradictions and surprises. It had happened slowly and almost despite herself—but it had happened, and she was now forced to consider what Harlan meant to her and why. Certainly sex was an important part of their intimacy, but it by no means accounted for all of it. Nor were they as companionable as she and Jigger or she and Philbrook Jamieson had been; they had many common interests, from going fishing to enjoying a good meal together, yet they still disagreed far more than they agreed. Like her attachment to Hell's Gate, where over the years she had encountered many setbacks and difficulties, and where still greater difficulties might lie ahead, Marie's attachment to Harlan Smith was ultimately a mystery to her.

She looked up at the mountains above the village. More than once she had heard city visitors to Hell's Gate say they felt closed in by the high, close peaks, that it was hard to breathe in the village because of them. To her, the mountains were as much a part of the town as the houses and factory, and she could not imagine being away from them for long. They were her first memory of Hell's Gate, the first sight she had seen as a girl coming out of Canada, and even on the darkest nights she could sense their great solid comforting bulk. Rachel Benedict had told the Baxters that she missed the mountains more than the Big House; and although Marie knew that, like Rachel, she too could move away from Hell's Gate and Kingdom County and make a fresh start if she had to, she did not have to and did not intend to do so. She had been away twice and come back both times, drawn to this remote northern settlement bordered by the towering granite mountains and mile after mile of deep cold water and deep woods. As Pia had told her years ago, it was her home.

It was beginning to grow dusky. Instead of dropping, as it often did toward night, the wind had come up stronger. Beyond the mouth of the cove, Marie saw some whitecaps curling up on the surface of the lake. She turned to Harlan. "You'll come back," she said. "You think you won't, but you will, and when you do, I'll be right here to go fishing with you."

She expected him to try to persuade her to change her mind, but he surprised her again by nodding as though he had foreseen her decision from the start. "Fine," he said. "Stay on here. Go down with the ship along with Benedict and all the rest. But don't expect old Smitty to come back and bail you out, because he's westward bound for good. I'm departing tonight."

"When did you decide that?"

"Just now. Get in the boat."

When they reached the dock twenty minutes later, twilight had settled over the village. The wind was blowing harder; sea gulls were flying in off the rough lake to perch on the rooftops. There was no doubt that a big storm was on its way, but Harlan insisted on going on to the Common in order to leave for Wisconsin that evening. He was already out of sight down the bay when Marie came out on the street and noticed the crowd milling around the station platform. Just beyond, on the siding near the roundhouse, stood the Philadelphia train, two days earlier than expected. In the middle of the crowd Stan Gregory was trying to answer half a dozen questions at once. Ned Baxter stood listening with his hands in his pockets, somewhat apart from most of the others.

"What is it, Uncle Ned?" Marie said. "What's all the commotion?"

He turned to look at her. "I'll tell you what it is," he said quietly. "That entire shipment of chairs made from green lumber just arrived back. Somewhere between here and Philadelphia they warped so badly not a one of them will sit straight. They aren't good for anything but firing the boiler with. Abie didn't get a penny for them."

"Good Lord!"

"Good Lord is right. Because you still haven't heard the worst. This afternoon in the mail Abie got a letter from U.S. Seating. He'd instructed Ellen to open all his correspondence while he was away, so she read it; but she soon wished she hadn't. Because it seems that the last batch of settees we sent out there were so rough they've canceled their standing order with us for chairs and settees both." He thought for a minute. "Over an eighty-dollar set of planing knives. And now these warped chairs on our hands."

"Does Abie know about the letter?"

"Yes. I gave it to him ten minutes ago, as soon as the train got in."

"What did he say?"

"Nothing."

"He didn't say anything at all?"

"No. He laughed instead. He just went off up the street laughing to himself."

Ned turned and started toward his house, walking slowly, bent into the wind. He stopped at his gate.

"There's an old saying, Marie. This storm coming reminds me of it. It's from the Bible, I believe, though I can't say where. 'Sow the wind, reap the whirlwind.' "

It was nearly full dark, and big drops of rain were starting to fall, but Ned looked at her searchingly for a long moment.

"I'm afraid that's what's going to happen next here," he said. "We're going to reap the whirlwind."

It was after midnight and the wind was blowing so hard that if she had not been sleeping fitfully she would never have heard the pounding on her front door. As she came fully awake she was quite sure it was Harlan, that he had changed his mind about going west or returned to try to persuade her to accompany him. But when she opened the door there were two men on her porch, wearing overcoats and holding their hats to keep them from blowing away. How they had gotten down the street without being blown away themselves was a wonder.

"Miss Blythe?"

"I'm Marie Blythe. Come in before the door comes off its hinges!"

She led them through the hallway out to the kitchen, where everyone in Hell's Gate received guests, and began to put on coffee.

"This isn't a social visit, Miss Blythe. We're with the United States Immigration Service. We're looking for Harlan Smith."

"I know who you are," Marie said, continuing to measure out coffee. "I knew who you were as soon as I opened the door. Who else would be out on a night like this besides whiskey runners and customs men?"

"We're with immigration, not customs," the spokesman said.

"Whatever, the government's the government. Harlan's not here."

"We'd like to look."

"Go ahead. You won't find him."

While the officers went from room to room with their hands on their guns, Marie sat at the kitchen table. When the coffee was ready she poured herself a cup and drank it. She was very angry, not only with the two men for ransacking her house in the middle of the night, but with Harlan for not telling her he was in some kind of trouble.

"What's Harlan been up to?" she said when the men reappeared in the kitchen.

"You know what he's been up to, Miss Blythe," the older man who did the talking said. "He's been smuggling in Chinks."

Marie stood up. "Mister," she said, "I've never yet turned anyone out of this house, and I don't like the idea of starting on a night like this. But that's a word I don't even like the sound of."

The man sighed. "He's been smuggling Chinese," he said. "You've been helping him. We've got a witness who saw four of them here one night. Do you want to tell us about it?"

"No," Marie said. "And I don't care what your so-called witness said he saw. You can't send somebody to jail for the color of their guests' skin."

"Maybe not," the man said. "But if you don't cooperate with us we can and will send you back to Canada, Miss Blythe."

"What do you mean, send me back to Canada?"

"I mean that our records show you've never been naturalized. You're as much an alien yourself as those people your friend's been bringing into the country illegally. Think it over. We won't bother you any more tonight, but we'll be back. You can count on it."

Sitting at her table after they had left, Marie looked at the cold coffee in the bottom of her cup and thought how Rachel Benedict had once asked Pia what future she saw in her teacup. Her own future, she realized, was still as uncertain as ever. No sooner had she decided to make Hell's Gate her permanent home than she was on the verge of being expelled not only from the village and county but from Vermont and the States, like Harlan Smith's line-bound uncle.

Marie did not think that the immigration officers could have much evidence against Harlan. As far as she knew, he had always worked alone and never said a word about his operation to anyone in Kingdom County, where it was still widely believed that he made his night trips up the lake for Canadian whiskey. It seemed obvious to her that while they were trying to build a case against him, the authorities had let him slip through their fingers. When they discovered that he had decamped, they'd panicked and tried to trick her into incriminating him.

What bothered her more was that someone in Hell's Gate had been spying on her or Harlan or both of them. Who the unnamed government witness could be she had no idea, except that it was probably someone she knew and trusted. Although Abie despised her and wanted her out of the village, she could not picture him lurking around her house like a peeping Tom; he had too many problems of his own now to have time for her. But she was seriously worried about the possibility that she might be deported, and the following Monday morning she postponed opening school for a day and took the early factory train to the Common to apply for United States citizenship.

"Where was you born?" the county clerk, Late Kinneson, asked her. He was a lanky middle-aged man with a perpetually aggrieved expression identical to his brother Early's.

"In the township of St. Francis, Quebec."

"Was you now?" the clerk said suspiciously. "Can you prove it?"

"I don't have a birth certificate, if that's what you mean."

"You have to have some documentation as to where you was born before I can process your request for naturalization."

Late went back to work on the deed he was copying, and Marie wheeled around and left his office and went down the hall into the chambers of Judge Scudder Pike.

Judge Pike was an old friend of Abraham Benedict, a genial, elderly man who was making a pot of coffee to fortify himself for a long day ahead hearing poaching cases.

"Judge Pike, excuse me for bursting in on you this way," Marie said, "but I need some help. I'm Marie Blythe. I met you years ago at Captain Benedict's house in Hell's Gate. I teach the school there now."

The judge nodded. "Sit down, Miss Blythe. Will you have a cup of coffee?"

"I'm too mad to sit down and too nervous to drink any coffee, thanks just the same. I came here this morning to apply for U.S. citizenship, and Late Kinneson says I can't do that until I have a birth certificate to prove I was born in Canada."

"Does he now?" the judge said. "Come with me."

He steered Marie back down the hall by her elbow and turned into the county clerk's office. "Late," he said in a booming voice, "sign this woman up to take the naturalization test straightaway. If I hear any more reports of your pettifogging lawyering, I'll have you brought up before me on the charge of practicing law without a license. Do you understand?"

Late understood, and three weeks later Marie, along with six other men and women, took the oath of citizenship in Burlington and became an American.

The same day she received the first postcard from Harlan Smith. He was in Buffalo, and he had written: *Toured truss factory here. Stocked up for trip west. Lost $1,200 at a cockfight in Albany, N.Y. Your friend and ex-student, Harlan "Smitty" Smith.*

Despite their threats, the immigration investigators had not returned, and Harlan's postcard amused Marie as much as it irritated her. But although she was pleased to have become a United States citizen, and relieved to think that she could no longer be deported as an undesirable alien, matters in the village were deteriorating so rapidly that her job and home seemed less secure than ever.

Soon after the fiasco of the Philadelphia chair shipment, the Boston consultant firm had charged six thousand dollars for preparing a two-hundred-page report, the gist of which was that the Mountain House was not, never had been, and never would be economically feasible.

Abie skimmed over the report, tore it up, and, since there wasn't work enough in the factory anyway, transferred the entire crew of day workers from the Common to the Mountain House. Most were unskilled at carpentry—hammer slingers, Ned called them—and they were worse than useless there, dropping plate glass windows, slamming up hallway partitions in the wrong places, plastering ceilings that fell down two days later.

At the factory, the work week was shortened to four days, then three. The day before Thanksgiving, Abie posted a list of men who should report the following week. Some of the men whose names had not been included appeared at the factory door Monday morning anyway, and Abie did not tell them to leave. But on the Friday before Christmas of 1921, for the first time in the history of the village, Benedict employees were not paid on time.

There were other difficulties at the factory. After Abie had pulled the cabinetmakers off the New England Life contract to make furniture for the Mountain House, several hundred backlogged desk orders piled up. Finally the insurance company, like U.S. Seating, grew tired of waiting and found another supplier in Grand Rapids.

To compensate for this major loss, Abie took an official American League baseball bat into the cabinet room one day and asked Herman to turn out five hundred exactly like it. He said that he planned to market these independently, at a reduced rate, to retail stores in New England. They were fine solid bats, made of seasoned white ash bought on credit, and Abie had no trouble selling them at his promotion price, which was about half the cost of an official bat. When he raised the price to break even, however, he was unable to sell more than a few dozen and gave up the venture.

By then Abie was hardly making a pretense of running the business. One morning in January he vanished without telling anyone where he was going. Two days late he reappeared in the village with two hard-looking women. One was about twenty, the other close to twice that age. Both were rumored to be Montreal prostitutes, with whom he ensconced himself in the Big House for a solid week during which the lights burned all night, every night, in every room. The next week Abie took them with him on the train to Chicago, reportedly to try to persuade United States Seating to reinstate their contract, but nothing came of the Chicago trip except a five-hundred-dollar hotel bill, which Ellen Baxter did not have cash on hand at the factory to pay.

As spring approached, conditions in the village worsened. The payroll was issued only irregularly. Many men worked on at the factory anyway, but others found jobs in Kingdom Common and elsewhere. Ned Baxter became more and more silent. He and Abie had said little to each other anyway since the warped chairs had been returned from Philadelphia. Even so, Ned was badly jolted when, two days after the ice went out of the bay, his name did not appear on the list of men to report to work the following week; after spending the weekend in dazed disbelief, he took a job at American Heritage and began commuting to Kingdom Common each day on the train, as most of the other men who remained in the village were doing.

On the day Ned began work in the Common, Abie went into the company store and bought a work shirt and a gray cloth cap. When the factory opened he appeared on the mill floor and began tailing a cut-off saw for Jump Simons. Apparently he hoped to improve morale by rolling up his sleeves and going to work beside the men, but the few remaining workers snickered behind their hands or regarded his performance as a sad parody. After less than an hour, he left the machine, went into the office, and asked Ellen Baxter for a financial statement. What she told him was as bleak as the rainy April sky over the village: There was no running cash on hand and the company owed more than forty thousand dollars, mainly for expenditures on the Mountain House. Except for a few of the softwood stickers formerly used to separate layers of stacked boards, the lumberyard was empty. New England Life's desk orders were down to thirty a month, and with only Herman Fischner and three other cabinetmakers left, they were having trouble meeting even that contract.

Appearing nearly desperate, Abie dictated a notice for Ellen to send to the Boston and New York newspapers, advertising the entire estate, including the factory, for half a million dollars. There were a number of inquiries from investors who seemed more curious than serious and a few mock offers from pranksters. But the ads did not result in a promising response until one day in late April, when the morning mail Stan Gregory brought in included a long buff-colored envelope addressed to Abie, with the word PRIVATE stamped on both sides in sharp black lettering.

The enclosed letter was typed on a sheet of heavy, expensive stationery matching the envelope and contained a formally phrased request from the agent of an unnamed furniture manufacturer, who wished to send a representative to Hell's Gate to view the property and examine the factory books. Oddly, the letter gave no return address but stated that Abie would be contacted soon by telephone.

Abie showed little interest until Ellen read the signature. Then he looked up sharply from clipping his fingernails. "What was that name?" he said.

"Greenwald. Phineas J. Greenwald."

"Give me that letter."

Ellen was surprised by his peremptoriness, since Abie had remained unfailingly polite to her, if to no one else. She handed the letter across his desk and watched with still more surprise as he studied it intently.

All he told her, however, was to put Greenwald through to him as soon as he called or, if he happened to be out when the call came in, to set up an appointment for the agent to visit at the earliest possible date.

Phineas Greenwald rode up to Hell's Gate late the following Saturday afternoon on the weekly shopping train Abie still ran to the Common. Marie, returning home from her Saturday normal school classes, watched him get on: a slim, well-dressed man in his late forties, with dark, slick hair scented with a pungently aromatic tonic, and a flat black briefcase, which he dropped in the vacant seat across from hers. He glanced at her once, incuriously, sat down, opened the briefcase, and removed a newspaper. Ellen had mentioned the mysterious buff-colored letter to her, and Marie suspected that the stranger was Greenwald. Something about him seemed very familiar, but she could not place him, and since he paid no attention to her or anyone else aboard the train but remained absorbed in his paper, she half forgot he was aboard until they arrived.

Abie was waiting at the station to greet the agent. Marie watched the two men shake hands and was amused to see that immediately afterward Abie seized the black briefcase and insisted on carrying it across the street to the factory office. Greenwald did not seem in the least discomposed by having a crippled man serve as his porter and walked briskly on ahead.

The rest Marie heard later that evening at the Baxters.

"Ellen," Abie had said, "I'd like you to meet Mr. Phineas Greenwald. Mr. Greenwald, this is Ellen Baxter, the factory auditor. She'll be sitting in with us."

Phineas Greenwald looked at Ellen. His eyes, she told Ned and Marie, were as dark as his polished black shoes.

"That's up to you, Mr. Benedict," he said. "But I want to advise you that my employer wishes to maintain the strictest confidentiality possible, so the fewer persons you involve in our discussions the better. He's planning to open a nationwide chain of woodworking plants, and above everything else he doesn't want competitive firms to learn what his plans are."

"Ellen will keep everything we say in confidence," Abie said evenly. He led the way into his private office, where after two hours of discussing the business and reviewing the books, Greenwald made an offer on behalf of his employer for three hundred and fifty thousand dollars. Although this figure was substantially below his asking price in the newspaper advertisements, Abie hesitated only a few moments before accepting. And as the discussion continued, Abie grew more and more deferential, much to Ellen's amazement.

The verbal agreement the two men worked out was that the factory would continue to operate with the same workers and with Abie as superintendent at an annual wage of ten thousand dollars. It would manufacture quality office furniture, as well as less expensive chairs and settees, as it had in the past, and most of the machine operators and foremen would be rehired.

"I'll believe that when it happens," Ned said. "This Greenwald sounds like too smooth a customer. Something's not right, Ellen. Tomorrow's Saturday, and at the risk of getting my head bitten off, which I don't much care if I do, I'm going to talk to Abie first thing in the morning."

"Don't go too early," Ellen said. "Those Montreal girls are back up there with him, and I doubt he'll be up and around tomorrow until noon or past."

The next morning about eleven, as Marie stepped onto her porch to shake out the hall runner, she saw Ned coming back down the street from the direction of the Big House. He looked neither to the right nor left and was walking very fast.

"What's the matter, Uncle Ned?" she said. "Wasn't he up yet?"

"He was," Ned told her grimly. "He's been up since daylight, he said, and I believe him."

"Didn't he listen to you?"

"Of course he didn't listen to me. He laughed in my face."

Ned's hands were shaking on the peeling yellow fence separating Marie's lawn from the walk. She had never seen him this angry before, and since she knew he had a heart condition, she was alarmed.

"It can't be that bad, Uncle Ned," she said. "Who cares about

Abie? It's a beautiful spring day. Now that Harlan's gone, I don't have anybody to take me fishing. What do you say we forget about Abie and take a look at the brook up in the park?"

"There isn't any park any more," Ned said. "And I can't forget about Abie. He's had those two trollops up on ladders all morning and do you know what they've been doing? I'll tell you. They're painting Abraham's house white."

Ned started off down the sidewalk, then turned back.

"He told me it was the last thing he wanted to do before he sells the town. And all the while that pair of French tarts were giggling to each other and slapping white paint on the front of the house while Abie stood there grinning.

"White paint," Marie heard him say again as he turned into his yard.

Although she understood how Ned felt about the Big House, Marie was more concerned about the sale of the town. If Greenwald's mysterious employer did buy Hell's Gate and revitalize the business, she could probably continue to live and teach in the village. But since Harlan's departure, she was no longer certain she wanted to stay on. She was no longer sure what she wanted to do, and as she continued her spring house-cleaning that morning, she wondered whether her own routine was beginning to become meaningless in the general unraveling of the village.

The following Friday, Abie left the village early in the morning for Boston, where Phineas Greenwald had asked to meet him in order to review some final details before closing the sale. He telephoned Ellen on Saturday to say that the meeting with Greenwald had gone well and they would take the *Montrealer* together from Boston to Kingdom Common Monday morning. He asked her to have Stan Gregory in the Common with the train at two-thirty sharp Monday afternoon, and to contact his lawyer and have him there to accompany them to Hell's Gate, where the closing would take place.

But when the Captain's private car pulled into Hell's Gate on Monday afternoon, Abie was the only passenger. Even from the factory office, Ellen could see that he looked fatigued, years older than when he had left a few days ago. He limped across the street and entered his office without speaking. He sat down at the big desk and stared out the window for a minute. Then he told Ellen to come in and shut the door and in a voice devoid of everything but weariness informed her that at yet another meeting Greenwald had called suddenly the previous afternoon, he had extorted a ten-thousand-dollar commission check from him, which as Greenwald knew from reviewing the books was the last running cash on hand in the factory; then he had vanished. The anonymous rich man, the chain of woodworking factories, the three hundred and fifty thousand dollars —all were as imaginary as the sale itself. Abie had no choice other than to admit he had been swindled by a professional confidence man, and although he wired his mother for a thousand dollars to hire a private detective to trace Greenwald, no word of the swindler was heard in the village again.

"I've lost it all, Ellen, haven't I?" Abie said one morning in mid-May.

It was the first time he had left the Big House, now a glossy white on the side facing the village, for two weeks.

Without waiting for an answer to his question—the factory had been shut for a week, though Ellen and a few of the other longtime employees continued to show up—Abie told her he was departing for Arizona that afternoon to make a final plea to his mother for cash to keep the business open a few weeks longer. Just before he left he extracted a promise from her that she and Ned would retain their scrip at least until he returned, and urge the others villagers who still held stock in the company to hold onto theirs. He stopped briefly at the school and made the same request of Marie, who listened politely without committing herself. Despite her contempt for his recent behavior, it bothered her deeply to see him reduced to this kind of pleading. Once he had been a proud young man with high spirits and hopes.

"Wish me luck with my mother, Marie," he said.

But she could not even do that in good conscience, and as he hitched off down the hill toward the station she felt a great sadness for his wasted life.

One day after school in early June, Marie cleaned the winter's accumulation of soot out of her chimney. Usually the villagers waited until fall to do this job, but not knowing what to expect in the months ahead, she wanted to get the job out of the way now. As she'd done once a year since moving into the teacher's house, she went across the bridge, walked a short distance up the lower slope of Canada Mountain, and cut a bushy skunk spruce tree about eight feet tall. Then she climbed up onto her kitchen roof with the tree, hitched a chain to the butt end, and shoved it top first down the chimney, using a beanpole to drive it all the way to the thimble hole where the stovepipe came in. She pulled the tree back up with the chain and repeated the process several times so that the stiff branches would scrub the accumulated soot off the inside of the chimney bricks. It was an old trick she'd learned from the gypsies, and she smiled to remember how many tricks they taught her; then she laughed out loud to think how they all had turned into staid business-men. It occurred to her that she had not really laughed hard like this for months, since before Harlan had left.

To her surprise, the auctioneer had stayed away all winter, though Wisconsin, when he finally got there and discovered that it resembled Vermont more than the great American West Marie had read to him about in Zane Grey stories, had proven to be a dreadful disillusionment, and he had quickly moved on to North Dakota and from there to Montana and, most recently, California. None of the places he had visited so far suited him—they were too hot or too cold, too high or too low, each activating one or more of his myriad phobias—and she expected to see him on her doorstep any day now, especially since the trouble with the immigration officers seemed to have blown over.

When she finished the kitchen chimney, she paused and looked around. It was a mild afternoon, and the air was so hazy that she could barely make out the Canada Mountain House, abandoned since fall, sitting high on the mountainside like a mirage. From far down the railroad track beside the bay she heard the factory train approaching, on its way back from the afternoon run to the Common. When the bright headlamp appeared through the haze, she thought of the first train she had ever seen, coming through the Canadian woods to take her to the States.

The train passed behind her garden. The lights were on in the single passenger carriage, and she could see Ned Baxter's profile at a window. His head was bent as though he was reading. He did not look up as she waved, and she suspected that he had finally bought the house he and Ellen had been looking at in the Common.

A few minutes later, just as she finished the main chimney, Ned appeared on the sidewalk, walking slowly toward his house with his head still bent. "Uncle Ned!" she called from the rooftop. As he looked up, she tossed the sooty tree down into the yard and said, "Merry Christmas!"

She hoped he would grin, but he continued to stare as though he couldn't quite make her out, though it was still only early dusk and there was plenty of light left to see by. She waved, then lowered herself to the roof of the porch and dropped lightly down beside him. "What's wrong, Uncle Ned?" she said. "Did you buy that place in the Common?"

He shook his head. "No," he said. "But I should have. I should have yesterday." He paused. "Do you know if Ellen's home yet?"

"No, I think she's still over at the office."

"Good. Because I've got to think how to tell her this."

He looked off into the dusk.

"Rachel died last night. I picked up the telegram with this morning's mail in the Common. Maybe that's a blessing, as they say, because she was terribly lonely and suffering more than she wanted to let on when we saw her. But that isn't all. When I went into the bank tonight after work, I found out they'd stopped payment on all scrip."

He looked straight at Marie and said, "Abie's filed for bankruptcy, Marie. Ellen and I have just lost twelve thousand dollars in savings."

Chapter Fifteen

She left the Common in the early evening on the train that had once taken more than one hundred workers to the factory each morning. She rode with the two dozen or so men from Hell's Gate who still commuted to and from the American Heritage factory in the Captain's private car, which by the late summer of 1922 was the only serviceable passenger car remaining, and once again she rode facing backward, as she had ridden backward years ago when she had first come to the yellow village on the cattle car with her parents, since the turntable was broken and there was no money to repair it.

As she moved north along the slow river, past swamp maples already reddening for fall, it did not seem to her that more than twenty years could have gone by since that morning in the early spring of 1899. Yet years seemed to have passed since the day less than three months ago that the telegram informing Ned of Rachel's death in Arizona had arrived, though it still did not seem possible to Marie that both the Captain and his wife were dead; she half expected them to be waiting in Hell's Gate to greet her, as they had greeted her and the other Canadians in 1899.

She shut her eyes and thought back over the events of the summer.

After settling his mother's estate—which had dwindled to

next to nothing, according to Ned—Abie had disappeared. All sorts of wild rumors about his disappearance were rampant in the village: he had committed suicide; he had been abducted for a ransom, then murdered; he had absconded to Mexico with a secret fund from the factory. But Abie had dropped out of sight before, and Marie was quite sure that he would reappear in a month or six months or a year, when whatever he had salvaged from his mother's estate was gone.

The village, in the meantime, was coming apart at the seams. After the company had gone into receivership, there had been several inquiries from prospective buyers, including a group of Shakers from Maine. But none had resulted in an offer, and through June and July and August, while Marie was in summer school, villagers had continued to move away, so that by now less than half of the original population remained. Neither the Baxters nor anyone else had been reimbursed for a single penny of their scrip. Fading away in desk and bureau drawers and private strongboxes and safety deposit boxes at the Common Bank, the quaint-looking squares of yellow paper were as worthless as Confederate money. Marie herself had lost eight hundred dollars' worth.

It had been a bad summer for her in other ways as well. Harlan had not written since May, and she was worried about him. Margaret and John Fellows had both been offered good jobs at the state university and had moved to Burlington in July. Ned and Ellen had finally rented a place near Ned's brother's house in the Common.

That morning Marie had waked up so discouraged that she had nearly skipped her graduation ceremony. For the first time since she had recovered from tuberculosis, she had to force herself to get out of bed and fix breakfast. She was further dispirited a few minutes later, when she discovered a few first gray hairs at her temples. Somehow she got ready and boarded the morning train, but she found herself continually raising her hand to her head to rearrange her hair all the way to the Common. Probably she would not have gone at all if she had

not been curious to see and hear the poet Robert Frost, who
was speaking to the graduates.

She spent the morning practicing with the other students, all
of whom were years younger than her. She felt no better at
noon, so to divert herself she walked over to the Commission
Sales barn; but although it was Saturday, auction day, the only
person she found there was Jehoshaphat, mooning about aim-
lessly, as he had since his mentor had gone west.

"Don't worry, Hosh," Marie said. "He'll be back. He'll get
sick of the West or the West will get sick of him, one or the
other." But her words had a hollow sound in the empty entranceway of the barn.

The ceremony began at one. At first Marie had to force
herself to be attentive, but when Robert Frost began his address, she found herself listening as intently as though he were
talking directly to her. He was a fine-looking man who began
by reading some of his poems. They were clear and straightfor-
ward, about people like the people she had grown up with and
worked with all her life. Then, instead of congratulating the
graduates on what they had already accomplished, or challeng-
ing them with achievements yet to be made, he simply advised
them to go their own way, like a brook that finds its own best
course down a mountainside.

As she rode back toward the disintegrating village, she
thought again about this advice. She found it both deeply
appealing and, at the same time, somewhat oversimplified,
since although she wished to go her own way, she could not
pretend to herself that her choices were not hemmed in by the
circumstances of the village, as the village itself was hemmed
in by the mountains and lake. It occurred to her that in order
to take Frost's advice she might have to see beyond those
borders. With her teaching degree in her handbag, she could
find work almost anywhere. Perhaps, she thought, she had
become too dependent on Hell's Gate; perhaps she was afraid
to try something new and unfamiliar. She sighed and shook her
head, too tired to think any longer.

Outside the window of the car, the vast cedar bog stretched away from the riverbank. The light haze of the first of the thirty smoky days before winter hung over the bog, mingling with haze that had drifted south from a distant forest fire in Canada. In the bird's-eye maple paneling above the window someone had carved the words *Hell's Gate or bust.* Someone else had tried to change the word *or* to *and.* Marie shut her eyes and did not open them again until the train stopped in the village.

Already it was growing dusky; what light remained seemed to come from the lake as much as the sky. Except for the men who had ridden up from the Common with her, the street was deserted. The factory was dark and empty; no one was loitering on the porch steps.

To stretch her legs she walked over to the roundhouse entrance and stood for a moment looking in. The disabled turntable was littered with broken boards, shards of glass, and pigeon droppings. All that was left was a small handcar used to keep the spur track in repair; she had no idea whether it was in working order.

"Echo," she said softly.

The Minotaur that had once terrified her and Abie said in a tired voice: *Echo.*

"Hello, Miss Marie."

She started. From the shadows to her right, a small figure appeared in the entranceway. It was Wheeler Mason, the ex-cleanup man from the mill floor.

"I weren't spying on you, Miss Marie. Honest I weren't. Just looking around."

"I know you weren't spying, Wheely. There's not much here to look at anymore, is there?"

"No, there ain't. Once I sneaked in here at night when they was two big locomotives in the stalls and drinked a whole gallon of hard cider all by myself. Then it looked like they was ten locomotives. Now they ain't any."

She nodded. "That's right, Wheely."

"You know, Miss Marie, I was thinking. A man could make a nice little home in here. If he didn't have nowhere else to go, this would make a man a good place. When my house is sold, I mean."

"You won't have to live in the roundhouse, Wheely. I'm sure you'll always have a home to go to."

"Well, I'm glad you are. But if I had to, I could come in here and make a place, as long as nobody minded."

He gave her a mysterious look, and she smiled at him and walked back down the street, past the double row of houses. In the twilight they looked shabby. Some had been shut up, like summer houses closed for the off-season, their boarded windows staring blankly back into empty interiors. Somewhere nearby someone was burning leaves.

"Ain't you going to speak?"

She heard him before she saw him, sitting on her porch in the dusk with his boots on the railing; then she realized that the smoke she had smelled was not from leaves burning but from his cigar.

"Harlan Smith."

"No other," he said. "Do you want to see something?"

She nodded, supposing he was going to show her something from his travels, maybe give her a present. Instead he stood up and came down the steps empty-handed, and as casually as though he'd been gone two days instead of a year he headed down the street, puffing on his cigar. She hurried after him.

The sign stood on two freshly peeled cedar posts between the railroad embankment and the foot of School Hill, facing south. There was just light enough left now to read it. It said in large pale yellow letters:

THIS ENTIRE VILLAGE OF HELL'S GATE
WILL BE SOLD AT AUCTION
ON SATURDAY, OCTOBER 7, 1922

September was a month of disintegration and decay. Everything seemed to be falling into ruin, from the Big House to the company store, which was running lower on supplies each day. The only persons in the village who did not seem worried were Madame Raspberry, who continued to go cheerfully to the woods to berry and fish, and the children, for whom Marie kept the school open until noon each day. Trying to maintain as normal a routine as possible, she rose at dawn, worked for half an hour in her garden, prepared a big breakfast of coffee and eggs and bacon and toast with homemade jam, and then walked up the hill in the mist under the horse chestnut trees to teach a dozen boys and girls.

The auctioneer arrived for a preliminary visit a month before the date of the sale. He took a room at the Common Hotel, where Armand St. Onge gave him a colorful and far from encapsulated history of the rise and decline of the village, which took up all of his first evening. The next morning he rode up to Hell's Gate on the factory train and was met at the station by Marie, who had volunteered to show him the village.

She was highly impressed by Joseph Stein of Stein and Sons, a leading Boston auctioneering firm specializing in early American art and furniture. He was a trim, energetic man in his fifties, interested in everything from the sagging roundhouse to the amount of closet space in the village homes. Several times during his tour he stopped and exclaimed that Hell's Gate must have been a beautiful place when Abraham Benedict was alive.

That evening he invited Marie and Harlan to eat with him at the hotel, and although at first the local auctioneer was intensely jealous and contradicted or qualified everything that was said, Stein was unperturbed and soon made friends by asking Harlan to assist with the sale.

To Marie's surprise, Joseph Stein was especially intrigued by the Canada Mountain View House. She smiled as she told him how Abie had originally planned to serve colored ices on the piazza, but the auctioneer said that a resort in Hell's Gate might not be a farfetched idea if the right person got behind it. He also asked how many of the remaining villagers might try to buy their houses and where they would work if they did.

"That's the trouble, Mr. Stein," Marie said. "Unless the factory opens up again or someone comes along and gets the Mountain House going, there isn't anything in Hell's Gate they can do for work. A few still commute to the Common, but Stan Gregory can't keep the train going much longer. He's burning scrap wood from the lumberyard instead of coal right now. I hope somebody does buy the Mountain House, or some company makes a bid on the town. At least that would mean jobs."

Joseph Stein shook his head doubtfully. "I have to be frank with you, Miss Blythe. We've had several inquiries about the factory, but I don't think anyone's seriously interested in buying it. Hell's Gate is simply too far from the rest of New England, or anywhere else for that matter, to make an industrial venture worthwhile here in these times. Your Captain Benedict was a remarkable man, of course; maybe if he were still alive he could make a success of it, if not with furniture then with some other product. But it would take an enormous investment, not just in money, but in time and energy, and that's the kind of investment hardly anyone's making these days. The more I hear about Abraham Benedict, the more impressed I am by him and his accomplishments. But I think he was essentially a nineteenth-century man. And this is no longer the nineteenth century."

"Maybe if the machinery were in better repair?" Marie said.

"Maybe. But some of those old saws and planers haven't been manufactured for twenty years or so, and spare parts aren't even available for them."

Harlan nodded sagely. "It's on the skids, all right," he said. "It's downhill all the way from here on out."

"What scares me, Mr. Stein, is that summer people are probably going to be bidding against local people for their houses."

"I'm afraid that's a strong possibility, Miss Blythe. I've never sold an entire town, so I can't say from experience. But certainly that's a possibility."

Joseph Stein paid for their meal and shook hands with Marie and Harlan.

"I'll see you again in a month," he said. "We'll keep doing the best we can to attract a buyer for the entire estate, or at least for the factory. But I don't want to mislead you. It won't be easy. If I lived in Hell's Gate, I'd look hard for employment elsewhere."

In the afternoons and evenings Marie worked at the Big House, which the auction firm had asked her to try to get into shape to sell; they were paying her a dollar an hour, and she needed the money. Sometimes Harlan came up after supper to help her, and on cool nights they made a fire in the central fireplace in the parlor, where once she had watched white birch logs burning on Christmas Eve. Often they worked until midnight, papering, painting, scrubbing woodwork. Squirrels had gotten into the wall partitions, and sometimes they rolled horse chestnuts back and forth. "Listen, Harlan," she said. "The red squirrels are playing ninepins."

"I'm glad someone's having fun," he said. "This is the damnedest job I've ever did, and when it's over and we're out from under this Christly village, I'm striking out for Alaska. You can come or not, as you please."

Yet he followed her everywhere, giving her advice and driving her distracted until she finally took refuge from him in the flower gardens, which were overrun with burdocks and Canadian bull thistles and crawling with several large families of garter snakes, which nested in the crumbling rear foundation of the house and terrified the big auctioneer as much as cobras. Marie hacked away at the weeds and poured kerosene on their roots, but they grew back taller than ever and she finally gave up trying to restore the grounds in the short time before the auction as an impossible task.

Entire armies of carpenter ants trooped in and out of the kitchen and pantry through holes in the foundation. Wild cucumber vines ran up the whale's jaw. In the evenings it glowed softly through the tangled foliage, which grew with a tropical profusion, creeping over the lawn and into the conservatory windows and sending exploring tendrils as far as the dining room. A vine got tangled in Harlan's boot one evening. "Jesus!" he shouted. "The snakes have broke into the house!"

Except for the haze from the forest fire to the north, the days were clear and fine, like Marie's first fall in Hell's Gate. But sometimes at night the wind gusted hard off the lake and loose slates went skittering down over the roof, thudding into the weeds and crashing through the glass roof of the conservatory.

The villagers watched the thickening haze from the fire with apprehension, and the talk on the store porch was full of real and fictitious disasters: fires and floods, suicides, unsolved murders, and disappearances, especially Abie's. During these uncertain weeks before the auction, the myth of the Captain grew dramatically. All sorts of dark deeds were ascribed to him —he had murdered the Indians who came to the peninsula to fish, or at least driven them away by dire threats which he was fully prepared to carry out; he'd deliberately sent Abie off to war because he couldn't stand the idea of anyone else owning Hell's Gate—yet one evening the talkers on the store porch discovered to their great surprise that none of them could recall exactly what Abraham Benedict had looked like, and a heated argument erupted over whether or not he had been six feet tall.

At the Big House, a bright green scum appeared on the goldfish pool in the conservatory. Marie raked it off and drained the stagnant water, but overnight it leached in again, and a few days later the algae returned thicker than ever, along with a bullfrog as large as a half-grown cat, with a wide saffron bib and huge staring eyes, which Harlan threatened to shoot with his .38 pistol. This angered Marie so much she refused to speak to him for two days, but he seemed hardly to notice.

Since returning from his travels, Harlan had seemed at odds with himself. He had not yet been questioned by the immigration officials, who, Marie suspected, had never had much evidence against him in the first place. Yet his wanderings had left him at loose ends. Although he spoke frequently of lighting out for Alaska, he did not talk about it with much conviction, as though he more than half suspected that, like Wisconsin, Alaska would disappoint him when he got there. In Marie's opinion, he did not know what he wanted, and she saw her own uncertainty reflected in his. For this reason, his presence often irritated her, and they could not seem to get back on comfortable terms with each other.

For weeks Marie had been racking her mind for a solution to her own dilemma. She still wanted to stay in Hell's Gate, or at least in Kingdom County, but very probably the school would close after the auction; she had not received a salary since the previous April. The fourteen hundred dollars she'd saved at the sanatorium had dwindled to less than a thousand, most of which she would probably need to buy her house. But what good would the house be if she had no job?

It was little consolation that everyone left in the village faced the same problem. Unless another business could somehow be established, Hell's Gate seemed doomed to dry up and blow away. Everyone, it seemed, was waiting to see what would happen at the auction, but now that the Baxters were gone, no one except Marie seemed to be doing the slightest thing to prepare for it, and most of her refurbishing work at the Big House seemed futile; one night it rained briefly but hard, and she and Harlan rushed from room to room upstairs trying to catch leaks in various pieces of Rachel's Haviland china.

Marie wished she could go to someone for advice. Margaret and John had both strongly urged her to leave Hell's Gate at the first opportunity, offering her the use of their farmhouse, which they had kept to summer in; but she did not want to go there except as a last resort. Ned and Ellen had always been as helpful to her as parents, but they had worries enough of their own now, and she was unwilling to add to their concerns. And even if he were not in a blue funk, Harlan was the last person she would go to for advice about anything. She tried to imagine what Captain Benedict would have done in her place, but quickly abandoned that line of speculation; she was not Captain Benedict. Nor was she Margaret, or Ellen or Ned, or Harlan; she was Marie Blythe, and she was determined, somehow, to follow the poet Robert Frost's advice and go her own best way, if she could only discover it. Yet the more she thought about it, the more confused she became, except when she forced herself to put her own problems aside by concentrating on the myriad small details of daily life in the village: teaching, cooking her meals, and preparing her house for another winter, as carefully as though she fully intended to spend it and the next forty there. She wished Abie would return from Arizona or wherever he was and at least make a pretense of taking charge of things.

Her idea came to her when she would have least expected it to, on her way up the hill to school one morning. She was thinking of the walking priest, Father Boisvert, as she often did when she walked anywhere, and wondering where he might be, and as usual at these times she remembered his advice to maintain a little faith in something, if only in fishing. With this in mind, she glanced up the long narrow lake between the Canadian mountains, just now emerging from the mist, and at that moment the solution to her problem presented itself fully formed; everything fell into place instantly, as though she were looking at a blueprint of her own future instead of the lake and mountains. She was as excited as she could remember being, though she had no intention of mentioning a word of her plan to anyone until after the auction. For its success or failure now depended entirely on the outcome of that event.

Toward the end of the month a few of the remaining villagers painted their houses with yellow paint from the storeroom at the back of the social hall. Most did not, in part from lassitude, in part because they were afraid that freshly painted houses would be more appealing to the hordes of people from Boston and New York rumored to be waiting for the auction to snap up summer houses in Hell's Gate for next to nothing—though contradictory rumors were equally prevalent. One day word swept through the village that Sears, Roebuck was going to buy the entire estate and reestablish the furniture business. The next day the excitement was even greater when Oat Morse, the night watchman at the factory for twenty years, swore he'd seen the Captain in his blue coat on the mill floor the previous evening, and feverish speculation spread that Abraham had never died at all but was coming back to save the town.

Oat Morse and several other villagers were certain that this was the case when some of Oat's bees left their hive the next afternoon and swarmed on the highest chimney of the Big House. On the same evening the Captain was allegedly sighted again, this time high in the brushy upper meadow, by Madame Laframboise. That night an electrical ball as large as the globe in Marie's classroom came bowling along over the surface of the lake out of Canada at a blinding rate of speed, ran up one side of the covered bridge and down the other, tore off down the south bay, and disappeared into the vast cedar bog to the southwest, all in a matter of seconds. There were several witnesses to this phenomenon, all of whom regarded it as a portent of the imminent end of Hell's Gate as a village.

In fact, no one had any real idea of what would happen at the auction, and the uncertainty was nearly unbearable. However it began, nearly every conversation ended with the sale of the village and what it would mean. And there were as many different opinions about that as there were inhabitants left in the village.

One day two officials from the St. Francis Pulp and Paper Company, whose forest lands were being devastated by the Canadian fire, came to visit Hell's Gate. Marie closed school in the middle of the morning and took them on a tour of the mountains, where once again, as before the Captain's time, softwoods were starting to proliferate. She remembered Ned's saying that a pulp mill would be the end of Hell's Gate, but at least it would be a way for residents to stay on in their homes and earn a living, and she hoped the Canadian firm would make an offer. The officials were noncommittal, saying only that a representative from the paper firm would attend the auction.

During the last week of September the prolonged hot weather hatched out a plague of cluster flies. They were everywhere, especially in the Big House. By the hundreds, then the thousands, then the tens of thousands they crawled out from between the cracks in the floorboards and window casings. As quickly as Marie swept them up, others appeared, filling the house with a low steady buzzing like the humming of the factory in better days. "We need to get Wyalia Kinneson up here," she told Harlan jokingly.

"We need to get the Christ out of this place," he said.

"I intend to."

"When?"

"Just as soon as the auction's over and everything's taken care of. Then I'll leave."

"Is that a promise?"

"Yes," Marie said. "That's a promise. I won't say how far. But I'm going."

If there was any doubt in her mind about leaving the village, it was totally eliminated the next morning when she went out to feed Applejack and found him lying dead in his stall with his throat slit like a hog's. It was as inexplicable as it was horrifying. Somewhere in the embattled village, someone had finally cracked under the strain.

Now all Marie wanted was to get on with her plan. Although she had not had much time to think about it, and she had still not mentioned it to anyone, she was determined to follow it through. She had no doubt that it would be difficult. Also she was going to need some luck; even the Captain, with all his resolution and ability, had relied to a degree on luck, on being in the right place at the right time. How much luck she would need was impossible to predict, so she tried not to think about it often. The important thing was to keep her routine as systematic and orderly as possible, no matter how chaotic everything around her became, so that when the auction arrived she would think clearly and carefully.

During the last month it had seemed to Marie as though nothing was happening in the village. Now everything seemed to be happening all at once. Early during the first week of October, newspaper reporters began to appear in Hell's Gate. That Tuesday the *Kingdom County Monitor* featured the following article on the impending sale:

HELL'S GATE RESIDENTS FACE LOSS OF HOMES AT AUCTION

Little Hope Left That Benedict Factory Will Ever Open Again

There is much serious speculation among the residents of Hell's Gate about the auction that is to take place at the local social hall at 9 A.M. on Saturday, October 7th. It may be that many of the 36 homes will be sold to city persons who will use them as summer cottages, or a syndicate may buy them as a unit and promote a summer colony. On the other hand, it is quite possible, many inhabitants believe, that few of the dwellings will be sold at this time unless they are disposed of at very low prices.

Most of the houses have had little or no work done on them for years. Before the War, it was the policy of the Benedict Company to keep them in excellent repair; a crew of painters was always kept busy each summer repainting the exteriors, and carpenters shingled the roofs and did other work whenever necessary. It is the consensus of most residents that many of the homes are at present in a deplorable state of disrepair. There are only a few, it is contended, that are in good condition.

The majority of the families in Hell's Gate are facing a difficult problem. The economic security they believed in and enjoyed for 30 years has been swept from under them, and now they are face to face with the strong probability that their homes will also slip from their grasp. Some of them would like to purchase their houses and remain in them, trusting to chance and industrial endeavor to make a living. A few others, who already have been doing cabinetwork in Kingdom Common, would like to buy their homes and commute from them. But because of the reasons already enumerated, everyone in the village agrees that if natives do buy their houses, the prices must be low. The factory was the economic hub of the place, and to the sharp regret of all, the factory is dead. Only a miracle can resurrect it.

The next day the *Boston Globe* headlined a column VERMONT HAMLET TELLS WORLD IT'S NOT WORTH BUYING and then, in smaller print, VILLAGERS, TRYING TO HALT SALE, SAY HOUSES ARE TERRIBLY RUN DOWN:

Hell's Gate, Vermont.—A battle of propaganda was raging today in anticipation of the auctioning Saturday morning of the factory and 36 homes in this northern Vermont hamlet on the Canadian border. The villagers, of whom there remain only about 30, have turned to the columns of the local press to inform outsiders who may seek to buy their homes that the dwellings are terribly dilapidated and that buyers had better beware.

Meanwhile Harlan Smith, a representative of the prominent Boston auctioneer Joseph Stein who will sell the place, was walking through the streets here from house to house today, interesting the villagers in bidding. Smith said that literature has gone out to metropolitan department stores, labor unions, religious and fraternal organizations, and to rosters of firemen, policemen, and schoolteachers all through Vermont and elsewhere, expatiating on the beauties of this village as a summer and winter resort for individual families or for large associations.

Smith, who ran his own auction firm for more than twenty years, said that first the whole village will be put up as a single unit. Then the factory will be auctioned, then the homes, then the land: about 100,000 acres. If the price on the village as a whole is higher than the sum of prices on individual parcels, Hell's Gate, founded by the Benedict family in 1890, will be sold as a whole. If the result is the other way around, it will be sold piecemeal.

The wildest rumors raged along the single street today, concerning possible buyers. The villagers, who have had almost no work in Hell's Gate for nearly a year, are praying for a factory owner, and several of them said they believed that a Montreal factory that was having trouble with labor unions might buy the place. There has never been a union here.

The only villager encountered who seemed absolutely unconcerned about what may happen was Mrs. Laframboise, who worked in the furniture factory for fifteen years. Mrs. Laframboise said she was a poor hand to worry and she guessed things would turn out all right, maybe.

The village was full of strangers, who came up on the daily excursion train Joseph Stein was running for prospective buyers. At about the time these visitors began arriving, some valuable silverware turned up missing from the Big House. The next day the Captain's harpoon disappeared from its iron brackets over the parlor mantel, and at the company store some staples were stolen out from under Early Kinneson's nose while he stood gossiping on the porch steps. Villagers began locking their doors and refusing to show their homes to anyone. The store was raided again two evenings later, after the excursion train had gone back to the Common, so Harlan, now wearing a card pinned to his hat that said *Stein and Sons Security Patrol,* sat up all the following night behind the meat counter, waiting for the thief. Nothing happened until dawn, when he heard the side window slide up and saw what he took for a child slip in and head for the canned goods shelves. As Harlan watched, the small figure filled a grocery sack with tinned beans, meat, and sardines, then headed for the window. "Stop right there," the auctioneer said.

"Don't shoot, don't shoot, it's just Wheely!" the little man cried.

Although Wheeler begged him not to, Harlan marched him over to Marie's house with the purloined tinned goods, issuing many threats about state's prison along the way. But Marie made him turn Wheeler loose and let him keep the food, which she paid for, after he promised not to steal anything else. "You won't go hungry, Wheely, I promise," she said. "You come here to eat from now on."

News of Wheeler's apprehension quickly got around the village, but most of the remaining families continued to lock their doors at night and to regard each other with suspicion. The uncertainty that had pervaded their lives for months had turned into outright fear. Because he had broken the village code of trust that for years had operated better than any police force, Wheeler was ostracized by everyone but Marie. And although she cooked three meals a day for him, he refused to eat with her and Harlan but spirited the food off to eat alone, then returned the dishes to her doorstep.

Harlan, in the meantime, was transferring many small articles from the factory, including hand tools, cans of varnish and shellac, and office supplies, to the roundhouse, where he planned to hold a small side sale before the main auction, which was scheduled to take place in the social hall. Although the proceeds of this venture were to go to the village's creditors, Harlan would retain half of the auctioneer's ten percent commission. He had called Jehoshaphat up from the Common to help move these odds and ends, and the ringman gobbled with excitement as he trundled Wheeler's old wheelbarrow back and forth between the factory and the roundhouse, raising a small cloud of dust in the drought.

The village had not been so busy since the days of the

Captain. Stein employees hurried from yard to yard driving stakes with numbered placards about the size of playing cards into baked lawns. On the Friday before the auction, Marie came home from school at noon to discover that her lot was labeled Parcel 4. Ned and Ellen Baxter's old place was Parcel 2. The factory was Parcel 1, the Big House Parcel 30, the school Parcel 34. On the store steps, villagers were exchanging parcel digits like telephone numbers.

Enervated by the carnival atmosphere, Marie went inside and poured herself a glass of cold water, but before she had time to drink it there was a knock at her front door, and a large, well-dressed woman with a high-pitched voice asked if she could see the house; she'd fallen in love, she said, with the pink hydrangea bush on the lawn. Overtired and discouraged—that morning Bill Kane's youngest son, a smart and impertinent ten-year-old, had asked why they had to learn to parse sentences when the town was being sold the next day, and her reply that an education was even more important in bad times than in good times had sounded so unconvincing, even to her, that she had dismissed school twenty minutes early—Marie was irritated by the woman's request. But she felt she had no choice other than showing her through the house, so she forced herself to be pleasant as the visitor enthusiastically admired the maple woodwork and view out the kitchen window down the bay and the hydrangea in the front lawn.

After the woman had left, Harlan stopped by and Marie told him about her. "I'd have put her out on her fat ass," he said. "You're probably better educated than her, and certainly better looking, and you would have had every right to."

Marie stared at him, almost too tired to be incredulous, but totally at a loss to discern how being educated and attractive entitled anyone to turn people out into the street—but Harlan's sense of justice had always worked in wondrous ways, and he had many stories of "putting this one and that one" off his own premises.

"You don't have to show your house to anybody you don't

want to show it to," he continued. "It's yours until that auction; but if you do it again be sure to stay right tight to them. You'd be surprised how much will fit into a coat pocket." He thought a minute. "I saw Stein going around talking to summer people in a low voice earlier today. I think he's conspiring to sell them these houses dirt cheap for a little kickback."

"That's the most ridiculous thing I've heard so far today, and that's saying something," Marie said.

"That's right, stand up for him," Harlan said. "Do you know what he told me not two hours ago? He told me he didn't think there'd be any need for me to carry my revolver tomorrow at the auction. Can you imagine that? 'What's that?' says I. 'Are you questioning my right to bear arms?'

" 'No,' he says smooth and easy. 'Not at all, Mr. Smith. I'm questioning your need to at the auction.' "

" 'I'll tend to my needs, my good man,' I says. I told him that right out quick. 'I'll tend to my needs myself.' "

"So what did he say?" Marie asked. She suspected that Harlan had not said any such thing, but you could never tell with the ex-auctioneer.

"He said if I intended to work that auction tomorrow I'd do so unarmed," Harlan said angrily. "So here. Keep this in your handbag. It might come in handy with all these strangers around. I'll pick it up again Sunday night. I'm going fishing. I lost that big lunker under the bridge again last night, and I intend to get him on dry land by dark today or know why."

He reached over and put his .38 revolver in Marie's pocketbook, which she set far back on the kitchen counter, intending to hide the gun in her dish cupboard later on. Then she started making tuna and cold meat sandwiches for the auction the next day, as most of the women in Hell's Gate were doing in hopes of making enough on the proceeds to bid on the social hall.

Later that afternoon, Joseph Stein dropped in to tell Marie that everything was set for the following day. "I had to ask Mr. Smith to put away his sidearm temporarily," he said. "I'm afraid he wasn't very happy about it."

"Mr. Smith isn't very happy about anything these days," Marie said. "He's still mad because he wasn't asked to auction off the town."

Joseph Stein nodded. "I can see that. I have the impression that everyone in the village, or nearly everyone, feels the same way toward out—"

Just then Jehoshaphat burst through the door. "Miss Blythe, Miss Blythe!" he shouted. "Come quick. Smitty's having a heart attack down on the bridge."

"What!" Marie exclaimed, jumping up from the table. "Good God!"

"Yes, yes, yes!" Jehoshaphat gobbled. "He was fishing and he latched onto the granddaddy of all granddaddies off the bridge and he wants his boat net and he wants his heart pills and he's all red in face like a man about to bust open. He's having a heart attack, all right!"

With Joseph Stein close behind her, Marie ran down to the covered bridge, where a crowd had already gathered to watch the excited auctioneer, who was talking a blue streak to the fish, the audience, and himself. "Now keep calm, Harlan, keep calm. Don't horse him, but for Christ's sake don't give him any slack. . . .

"This is it," he shouted when he spotted Marie. "This is the one I've been waiting for. Now we're going to find out how strong this old ticker of mine is. I'm going now if I ever do. Is my face red?"

"Very," Marie said. "Mine would be too if I talked that much without stopping for breath."

"Breath? Breath? Jesus, what did you say that for? If I get to breathing I'm through here. Grab the rod if I pass out. Give me those pills, quick." Harlan opened his mouth and Marie tossed in half a handful of Dr. Rupp's heart pills. "Quick," he mumbled. "Get me a beer. You know I can't swallow pills. It's under the feed sacks in the back of the boat. Get the net too."

Marie went down to the dock and got the net and beer, which Harlan drained in four or five gulps.

Meanwhile his fly rod bent nearly to the railing as the big fish moved slowly back and forth through the deep channel between the bay and the lake, sometimes swimming far back under the bridge toward the bay, sometimes heading up the lake. Such a powerful fish had to be a brown trout or a land-locked salmon, but none of the natives of Hell's Gate could understand why it didn't break water. It had not come near the surface once since Harlan had hooked it. Sweat poured off Harlan's face, staining his white shirt through to the jacket. His wrist muscles twitched from the terrific tension, and he took bets on whether he would land the fish, how long it would take, and how much it would weigh.

As the afternoon wore on and the sun sank below the shoulder of the mountain, more people appeared along the walkway. Stan Gregory held the afternoon train so everyone would know the outcome of the battle. It was a classic struggle of man against fish, a professor from New York said.

"He's tiring out, boys," Harlan said. "We're tiring him out on light tackle." Time and again he brought the line to its breaking point, so it vibrated like a plucked guitar string, but the fish refused to come up and roll onto its side.

Just before dark, Harlan began edging along the walkway toward the long street. Holding his rod high above his head for maximum leverage and showmanship, he proceeded slowly down the bank to the edge of the water and, reeling slowly, brought his catch toward shore, where it swirled angrily in the shallow water. He reached down and grasped its tail and gave an enormous heave; a great cheer went up from the gallery. But it was not a trout, or a fish of any kind. It was the largest snapping turtle ever seen in Hell's Gate, and it was not pleased to have a size two treble hook in the side of its mouth and an ex-auctioneer holding its tail.

Turning like a striking snake, the turtle hissed loudly enough to be heard by everyone on the bridge and fastened its beak in Harlan's boot. Then it started toward the water. Harlan shouted, cursed, did a fast jig on one foot. He screamed for

Marie to cut the line with his fish knife, which she did just as the huge snapper seemed about to yank him into the lake.

"That does it," he said calmly when he was able to talk. "I'm going to Alaska on the next train."

"You better come up to the house and have supper first," Marie said. "It's a long way on an empty stomach."

That evening Marie and Harlan sat visiting for a long time on her front porch. While he recounted his epic struggle with the turtle, she found herself reflecting on a strange experience she'd had on the bridge that afternoon. Looking down through the crowd, she thought for a moment that she glimpsed Pia, not as she had become in recent years but as she used to be. Of course she was mistaken; it turned out to be the large woman who had gone through her house and admired her hydrangea. She was now wearing a vivid red fall coat, which she had carried folded over her arm earlier. Yet Marie could not stop thinking about the gypsy woman and how right she had been, about the future and human affairs in general.

Harlan lighted a cigar and put his boots on the porch railing. He talked on and on, telling one anecdote after another. Half listening to the stories, Marie watched the glow of the Canadian fire, bright as the northern lights. It was much closer, only twenty or twenty-five miles away, just beyond the mountains on the northwest side of the lake, and if the wind should change suddenly the village would be in serious jeopardy. Yet Pia had once said that when at last trouble came to Hell's Gate it would not come from the outside, and so far she had been right. The failure of the business and the general deterioration had resulted almost entirely from mismanagement and bad judgment and sheer self-destructiveness on Abie's part; although he had not succeeded in getting rid of her, as he had promised he would, he had done something far more subtle, she thought, in ruining the place that was her home.

"Harlan, I have to go to bed. Tomorrow's a big day."

Just warming to his subject—himself, as usual—Harlan was indignant. Then it occurred to him that he should make one more swing through the town in his official capacity as security agent, so he went off down the street and Marie went inside, washed, laid the kindling in the kitchen stove for her breakfast fire, and went to bed.

For a minute she thought about her plan, but she was too tired to concentrate on it, or on anything. When Harlan returned half an hour later she was asleep, and she did not wake up until dawn.

Auction day had arrived.

Chapter Sixteen

It was an overcast morning. Prospective buyers coming in on the early train worried that it might rain, but the villagers explained that it was only the fall mist rising off the lake and mingling with the haze from the forest fire in Canada. The sun would rise around eight thirty, when it cleared the south shoulder of Canada Mountain, and it would be another clear day. At sunrise the woman who had toured Marie's house the day before looked up at Kingdom Mountain and exclaimed, "My goodness, it's the forest fire!" But it was only the low rays of the sun striking the pink granite shell of the Canada Mountain House, and when Marie explained this to her the woman laughed at herself good-naturedly.

The Baxters were nowhere to be seen. When the second train appeared at nine and they did not get off, Marie realized that they could not bear the thought of seeing the town auctioned. She was disappointed because she'd hoped to sit with them, but she could not blame them for staying away.

By nine fifteen the social hall was filling up. Near the door was a long table displaying a scale model of the village that Herman Fischner had made at Joseph Stein's request. It was a remarkable replica of Hell's Gate, with each parcel numbered with a tiny placard, yet it resembled the village during its heyday more than in its current state of dilapidation, since each miniature building including the Big House had been carefully painted pale yellow and the lumberyard across the yellow covered bridge was full and the factory had a busy air about it.

Near the table with the model, Harlan was selling catalogues printed by Stein and Sons with glossy aerial photographs of the village and lake and exhaustive listing of the buildings and their contents.

There is not another similar industrial community in the whole United States which has the natural beauty and advantages of Hell's Gate [the catalogue began]. Founded by an idealist with a great and sustaining vision and located in the heart of what the *Encyclopaedia Britannica* calls a "beautiful country," the Benedict factory has long enjoyed an enviable reputation for the manufacture of fine office furniture. This plant covering 16,000 square feet of floor space could be used for the manufacture of almost any article made from hardwood, which still abounds in the one hundred thousand acres of surrounding land. The company-owned residences would make it very feasible for families to do piecework at home . . . several excellent woodworkers are available to help run the factory . . . the name of the village could be changed to that of the new owner or institution . . . this is an opportunity to help our fellow citizens.

Marie's eyes ran quickly from one inflated statement to another. She laid the folder on a chair and walked to the front of the room, near the right side, and sat down. She noticed that her chair did not sit quite level and realized that it was one of the warped chairs sent to Philadelphia and returned unpaid for; sometime during the past week, Joseph Stein's employees had brought several dozen of these seats into the hall to augment the folding wooden chairs used by villagers for meetings and social affairs.

Stan Gregory sat beside her. His brown eyes were steady, but she knew that, like most of the other villagers, he was afraid he wouldn't be able to buy his home. "Marie," he said in a low voice, as though they were sitting in church, "I saw old Wheeler standing on the walk outside and I asked him if he wasn't coming in. He just shook his head and told me he couldn't buy his home, so he wasn't going inside to watch somebody else buy it. He had tears in his eyes."

Marie shook her head. Just then Johnny Moon, the lathe operator in the factory for thirty years, came in and sat down next to Stan. "You going to bid, Johnny M?" Stan said.

"Hell, no," Johnny said. "I don't want none of their old crows' nests. I'll tell you, Stanford. If a man ain't got nothing, he can get something; but if he's got something, he can't get nothing."

By nine twenty the hall was packed, though many of the villagers had been reluctant to sit in the first several rows of seats, some of which remained vacant until the last moment. Marie had never before seen so many persons together in one place in Hell's Gate at the same time. While most of the villagers wore their best clothes, many of the strangers were dressed the way they supposed country people dressed, in plaid flannel shirts, khaki or denim slacks, and expensive walking shoes.

At precisely nine thirty Joseph Stein walked onto the stage in a dark suit and a sober dark tie. He stood behind the gold medal desk from the factory office. Once, lightly, he tapped the edge of the desk with a small black gavel; the hall fell silent.

The auctioneer looked the crowd over quietly, as though appraising its spending potential. Marie glanced at Harlan, lounging in his bottle-green sports jacket and a bright blue necktie by one of the windows. His face was full of envy as Stein read the terms of the sale in a distinct voice.

"The entire gore of Hell's Gate will first be offered as a single unit," he said. "There is a scale model of the village and factory on the table near the door, and I assume that most of you have had a chance to see it or to tour the property itself. It consists of sixty-seven buildings, including the factory, a store, the railroad station and roundhouse, the school, this building, the Benedict house and most of its contents, thirty-six houses on this side of the bridge and twenty-two on the far side, as well as one hundred thousand acres, more or less, of mountain land. The bidding will start at five hundred thousand dollars."

The hall was silent. Then from the side Harlan Smith said, "One thousand dollars firm."

There were a few laughs, not many.

"Is there a bid for five hundred thousand dollars?" the auctioneer said.

"One hundred thousand dollars."

It was the representative from the St. Francis Paper Company.

"Do I have a bid for five hundred thousand dollars?"

Silence.

"Then the bidding will be reopened at one this afternoon and we will offer the property as a unit once more, with the understanding that it is on reserve for five hundred thousand dollars. If there is no minimum bid at that time, we will offer individual parcels, beginning with Parcel Number 1, the factory. In the meantime, there will be a sale of small items from the factory and lumberyard in the roundhouse at the end of the street, adjacent to the west end of the covered bridge. This auction is now adjourned until one o'clock."

Harlan's side auction began at ten thirty. Standing on the broken turntable with Jehoshaphat beside him to hold up items and point out bidders, he had no difficulty selling the array of odds and ends from the factory. Marie stayed only long enough to buy for a dollar a large pasteboard box containing some old ledgers and miscellaneous records Harlan had discovered while rummaging through a compartment behind the filing drawer in the Captain's desk, including some of his diaries and a set of eight red account books in which he kept his own private financial records. The desk itself would be sold at the main auction.

Although it was still hazy, the sun shone quite brightly on the town. Except for the gaudy colors on the mountains, it was more like August than early October. The city people were seeing Hell's Gate weather at its best.

At one o'clock Joseph Stein once again offered the entire package of the village for half a million dollars. Another train had come in around noon, and it had been rumored that two prospective buyers were aboard. But this time not even the representative from the paper company offered to bid. The reserve clause was firm, so, as he had warned, the auctioneer took the village off the block and opened bids on the factory.

Harlan bid five hundred dollars. Willis Yates, a junk dealer from Pond in the Sky, bid a thousand. Harlan raised his bid to fifteen hundred but refused to go higher, and Yates bought the building and its machinery, much of which was good for nothing but scrap iron, for eighteen hundred dollars.

St. Francis Pulp and Paper bought all of Kingdom and Canada mountains, including the half-completed Mountain House, for twenty dollars an acre. At that price they could afford to wait for the fir and spruce to grow taller. The representative had told reporters that when the time came to start cutting they would probably drive roads through the mountains on both sides of the lake and truck the logs north to their mill in Magog rather than invest heavily in a plant in Hell's Gate. Otherwise, they would have purchased the factory building, which Willis Yates would now undoubtedly tear down for its lumber. The woodworking business was dead.

Marie had dreaded this moment for weeks, but now that it had arrived she was only impatient to get the whole thing over with. If she could carry out her plan, she would. There was nothing she could do now but wait and see what happened. She felt oddly detached, like a person watching a play.

Joseph Stein rapped with his gavel. "The village houses will now be put up for sale individually," he said. "Most need a coat of paint but all are still structurally sound, with running water and electricity. About half have coal or wood furnaces in their cellars."

He looked carefully out over the crowded hall. "I wish to remind you of something. A number of these houses are still occupied. Some of the families in Hell's Gate have been here for many years and would like to bid on their homes."

Except for the buzzing of the cluster flies, the room was still. "That's all," Joseph Stein said. "The bidding will now continue with Parcel Two, known as the Baxter place, located directly across from the store. The Baxter place is unoccupied, and my understanding is that the previous occupants live in a nearby village and don't plan to bid on it. It's one of the half dozen houses in the village that have been kept painted and is in excellent repair."

A man from Montreal promptly bought Ned and Ellen Baxter's home for seven hundred dollars. The next parcel to go up on the block was Stan Gregory's home. "Is there a bid on Parcel Three?" the auctioneer asked.

Stan raised his hand. "I bid four hundred dollars."

"Are you the present occupant of the house?"

Stand nodded.

With particular stress Joseph Stein said, "The *occupant* of Parcel Three has bid four hundred dollars on that property. Is there another bid?"

There was not.

"Parcel Four," Joseph Stein said. "The house occupied by Miss Marie Blythe, the Hell's Gate schoolteacher." He looked at Marie. "Does the occupant of Parcel Four wish to bid on her house?"

Someone joggled Marie's arm. Harlan had slipped into the chair beside her. "Put up your Christly hand," he said.

Stein looked inquiringly in her direction.

Marie shook her head.

"Good Christ, what's the matter, don't you have the money?" Harlan said. "Hurry up and bid. I'll help you out."

Marie shook her head. In a firm voice she said to Joseph Stein, "I don't wish to enter a bid on the teacher's house."

Everyone who knew her was surprised, Harlan most of all. But by the time the woman who had looked at Marie's house the day before had bought it, a cynical smile had appeared on his face. "Now I see," he whispered. "It's the Big House you're after, ain't it? That's why you've been spending every night for the past month up there papering and painting and such. Do you have any idea what it'll cost to heat and maintain that barn?"

"Shh!" she said. "I have to pay attention."

Shaking his head in disgust, Harlan got up and started for the door. But before he'd gotten halfway, he turned and came back and leaned against the wall.

The bidding progressed rapidly. Usually, though not always, when a villager put in a bid on the house he was occupying, people from outside Hell's Gate abstained from bidding against him. By three fifteen, all the houses had been sold. About half had been bought by city people as vacation homes; the rest were purchased by villagers.

Wheeler Mason was one of the few villagers who wanted to purchase their homes but simply couldn't afford to. Nor would he accept Marie's offer of a small loan—two hundred dollars would have been enough to buy the place—but stalked up and down in front of the social hall mumbling threats against the paper company, which had acquired his house and most of the battened houses across the bridge for one or two hundred dollars apiece.

Early Kinneson bought the store, the schoolhouse, and the social hall, apparently with the idea of operating the store and renting or selling the two other buildings back to whatever new village corporation was formed.

"Parcel Thirty," Joseph Stein said. "The Benedict house."

There had been a good deal of speculation in the village during the past month about the probable fate of the Big House. Many people thought Abie would show up to bid for it. Others pointed out that, as the bankrupt previous owner, he could not do this. Still others believed that Abie had left Hell's Gate for good and had no interest in his family house. It did not occur to anyone but Harlan that Marie might want the place.

But to his surprise she made no attempt to bid for the mansion, which was sold with its contents to a doctor from Boston for only four thousand dollars.

"The next item is an island consisting of eighty-two acres, more or less, approximately five miles north of the village," Joseph Stein said. He smiled. "I won't try to pronounce the name of the lake it's in; I haven't gotten it right yet. There are no habitable buildings on this property, part of which is situated in Canada. The fishing nearby is excellent, I'm told. That's its main attraction."

"Five hundred dollars." It was the representative from the paper company.

"Five hundred dollars," Joseph Stein said evenly. "Is there a bid for six hundred?"

Marie waited as long as she dared before lifting her hand. Harlan looked at her incredulously.

The representative glanced at her. "Seven hundred," he said.

After a short interval Marie raised the bid to eight hundred. Except for a few dollars in her purse, grocery money, it was all she had.

The auctioneer looked at the man from the paper company, who shrugged and shook his head, and only then did Marie realize how much she had wanted the island.

The locomotive and some of the freight cars and passenger carriages were sold to the paper company. Then it was Harlan's turn to surprise Marie, as he got up, walked forward, changed places with Joseph Stein, and asked for bids on the last items to be auctioned: the Captain's gold medal desk and private railway car, which Stein bought himself for six hundred and two thousand dollars, respectively.

It was six o'clock and the auction was over.

The sky above the village was thickly hazed, and through the haze the lowering sun glowed huge and red, like an overheated stove lid. The wind had shifted into the northwest and was stripping the trees of their leaves. If it kept up all night, most of the hardwoods on the mountain would be bare by morning. The air smelled acrid; smoke from the fire in Quebec was so thick that some of the people coming out of the social hall covered their mouths and noses with handkerchiefs. Singly and in pairs, sea gulls came flapping in off the lake, as they did before a storm, perching on the rooftops and hunching themselves into the hot wind.

"Them birds know something we don't," Harlan said.

"Maybe it's going to rain," Marie said without conviction. "We need a good long soaking rain to clear the air and put out that fire."

For a few minutes successful buyers walked up and down the street, looking at their new property and talking quietly. The doctor who had bought the Big House asked Marie to hold on to the key for him until he and his wife could get back up to see what needed to be done there. Soon it was time for the last train to leave; all of the city people crowded onto the cars. The engine whistled and started down the track along the bay toward the causeway. Instead of a caboose, the Captain's private car brought up the rear. Inside, Joseph Stein sat writing at the gold medal desk. He glanced up briefly and Marie waved. He gave her a brief salute and returned to his writing.

"There goes a most fortunate man," Harlan said as they walked across the littered street toward her house. "He don't have to stay here and face the music."

"Neither do you," Marie said wearily. "Neither do I, now that I think of it."

He looked at her. "What did you go and buy that island for?"

She had intended to reveal her plan to him that evening, but now, at the frayed end of the long sad day, she was too tired. All she wanted now was to go inside and take a hot bath and sleep until morning.

"Do you want a sandwich, Harlan?"

He glared at her. "I want to know what you intend to do out on that island."

"That's for me to know and you to find out," she snapped.

"If you're intending to farm it, count me out. I won't be tied down to a farm."

"I'm not intending to farm it, and I never counted you in."

He stopped with one foot in her yard and one foot on her porch steps, looking up at her on the porch. "Fine," he said. "Because I'm lighting out tonight to Alaska. And now that you're a woman of property I ain't even going to ask if you want to come along. I doubt I'd take you if you did."

"I'll remember that."

Marie slammed the door in his face, and he whirled around and went off fast down the street toward the dock. A minute later she heard the *Ice Chopper* roaring down the bay, and although she was already angry with herself for fighting with him, she was relieved to be alone. At this point, she hardly cared where Harlan went.

She supposed that she should feel a sense of satisfaction, since she had accomplished the first part of her plan, but she did not. Nor did she any longer feel like sleeping; she was too wrought up from quarreling with Harlan. She sat down at the kitchen table and watched it grow dark. After a while she lighted a kerosene lamp. She knew she would feel better if she ate, but could not summon the energy to get up and fix anything.

For some time, Marie had been staring at a cardboard box on the table. In it were the red leather diaries and ledgers she'd purchased earlier in the day at Harlan's side auction, which now seemed weeks ago.

To keep herself from growing more dejected, she began to arrange the diaries in chronological order. This took only a few minutes, since the year of each book was stamped in gold lettering on its spine. When she had finished, she began to scan through them, beginning with the year 1884, six years before the Captain had come to Hell's Gate.

As she leafed through the volume, she realized that it served a double purpose: it was both a diary and a ship's log. Each day's entry contained his ship's position, the distance covered in the past twenty-four hours, the weather, the names of any other ships sighted. Here and there, ports of call were mentioned, with notations indicating how much lumber he had discharged at each port. *Mailed packet of letters,* he had written on December 8, 1884, in Rio de Janeiro. And on February 14, 1885, in Sydney: *Received packet of letters. R. and H. and C. fine. Mother still listless since Father's death.*

She skipped two years and opened the diary for 1887, which she skimmed through until she came to a longer entry than usual, dated June 23, in Bombay: *Visited American consul with H., who had his first elephant ride. Left C. on board because of extreme heat, but plan to take him and H. both on an excursion early tomorrow morning. Picked up packet of letters at consul's. R. well, G. recovered from croupy cough and flourishing. Mother the same. Left letters for home with consul.*

The unfamiliar initials baffled Marie. R. must be Rachel, but she had never heard him mention H. or C. or G. She assumed that the initials might refer to nephews, or perhaps younger brothers. But if this were the case, what on earth had become of them, and why would the Captain turn his back completely on his own relatives, or vice versa? It was very puzzling, unless —a forbidding thought crossed her mind. She remembered Pia's certainty that the Captain labored under a great and dreadful secret, which the gypsy, for all her enormous curiosity, had refused to tamper with. Yet Marie could no more stop reading at this point than she could stop breathing.

There had been no voyage during 1888, when the Captain had been busy supervising the construction of a new ship, which he christened the *Kennebec* and launched in the mouth of that river on March 5, 1889, with a cargo of newly cut spruce and fir lumber, bound for Japan by way of the Cape of Good Hope: *Embarked an hour before dawn this morning with H., C., and G., leaving R. well but expecting in September and so unable to make the trip as she had hoped. Have R's hope chest for sea things and plan to return by mid-October, at latest.* The usual nautical observations followed. The trip had started out well. There were several entries remarking upon the favorable weather and the progress in various navigational skills of H., C., and G. Then, skipping ahead to July, Marie found only blank pages. She backtracked and found nothing for the entire month. There was nothing for the last week of June. Hurriedly she leafed back to the first week of that month and found four entries written in blue ink instead of the Captain's customary black, and with a somewhat broader pen point, prefaced with this notation:

July 14, 1899: I write from a bed in the British Seamen's Hospital in Alexandria, thirty-four days after the accident. Until now fever, delerium, and weeks of subsequent weakness have prevented my completing this log.

June 1: On this day, shortly before midnight, in the midst of the Indian Ocean at approximately 15 degrees 10 minutes of latitude, 62 degrees 4 minutes of longitude, the *Kennebec* was unaccountably struck by lightning on an otherwise clear night. Instantly a great fire broke out in the hold. The entire cargo was engulfed in flames, the pitchy lumber below exploding like boxes of ammunition. As the conflagration erupted onto the deck immediately, there was no time to think of lowering boats. It was all I could do to heave the chest overboard and H., C., and G. after it. I leaped in after them and managed to get them to the chest and away from the ship. When I looked back the *Kennebec* was a gigantic floating mass of flames.

June 2: Drifted at sea all day and night with three boys.

June 3: Drifted this day and part of night with two boys.

June 4: Drifted at sea this day until shortly before noon with one boy, whose body, I was informed, I refused to relinquish until sunset, six hours after being picked up by the vessel *Calcutta*. I have, besides losing my ship and cargo, broken my promise to Rachel, whose sons, one after another, I had to consign to the ocean, to which I now consign my profession.

This was the final entry in the Captain's log.
Although she had guessed the identity of the three boys

even before she began to read the last diary, Marie was stunned
by the revelation of the Captain's secret. Now she saw why
Rachel had grieved on her way to Hell's Gate the first time,
moving each minute farther away from the ocean that was her
only remaining link with her three dead sons. For the first time
she understood the terrible significance to the Captain of the
whale's jaw and why he had come to this remote place to
establish a new life for himself and what was left of his family.
She realized too why he had reproved her so sharply that
morning when she had thoughtlessly started up the stairs with
the live coals for Rachel's fire, and why Rachel told her that fire
was the one thing her husband feared. Everything fell into
place—the Benedicts' indulgence of Abie, the Captain's determination to keep him close to the safe world he had created,
and his refusal to speak of the past or acknowledge it at all
except through the whale's jaw, which he had clearly meant to
remind him of the awfulness of chance and the importance of
leaving as little to chance as possible.

Now she could not have slept if her life had depended on it.
She made herself a pot of coffee and opened the volume for
1890, the year Abraham Benedict had come to Hell's Gate.
There were no further references to the fire at sea or his first
three sons; it was as though neither they nor any other part of
his past had ever existed. But as she read through the Captain's
early accounts of establishing the village, his actual history
began to emerge distinctly and separately from the myth.

She had never doubted that he was a remarkable man with a
great vision. Now, for the first time, she realized that he was also
a human being with all the ordinary small and large worries and
doubts and self-doubts of anyone else. He fretted over his
wife's health. He referred frequently to Abie's waywardness,
for which he blamed himself without seeming to know what to
do about it. Occasionally he worried about a contract that had
been held up or a problem in the factory. He worried about his
own periods of unrest and morbidness, which so far as Marie
knew he had never revealed to anyone. On one occasion he
reprimanded himself strongly for self-destructive thoughts. On

another he vowed to give up his daily glass of wine before supper because he believed it had a dispiriting effect on his mood the following morning. Like a guilt-ridden man, he worried about dreams in which he sought various ways of doing away with his entire creation. And to Marie's surprise, after 1904, the year she had gone to the Big House to live, he often worried about her, expressing concern that she was becoming "too attached," first to Rachel, then Abie; that she had not been sent to school; that her future had not been "settled."

On April 20, 1906, he had written:

> Today M. announced that she is pregnant. A. seems to be the author of this event. R. greatly wishes to raise the child as our own, a plan that has a certain merit, and to which I have given my conditional approval. Yet this complicates matters and will require the most careful handling.

For May 5 of the same spring:

> Two more totally unexpected events have taken place. A. has decamped from St. Mark's with C. Pike and the Pike lad's bank account. M., too, has run off, and R. is close to distraction. Have hired a private detective, P. Greenwald of New York City, where I lost Abie's trail last Wednesday, to find all three. It was a mistake to take the girl into the household in the first place, as I clearly see now, and when she is located, different provisions will be made.

Marie reread the reference to the detective. Greenwald was also the name of the swindler who had extorted Abie's last ten thousand dollars, the man she thought looked familiar that day on the train. Yet the pieces of the puzzle did not seem to fit together.

She read on.

> May 10. Greenwald has discovered that A. and his friend left N.Y. City on the steam vessel *Glasgow* on May 7. Apparently they intend nothing more adventurous than an impromptu tour

of Europe; I will reimburse Mr. Pike for C.'s savings and leave them to their own devices. No word yet of M., who R. fears may have drowned herself or wandered off into the woods. I think not, however, from certain leads Greenwald has been following. I have worked out a plan with him, to be implemented upon her discovery.

May 16. Met with Greenwald in Boston last night. Informed me that he has discovered M. and her infant son in a shabby district of Montreal. Both seem to be in good health, though the girl is living from hand to mouth. Have arranged an annuity to be handled by Greenwald and paid in monthly installments by an agent in Montreal to whom my identity is to remain a secret, with the condition that neither she nor the boy return to Hell's Gate or try to contact any member of my family, and that neither ever assume the name Benedict.

Then finally on May 22:

Greenwald has met with the girl and secured her agreement to the conditions of the annuity. An enormous service to me, for which I have rewarded him appropriately. Have decided not to mention any of this to R., who remains convinced that M. has drowned. I think it best to leave things this way, in order that this unfortunate matter may be resolved permanently. I plan to take R. on a trip west this coming winter to distract her from this unpleasantness. My lack of foresight astonishes me.

It was not the Captain's lack of foresight that astonished Marie, though; it was his ruthlessness. Even as she read the words, then read them over and over again, she could not accept them. Yet she had to. He had put her out of his life and, worse yet, out of his wife's, as completely as his first three sons and the past itself.

The myth was that the Captain kept a second set of factory books in the deep bottom drawer of the gold medal desk, in which, for purposes of his own, he made daily entries. He made them carefully and accurately, according to the myth, checking them against Ellen Baxter's at the end of each month. Nearly everyone in the village believed this, partly because on the last working day of each month Abraham Benedict did in fact spend several hours going over Ellen's books, then his own: tall, handsome volumes, bound in red leather, like the diaries, and like the diaries embossed at the base of the spine in gold lettering with the dates they covered and his first initial and last name.

As she began to leaf through them, Marie quickly realized that once again the myth was inaccurate. The private ledgers did not constitute a second set of factory accounts. They had nothing to do with the factory at all, but contained a detailed itemization of Abraham Benedict's personal expenditures, including the money he spent on the Big House, the upkeep of the village and park, Abie's education, and, after 1906, the secret annuity intended for her. She discovered that from 1906 until his death, he had drawn on his bank account each year, first for five thousand dollars and then, after 1914, for seventy-five hundred dollars, which he had paid to P. Greenwald of New York City, who presumably had pocketed the entire amount of each draft.

Now it was clear to Marie why the Captain had never discovered her when she was working in Pond in the Sky and at the sanatorium, almost under his nose; he had stopped looking. He thought he had already found her and the illegitimate grandchild, who in fact was long since dead, and that so long as the money kept coming, they would stay out of his and Abie's life. What surprised her was that a shrewd businessman and judge of human character like the Captain had been fooled so completely by Greenwald. The man did not seem to be connected with the Pinkertons or any other reputable agency. For a few thousand dollars a year, he was taking a considerable risk by assuming, or at least hoping, that both she and the child were dead; obviously he was a second-rate detective, besides being dishonest.

A disturbing thought occurred to Marie. If Greenwald had been a little smarter and a little less scrupulous, he might have tried to find her and do—what she did not care to guess. Suddenly she remembered where she had seen the swindler before, smelled the strong clove scent of his hair oil. He was the man who had spoken to Bull Francis about her at Pond in the Sky. Something else came to her: Greenwald sounded like the name the crazy little thief Tuque had let slip when he and Hiram and the man they called Preacher had come to Pond Number Four to kill her. Now she realized that Greenwald had been much smarter and much more dangerous than she had assumed at first. She remembered the way he had looked at her on the train up from the Common when he was impersonating the purchasing agent for the woodworking-chain entepreneur, glancing her way with total disinterest, as though she meant absolutely nothing at all to him. She remembered finding Applejack with his throat slit, remembered the anonymous informer who had reported her and Harlan to the immigration officials. Maybe Greenwald had been the person who had tried to frighten her away from Hell's Gate, though why he would bother after the Captain's accident she had no idea.

"It's late," she said aloud. "You're too tired to think about this now."

The ledgers had told her what she wanted to know, so she returned to the diaries. She skimmed quickly through 1907, 1908, 1909. She found no further entry in these years pertaining to herself or the grandchild the Captain still supposed to be living. Except for the annual payments, they both might as well be dead, as Rachel had assumed they were.

Again she was struck by the mundane anxieties of the man about whom the myth had evolved. He worried to his diary about Abie's lack of interest in college, then about his lack of interest in the family business. He continued to fret about Rachel's health until 1912, when he bought the winter home in Arizona.

She did not find anything else of great interest, however, until 1914, when Abie enlisted in the Canadian forces. Again the Captain had hired Greenwald to find his son, and Greenwald had promptly done what he was paid to do, reporting Abie's enlistment to the Captain four days later and no doubt bolstering his employer's confidence in him still further. After that, Marie reasoned, the swindler would have worried even less about being checked up on and exposed, if he was the type of man who worried at all.

During the war years, the Captain himself had worried a great deal. By 1915 and 1916, though the secret payments to Greenwald not only continued but increased by fifty percent, the Captain was also fretting over his own wish for a more stable family, which to Marie could mean only one thing. He wanted Abie to return, get married, have children, and settle down. As she had so many times in the past, she felt indignant and defensive on Abie's behalf. Why couldn't his father have left him alone to lead his life as he pleased? No one had told the Captain how to live, and if anyone had tried he wouldn't have listened. What would he have done if someone had told him not to come to Hell's Gate? What if his own father had told him that creating the village was folly? Without knowing anything at all about the Captain's father, Marie was positive it wouldn't have mattered. He would have come here anyway, for he had an all-consuming vision that inspired and drove him —and to which he alluded once more, on the last page of the last diary.

It was a concise entry, like the others, and like the others written in the same abbreviated style he had used when making daily entries in his ship's log. It was dated July 28, 1918.

A. has just informed me of the most disturbing news of my life since coming to Hell's Gate, nearly thirty years ago. In consequence of this I can no longer consider him as my heir. I have set aside $50,000 marked "Marie and my grandson," with instructions for locating them through Greenwald. Furthermore I have hand-drafted a will leaving Ned Baxter the sum of $10,000 and his house, and H. Fischner his house. The remainder of the estate is to go to R., with the provision that upon her death it pass in its entirety to my grandson, Marie's son. I have placed these documents inside R.'s conch shell, where she and she alone will find them, along with a private letter to her explaining my intentions.

Words, phrases from the Captain's last entry whirled through Marie's mind. What could Abie possibly have told him to cause him to rewrite his will so hastily? Was the private letter to Rachel a suicide note? Apparently so, though in spite of his secret brooding, suicide seemed totally out of character for the Captain. Was it possible that he had arranged to meet Greenwald on the mountain that afternoon and been murdered by the extortioner?

Another possibility occurred to her as she thought of the recent reports that the Captain had been sighted in and near Hell's Gate. Perhaps there had never been any accident at all. She knew there had been no funeral. The Captain might still be alive, living in Arizona; this would account for Rachel's reclusiveness.

No. She was certain he was dead. And since she did not believe in ghosts, she concluded that the rumors of the Captain's presence were just that, rumors, as groundless as the rumors that Hell's Gate was being sold to Sears, Roebuck. He was not a myth but a man like any other, who had lost three children in a tragic accident, put all his hopes in the fourth, and been disappointed. He had gone riding. He had let his mind wander, and he had died accidentally, though not before leaving her and the grandson he thought existed an enormous amount of money, which Rachel, who had left immediately for Arizona with his body, had never found.

Marie closed the last diary and looked at her kitchen clock. It was past one. She had read steadily for more than four hours. She stood stiffly and picked up the lantern. Half a minute later she was walking up the hill toward the dark bulk of the Big House. Not a light was burning in the village, but as usual the whale's jaw was glowing pale in the darkness over the entrance of the drive. As she passed between the stone pillars, she reached up toward the jaw with her free hand. Her fingers seemed to acquire a phosphorescent transparency, like fingers in an X-ray film, and she had the startling sensation that she could see through to her own narrow, jointed bones. She jerked her hand away.

She was not thinking so much about the money as about her plan, how the legacy would help make it easier and quicker. Like the Captain when he had first come to Hell's Gate, she had estimated that it would take ten years to accomplish what she wanted. Now she could do it in less than half that time, less than a third probably. Pia had been right again, she thought. It had taken more than twenty years, but the debt owed to her by Abraham Benedict was about to be paid.

She unlocked the large front door where once the Captain and Rachel had greeted her and her parents on Christmas Eve, and she was nearly as excited now as she had been then. She knew exactly where the shell was, tucked away in the bottom of the trunk on the landing at the head of the stairs, where she had seen it two weeks ago, when she was itemizing the contents of the house for Joseph Stein. She opened the trunk lid and reached inside. The shell was there. And deep inside it, where she would not have felt it at all if her fingers had not been long and slender, was a pale yellow envelope with her name written on it in the same plain, clear hand she had been reading all evening.

She wondered where the other documents were, and as she opened the flap it occurred to her that the legacy inside might very well be in scrip instead of cash. If so, it would now be worthless to her. But it was not scrip that she shook out of the envelope.

It was a single piece of yellow stationery with three lines scrawled slantwise across it in large characters, written so hurriedly that she had to study them twice to be sure that they said:

I. O. U. $50,000
Abraham Benedict, Jr.
October 13, 1919

"I understand."

This was all she said. Her thoughts were coming so fast, one tumbling after the other that if she had tried to say anything else she probably could not have. She understood. She understood Abie's uneasiness when she had first returned to Hell's Gate. She understood his fear of her, which had gradually turned into outright hatred. And she understood why Abie had continued to hate his father and the factory after the Captain's death.

Until this moment, she had always been able to give him the benefit of her doubts. She had even taken his side in arguments with Ned and others. He was trying, wasn't he? Who in Abie's situation could possibly have lived up to the expectations of a man like the Captain? And there was his war wound to consider, the injured leg that had precluded other careers where he might very well have been successful—and so forth.

She knew now that despite her travels and her education and her instinctive understanding of most people, Abie had fooled her too, and badly; he had fooled everyone except possibly Ned, who out of respect and friendship for the Captain had never been able to bring himself to say what he really thought.

Now she began to understand why she had returned to Hell's Gate in the first place. It had little to do with acquiring an education and less to do with wanting to come home. She had returned because of Abie. Despite her better judgment she had remained in Hell's Gate less from affection for the dying village, of which she had never been more than peripherally a part, than in the hope that somehow Abie would change, become responsible, fulfill the bright potential of his youth, and then—she was not sure what. And she was ashamed of herself equally for this hope and for her ambivalence toward Harlan, her unwillingness to make as full a commitment to him as he was ready to make to her, which had nothing to do with his own inconsistencies but with her false hopes.

She put the envelope in her pocketbook, replaced the shell in the trunk, shut the lid, and left the house. On the way down the hill she noticed that the sky behind the mountains in the northwest was pulsing with a rosy glow, which she mistook for the northern lights until, just as she turned into her yard, she remembered the forest fire. It seemed much closer now, but she was too tired to care. Now all she wanted was a few hours of sleep before going to see Harlan.

She tucked the envelope into one of the diaries for safekeeping and then lay down on her bed without undressing and fell asleep immediately. But an hour later, in the restless time just before dawn, she began to dream the old dream of being trapped between Canada and the States. This time in her dream the air smelled sulfurous, and to both the north and south the sky was hazed and flushed with red.

"Miss Marie! Wake up!"

Someone was rapping on the front door. But the dream was so vivid and powerful, and she was so exhausted, that she thought it was her father calling to her in the covered bridge while she hid in the rafters. She did not actually wake up until she stood on the porch at dawn with Stan Gregory, feeling the hot wind on her face and looking at the fiery orange sky behind Kingdom Mountain, and even then she felt she might still be dreaming, since the half-deserted town with its peeling buildings, gray in the dawn light, and the flat gray lake and bay, and the gray, nearly leafless trees in the mountain framed by an orange sky resembled Pia's mysterious tableau on the north wall of the Mountain House rotunda more than the Hell's Gate she had gone to sleep in.

"We have to get the people out of here," Stan said. "That fire's only a few miles away."

Although Marie heard him, she had noticed something that she found as disquieting as the Canadian fire. "The sea gulls," she said. "Where are they?"

"Wake up!" Stan shouted at her. "You're still dreaming."

"I am awake. The sea gulls are gone."

He stared at her, then at the rooftops. They were empty; not a single bird had remained. Even the pigeons that roosted on the roof of the covered bridge had disappeared.

"You take this side of the street," Stan said. "I'll take the other."

Marie started up the south side of the street, pounding on doors, alerting the dozen or so remaining families. Just as she reached the last occupied house, she saw a small figure scuttle out of the grown-up weeds in the Mason yard and start up School Hill. "No classes today!" she shouted. "Go home as fast as you can."

She repeated her warning, then ran back down the street to the station, where the villagers were already gathering on the platform. Stan had sent Clayton and Slayton across the bridge to the lumberyard to bring back anything they could find that would fuel the locomotive. A minute after Marie arrived they returned to report that there wasn't a single sticker or scrap of lumber available.

Tiny flakes of ash were falling on the street like snow. It was difficult to breathe in the gusting, ash-filled wind. Marie thought fast. "Get the chairs from the social hall. Break them up, we'll burn them."

"Don't you dare," Early Kinneson said. He was standing in the street in his nightshirt and a pair of black rubber knee boots, holding the bucket of water he kept by his bedside in case of fire. "Those chairs belong to me now and I won't have them destroyed."

Clayton and Slayton looked from Early to Marie.

"You'll go to jail if you do," Early said.

"Get those chairs!" Marie shouted. She whirled toward Early. "Would you rather burn up yourself?"

"What should we do, Pa?" Clayton said.

"You go down the street and bring up them chairs, just like your teacher says," Bill Kane roared. "I'll fetch a wagon to load them on."

As he passed Marie on his way toward the lumberyard for the wagon, Bill gave her the high sign. "One hundred percent!" he said in a low voice.

Except for one of the original cattle cars on which Marie had ridden to the States as a child, all the Company's rolling stock had been sold at the auction. The cattle car had been stripped down and used as a flatbed for bringing heavy equipment up to work on the Mountain House, and there was not much room for furniture. People were racing back and forth between the flatbed and their houses with framed family photographs, mantel clocks, parlor chairs, bedding. Oat Morse's wife held a kitchen calendar in one hand and a frying pan in the other. Oat came running with his bee-keeping mask. Johnny Moon had his shotgun and two blue-tick hounds.

Early ran across the street to the store and returned with his ledger of outstanding accounts.

Bill Kane appeared pulling a wagon, which Marie and Clayton and Slayton began to load with the warped chairs from the Philadelphia shipment. Once again, the Kane boys were the heroes of the village as they pulled the wagon back along the street like two young oxen and threw the chairs down to Stan Gregory, who smashed them into kindling and tossed the pieces onto the flatbed behind the locomotive. While Bill and his sons returned for a second load, Marie checked the houses once more to make sure no one was left behind. She could not shake off the sensation that she was still dreaming. On her way back to the station she ran into her own house and got her pocketbook and the box of diaries and ledgers.

By this time the sky was much lighter, though so smoky the mountaintops were invisible. The orange glow behind the haze seemed paler, farther away, and Marie was less certain that the danger was imminent. The fire might still be many miles away;

it was impossible to tell for sure. But Stan had fired the locomotive boiler, and most of the villagers were already aboard
the cattle car.

Stan leaned out of the engine cab. "All right?" he said.

For the twentieth time that morning Marie wished Ned Baxter were there to tell her what to do.

"All right?" Stan called again.

"Blow the whistle," she told him.

He gave three long blasts on the whistle. Just as Marie was
ready to jump onto the flatbed, Madame Raspberry appeared
at the foot of School Hill.

Although Marie waved to her frantically, the big woman did
not quicken her stately, rolling gait at all. She ambled along at
a leisurely pace, stopping to look between the houses at the
bay as though assessing the angling prospects for the day
ahead. As she came closer, Marie saw that she held a heaping
quart of late-bearing red raspberries. From time to time she
paused to pop one into her mouth.

"Hurry!" Marie shouted. "Hurry up, Madame. The mountains are on fire."

Madame Raspberry did not seem at all curious about the
flatbed crowded with people holding incongruous household
items. To her, the entire commotion of the past several days
had seemed pointless when there were still berries to be picked
in the woods, perch waiting to be caught in the bay.

Marie ran toward her, grabbed one of her massive arms, and
steered her toward the car. Hands reached out to help her
aboard.

"What's all this big hubbub?" Madame said with considerable amusement. "Don't spill these berries, Marie. It took me an
hour to get them. We going to a circus this morning?"

"Quick," Marie told her, boosting her from behind while
Oat Morse hauled her aboard. "Everyone's leaving right now."

"Not everyone," Madame said, chuckling. "I know one
who's not."

"All right?" Stan shouted. "All right? Can we go?"

"Yes, for Christ's sake, go, go!" Early called. "Do you want to burn up to a crisp?"

"No!" Marie called. "Wait."

She looked up at Madame Raspberry, sitting with her legs dangling off the edge of the flatbed. "What do you mean, you know one who's not?"

"Wheely," she said, nodding and winking cannily. "Wheely ain't a-going."

"Good Lord! I forgot all about Wheely."

She thought of the small form she had seen stealing away from the Mason home at the foot of the hill at dawn.

"Where is he, Madame? Where did you see him?"

"I promised I wouldn't tell."

"Do you want him to get caught in the fire? Where is he?"

The huge woman sat eating berries with her legs dangling, impassive as a Buddha. Marie jumped up beside her and whispered something to her, and Madame's hand shot up to her ear, as it had once before, late at night on the floor of the varnish room. Before she knew what she'd done she pointed toward Kingdom Mountain and said, "Up there. In that big pink building."

The train had started to move. It was already passing Marie's old garden plot, raked clean now for winter.

"Tell Stan I'm bringing Wheely down on the handcar," she shouted at Bill Kane, who was handing legs and backs of broken chairs to Clayton and Slayton, who in turn were feeding the boiler fire.

As Bill started to object she thrust the box of diaries into his arms. "Give these to Harlan Smith to hold for me."

Bill turned, set down the box, turned back, and reached out to stop her, but he was too late. She had already jumped, hit the cinder embankment behind Herman Fischner's back yard, rolled with her momentum as John Trinity had taught her to do years ago, and come to her feet unhurt.

All Bill could do was give her the high sign and shout his old slogan: "One hundred percent!"

Then she was out of sight between the houses.

Bill Kane turned back toward the front of the car.

"Where's that box?" he growled at Clayton. "Where's that Christly box of books she give me?"

Slowly, through the smoke and sweat on Slayton's face, came an expression of painful comprehension.

"Haw," Clayton said disgustedly. "The dummy throwed it in the fire."

Carrying her pocketbook under her arm, Marie headed up the low road into the ruined park, running as she had once run playing fox and the geese with schoolchildren. But she was not thinking about her schooldays. She was not thinking about her plan for the future or about Abie or Harlan or the Captain or her stolen legacy. She was thinking only of the absolute necessity of finding Wheeler Mason and getting him back down to the village and then getting both herself and him to safety.

The low road and the brook beside it were still blocked in spots with limbs and brush from the big trees cut in the park. Sometimes Marie had to go out around the slash or fight her way through it. The haze stung her eyes. She was panting hard by the time she reached the falls below the waterwheel, now just a trickle. The meadow above was brown and dry, with no trace of the golf course, but a narrow trail like an animal path had been beaten through the sere grass toward the abandoned shell of the Mountain House, looming in the haze like a ruins that had stood empty for centuries. She ran along the path, with the wind gusting hot on her face.

"Wheely! Wheely!"

Standing on the flagstone piazza, she called his name repeatedly. It occurred to her that he might be hiding somewhere in the labyrinth of empty rooms inside, where it could take hours to find him. For weeks Wheeler had been growing increasingly timid and wild, like a cat whose owners had moved away and abandoned it, and he might not let her approach him at all.

"Wheely, it's Marie. It's me, Marie."

Except for the crickets under the flagstones, it was still.

She stepped through the open entrance into the great rotunda. In the hazy light coming through the glass roof, the colorful tableaux on the walls made her head swim.

"Wheely!"

Her voice bounced off the ceiling. The echo boomed: *Wheely! Wheely! Wheely!*

She did not shout again, but started up the wide marble staircase to the second floor. When she reached the top, she began going quickly from room to room. Once she went to a window and looked out, but it was too hazy to see more than a mile or two up the lake, and across the narrows, Canada Mountain was as indistinct as a mountain fifty miles away.

As she turned back toward the door, Wheeler appeared in the hallway, grinning at her like a guilty child.

"Wheely! For heaven's sake, I've been looking all over for you. Didn't you hear me? The mountains are on fire. We have to get out of here fast. We have to get out of Hell's Gate."

She started toward him, but with surprising agility he scampered down the hall. At the head of the stairs he paused briefly to make sure she was following him, then started down. As Marie ran along the empty hall after him, she thought she heard the echo of her own footsteps behind her. The sound disconcerted her, and she ran faster.

By the time she reached the top of the steps he was at the bottom. Again he paused, grinning guiltily but also with a kind of happy excitement, like a child playing a new and daring game.

"Wheely," Marie shouted, "I'm not going to play cat-and-mouse with you any longer. I'll catch you and when I do I'm going to slap you until your ears ring."

He dodged out of sight into the corridor leading to the kitchen at the back of the building.

She ran downstairs, taking the steps two and three at a jump. At the bottom, as she crossed the rotunda, she heard the echo of her own footsteps, and the delayed echo of her voice calling: *ears ring, ears ring, ears ring.* It was uncanny and terrifying, and as she entered the dusky corridor to the kitchen she wondered again whether Greenwald might be after her. In her fear she stopped abruptly and listened, but the echo had ceased.

"Wheely, you come here!"

Wheely, you come here, come here, here.

She ran, with the echo following her.

She arrived in the huge, barren kitchen just in time to see Wheeler disappear through a door leading to the basement. She started down after him in the dimness, tripped, and fell the last four steps. One of her knees was badly bruised, she had dropped her pocketbook, and she was so frightened and so furious at Wheeler she wanted to thrash him within an inch of his life. She imagined that she could hear laughter. Nearly crying with pain and fear, she found her pocketbook, got up, and looked around.

Half-completed heating conduits and plumbing fixtures ran here and there in the dusky light admitted by a row of small windows in the wall above her head. Moldering crates and unidentifiable debris lay in pools of stagnant, reeking water. Wheeler was nowhere to be seen, but somewhere in the dark she could hear him laughing.

Cautiously, Marie picked her way through the maze of dripping pipes and junk, around the standing water, toward the furnace room at the far end of the basement. The door was ajar. She squeezed through and knew she had found Wheeler's hideout.

Near the coal furnace, which like everything else in the Mountain House was unfinished, squatting like an armless octopus above a jumbled heap of rusting boiler plates, were the housekeeping utensils of a man camping out, including the missing silverware from the Big House. A couple of Marie's pie plates sat on the floor nearby like a dog's dishes, and through the open door of the furnace Marie could see, dimly, a heap of empty tin cans. A few magazines were scattered near some blankets, but Wheeler himself seemed to have slipped through Marie's fingers again.

"Damn!" she said.

The small man stepped out into view from behind the furnace, still grinning.

"Wheely, what are you doing?" she said angrily. "I ought to cuff you until you can't see straight, running away from me like that. What did I ever do to you to make you run away from me?"

Wheeler cringed back against the furnace. "Don't cuff me, Miss Marie," he said. "I didn't mean to make you mad. No, sir. I'd never make you mad, you've always been good to me, and I'd never have run away from you except Captain said to. He said to do it, and he wouldn't let nobody send me off. He said he'd stand right by me, he did."

Marie shook her head. "What are you frightened of, Wheely? No one's going to send you anywhere. I promise. Come on." She put out her hand, as if to a child. "We have to leave this place. That big fire's heading this way."

Wheeler drew back, shaking his head. "No! You ain't going to trick me. Old Wheely may not be smart, but he's too smart to be tricked like that. Captain said they'd try to trick me."

"Wheely, the Captain's dead. He's been dead for years."

"No, he ain't, Miss Marie."

Again Wheeler was grinning, despite his obvious terror.

"Where is he then?"

Wheeler's grin was triumphant as he shouted, "He's out there, and he'll be in directly!"

Knowing that he would dash for the door the moment she turned, Marie glanced quickly over her shoulder. She saw nothing but the open doorway.

"Hark!" Wheely said, putting his forefinger to his lips. "Hear him?"

Marie listened. Except for the steady plinking of waterdrops falling from broken pipes, it was still. She shook her head, turned back to Wheely, started to speak; then she heard the footfalls on the concrete floor outside the door.

Wheeler nodded excitedly. "Oh, yes," he said. "Yes, yes. The Captain's coming."

The steps stopped outside the room.

"Come in, Captain," Wheely called. "I got her here. She's right here."

The figure of a man appeared in the doorway. "Well, Marie," it said. "Is the morning wiser than the evening?"

Although he spoke in the Captain's voice, she knew immediately that it was not the Captain. In spite of the voice and the coat that hung nearly to his knees and still shone faintly blue in places under the filth and grime, in spite of the fact that he was holding the Captain's harpoon, this man was not Abraham Benedict. This man was at least four inches taller and had to stoop to avoid scraping his head on the ceiling of the room; and the Captain, if still living, would have been over sixty, but this man's beard and tangled, greasy hair were still quite light where the light from the single window of the furnace room fell on them.

"Can I go now, Captain?"

Marie glanced at the little gray-headed man behind her. He was dancing eagerly, like an ancient, grizzled child.

"Did you get what I told you to get, Wheeler?"

"Yes, sir! Yes, sir, Captain!"

"Can you remember everything I told you to do? Where to go first? What to do when you get there? What to do next? What to do after that?"

"Yes, sir, Captain. You're sure nobody's going to put me away?"

"No one will put you away, Wheeler. I promise. Now you can go."

Wheeler grinned at Marie, exactly like a guilty child. Then he scampered past her and was gone. The figure holding the harpoon stepped inside the room and shut the door.

"Hello, Abie," Marie said quietly.

"Hello, Marie," he said in his own voice.

"You're walking."

"Yes."

"Why?"

"Because I have a reason to."

He spoke quietly, in a tone devoid even of hatred, though she already knew that he intended to kill her and was so terrified that for the first time in her life she thought she might actually faint.

But she did not. And when she spoke she was amazed to realize that her voice was shaking not with fear but anger.

"I want my money," she said. "Give me my money, Abie Benedict."

He sneered at her. "What money?"

"The fifty thousand dollars you stole from me. I want it."

"Oh. That."

It was as though she had said, "The ten dollars you borrowed from me last month."

He made a short gesture with the harpoon, apparently meant to encompass the ruined Mountain House. "Here's your money," he said in the same toneless voice. "It didn't go very far, did it? How did you find out?"

"The same way I found out about your father's will. In his diaries. They make it all very clear. He set the money aside for me, and you stumbled onto it, or maybe you read the diaries and knew where to look. It doesn't matter. You stole it."

"How do you know my mother didn't take it, dear?"

Abie mimicked the tone and modulation of Rachel's voice so perfectly that Marie started.

"That's crazy. Your mother was the most honest person I've ever known. Nothing in the world could make her do such a thing. Besides, I've got your I.O.U. right here in my pocket-book. I'm surprised you bothered with that formality."

He looked at her mockingly. "All right. You're right. Mother didn't know. She didn't know anything about the money. Why would she? He never spoke about business with her.

What was she to him? A way to make heirs legitimately. And when she couldn't do that any longer, a graceful adjunct to his estate. Nothing more. So he squirreled the money away in the shell, like the pirate he was, where he planned for her to find it and follow his directions to the letter after he was gone, and then he came up here and had his neat little accident. If he'd had a regular notarized will like everybody else he might have waited and put it in that. But he didn't have a notarized will, or any other will except that note in the shell, which he didn't write in his right mind anyway."

Abie laughed.

"You see, Marie, it never occurred to him before that day that he was going to die. At least not until he'd finished everything he wanted to finish."

Abie's voice was no longer neutral. Now there was absolute hatred in his words, which terrified her even more than his ghoulish imitations. Yet she had to keep him talking until she could distract him long enough to try for the furnace room door.

"You once told me yourself he'd finished everything. You told me he was bored and ready for a change. What hadn't he finished?"

"Me."

She looked at him.

"I wasn't finished. I wasn't running the factory. I wasn't building parks and stone walls and dams and monuments. I wasn't married, with sons of my own. There was still a good deal of work to be done on me. And when I came home and finally worked up the courage to tell him face to face that I wasn't ever going to run the factory and build walls and have sons, or even daughters, and why, he simply couldn't accept the fact. Any more than he could accept the fact that you had tossed me out of a ring in the factory yard when I was fourteen. He killed himself, Marie. The great brave Captain came up here and killed himself."

"I don't believe that," she said.

"What don't you believe?"

"I don't believe your father killed himself."

He started; the harpoon in his hand wavered slightly but remained pointed at her.

"You read the last entry in the diary. How don't you believe it?"

Her challenge had been a shot in the dark. But his reaction told her she had hit something she hadn't aimed at, and suddenly she realized that she really did not believe that the Captain had killed himself. It was not only unacceptable; as Pia had once told her, many true things are unacceptable. It simply didn't happen. It was the last recourse in the world that a man like Abraham Benedict would take, no matter how desperate.

She shook her head slowly. "Maybe he considered killing himself. Maybe he even came up here to kill himself. But he didn't."

Abie looked at her wildly, and for a moment she thought he was going to throw the harpoon. She tensed to dodge.

"All right," he said, his voice shaking. "It was an accident. Just the way he planned to make it appear. He rode up here and got down to look in the quarry the way he did from time to time, and somehow he slipped and fell. He fell a hundred feet. There wasn't a thing anyone could do."

Abie's voice was shaking badly. His hand was shaking on the harpoon.

"No," Marie said. "That's not what happened either."

This was not even a shot in the dark, but merely a ploy to sustain the argument long enough for her to pick up a length of pipe, a tool, anything heavy, since she had made up her mind that she would have to attack him very soon.

But instead of objecting to what she had said, he looked at her for perhaps twenty seconds without speaking; and when he did speak at last, his voice was so low she could just make out the words.

"You're right," he said. "It wasn't an accident."

She stared at him, beyond even surprise now, as though

nothing he could say or she could discover about him or his family or Hell's Gate would surprise her ever again. As he began to speak, speaking quietly, wearily now, she listened with a fascination that had nothing to do with surprise.

"When I was recuperating in the London hospital—to the extent that a person can recuperate from that type of injury—they sent me a box of clothes and some other personal things. On top was a cheery little note from my mother, who wrote to me nearly every day I was there, and a letter on Company stationery from my father, full of man-to-man nonsense about how proud he was of me for getting myself shot. In the very bottom of the box, wrapped in tissue paper, there was a baseball.

"It was an ordinary baseball except for one thing; it had been signed by all the 1918 Red Sox players. The team that turned out to be world champions. The names had been scrawled on in a hurry, and some I had to study a long time to make out. But they were all there. Harry Hooper, Carl Mays, Babe Ruth, Ernie Shore. All of them. And all I could think at first was that now that it was probably too late for me to do anything about it, the bastard was willing to indulge me a little. Or maybe this was his way of showing me he'd won, beaten me at last, and I had no choice but to come home and run his goddamn factory. There was no explanation in his letter. Just that ball.

"Until then, I hadn't mentioned the nature of my wound to my parents. I let them think it was my leg. I'd planned to tell them later, as gently as possible. But that ball changed my mind. It made me want to tell him, hurt him the way he'd hurt me. For the next week or so I composed dozens of letters in my head to him, each one more vicious than the last. I suppose I got rid of some of the anger that way, because I never did write the letter, and as the days went on, I began to have second thoughts about why he'd sent that baseball. It occurred to me that maybe he was asking for a reconciliation. Certainly he had gone out of his way to get the signatures.

"After that I began to look at the ball differently. The nights were long and empty, and there wasn't much to do. I'd been put in a bed next to an English officer with the same injury, and the idiot kept making jokes about it—'At least we can still keep our chins up'—until I told him to shut up or I'd kill him. When I couldn't sleep, I'd look at the signatures in the nightlight and play an imaginary game where I'd pitch to the Boston lineup. It was fun in a way, holding the ball differently for different pitches, counting the balls and strikes and inventing situations in my head. When I got tired of that I'd write up imaginary headlines for the games I'd won. *Impotent Pitcher Shuts Out Sox on Three-Hitter.* Sometimes I'd make up whole newspaper accounts of games. It gave me something to do.

"It gave me something else. It gave me some hope. I thought I might get into sportswriting, maybe. Or coaching. I knew that would disappoint my father, but because of the gift, the signed ball, I thought maybe he'd understand. Though I still didn't know if I had guts enough to tell him, or tell him how I'd really been wounded. When I was ready to go home, I decided not to, just to continue the ruse about my leg for a while.

"He seemed pleased to see me when I got home. He didn't mention the leg, except to say he'd see to it that I had the best medical care available.

"By then I was carrying the ball in my coat pocket, like some sort of talisman. I'd rubbed off most of the signatures from fingering it different ways, and I think it pleased him that I carried it around with me. I told him about the made-up games I'd played while I was in the hospital and he said that was just what he would have done to keep his mind occupied. He was interested in what I'd done in the war. We had some good late-night visits in the library, and one night I think he almost told me about my brothers. Do you know about them too?"

She nodded.

"It happened late one evening, long after Mother had gone to bed, over a bottle of Scotch I'd brought him. I was telling him how for the fun of it we used to fly in over the Turkish docks to see what we could hit with our hand pistols, and he shook his head and said, 'My God, son, weren't you afraid?'

"I was surprised. Surprised that he'd think I might have been afraid. 'No, of course not,' I said. Then I laughed and said, 'What were you ever afraid of?'

"Without any hesitation he looked at me seriously and said, 'Fire. I'm afraid of fire, Abie, and you should be too. A fire would wipe out our village in an hour, destroy everything we've got here.'

"He paused then, as though he was debating something with himself. I had no idea what at the time; but when he started talking again he asked me something about the planes we flew, and a short while later we went to bed."

Abie had let the blade of the harpoon touch the floor. With his other hand he held the doorjamb, as though it was still an effort for him to support himself on the leg he had not used in public for years. Now, she thought. Now. But she was fascinated by his story, and he seemed much less dangerous supporting himself on the harpoon and doorway and talking so frankly. So she stood where she was.

"If only he'd gone on and told me about the fire and my brothers and why he'd come here in the first place, done what he'd done here, I never would have gone to him and told him about the injury and that I was leaving. By then the last thing I wanted was to hurt him. I just believed he should know the truth, and know my plans, and he'd either sympathize with them because of what I'd been through, or be angry, which I could have understood. I could have handled his anger. That can be a way of acceptance, as much as sympathy. But he hardly ever got angry with me, and he didn't the next morning when I finally worked up the courage to go to his office and tell him. He didn't show any feeling at all, or speak a word. He just stared past my head at that picture on his wall that the gypsy woman painted of me as a boy in my ball uniform. Then he got up and walked out the door, not looking at me at all, and went out of the factory and up to the Big House and sat down in the library and changed the will he hadn't yet prepared because it had never occurred to him that he might die. When he finished, he put it and the money in the shell. He was very methodical about everything. He went back and made his diary entry, like the good captain who sees the icebergs all around the ship, and closing in, and can't do a thing about it but has time at least to write in the log what's going to happen, and then he locked up his diaries and came up here on the mountain.

"I sat in his office a long time. I kept hoping he'd come back and say something to me, say anything to show he knew I was there. I must have waited the better part of an hour. Because when I finally went up to the house and passed the library window and looked inside he was just closing his diary. He left by the back way and never saw me, and I went straight to the desk and read what he'd written and then I read what he'd put in the shell.

"At first I was just going to leave town, only sooner than I'd planned. I was packing when Mother came up to my room. She was all out of breath, and told me that his horse had come back without him. She begged me to go see what had happened. I'd never seen her so upset, and I couldn't very well say no. So I hitched up her buggy and drove up through the park, holding the reins in one hand and rolling that baseball inside my pocket with the other, twirling it faster and faster. When I got to the quarry I saw him—standing on the edge, looking down into it. It was a dry summer and the water in the pit was lower than usual. Part of that broken obelisk was sticking out, and he was looking down at it, as though at his ruined dream.

"I called to him. He stood there, not moving. I called again. Nothing. As though I wasn't even there and never had been. As though I'd never existed. And all the time I was twirling that ball in my pocket."

"He didn't turn around?"

It was the first time Marie had spoken since he had begun the story.

"He turned just as I threw. To this day I don't know whether

I wanted to get his attention or hit him, though I had no reason to think I could hit him from that distance. I was at least a hundred feet away and I hadn't thrown a ball in years. I didn't stop to think at all. I was twirling the ball in my pocket, and he wouldn't turn, and then he did, too late; the ball was in the air and I was on the ground from the force of the throw. I doubt he ever saw it coming.

"I heard the crack, first. Then his hand went up, and he fell backwards and hit on the obelisk. Ned found the ball floating near his body and gave it to me. He was suspicious, I think, but he didn't have any real proof, and he couldn't quite bring himself to believe that I'd go that far. But I had. And I wasn't sorry except that I had to do so much pretending from the start, and now I would have to continue pretending to be crippled. Or if I didn't have to, I decided to. It wasn't hard. At first I couldn't go faster than a slow shuffle anyway, and I just decided to keep on that way. It gave me an advantage, in certain ways, to be able to walk when people thought I couldn't. In some ways it was even amusing.

"For instance, there was the memorial service. You missed that, Marie. That was very amusing. I knew the village would know that he wouldn't want a funeral. But the village wouldn't allow me to get away without giving them some sort of opportunity to show what a great man they thought he was, so I had to have a memorial service. I shut down the factory in the middle of the afternoon, and blew the whistle because there wasn't any church bell to ring. Afterward Johnny Moon told how his hunting dogs howled because they knew the Captain had died when everybody in Hell's Gate had heard them howl exactly the same way for years every morning, noon, and evening when the whistle blew. Then that superstitious fool Oat Morse went out behind his house and told his bees the Captain was dead so they wouldn't fly away. Then my mother retreated even further into her isolation, twenty-five hundred miles away, less for her health than because it was the last place the man she'd spent her whole life making excuses for had been happy—that was especially amusing.

"Not to mention the diaries and ledgers, Marie. They were very entertaining. I read them all. Carefully, carefully enough to learn how Phineas Greenwald had told him that child of yours was still alive, and you and he were in Montreal or wherever, though of course I didn't know myself yet that none of that was true. At the time I believed it all, even when I tried to locate Greenwald and couldn't. When my father died he must have figured that he'd run his luck as far as he could reasonably expect to, since I was an unknown quantity and might investigate the matter and discover the truth; so he dropped out of sight and didn't come back here for some years, and then in a different role.

"But even when Greenwald didn't show up, I still thought you would, Marie. I lived in dread of that time. And when it came, as I knew it would, I was positive you wanted more money, for yourself and your son. I believed he was still alive, you see, until I began to check your story. Only then, when what I discovered seemed to tally with what you'd told me, did I finally realize that Greenwald had fooled my father—as he later tried to fool me."

"Wait. If you knew about Greenwald, why would you let him come up here posing as that agent and swindle you?"

"I told you, Marie. Certain things amused me. I had to find unusual ways to entertain myself, and by the time Greenwald arrived, I thought it would be entertaining to let him play out his game."

"You mean that you let him swindle you out of ten thousand dollars for a joke?"

"I let the village *think* he swindled me out of ten thousand dollars. I left him dead in his hotel room in Boston. Nobody there knew me or him, and by the time I was finished I doubt he could have been identified anyway. When I got back here and saw that the village was laughing at me, as I'd intended them to, I was laughing up my sleeve at them and already planning my next step.

"That money, Marie. All that money my father gave Greenwald to pay you to stay away. That was reason enough for me to kill him. And all that money my father left in the shell for you. That might have been reason enough for me to kill you. But the thought didn't even cross my mind when I discovered it, though I destroyed that so-called will and the letter to my mother immediately. The money I intended to give to you, as a bribe I suppose, when you showed up. I was in a hurry, so I put the shell with your money in it in the office safe, where Mother wouldn't stumble onto it, and after she left for Arizona I put it back in the trunk.

"And when you did show up, as I'd known you would, and I had to bear seeing you here, where I'd be reminded every day of whom my father favored over me, and why, I still intended to give you your legacy, indirectly at least; let you use it for your education or whatever you wanted, as long as you'd agree to leave Hell's Gate. But you wouldn't leave, so I took the money—it was that rainy night you moved into the teacher's house, and by then I needed it, since mine and my mother's was about gone—and left the I.O.U. for a joke, to amuse myself. It never occurred to me you'd find it. I should have destroyed those diaries too, of course. But it doesn't matter. I think I like it better this way.

"But you still didn't leave, Marie, so then I thought I really might kill you. I lay awake nights imagining interesting ways to do it. The way I'd imagined pitching against the Red Sox. It was amusing to think of killing you nights while during the day I was spending your money. But even before the money was gone, that satisfaction began to pall. Like all the others, including this resort; and then I began thinking along different lines, for both you and my father's little kingdom. I began to think it would be more fun to destroy it and you both, slowly, by degrees. That's why I tried to get you fired from your job, Marie. I knew you wouldn't go to bed with me, when I propositioned you that day in my office. I merely wanted to give you an unpleasant choice. Sleep with a cripple or lose your job.

"When you found a way around that, I was tempted again to kill you. Once I almost did. Remember the night you and

Smith came down the lake in the storm? It wasn't Belliveau who shot at you. It was me. I was waiting on the hill for the Frenchman with that punt gun I bought; but by the time I heard Smith's boat coming along, I doubted that Belliveau would show, so I thought I'd have some fun and give him a little scare, and maybe kill him into the bargain for coming out onto the lake after I'd told him not to. I didn't know you were with him until I'd already fired, though I might have done it anyway. I had the thing loaded with everything from cuff links to shotgun slugs, and it's a wonder you both weren't blown to bits like that plane. You would have been if I'd had another shot; but by then Belliveau was coming, and I figured he was more important, so I saved the next charge for him. You didn't really suppose Smith shot down that plane with a pocket pistol, did you?"

He paused to enjoy her astonishment. "Who do you think slit your horse's throat, Marie? Who put the immigration authorities on you and nearly had you deported? Before that even —who do you suppose offered Madame Raspberry a dollar to throw you in the stain tank? Paid Clayton and Slayton to ambush you? And each time you came up grinning your foolish little grin and plodding on with your damnable petty ambitiousness and your petty little accomplishments—once I actually thought of having you run the Mountain House for me because I knew you'd make it succeed; but by then I wasn't at all sure I wanted it to—each time, I'd think with amusement that it would all come to exactly nothing. To this, Marie."

He raised the harpoon, and instantly she regretted not having rushed him when she'd had the chance. His eyes and voice and manner were too calm, she thought, as he continued talking with the harpoon pointed at her. Only a madman could be that calm, address her amiably by name while holding a weapon at her throat.

"But I still had the village to tend to. After the Mountain House fell through, as I'd half suspected it would all along and then planned for it to, I went to work on the village. For a while that was entertaining too. I don't understand much about woodworking, God knows, but I understand that you can't put green lumber through a kiln and expect it to come out seasoned. That was to pay Ned back for badgering me when I was a boy and for being so goddamned right about everything around the factory. And for the way he looked at me at the memorial service and various times afterward when he thought I didn't notice, wondering if I really did help my father fall into the quarry. I liked seeing those warped chairs, Marie. 'They're like you, Ab, my boy,' I said to myself. I laughed all the way home from Philadelphia.

"I liked my final meetings with Ned and Herman and a few other old-timers just before the bankruptcy, when I begged them to hold onto their scrip for just a few more weeks, knowing all the time what was going to happen. Herman was too smart for me; he cashed his in anyway and cleared out. Some of the others weren't.

"I especially liked cutting those trees in the park. That was very satisfying. I hoped wherever my father was, he was watching. It was enough, though, to know the village was watching. Watching their home destroyed, bit by bit by bit. 'Ab,' I thought, 'you're actually good at this business of laying waste by degrees. Maybe even better than he was at building it all up. Don't go too fast now; savor all this a bit.'

"So I did. I savored all of it, right through the auction. I savored masquerading as the Captain, scaring idiots like Oat Morse a little, actually making poor Wheeler believe I was my father." With sudden irrelevance, he said in an interested voice, "What did you buy at the auction, Marie? Your house?"

"No. Nothing at all in Hell's Gate."

"I don't believe you. You must have bought something. The Big House?"

"No."

"That's too bad. I know you've been working hard on it. I hoped you'd buy it. I thought I might meet you there some night and finish our business, but you always had that loud-

mouth cattle auctioneer with you. To get back to what you
bought, though. I know what you bought. You bought that
worthless island. What did you propose to do out there, set up
a colony for Harlan Smith's Chinese friends?"

He smiled, and Marie thought that he must certainly be mad,
though perhaps not quite as mad as he wished to appear.
Several times as he spoke he had glanced out the window
above her head, as though he was waiting for something to
appear there—the way he had looked out the window of his
office the morning in the fall of 1918 that she returned to Hell's
Gate.

She had to keep him talking.

"What about those girls from Montreal or wherever?" she
said. "What did you bring them here for if you were . . ."

He laughed. "Mainly to outrage old women like Gertrude
Fischner and Ned Baxter. And to make the men in the factory
jealous. I knew what they were saying. I overheard them, as
they intended for me to. 'Young Mr. Abie would go for a snake
if it had ears to grab onto,' they said. Toward the end, though,
I'd even lost interest in outraging people. So I began to look for
girls who had other tastes. Girls who liked being hurt, the way
I wanted to hurt you. It wasn't hard to find them once I knew
where to look. Some of those girls enjoyed what I did to them
even more than the money I paid them to let me do it. Even
more than I enjoyed obliging them.

"But after a while, I got weary of all those games too. They
weren't gratifying to me anymore. And I hadn't been wholly
successful with all of them, since some of you found ways to
stay on in the village and keep going even after there was no
work and no money. And there was always the chance that a
new business would come in and put the village back on its
feet and spoil my plans altogether, though what I told those
few that were interested pretty much ruled out that possibility. My idea was for things to continue to crumble slowly,
for Hell's Gate eventually to turn into a ghost town, a re-
minder to anyone who cared of my father's ultimate failure.

I had similar plans for you, Marie. I wanted to see you grow old poor and alone, wondering what had gone wrong and why. But when St. Francis bought the village and some rich man bought the Big House and you bought that island to farm on or whatever you decided to do out there, I began to have doubts. I thought maybe my plan wasn't the best one, even though I'd be here in the background to help it along, at least for a while. So I began thinking along different lines. It occurred to me that it might not be such a bad thing if that Canadian fire swept right over the top of the mountain and finished everything for me in a few hours. How close is the fire, Marie?"

"It's miles away. There's very little chance of its getting here at all."

"Good. Because after I'd thought about it, I didn't want some freak of nature to be responsible for finishing Hell's Gate after all. I wanted to do that myself, in my own way. And I intend to. But first, Marie, there's you."

He lifted the harpoon so that the tip was inches from her throat.

"Take off your clothes," he said.

"What?"

"Undress."

"What do you mean? What are you talking about? What is it you want?"

"You'll see soon enough. Undress."

"What are you going to do, Abie?"

"Now!" he said. "Undress, you bitch, or I'll cut off your clothes."

It was the word bitch that jolted her out of her terror, restored the anger she had relied on earlier to keep from giving in to him. She thought of the snowy Christmas Eve years ago in Pond in the Sky when she had used her wits to prevent Bull Francis from raping her and perhaps killing her; although Bull Francis had not been mad, only vicious and drunk, and she was positive Abie was mad and had been for months, she believed that she could still outwit him too if only she did not lose her head.

She looked at him and shook her head.

Before she knew what he meant to do he had ripped open her dress with the lance. She looked down on the floor at the dress buttons, more surprised than frightened, though she was frightened too. She felt a trickle of blood slide down her left side. Then she felt the stinging, as though she had brushed against nettles; but the pain, like the anger, helped clear her head.

Slowly, not taking her eyes off him, she knelt and removed first one shoe, then the other. She stood up and removed her dress and folded it and placed it on the floor beside her shoes and pocketbook. She took off her slip, undressing slowly and methodically, as though getting ready to go to bed, thinking as she removed each article of clothing exactly what she would do when the time came. She unsnapped her garters, unrolled her stockings, paying no attention to the blood still running down her left thigh. She took off her bra and underpants and stood naked in front of him.

"Lie down," he snarled. "On those blankets."

Looking at him steadily, she said, "Why don't you have me put on my lipstick first? Fix my face?"

He glanced over her head out the window.

"Fix your face," he said.

Watching him, steadily, never taking her eyes from his face, she knelt and picked up her pocketbook. Her eyes never left his as she unclasped it. So that he would watch her face, not her hands, she stared steadily into his eyes as she reached inside. Momentarily, she panicked because she did not feel what she was searching for immediately. Then her hand touched something hard and flat; it had worked its way to the bottom, under her change purse and compact. Now, more than at any time in her life, it was essential to be methodical, not hurry. She turned it slowly until she was holding the handle. There was a faint click inside the pocketbook.

"Fix your face," he repeated, and then she was pointing Harlan's .38 squarely at his chest.

"Put down that spear and turn around," she said. "It's indecent of you to stare at an undressed woman this way."

"You won't pull that trigger, Marie."

"I'll pull the trigger, Abie. Do as I say."

"You won't pull the trigger. I'll tell you why. Despite everything I've done to you and what I'm going to do to you, you're still in love with me. You always have been. You know it. I know it. You won't pull the trigger."

She shook her head. "There's nothing left of you to love, Abie. Put down the harpoon."

She saw him stiffen, heard the noise in his throat. She saw the hand holding the lance start to come up, and then she heard the explosion of the gun, deafening in the small room, though neither then nor later did she remember firing it.

Her ears were ringing too loudly to hear the harpoon clatter on the floor as he spun around, grasping his left leg. The room smelled strongly of smoke, and she was astonished that at such a moment she would think with chagrin that Harlan had been right once again—the gun had come in handy.

She did not bother with any of her underclothes but hastily put on her dress and shoes.

Abie lay half propped against the wall, holding his upper leg.

"Get up," she said. "We're going down the mountain."

He shook his head and smiled, almost sadly. "No, we aren't, Marie."

She shrugged. "All right. I'm through fighting you. I'm going down the mountain."

"No. You're not going down the mountain."

She looked at him. She supposed he was totally mad now, but she could not feel pity for him. She had no feeling about him at all.

As she started to step out around him, he spoke again, and she paused in the doorway.

"You're dead, Marie. You're as dead as though I'd spitted

you like a whale. I sent Wheeler down to the park to set the brush on fire. He's done it already; he's probably on his way to the Common on the handcar. When he reaches the causeway he's going to light another fire. That will do it. You and I and Hell's Gate and everyone in it are going to vanish from the face of the earth."

"Wheeler wouldn't do that. He's not crazy."

"Wheeler's a firebug. Had you forgotten that? Wheeler loves fire, and he loved my father, and he thinks he has my father's permission to do what he likes best, which is to set something on fire. The Captain told him that he could set a whole mountain on fire, avenge himself on the paper company that took his house, avenge himself on all the people who made fun of him and played tricks on him for years. Look out the window."

She glanced out the window and saw the smoke, already thick below the Mountain House.

"Good God!" she said, and began to run fast down the damp passageway toward the cellar steps.

Then she stopped, turned around, ran back, and did the only merciful thing left to do for Abie Benedict. She tossed the gun through the open door into the furnace room.

A minute later she was racing across the piazza toward the burning woods below her.

Chapter Seventeen

Today only a very few, very old natives of Kingdom County can remember the big unrelieved woods that once covered the gore of Hell's Gate from the east shore of Lake Memphremagog all the way to the New Hampshire line and extended even farther to the north into Quebec, as well as south along both sides of the bay to the edge of the vast cedar swamp between the south end of the bay and Kingdom Common. Although somewhat less extensive, the woods on the west side of the lake, the Kingdom Mountain side, were also dense and wild. Some nearly inaccessible parts of this land held sizable tracts of virgin spruce and fir until the middle of the 1880s, when the last big softwoods were cut and floated north up the lake. In the 1890s Abraham Benedict had begun cutting the hardwood, judiciously but steadily. Finally his son took the maples and birch, the ash and wild cherry and butternut, indiscriminately and spitefully, so that most of what remained was young soft-wood forest, spruce and fir again, which the St. Francis Paper Company officials hoped someday to convert into sheets of newsprint. Along with the dry brush in the park, which Abie had never picked up and disposed of after cutting the big trees, these young softwoods and the foot-deep duff of dry needles beneath them burned like tinder, causing many of the weird pyrotechnics of what was erroneously called the Great Canadian Fire of 1922.

People who did not see the fire assumed that the descriptions from those who did were embellishments to aggrandize a natural disaster into part of the myth of Hell's Gate and Abraham Benedict. Yet the tales of illusions in the sky, of fire cyclones hundreds of feet high and sparks as large as armchairs, of whole trees bursting instantly into flame, and of tributary fires that burned underground like fires burning in a coal mine, then surfaced weeks later, were for the most part accurate. Once started, the fire burned with a nearly unbelievable fury, and Marie thought at first that her only chance was to reach the handcar before Wheeler did. But as she raced down through the meadow, she could hear the flames roaring in the brush on the mountainside below, and when she reached the woods at the foot of the meadow, where the low and high road divided at the upper entrance of the park, she knew it was too late to try to reach the village. The entire lower east side of Kingdom Mountain was already burning.

Her feet hurt terribly from running in her good shoes. Leaning against the Captain's waterwheel, she removed them for the second time that morning. As she looked down the mountain over the pool near where she had once bathed before parting with Pia, and later made love to Abie, and still later watched the single battered trout try again and again to clear the falls, she thought she might find refuge from the fire in the water. Hurriedly she waded out toward the middle; but now, in the drought, the deepest part was not up to her knees.

Below her, Hell's Gate was invisible through the smoke. The fire had now gotten into the big hemlocks left standing in the park. One by one they flared into flames and exploded like gigantic Roman candles. The flames were jumping through the crowns of the trees, traveling faster than Marie could believe possible, and she was terrified to see a river of fire burning its way toward her up the slash and brush that had been thrown in the brook, as though the water itself was on fire. Holding her shoes in her hand, she started running back up through the meadow, but stopped before she'd gone twenty steps. Even if she outdistanced the fire below her, she would only be running straight into the fire coming out of Canada, and then she would be trapped.

When she turned back toward the park, she could feel the heat from the advancing flames on her face and neck. The dense smoke rolling up the mountainside like lifting fog made her weep, but her tear ducts were already drying out in the intense heat, and as the firestorm advanced, destroying everything in its path, it roared louder than any sound she had ever heard, like the steady thundering roar of artillery before an attack that the soldiers in the army hospital had described to her.

Marie realized that she had one chance left, and that was to run obliquely down the southeast slope of the mountain toward the causeway at the south end of the bay. She knew that it was not a good chance. Even if Wheeler hadn't already set the second fire, the flames below her were moving laterally across the mountainside as well as upward and might well reach the causeway before she did and cut off her retreat. But it was the only chance she had. Dropping her shoes, she plunged down the bank toward the brook.

Just ahead of the ascending wall of flames, she crossed the water and headed into the woods, running on an animal path roughly parallel to the bay and the spur track. The fire had created its own high wind, and all around her burning brands carried by the wind were falling and starting smaller fires. A brush fire close beside the path forced her to detour higher up the mountain, and when she angled back down she crossed the narrow animal trail without seeing it and had to blunder on by guesswork.

Her dress was catching on tree branches and brush piles, so she ripped it off and ran faster.

Without the dress to protect her, branches tore at her skin, reopening the long slicing wound from the harpoon. Brambles caught on her bare legs, leaving long red scratches. Her bare feet were bruised and bleeding from pounding over exposed granite and jutting roots.

Marie was not the only fugitive. Wild animals were running beside her: porcupines, snowshoe rabbits still as brown as the leaves underfoot, raccoons hurrying by, humpbacked in their flight. All were heading in the general direction of the causeway.

Huge sparks, some larger than bushel baskets, were drifting through the air, weaving with erratic purposelessness and instantly consuming whatever they landed on. One had apparently blown all the way across the bay to Canada Mountain, which was burning brightly through the smoke. Or perhaps, Marie thought, that was another piece of Wheeler's handiwork.

Her neck throbbed badly. She touched it with her hand, and the hair on the back of her neck felt dry and brittle. She ran beside the fleeing animals, no longer thinking of anything but her own survival. Her breath came in searing gasps. Twice she fell. As she got to her feet the second time, she saw a large bear sprinting toward a brush pile, and then not around it or over it or under it but directly through it.

For some time she had been running through cedar trees on level ground, but she had no idea where she was until it occurred to her that somehow she had come out on the edge of the bog, west of the causeway, where as a girl of ten she had tracked the deer. All around her animals were running into the swamp. She paused, then started after the animals, which continued to rush past her: a mink, two muskrats, another mink. Once she had helped trap these creatures. Now she and they were fleeing together.

The footing grew marshier. The trees were thinning out into small islands of cedars and tamaracks packed close together on hummocks of drier ground. She could not move fast because of the treacherous going; even the porcupines passed her. Birds were flying from one island of trees to another, until finally there were no more islands, no more trees, just a flat expanse of waist-high marsh grass. The place through which she was moving seemed as infinite as the flatland in her recurrent nightmare, though she knew it was closed in by the fire behind her and the vast bog ahead. She moved forward, knowing too that when the fire reached the tall grass it would sweep through like the wind on which it was borne. She followed a family of half-grown raccoons, thinking they would go to water instinctively; but suddenly she saw flames jumping high above the marsh grass just ahead of her. She turned and ran.

She was not sure how long she had been running. The sun was obscured by a huge cloud of thick yellow smoke that now hung over mountains, lake, and swamp. It might have been noon or six o'clock; there was no way to tell, and she thought of Father Boisvert, walking through smoky fields as a small boy and losing track of time and direction. She was wading in knee-deep water between tussocks of grass, which she grasped to keep from stumbling since she could not see where her feet were in the murky, cedar-stained water.

The tussocks ended abruptly, and she emerged onto the edge of a large backwater, dotted with a dozen or so muskrat houses. Sitting on top of the stick houses were all kinds of animals: minks, otters, muskrats, raccoons, porcupines, fisher cats. Some of the animals were crowded close together with their natural enemies—fisher cats and porcupines, minks and muskrats, foxes and rabbits. There were dozens of them, and more were coming out of the marsh grass every minute. Some paused and stood up on their hind legs to look back at the fire, as though entranced. Others began to swim without breaking stride at all. She stepped into the water and waded toward the nearest muskrat house. As she approached, a large beaver slid off and swam to another lodge thirty feet away.

Instead of sitting on the lodge, Marie leaned against it, keeping as low in the water as possible because of the scorching heat. Gigantic orange sparks were wafting out over the bog, veering crazily, and though most extinguished themselves in the air, one huge fireball landed on a muskrat house across the backwater. Instantly the mud and stick structure vanished in flames.

The fire was racing through the marsh, leaping from one island of trees to another. Small animals that had been safe in the tussocks of grass came running before the blasting heat, emerging confused on the edge of the cove. There were chipmunks and red squirrels, jumping deer mice, garter snakes, frogs. Some were so badly singed she could not identify them. And then, from where Marie had no idea, hawks began to descend on the small fleeing animals. The hawks screamed as they swooped down to pick up their prey in front of the onrushing flames. The air over the cove seemed full of their bloodthirsty cries. There were hawks of every variety native to Kingdom County: vivid red and yellow and blue sparrow hawks, great red-tailed hawks, low-flying marsh hawks. Instead of carrying off their prey, the birds lifted them a few feet above the ground and in their frenzy dropped them to pick up others. The old hawks seemed to be encouraging and instructing their young, and the young ones seemed to be competing with each other. Marie recalled watching the skunks dig up the turtle eggs and the owl catching a skunk on the night she ran away from Hell's Gate and had the miscarriage. Yet, the blind chaotic fury of the screaming hawks was far more terrifying, until finally she could no longer hear them over the roaring of the fire.

Because the shoulder of Kingdom Mountain intervened between the peninsula to the north and the backwater where she had sought refuge, Marie had no idea whether the fire had reached the village. But when she looked up at the enormous pillar of yellow smoke above the notch, she saw the inverted burning image of Kingdom Mountain reflected in its thick underlayer. The reflection was magnified so that she could plainly see individual trees burning, and then she saw the burning image of the Canada Mountain House and realized that no person could survive in that inferno. But she could not help looking; and now, reflected in the smoke, she saw not only Kingdom Mountain but Canada Mountain as well, and between them the village, still intact; and the inverted images were so exact she could make out each house, including her own, and the bridge and factory and the Big House, all suspended bottom-side-up a thousand feet in the air. Great tongues of flames leaped hundreds of feet high, jumping toward the hanging village.

Marie's eyes hurt from the smoke and heat. She splashed water into them and looked away for a moment. There was a sudden intensity in the roaring, and when she looked up again at the mirror image in the smoke, there was nothing in the notch between the mountains but a great gulf of fire. The entire village had combusted as spontaneously as a haystack. The air itself seemed to be on fire, and a few minutes later the fire engulfed its own pillar of gaseous smoke in a flash so bright Marie could not look at it or at anything else for a matter of minutes.

Then there was just the fire, feeding on itself, consuming itself.

She thought it might be night because to the south over the bog the sky was dusky. In the north it was still as bright as day, though the brightness was harsh and metallic, not like a bright fall day when the sun was shining. The roaring had abated but the heat seemed more intense, as though the fire had eaten its way into the granite heart of the mountain and the mountain was burning from the inside out, fueled by its own molten core. She huddled behind the muskrat house; it was warm to the touch. Her face burned badly, as if she had lain face up in the blazing sun all day. The animals surrounding her were quiet, gazing toward the fire. Her throat hurt each time she swallowed.

Later the heat forced her deeper into the bog. Wading slowly, sometimes shoulder-deep in the cold swamp water, she headed in what she thought was an easterly direction, hoping she might eventually strike the spur track. Repeatedly she ducked completely under the water to escape the heat. She passed a few dead tamarack snags and some isolated red alders, and then there were no trees or bushes at all.

She recalled the St. Francis Indian myth that her mother had told her soon after they had come to the States. "Of those persons foolish enough to enter the cedar bog," she heard her mother saying, "few have emerged. And those few have lost all memory of their past lives. In the swamp there is no direction, no night or day. There is only the absence of all light, darkness, sound, life, and time."

She had no idea whether it was night or day or how much time had passed since the fire had started or in which direction she was moving. It was just a gray, desolate expanse where, because of the haze, water and air seemed to mingle. Peculiarly trivial anxieties tormented her. She regretted that she had not made time to take Latin when she was at normal school. At the same time, she realized the absurdity of such a regret. What would she do with a year of Latin, naked in the swamp as she was, surrounded by fire—go back to the last stand of tamaracks and identify them by their technical names?

She thought of the remark she had once made to Harlan, that she expected to leave the world as she had entered it, and was struck by the terrible irony of her cavalier prophecy.

She could not remember what she had done with her dress. For a moment she could not remember anything at all, and a wave of panic swept over her. She had heard about the panic that sometimes causes persons wandering in desolate places to lose their senses; she had never believed she would succumb to it. For a moment she was overwhelmed. She actually could not remember who she was. "Marie!" someone said aloud. She realized that she had called out her own name, but it sounded like someone else calling to a stranger. She lost her breath, then lost her footing and went in over her head. Gasping, she struggled to the surface. She had to fight down a powerful impulse to run blindly.

"Marie Blythe," she shouted. "My name is Marie Blythe!"

Over and over she shouted her name, until at last the panic subsided and she was breathing evenly again. Her face continued to crack and peel; bubbles pushed out her skin and burned fiercely. After a while applications of the cold swamp water only made the pain worse. The air was still hot. The smoke was too thick to see more than a few feet. She had to walk with her eyes shut much of the time because they had been seared by the heat from the sudden flash of light when the pillar of smoke had ignited.

She did not see the floating log until she bumped into it. It was stark white, from a cedar tree probably, and about eight feet long with a jutting prong where a limb had branched off. She clung to it for support and found she could put her entire weight on it and push it ahead of herself through the water. She could even doze a little while leaning on it, though her scalded face hurt too much to allow her to sleep.

She thought several hours might have passed this way, but she could not be sure. She half slept, dreaming that she was riding roped to the top of a freight train rumbling through deep woods. A stream of fiery red cinders fell beside the track, setting dozens of small fires. She felt something sting her face and thought it was a live cinder from the locomotive.

When she came fully awake, it was raining. The rain stung her face, and she was drifting through an eerie watery forest of dead trees. Each tree glowed like the glowing whale's jaw at the foot of the drive winding up to the Big House. The prong of the log she was clinging to glowed faintly and the burned skin on the back of her hands seemed to glow. In the far distance she saw the two great mountains glowing pink, as they had the morning she first saw them. Drifting between the phosphorescent trees and looking at the pink mountains was strangely peaceful and beautiful. The rain stung her face but at the same time seemed to soothe it. It was quite cool. It would start bringing down the leaves on the mountains, she thought. Then she remembered that there were no leaves left to come down because there were no trees. She climbed onto the log, stretched out with her arms around it, and slept. . . .

It was daylight. Again the sun shone huge and red over the shoulder of Canada Mountain. The smoke had dissipated into a thick haze through which Marie could see the outlines of the mountains, still faintly lavender in places where the fire was not yet out, but elsewhere as black as two blackened cinder cones. Her log was moving a little. The dead trees were going by slowly.

A kingfisher with a bright blue crest went chattering off ahead of her, bobbing up and down over the water in the manner of all kingfishers. A blue heron standing on one leg in a backwater watched her go by. A foot or so off the end of her log, a trout rose and took a large pale-green fly off the surface. Far up the river a fish hawk dove, slamming the surface hard. Something pertaining to fishing kept nagging at her, but she could not think what it was.

The current quickened. Marie was gliding between an alley of burned woods, still smoking. Periodically a breeze rose and flames would fan up from a smoldering stump. Ahead was a small copse of young live birch trees inexplicably spared by the fire. For no apparent reason, the entire copse suddenly burst into flames. In places little tongues of flame lapped out of the ground. The charred carcasses of animals hung on the lower branches of bankside trees. Apparently they had caught fire, then plunged into the river and drifted down in the rising water. Somewhere to the south, toward the Common, it must have rained hard. Or perhaps, Marie thought, it had rained hard everywhere and she had slept through most of it.

Later she realized that she was facing backwards on the log. She turned carefully, and saw ahead a wide expanse of water, though she did not realize where she was until the log bumped up against the slag along the base of the causeway at the mouth of the river. The railroad bridge was gone, burned down to its submerged pilings. The ties had been burned to ashes. On the causeway, the rails had been heaved up at grotesque angles by the heat.

She tried to stand but her legs refused to support her, and she had to crawl out onto the sand. She sat with her back

against the collapsed embankment and shut her eyes. Again
she slept.

When she woke her blistered face was a mask of fiery pain.
She was thirsty but did not have strength left to reach the
water, a few feet away. She raised her hand to her face and
could not feel her eyelashes or eyebrows; they had been
burned off. The backs of her hands were blistered. She drifted
again into fevered sleep and dreamed that she was home on the
St. Francis during the epidemic. Then she was walking through
the rain between two borders, then waiting for the train in a
long narrow cut through the woods. "Listen, Marie," her father
said to her in the dream; and in the distance she heard the faint
sound of the train engine.

She opened her eyes. Upriver she heard an engine. At first
she thought it was a train, but no train could possibly pass
along that twisted track. The noise grew fainter, then louder.
A boat with two men in it appeared in the mouth of the river.
She tried to call to them; but her voice was gone.

Somehow, she lifted an arm. The engine roared as the boat
swung in to shore, and then Ned Baxter and Harlan were
beside her, though she could not think of their names at first.

"Jesus Christ," Harlan said. "Oh, Jesus Christ!"

Marie was quite surprised and somewhat annoyed that he
seemed to be crying.

"Stop that," she whispered. "Get me a drink of water."

But by the time he cupped his hands and dipped them in the
bay and brought them to her lips, her eyes were shut and she
was dreaming again, dreaming that she was a little girl in
Canada, walking through the rain toward a place of many
opportunities.

Chapter Eighteen

Formerly it was Portes de L'Enfer. According to the myth, the name was conferred by one Grenadier Bonhomme, a fur trader and would-be explorer who, after being drummed out of the garrison force at Quebec City for chronic drunkenness, had converted his rank into a first name. Characteristically, when Bonhomme came south down Lake Memphremagog in the fall of 1740, he was looking for something that didn't exist: a navigable waterway between the St. Lawrence and Connecticut rivers. Most of the leaves were down, but it was a mild, hazy morning, one of the last of the thirty smoky days before winter, and as the Canadian expeditionary paddled around the north point of the island, he glanced down the lake, took one quick look at the two dark, close-set mountains towering over the peninsula with the darker bay and still darker bog and mountains beyond, and began to backwater fast.

Whether this account is strictly accurate or not, it seems evident that Bonhomme wanted no part of the place he named the Gates of Hell. He hastened back to settled Canada (though not to Quebec City), where he told every fur trader, homesteader, missionary, fisherman, trapper, and soldier who would listen that he had smelled brimstone and seen fire on the peninsula—and perhaps he really had, since for generations before he arrived the St. Francis Indians had camped there and on the big island to the north, to make maple sugar in the spring and to smoke salmon and trout in the fall on high hardwood racks: some of which were still standing when Abraham Benedict arrived one hundred and fifty years later. So even taking into consideration the fact that Bonhomme was probably already drunk when he came down the lake that September morning, it is quite possible that he was telling the truth, even about the scent of smoke, since the green maplewood used by the Indians for curing their fish would have produced a strong, heavy smoke with an acrid redolence that would carry many miles if the wind was right.

During the century and a half between Bonhomme's brief visit and the Captain's arrival, no one, including the Indians, evinced much interest in settling year-round on the peninsula. Robert Rogers was probably the first white man to set foot there, and he did so only lightly since he was being pursued by a group of enraged St. Francis warriors whose village on the north shore of the lake he and his Rangers had wiped out three days earlier. Around 1800 a scapegrace grandson of the Grenadier passed through the narrows between the tip of the peninsula and Canada Mountain and established a tavern and fur post on the spot later occupied by the Commission Sales barn in Kingdom Common. (The Indians themselves apparently rarely if ever ventured south of the bay, either because of the myth of the cedar bog or, more probably, because they saw no point in going there; to reach the Connecticut, they preferred the easier route to the east, through what is now the northern tip of New Hampshire.)

Other parts of Kingdom County were settled slowly and incompletely during the first half of the nineteenth century, until, just before the Civil War, the population reached about fifty thousand, where it has more or less remained ever since. Except to be logged over, much of the county was never settled at all, and it is unlikely that Hell's Gate ever would have been if Abraham Benedict had not looked at a map and picked the peninsula as the most desirable place to establish his second home.

Then for a single generation Hell's Gate was unique among American villages—or villages anywhere, for that matter: a strange yet lovely anomaly, a model community where you would least expect to find one.

Then the Captain died and a few years later his entire estate caught fire, so except for the fact that the trees were gone, or charred almost beyond recognition, when the snow went off the mountains and the peninsula in the spring of 1923, they looked no different than they had on that fall day in 1890 when he had first arrived and written in his diary: "Ten years."

The tiny shoots came first, the palest blush of green-gold where there had been only black. In the bog, new alders appeared from nowhere, and here and there a few isolated brakes of tamaracks and cedars put out sticky new buds. On the lower slopes of the mountains, raspberry roots buried deep in ravines over which the fire had raged put up new green canes. Descendants of the rainbow trout brought to Hell's Gate by the Captain swam up the brook on Kingdom Mountain and spawned there, as usual.

As summer progressed, red and orange paintbrush blossomed along the edge of the hanging meadow; and far below, pink fireweed and blue-flowered chicory came up on the embankment where the spur track had run. But on the peninsula itself the topsoil had been burned almost down to the rock, and it remained as barren as the coast of Labrador until the following spring, when a few young poplars and soft maples established themselves near the water. That summer blueberry bushes spread over the upper slopes of the mountains in great profusion, as though by magic, and by August of 1924 partridges had begun to move back in, like dun-colored northern phoenixes sprung from their own ashes, though in fact they had merely flown over from the back side of the mountain, which had remained mostly unburned since the Canadian fires never did reach the gore of Hell's Gate. At about the same time, the rainbow trout hatched as fingerlings two springs ago went down the brook to the lake.

Now it was the spring of 1925. Although the ice had been out only two weeks and there was still snow on the tops of the mountains, the lower slopes were already pale gold with small new leaves of new growth, and the mountains looked like mountains again, instead of volcanic cinder cones.

On the hill that dominated the island five miles to the north, wild cherry trees were in flower. The tall maples once tapped by the Indians, the great smooth-boled beeches, the white and yellow birches, and the scattering of elms had been in leaf for a week, and at the foot of the hill, on the slope just above the south cove, a blue plume of woodsmoke drifted out of a stone chimney above a two-story log house and mingled with the early-morning mist.

Inside the house, a man and a woman sat eating breakfast at one of several good-sized tables in a large dining room overlooking the lake. It was a big breakfast—coffee, bacon and eggs, homemade bread toasted, fried potatoes, and pie—and for a time they ate steadily, without speaking.

When she finished her second cup of coffee, the woman stood up, went to one of the windows, and looked off down the lake. She glanced at her reflection in the window glass and critically smoothed her hair. Although it had grown back as thick as ever, it had come in streaked with gray, and she was still somewhat self-conscious about it, and about her face, which was scarred in three places: her forehead above her right eye, her right cheek, and (from her childhood) just under her left ear.

"I hope they don't turn around and run as soon as they see me," she said.

"Stop fishing for compliments," the man said in the harsh voice that still reminded her of gravel sliding out of a wagon. "The second Mrs. Smith was forever fishing for compliments, and it's a tactic I can't and won't abide. For a woman fast approaching thirty-five Christly years old, you look fine. Do you think I'd still be interested in you if you didn't, after all the trouble you've caused me?"

She looked at him solemnly. "Well," she said. "I hope they aren't disappointed by the accommodations or the fishing. Margaret wrote that they've been to northern Canada and out west and nearly any place you can name where there's good fishing. I just hope they don't experience a big let-down."

"How can they experience a let-down with me guiding them? If the fishing's half as good as it has been since ice-out, they won't know what to do with all they catch. Stop worrying. Next thing you know, I'll commence to worry too, and have a spell halfway up the lake and swamp your party before they get here. Just stop worrying."

He pushed back his chair and stood up from the table. He brushed a toast crumb off his flaring red tie and straightened it.

"I'd best start out," he said. "They're due into the Common at, what, ten o'clock?"

"It's still early," she said. "You've got lots of time."

But he was nervous too, as eager as she was for things to go smoothly. "I'd best start out," he repeated.

"All right. I'll have lunch ready when you get back. This afternoon you can take them over to the St. John. John said they were interested in brook trout mainly, and that's the place to go for brookies."

"I believe I know where to take them," he said angrily. "I've been fishing this lake for nearly fifty years." But he looked disgruntled. "I don't know, though. As good as it may still be, the trout fishing ain't what it was when I was younger. If this so-called camp goes good, and we build up a little nest egg, we ought to think about doing the same thing up to Alaska. I'd still like to strike off for that country sometime."

"Don't strike off this morning," she said. "I want my party up here safely first."

She walked down the path to the cove with him, and he climbed into his boat, awkwardly, as always, causing her to wonder for the hundredth time how a man who had been around boats all his life could possibly be so ungainly every time he got into one. He pulled four times before the old make-and-break engine caught, and that annoyed her too, and then she was annoyed with herself for being so edgy, even though it was their first opening day.

"Don't capsize before you get away from the dock," she said. "I'd at least like to see what they look like."

But he was already on his way, roaring out of the cove as though a boatload of immigration officers were in hot pursuit, though he had smuggled nothing for years.

Remembering the advice Pia had given her years ago about never watching anyone out of sight, Marie turned and started back up the path toward the lodge. It was, she thought, a handsome building, somewhat cruder than what she had once planned but in a way even better because, with some help from Ned Baxter, she and Harlan had built it themselves, cutting the spruce logs on the back side of the hill, raising them log by log, putting the long cedar shakes on the roof, laying up the fireplace.

As she entered her dooryard a V of geese went over, honking eagerly, and although they were quite high she could tell from their dark wingtips that they were snow geese, and she thought of her mother, whose ancestors had come to this island to make maple sugar. In February she and Harlan had thinned and cleaned out the maples behind the house, and she hoped to start making her own maple sugar next March; but now the wood they had cut was waiting behind the lodge to be split and stacked for winter, and it occurred to her that she might as well work on it, since it would be at least four hours before their fishermen arrived.

She got her ax and began chopping methodically, stacking the split sections crosswise, neatly, as she had once done while hitched to her mother on a spruce root.

The scent of the new leaves hung on the air, mingling with the smell of the split wood. The mild sun warmed her back and shoulders, and she removed her jacket and draped it over the pile of logs. She had at least twelve cords, she thought, which should be plenty. But as she admired the wood, she remembered something Jigger Johnson had once told her at Pond Number Four.

"Marie," he'd said, "when you've cut as much wood as you think you'll need to get through the winter, go straight back and cut just that much again. Then, if you're fortunate, and the snow goes off before July, you'll have enough to see yourself through to spring."

She smiled and picked up her ax. Along with something a priest had once told her, it was as useful a piece of advice as any she had ever been given.

FOR THE BEST IN PAPERBACKS, LOOK FOR THE

In every corner of the world, on every subject under the sun, Penguin represents quality and variety—the very best in publishing today.

For complete information about books available from Penguin—including Puffins, Penguin Classics, and Arkana—and how to order them, write to us at the appropriate address below. Please note that for copyright reasons the selection of books varies from country to country.

In the United Kingdom: Please write to *Dept. JC, Penguin Books Ltd, FREEPOST, West Drayton, Middlesex UB7 0BR.*

If you have any difficulty in obtaining a title, please send your order with the correct money, plus ten percent for postage and packaging, to *P.O. Box No. 11, West Drayton, Middlesex UB7 0BR*

In the United States: Please write to *Consumer Sales, Penguin USA, P.O. Box 999, Dept. 17109, Bergenfield, New Jersey 07621-0120.* VISA and MasterCard holders call 1-800-253-6476 to order all Penguin titles

In Canada: Please write to *Penguin Books Canada Ltd, 10 Alcorn Avenue, Suite 300, Toronto, Ontario M4V 3B2*

In Australia: Please write to *Penguin Books Australia Ltd, P.O. Box 257, Ringwood, Victoria 3134*

In New Zealand: Please write to *Penguin Books (NZ) Ltd, Private Bag 102902, North Shore Mail Centre, Auckland 10*

In India: Please write to *Penguin Books India Pvt Ltd, 706 Eros Apartments, 56 Nehru Place, New Delhi 110 019*

In the Netherlands: Please write to *Penguin Books Netherlands bv, Postbus 3507, NL-1001 AH Amsterdam*

In Germany: Please write to *Penguin Books Deutschland GmbH, Metzlerstrasse 26, 60594 Frankfurt am Main*

In Spain: Please write to *Penguin Books S.A., Bravo Murillo 19, 1° B, 28015 Madrid*

In Italy: Please write to *Penguin Italia s.r.l., Via Felice Casati 20, I-20124 Milano*

In France: Please write to *Penguin France S.A., 17 rue Lejeune, F–31000 Toulouse*

In Japan: Please write to *Penguin Books Japan, Ishikiribashi Building, 2–5–4, Suido, Bunkyo-ku, Tokyo 112*

In Greece: Please write to *Penguin Hellas Ltd, Dimocritou 3, GR–106 71 Athens*

In South Africa: Please write to *Longman Penguin Southern Africa (Pty) Ltd, Private Bag X08, Bertsham 2013*